Also by J

Did I Mention I Won The Lottery?

Google Your Husband Back

Did I Mention I was Getting Married?

By
Julie Butterfield

Part 1
New Beginnings

Chapter 1

'Rebecca? Rebecca? Did you hear what I said?'

Rebecca stared at the phone. She was holding a half-eaten bacon sandwich in her hand listening to her ex-husband telling her that he was getting married again.

'To Annabelle?'

'Well yes, of course to Annabelle.'

Rebecca shook herself. It was a stupid question, it wasn't as though Daniel had a number of women he may have asked to marry him. He'd mentioned Annabelle several times during their infrequent conversations and Rebecca knew that they'd finally moved in together.

'That's wonderful news Daniel.' She put down her bacon sandwich and wiped her hand on a towel. 'Really, I'm very pleased for you.'

'Are you okay? I mean I know we - well things are over between us.'

Divorce had a tendency to do that, thought Rebecca.

'But I wanted to be the one to tell you. I didn't want you to be upset or think that I didn't care for you, or that I didn't...'

Rebecca took pity on him. 'Daniel I think it's wonderful, really. There's absolutely no reason why you shouldn't get married again. I'm very pleased for both of you.'

She heard Daniel's relieved sigh gust down the phone and caught a glimpse of her reflection in the kitchen window. She was standing straight and tense, her face serious. She didn't look very pleased.

'Really pleased,' she tried again, frowning at her reflection. There was no reason to begrudge Daniel happiness. They had divorced and moved on with their lives. At least Daniel had moved on. Rebecca turned her back so she could no longer see her pale face in the window. She hadn't moved very far at all.

'I would like you to meet her.'

Rebecca brought her thoughts back to the conversation. 'You want us to meet?'

'Well Annabelle is very concerned that this works for the whole family. She wants the children to feel comfortable about visiting us and doesn't want you to feel left out. She doesn't want any arguments about who goes where at birthdays and holidays.'

'That's very thoughtful of her.'

'She's a lovely person Bec, you'll really like her!'

Rebecca frowned, did ex-wives traditionally get on with their replacements? Were they expected to be best friends for the sake of the family?

'She actually said there's nothing worse than families being split up at times when they should be celebrating together. She wants to meet you, she's sure you'll be great friends and then we can all come to visit you at Christmas, have a real family get together!'

Rebecca's eyebrows shot up as far as they would go. She hadn't even met the woman and she was already inviting herself round for Christmas lunch.

'Christmas is a long way off Daniel.'

'I know,' he chuckled, 'but Annabelle likes to plan ahead, she's always thinking of others.'

'Right,' said Rebecca faintly.

'So we thought we'd visit you at the weekend. Maybe come on Saturday morning so we can have a few days together, time for my girls to get to know each other. You can give us your blessing!' Another chuckle. 'That okay with you Bec?'

His girls? He had never seemed particularly interested in Rebecca's opinion when they were married, she thought wryly, why was it important to him now?

'Well I suppose …'

'Perfect! Annabelle said you would want to meet her, get it out of the way!'

'Out of the way?'

'Well you know, the old Mrs Miles meeting the new Mrs Miles.'

Rebecca stared at the phone. He made it sound like a relay race where she would hand over the baton to her successor.

'Annabelle said it might be a bit awkward, the first meeting, so why not get it over and done with?'

'It won't be a problem Daniel,' she said lightly. 'After all we have been apart for two years.'

'That's my girl I knew you'd be brave about it.'

'Daniel There's nothing to be brave about …'

'You'll always be the mother of my children Bec, you know that.'

'I don't think I'll forget.'

'And no-one will take your place in that respect.'

Rebecca resisted the urge to hit her head against the wall. 'Daniel I really don't mind you getting married again.'

'Excellent! So we'll see you on Saturday?'

Rebecca was beaten. 'Yes, I'm looking forward to it,' she insisted through clenched teeth. 'Can't wait.'

'Great and - thank you Bec, thanks for being so reasonable about it all.'

'Why on earth would I not…' but he had gone leaving Rebecca to slam the phone down and stare at her now cold sandwich. Pouring herself a coffee, she threw the sandwich in the bin and walked out of the kitchen to sit in her courtyard amongst the herbs. It was a place that never failed to relax her, the scent of mint and basil drifting through the air was a tonic for most worries. But today she ignored their appeal, staring down the garden to the tennis court that lay beyond the lawn and the trees.

It was two years since she had asked Daniel to leave. Two years since she had discovered that their hasty move from the house and friends she had loved in Leeds to an unappealing house in Darlington where she knew no-one, had been prompted by Daniel's affair with a woman called Christine. He'd successfully hidden the sordid details by uprooting the family and insisting that he needed to live closer to his head office. Friends had been told Rebecca was too upset to discuss the matter and wanted to move away and forget it had happened and for five years they had lived in a place she hated with a husband who had changed into an irritable, overbearing man without a good word to say for anyone, in particular Rebecca. Her marriage had disintegrated, her life had become stale and unhappy. But Rebecca's fortunes had changed when she won 15 million pounds on the lottery and suddenly the cold, impersonal house in Darlington could be replaced with the luxurious house of her dreams back in Leeds. She could move back to where she belonged, close to her mother and the friends she had left behind. She'd been given another chance at happiness.

It hadn't been the easiest of transitions and Rebecca had struggled on with her marriage, hoping to find the man she had once loved somewhere inside the man Daniel had become. But eventually she had come to the realisation that when a marriage has reached its end, it couldn't be saved, even with millions of pounds in the bank.

Rebecca sighed and shifted in her seat. She and Daniel had reached a level of harmony over the last few years. He had been truly devastated when she'd found out his secret and she'd accepted that in a strange way he had been trying to save their marriage by whisking her away to Darlington. And although his contrition had come too late, with time and space between them they could now enjoy the occasional civilised conversation.

Rebecca had wanted to share the money with Daniel and he had wanted to walk away empty handed, atonement for his behaviour. At Rebecca's insistence, he had finally taken a million pounds and the new Mercedes sitting on the drive. To her annoyance, having refused for years to move out of Darlington despite knowing Rebecca hated every minute she spent there, Daniel had decided not to return North but moved to Devon where he'd used the money to set up a business selling cherished cars, which was surprisingly successful. His bombastic nature suited an industry which was obsessive about whether the speedometer in a 50 year old Rolls Royce was in fact the original and not a clever copy.

Rebecca had stayed in her lovely house in Leeds and free of Daniel's dour and unpleasant presence, she had decided that whilst she could never recover the wasted years they had spent living a lie in Darlington, she could start again. When Rebecca won her millions, the residential home her mother lived in was on the verge of being sold and Rebecca had stepped in to buy and restore the beautiful building. It was now a hugely successful home with a waiting list and a host of very happy residents. In fact, it needed very little attention these days, the restoration work had been finished, the changes made and with the fine details of day to day life taken care of by the manager Brenda Wendover, it ticked along without needing anything from Rebecca.

After the shock of their mother's win, her children had carried on with their lives. Toby had left university and stayed in Bristol and Sarah was now in the midst of her final exams at Leeds university and had already been offered a job which would start in September.

Rebecca still loved her beautiful house; the gardens were now tended to by Colin who came in a few times each week and nourished the flower beds, the lawns and the orchard as though they were his children. Her friends had been delighted at Rebecca's return and they all met regularly for lunch and gossip and Rebecca still travelled north to Darlington to catch up with Carol and Susie at the little deli where Rebecca had worked. She had everything she could possibly need.

Rebecca stood up and took her cup back into the kitchen. The last few months she had started to feel a small niggle of something she hadn't been able to place. It had first appeared in the evenings when she would curl up in her living room and turn on the TV or grab a book. Then it started to surface more and more during the day, on days like this for example when the weather was cold but dry, the sky blue and clear and Rebecca would sit in her herb garden deciding what to do with her day. Eventually she had realised that the strange little knot in her stomach was actually loneliness. Rebecca Miles may have won the lottery, she may have a wonderful house and a successful business. She may have rid herself of her overbearing husband and moved back to a place she loved close to her family and friends. But she had failed to take her second chance and move on with her life and now, after two years she had reached the inescapable conclusion that she was lonely. She really didn't mind Daniel getting married, she didn't mind at all that he had someone new. But she was envious that he had managed to start again whereas Rebecca seemed suspended in time, going neither forwards nor backwards.

She shook herself. It was the talk of weddings that was making her feel so down, she decided. Weddings were all about the future, spending the rest of your life with someone you loved and that was something she simply didn't have.

Sighing Rebecca flicked on the kettle for a fresh coffee as the phone rang again.

'Mum! Guess what?'

Rebecca smiled. One definite benefit to moving back to Leeds was her ability to see more of her daughter. She visited Toby regularly and he often came up for a weekend when work allowed, but Sarah she could see every week.

'Oh I don't know darling but I'm feeling a little down so tell me your news, it might just cheer me up.'

'Dominic has asked me to marry him! Oh mum, I'm getting married! Isn't that wonderful news?'

Chapter 2

Rebecca stared at the phone for the second time that day as Sarah continued.

'It was a complete surprise,' she giggled. 'He took me out to dinner and I thought he was acting a little twitchy. We ordered desert but then the waiter brought over a bottle of champagne and a cake with little sparklers, two of them. And I was staring at the sparklers and wondering where my cheesecake was and then Dominic took out a ring and went down on one knee. He actually went on his knee mum! In the middle of the restaurant with everyone looking and pointing. I still didn't know what was happening, I was worrying about my cheesecake! Then he asked me to marry him and I was so surprised I just stared at him. Everyone was really quiet - they were all waiting for an answer. Suddenly I realised he was proposing and I said yes and everyone in the restaurant started clapping, even the waiters. Oh, it was so romantic Mum.'

Rebecca was standing very still, Sarah's words rolling over her. 'Dominic has proposed?'

'Haven't you been listening Mum?' Sarah giggled. 'Yes, I'm getting married!'

'But I ...' Rebecca took a deep breath. 'Sorry darling, I think it's just the shock. How wonderful, how very exciting!'

'I know! And such a surprise.'

Rebecca carried on, choosing her words with care. 'I just wasn't aware things were quite so serious between you two.'

'But mum we've been together for over a year now.'

'I know sweetheart, I just didn't know that weddings were in the air, that's all.' Rebecca held onto the edge of the kitchen counter wondering if she should phone Toby and check if he had anything to tell her.

'I know, it's a bit of a shock. I mean, we hadn't really talked about it, I thought Dominic would want to focus on his career before thinking about weddings. But apparently,' Sarah's voice was dreamy as she continued, 'he decided that although he needs to work really hard over the next few years to get his next promotion, he didn't want to wait any longer before asking me to marry him.'

Rebecca couldn't help smiling at the delight in her daughter's voice even as she offered a word of caution.

'But it is something you want isn't it darling, I mean you haven't said yes just because he asked?'

'Mum! Of course not. I love him and I'm so happy. And all we've done is decide to get married, it's not as though we're actually tying the knot in the next couple of weeks!'

'Good, I mean I'm glad you're taking it slowly.'

There was a tiny pause before Sarah spoke.

'Mum, it is okay you know.'

'What is darling?'

'Dominic. I mean, he's okay. We've been together long enough for me to know him, he isn't after my money, well - your money. His family have money of their own, they live in Gloucestershire in the most wonderful old house and he doesn't need my trust fund to get by.'

It was an ever present worry for Rebecca. She had insisted that her children shared in her good fortune and had allocated generous trust funds for both of them, against Daniel's wishes. But she was always anxious that friends, in particular partners, were with Sarah and Toby for the right reasons. It was something that amused both of her children but was a concern for Rebecca.

'Dominic and I are perfect for each other mum, really.'

It was something that had seeped into Rebecca's own life and since her divorce she had tended to view interest shown by anyone new as suspicious. Helen had told her to stop being so sensitive but Rebecca still felt ill at ease, wondering if they were chatting to her or her bank balance. She had embarked on a brief relationship with her bank manager a few months after her divorce. He knew more about her financial position than anyone else could and Rebecca had trusted him implicitly. The relationship had still floundered. If anything Richard knew too much, he knew that Rebecca hadn't told her husband as soon as she had won the money. He knew of Daniel's behaviour, how he had tried to stop her setting up the trust funds, how he'd tried to sell Rebecca's new house without her knowledge and how Rebecca had been so concerned about her husband's need for control that she'd refused to put the money into their joint bank account where he would have access. Rebecca had initially felt relieved that she was with someone who didn't need explanations about her money and the end of her marriage. But strangely it had worked against them and she had struggled to feel truly at ease in Richard's company despite his innate good manners and courtesy. After only a few months they had agreed the relationship wasn't working and since then Rebecca had been alone.

'Mum?'

'Sorry darling, deep in thought! Ignore me Sarah, you know what an old worry I am. I couldn't be happier for you.' She took a deep breath, 'It must be something in the air. Your father phoned me this morning, he's getting married as well.'

'Dad! Dad and Annabelle are getting married?'

'Yes. Isn't it wonderful?'

'And are you okay with that?'

Rebecca frowned. Why did everyone think she would go to pieces because Daniel was marrying again. 'Of course I am! Why would I not be happy for them?'

Rebecca could hear Sarah's thoughts whirling across the phone line. 'Well, it's just that he's your husband.'

'Ex-husband.'

'Well okay ex-husband, but he was *your* husband. Even if you didn't want him. And now he'll be someone else's husband. I could see that you might be a bit upset.'

'Well I'm not,' said Rebecca shortly. 'Not at all.'

Except, thought Rebecca, she hadn't really felt at all herself since the news broke.

'Why don't you and Dominic come over for the weekend,' she found herself saying impulsively. 'Dad is bringing Annabelle, apparently she wants to meet me and plan Christmas.'

'Christmas?'

'Mmm, well she wants to meet me anyway, make sure we all get on.'

'Oh that's nice,' said Sarah warmly.

Rebecca smiled, her daughter always saw the best in everyone. She tried to banish her own scepticism at Anabelle's request. 'I suppose it is. So why don't you and Dominic come over and join us. I've only met him a few times, if he's about to be my son in law it's time I got to know him better.'

'Oh mum, what a great idea,' enthused Sarah. 'You should spend more time with him, you'll love him, I know you will. He's so kind and thoughtful and - well lovely!'

Rebecca laughed. 'Okay, that's a plan. We'll introduce Dominic and Annabelle and start the whole getting to know you ball rolling.'

When Rebecca put the phone down she stared at the kettle then walked to the fridge to pour herself a glass of wine. Her daughter was getting married, her ex-husband was getting married, all these people embarking on a new relationship, a new life. What on earth was Rebecca doing wrong?

The phone rang and for a while Rebecca just stared. She'd had all the news she could cope with for one day.

Sighing she took a large sip of wine then answered.

'I was just about to hang up, I thought you might be out doing something exciting!'

'Helen, thank goodness!'

'What?'

Rebecca settled down on one of the raspberry settees by the French windows where she could see her courtyard and her herbs, the glass still in her hand. 'Oh nothing, just pleased it's you.'

'Why, who else has been phoning you?' asked Helen intrigued.

Rebecca paused, 'Sarah phoned, she and Dominic have just gotten engaged.'

'Engaged! Oh how lovely. Has that made you feel old?'

'Well no actually, it hadn't until you just mentioned it!'

Helen chuckled. 'Sorry, just wondering why you don't sound more cheerful about it.'

Rebecca sighed. 'Oh I don't know, she just seems awfully young to be thinking about getting married.'

'I bet you were younger than her when you and Daniel tied the knot.'

'Yes, and look how that turned out!'

Helen laughed again, 'Relax Rebecca, Sarah is a sensible young woman, she wouldn't marry someone like Daniel.'

There was a pause.

'Oh God I didn't mean it to sound like that, I just meant that she would be too intelligent to fall …. oh that's even worse! I mean …'

'Don't worry Helen, I know exactly what you mean! And I am happy for her, it was just a bit of a surprise that's all. Especially after Daniel's news.'

'Daniel's news?' echoed Helen. 'What did Daniel have to say for himself?'

'He's getting married as well.'

'What? Daniel! Dear God, who is the poor unfortunate woman?'

Rebecca couldn't help but laugh. 'Her name is Annabelle, I told you they'd moved in together.'

'Yes but I presumed she would have moved straight back out!'

'Don't be mean, Daniel used to be okay, I loved him once.'

Neither of them said anything for a moment and Rebecca felt the usual twinge of sadness at the loss of a man she had spent several happy years alongside.

Helen sniffed, 'Well that's as maybe but people change and Daniel certainly didn't change for the better!'

Rebecca sighed, 'You're right. But anyway, he's asked Annabelle to marry him and she wants to come and meet me.'

'What on earth for?'

'Well, she wants us all to be one big happy family and get on and not argue about who spends Christmas together...'

'Christmas! Did you say Christmas? It's only February!'

'Apparently she likes to plan ahead. Anyway, she wants us to be comfortable with each other so they're coming up for the weekend so we can bond.'

'I suppose that's quite a sensible idea when you think about it.'

'It is,' agreed Rebecca in a neutral tone.

'And yet I can't help feeling you're not looking forward to it?'

'Oh I don't know Helen. I really don't mind Daniel getting married. I'm not sure why I have to get involved. And it just made me feel so ...'

'Unhappy?' suggested Helen.

'No.'

'Angry?'

'No.'

'Annoyed?'

'No.'

Then you're going to have to help me out here Bec, what is it making you feel?'

'But that's the trouble Helen, I don't really know but I suspect I'm feeling, well I think I'm feeling ...'

'Oh for heaven's sake Bec tell me!'

'I think I feel lonely.'

'Lonely? Why on earth would Daniel getting married make you feel lonely. You speak to him every six months.'

'Well that's the bit I don't really understand but I think it's because he's done what I wanted to do.'

'You want to get married?'

'No! Of course not. But I asked Daniel to leave because I wanted to move on with my life. I was so angry at the wasted years I'd spent in Darlington being miserable and I wanted to start again, be happy, meet someone new.'

'Ah. And you haven't but ...'

'Daniel has,' finished Rebecca. 'He gets a second chance, why don't I?'

'Bec darling, you could have had no end of second chances, you just won't take them. All you need to do to have your new start in life is to let down a few of those barriers you've erected and let someone in.'

'But...'

'There are no buts Rebecca, I know you worry about men being interested in your bank balance instead of you but let's face it, even if they were, you could still have some fun, get out occasionally. Remember what it's like being taken to dinner, flirting?'

'But ...'

'Look at Richard. He was lovely and you know he wasn't at all interested in your money but you pushed him away.'

'I didn't!'

'Yes, you did! If you're lonely Bec you can do something about it, but you need to stop worrying about the motives of every new man you meet.'

Rebecca pulled a face and sighed. 'I suppose you're right but it's not easy.'

'Ah well, life isn't meant to be easy darling,' said Helen good naturedly. 'But you could stop making it quite so hard. Let this be a little wake-up call Bec, let's face it if Daniel can find someone new, anyone can. I've introduced you to several potentials - you just get all uptight and touch me not!'

Rebecca couldn't help but giggle. The last man Helen had introduced to Rebecca had been a single dad of five who had arrived for their date looking exhausted. He had grilled her about how many bedrooms she had, whether she felt she could take onboard somebody else's children and did she think nannies were a good idea. Then he suggested that people could save a lot of time and energy if they just cut to the chase and went to bed without wasting time with all the getting to know each other bit first. Rebecca had spent the last hour of the evening slapping his hand away until he actually dozed off briefly as they waited for their desert to arrive and she had taken her chance and fled. Before that had been Simon. Their first date was in a restaurant and he had insisted on paying the bill. The second date had been to the cinema and he had paid for her taxi home. She was just starting to relax in his company when he produced several travel brochures featuring exotic and very expensive locations and said that it was Rebecca's turn to pay for their next date and why didn't they make it a fortnight in St Lucia. And before Simon was Nick, who had turned up at Rebecca's house the morning after their very first date with eight members of his family in tow. They had emptied Rebecca's fridge and her wine rack and announced that they were happy to keep her company every weekend and had she ever thought about installing an indoor swimming pool.

'Maybe I need to try again,' she suggested thoughtfully. It had been months since she'd spoken to an unattached man in anything remotely resembling a flirtatious way, ever since she'd banned Helen from organising any more of her fix up dinner parties. They had become quite mortifying. She would arrive to find the unattached male sitting at the table, waiting for her inspection whilst the rest of the dinner guests watched their every move with bated breath and a level of expectation that had left Rebecca quite nauseous.

'You mean it?' demanded Helen eagerly. 'Really?'

Rebecca chewed. She hated the very thought. 'I suppose so,' she agreed reluctantly. 'But ...'

'Leave it with me!' trilled Helen. 'I've actually got someone in mind, I've had him under surveillance for a while, waiting until you gave in!'

'Surveillance! What do you mean?'

'Oh you know, checking out his story, his personality, his habits.'

It sounded like something from a David Bellamy programme, a study of the lesser crested unattached male. Rebecca screwed up her nose.

'I don't know.'

'Yes,' Helen interrupted firmly, 'we are doing this. He's nice, trust me. He's single but not so recently that he's on the rebound, he has a good job and a nice house so he's not desperate for money, he goes on dates so he's not some kind of freak, he's looking for company - just like you.'

'But ...'

'No buts Bec darling. You've just told me you're lonely. Here is a perfect opportunity to meet someone new. And this time give it a chance, get to know him before you decide it's not going to work!'

Rebecca was silent and Helen played her ace. 'After all, Daniel didn't waste any time did he. And now he's getting married again. A great new life ahead of him.'

'Oh okay,' she said ignoring Helen's whoop of joy, 'but he better be nice Helen. And normal. And not just looking for someone to help look after his children. Or ...'

'Stop!' laughed Helen. 'Relax, he's lovely and a perfect match for you. Trust me,' and she rang off leaving Rebecca feeling hopeful and worried in equal measures.

Chapter 3

Daniel and Annabelle arrived early Friday afternoon. Daniel had phoned at 12.30 and said he presumed Rebecca wouldn't mind them coming a day earlier than planned and that they were already on the motorway and would be with her in half an hour.

'What! Now?' Rebecca had spluttered.

'No - in half an hour,' repeated Daniel patiently. 'That's okay isn't it?'

'But you said tomorrow. I mean, I was ready for you to come tomorrow.'

'You don't want us to come? You'd rather we stayed in a hotel?'

Yes, thought Rebecca, she would much rather they stayed in a hotel but when Daniel said it like that, it sounded very churlish.

'Of course not, it's just …'

'Okay, so we'll be with you in half an hour then,' said Daniel before hanging up and leaving Rebecca standing in the kitchen with the phone dangling between her fingers. She looked down at her grubby trousers and dirty hands. She'd decided that she would give Colin a hand by clearing out the greenhouse ready for spring. Her hair was pulled back from her face with an elastic band she'd found in her pocket and there wasn't a scrap of make up on her face.

It wasn't meant to be like this. She had planned on spending Saturday morning in the bath - a long scented bath with some of her expensive Jo Malone bath oil which impregnated her skin with the delicious aroma of orange blossom and left her glowing for the rest of the day. And then she would spend some time on her hair and her face before getting dressed, ready for the arrival of her guests.

She didn't mind that Daniel was getting married again. She didn't mind that there was someone new in his life. But she was about to meet her ex-husband's new partner and she had every intention of making sure she looked her very best when that moment arrived, this was a meeting of the wives and she had no intention of emerging as runner up.

But with Daniel's imminent arrival she would have no time to put her plans into action. She could fit in a quick shower but she didn't have time to wash and dry her hair, she would have to spend some time scrubbing at her hands and nails to banish the dirt from all the plant pots she'd just sorted. And she certainly didn't have time to browse through her wardrobe for the perfect outfit. Come to think of it she needed to put some towels in the spare room and there was a bunch of flowers still standing in water in the sink that she'd planned to put in a vase on the dressing table. She didn't have time to do all that and spend time on her makeup. She had been caught well and truly unawares!

Half an hour later, on the dot, the bell pealed out just as Rebecca was putting a pile of soft fluffy towels in the spare bathroom. She'd pulled on a pair of trousers and a silk blouse and run a brush hastily through her hair, but she felt unready and far from her best. Not how she had wanted to feel when she greeted the new Mrs Miles to be.

Running down the stairs as the bell rang out impatiently once more, she flung open the door and tried not to glare at her ex-husband who stood there surrounded by suitcases and a petite dark haired woman who was hanging onto his arm.

'Bec old girl. You took your time!' and greeting over, he dropped Annabelle's arm, grabbed some of the cases and pushed past Rebecca into the hallway.

Old girl? Had her ex just called her old girl?

Still standing on the door step was a tiny creature, only an inch or so shorter than Rebecca but with an incredibly petite frame, a narrow waist that made Rebecca instinctively pull in her stomach and tiny sparrow hands that fluttered in the air, showing off an immaculate manicure and a large diamond ring.

Rebecca took in the glossy brown bob, shimmering pink lips and the limpid brown eyes framed in dark curling lashes that had most definitely spent a considerable amount of time with a mascara brush. Rebecca thought longingly of her lipstick still laying on the dressing table, top off, ready to apply a slick coat of shiny pink to her own lips and berated herself for not leaving her guests on the doorstep to continue ringing the bell while she took a little more time with her appearance. Was it too late, she wondered, to shut the door and declare that the meeting would take place at the designated time the following day, when she also had glossy hair, carefully applied makeup and an outfit that hadn't been pulled from the back of the wardrobe in desperation.

Sighing inwardly she stepped forward to greet the new Mrs Miles. At second glance Annabelle wasn't quite as young as she first appeared, maybe Rebecca's own age. Despite the skillful makeup, there was a fine web of lines creeping in around her eyes and the tiniest hint of a sag beginning to develop under her chin. Her nose was a little on the large side, her lips a little on the thin side despite the pink gloss. But she was undoubtedly an attractive woman Rebecca conceded. Slim ivory trousers emphasised her narrow legs and waist and her brown cashmere jumper, almost the exact shade of her hair, made her look like a rather delicious chocolate treat. Rebecca couldn't help but wonder what on earth had attracted her to Daniel.

'Hello Annabelle. Come in please,' she said holding out her hand. Much to her surprise, Annabelle threw her arms around Rebecca and they became wedged in the doorway briefly as Annabelle squeezed her tight, planting a scented kiss on her cheek.

'Oh how wonderful to meet you Rebecca. How absolutely lovely that we can spend some time getting to know each other!'

Startled, Rebecca tried to pull out of her embrace but Annabelle hung on, keeping her close by her side. 'I know we're going to be great friends' breathed Annabelle, 'united by Daniel, always there for each other, giving support, a helping hand whenever it's needed. Just the best of friends!'

Rebecca smiled uncertainly, that was quite a list of expectations. She liked the current set up where Daniel lived many miles away and they exchanged pleasantries a couple of times each year. She felt no need for a new best friend and if she did, she certainly wouldn't be looking in Annabelle's direction.

'That's nice of you.'

'Oh not nice at all! It's absolutely essential, don't you think?'

'Er…?'

'We don't want anybody feeling left out, do we?'

'Left out?'

'Well with a new stepmother on the scene,' Annabelle giggled, 'I really have trouble thinking of myself as a stepmother! But we don't want anyone feeling unhappy or worried. It's important that everyone still feels part of the family, still feels loved and cherished. Especially the children, they must still feel wanted, don't you think?' she asked sincerely.

Rebecca wondered if Annabelle knew how old Sarah and Toby were.

'Well,' she began doubtfully, 'I don't ….'

'And you too Becky darling.'

'It's Rebecca, or Bec,' corrected Rebecca. 'Me?'

'Of course! I may be about to get married to Daniel but you'll always be part of each other's lives.

Rebecca shuddered at the thought. 'Oh no! We're divorced and we don't need to be….'

'And it's important that you still feel part of the family.'

'Well it's my family, of course I will still feel part …'

'And that's going to be so much easier if we're best friends, don't you think?' finished Anabelle on a bright note giving Rebecca a last little squeeze before turning to

Daniel who was standing at the foot of the stairs impatiently waiting for her attention.

Looking smug he threw his arms out to encompass the striking entrance hall.

'What do you think then Belles? Didn't I tell you it was a beautiful house?'

Annabelle stepped daintily into the hall, looking obediently at the staircase and the window, the oak floor and the panelled walls in turn as Daniel's pointed each one out.

'It's amazing,' agreed Annabelle in wonder, her hands fluttering in the air. 'How beautiful Daniel, how absolutely beautiful.'

'Yes,' said Daniel pompously. 'It's the sort of house you see and just have to buy.'

Rebecca's eyebrows shot upwards. She had bought the house on a whim, before telling Daniel about her lottery windfall and when he found out, he'd told her she was stupid to buy such a large house, stupid to buy a house in Leeds and incredibly stupid to buy anything without consulting him first.

'I'll show you the living room later, beautiful room, and the bedrooms – gorgeous all of them. Bec – you've got a bedroom ready for us haven't you,' he barked in her direction.

'Of course I have!'

'Just checking. I know how forgetful you can be, especially when you have your nose in a book.' He turned back to Annabelle. 'The grounds are incredible, absolutely wonderful in summer. Great for a family party. This is … was my study,' he pointed to a closed door that led off the hallway receiving a glare from Rebecca. Daniel had used that room for all of two weeks when he'd been trying to buy his old firm to teach them a lesson for not promoting him. It had been Rebecca's study for the last two years.

'My study,' she muttered.

Daniel ignored her. 'But you must see the kitchen. It will take your breath away. One of the main reasons we bought the house.'

Rebecca gasped. Daniel had admitted the kitchen was superb, just before he announced it was too big and she should sell the house immediately.

'Actually, I bought the house ....' she started firmly but he had already grabbed Annabelle's arm and was escorting her down the hallway into the huge kitchen which Rebecca had fallen in love with at first sight.

Rebecca glared at Daniel's back and slammed the front door shut. She had forgotten just how irritating she found him but three minutes in his presence had brought it all flooding back. What on earth had she been thinking, saying he could stay with her? They were divorced, surely it would have been okay to tell him to stay in a hotel. She could have met them for a meal, said hello and left again as quickly as possible with her sanity still intact. Sighing she climbed over the huge pile of cases piled on the floor, briefly worrying about just how long they planned on staying and stamped down the hallway to join them in her kitchen.

'Oh my word! This is superb.' Annabelle was standing in front of the huge range cooker, admiring the array of copper pans. She threw out her arms and walked towards the French windows and the two raspberry settees that gave a superb view onto the garden. 'Delightful, just delightful!'

Daniel looked on indulgently as Annabelle continued to explore the vast kitchen and Rebecca had to elbow him out of the way so she could get through the doorway.

'Oh Daniel, can you imagine the meals I could produce in this kitchen? Can you imagine the wonderful time we would have!'

She turned to Rebecca. 'We love entertaining Rebecca, I love to cook.'

She would have to, thought Rebecca caustically, Daniel hadn't so much as boiled the kettle in the last five years of their relationship.

'But our kitchen is so tiny!' The silver tinkling laugh filled the room. 'If I want to open the fridge Daniel has to stand in the hallway. You're so lucky, having this wonderful room. In fact, having this whole house. So lucky.'

Rebecca stared, of course she was lucky. She had won the lottery.

'We have a tiny little house, don't we Daniel. But it's enough for us. We're happy there, just the two of us, aren't we?'

A tiny house? Daniel had sent a photograph of the house he bought in Devon and it was exactly the sort of house Rebecca knew he would choose, a brand new square box with 'luxury' and 'executive' appearing frequently in the description and as far as Rebecca could remember, it had been far from tiny.

'You have to be happy with what you can afford,' continued Annabelle firmly, 'there's no point hankering after things out of your reach. We can't afford a house like this,' she added pointedly.

'Well yes, I am lucky,' said Rebecca, getting the distinct feeling she was being chastised.

'Do you cook?'

Rebecca looked sideways at Daniel who was standing in front of the double doors to the garden puffing out his chest in appreciation

'Well yes I do …'

'It must be nice not having to work. All that free time to spend in the kitchen.' Annabelle sighed, trailing one hand elegantly across the huge, range cooker. 'By the time Daniel and I get home from work we're just so exhausted!'

Rebecca blinked. Daniel must have changed a great deal if he was coming home from work exhausted. Grumpy yes. Belligerent, bad tempered and full of complaints definitely, but Rebecca couldn't remember the last time Daniel had exhausted himself at work.

'I do work actually …'

'Yes, Daniel mentioned you bought a retirement home for your mother to live in. You have a manager, don't you?'

'I didn't buy it for my mum to live in!' She thought of all the hard work and effort that she had put into turning Parklands around, the success she'd made of the project. 'And I do have a manager but …'

'Do you entertain a lot?'

Rebecca blinked again, this was like a high speed interview.

'Entertain?'

'It's such a lovely big kitchen, it would be a waste not to use it properly. I would have friends round all the time, lots of chatter and good food.' Annabelle had a wistful look in her eyes, 'I can imagine the wonderful evenings Daniel and I would have.'

Rebecca couldn't begin to imagine a wonderful evening with Daniel but she nodded politely. 'Well yes it's perfect for …'

'It's a bit of a waste if you sit in here every night on your own! Eating macaroni cheese for one!' and the tinkle of laughter filled the air again.

'I don't sit by myself,' started Rebecca indignantly before pausing and flushing slightly. 'I don't sit by myself every night …'

Annabelle stopped her patrol of the kitchen to press a hand on Rebecca's arm, a slender hand with long slim fingers, the hand where her huge diamond ring nestled. They both looked downwards at the prisms of light that shot outwards and Annabelle allowed herself a happy smile before lifting her deep brown eyes to meet Rebecca's own. 'I'm sorry, I didn't mean to upset you. Daniel said you still lived on your own.'

'Well, yes I am on my own at the moment but …'

Annabelle patted Rebecca's arm again in sympathy. 'Poor you!' she cooed.

'No! I'm happy,' insisted Rebecca wondering why it didn't sound as though she meant it. 'Really!' she tried again.

'Of course,' Annabelle said disbelievingly. 'Of course you are.'

'Bec is that kettle broken. Aren't you going to offer us a cup of tea?'

'Oh that would be lovely. We seem to have been driving for ever.'

'Sorry, of course you must be parched.' Wondering why she was apologising when they had arrived a day early, Rebecca took the opportunity to escape Annabelle's sympathetic patting and filled the kettle with water. She really could do with a brandy she thought desperately, reaching for some mugs. Five minutes into the visit she was left feeling thoroughly inadequate for not having a sparkling social life and at least 8 guests sitting round her kitchen table every evening.

'Actually, do you think we could go to our room Rebecca darling. I need to freshen up after that long drive?'

There was a definite note of censure in Annabelle's voice and Rebecca slammed the mugs onto the surface feeling like a rather inefficient bellboy.

'Of course,' she said through gritted teeth, 'Let me show you the way.'

Grabbing Annabelle's arm she hauled her to the kitchen door before she could change her mind and gave Rebecca another task. 'Daniel, get the cases,' she commanded over her shoulder and ignoring his startled look, she propelled Annabelle at speed up the staircase.

Opening the door to the spare room, Rebecca stood back and let Annabelle appreciate the large airy space decorated in cream and yellow with touches of fresh apple green.

'Oh it's lovely!'

Rebecca nodded in satisfaction. Her house was beautiful, she had made sure each room had its own personality and it was a warm and welcoming home. She stepped past Annabelle to open another door to the ensuite bathroom and one of the wardrobe doors to show her the space.

'You seem to have a lot of luggage,' she said dubiously, 'but I think you'll have enough room to put everything in here.'

Annabelle stopped in her admiration of the room spinning round to stare into the wardrobe and Rebecca suddenly felt a little surge of sympathy. It couldn't be easy for her either, meeting the first wife. She probably felt as though she was being judged at every turn.

'Oh I like to be prepared,' Annabelle said, casting a quick look at Rebecca's slightly crumpled silk blouse.

Rebecca's sympathy disappeared.

'Is this your only spare room?' asked Annabelle, wandering over towards the window and peeping down at the vast sweep of drive.

'What? I'm sorry, don't you like this room?' asked Rebecca in confusion.

'Oh it's lovely,' Annabelle reassured her. 'I just wondered where everybody else stayed when they visited.'

Rebecca frowned. 'Well,' she began cautiously, 'Sarah and Toby both have their own room. I want them to feel as though this is their home, somewhere they can turn up and stay whenever they want.'

'How wonderful,' beamed Annabelle. 'And?'

Rebecca stared. 'And what?'

'And do you have any other rooms?'

Rooms? It wasn't a bed and breakfast. 'There is another spare room,' Rebecca said, a little confused.

'Wonderful! So this could be our room?'

'Your room?'

'Yes. For when we come and stay. You know, part of the family, a big extended unit, all with their own room, all with their own little part of the house.'

Rebecca tried not to look too horrified. Was Annabel seriously suggesting that she and Daniel should have their own room in Rebecca's house? Beech Grange may be big, but it definitely wasn't big enough for Daniel and his new wife to use on a regular basis

'Oh I don't think …'

'Is this the room Daniel used when he lived here?'

'What?'

Annabelle didn't answer but walked around to the far side of the bed, picking up one of the pillows and examining it closely, leaving a silence for Rebecca to fill.

Rebecca's eyes narrowed as she watched her. Did Annabelle want her to know that Daniel had not kept anything secret about his previous life, was Rebecca meant to feel guilty that Daniel had been pushed into the spare room as soon as she had won the lottery?

'Yes, it is,' she finally offered coolly.

'So it would be a good room for us to have?'

Rebecca shook her head. 'I don't think that's really necessary Annabelle,' she said pleasantly. 'I can't imagine that you and Daniel will be here frequently enough to need your own room. After all,' she tried to laugh although it came out more as a bark, 'you will want to get on with your own lives, in Devon, where you live.'

The conversation was halted by Daniel appearing in the doorway, laden down with bags and puffing slightly.

'I'll leave you to get settled in and I'll finish making the tea,' said Rebecca walking away. 'Come down when you're ready,' and she closed the door with a snap behind her. Fleeing in the direction of the kitchen, she ignored the kettle and reached into the fridge for a bottle of wine. It had been a meeting of the wives, old versus new and Rebecca had been left in no doubt, Annabelle had emerged victorious.

Chapter 4

Taking a large slug of wine, Rebecca berated herself for agreeing to let Daniel stay in her house. What had she been thinking! The phone rang and Rebecca snatched at it, hoping it was some kind of emergency that meant she would have to leave the house for the next few days. It was Helen.

'I can't talk,' whispered Rebecca into the receiver. 'They're here!'

'Whose there?' asked Helen, 'and why are you whispering?'

Rebecca frowned. She wasn't sure why she felt the need to whisper, Daniel and Annabelle were still upstairs but since they'd arrived the house had started to feel very small.

She spoke a little louder but still in a soft undertone. 'Daniel and Annabelle.'

'I thought they were coming tomorrow?'

'They were but then Daniel phoned and said they were coming early. I only got half an hour's notice!'

'No! How did you look when they arrived, did you have chance to tart yourself up a bit?'

'No I didn't,' wailed Rebecca. 'I was clearing out the greenhouse, I didn't have time to even wash my hair.'

There was a sympathetic gasp from Helen. 'What's she like?'

'Horrendous!'

'Oh I knew it! I knew if she had fallen for Daniel she'd be awful! Is she like Miss Trunchbull? Is she wearing a tweed jacket and a moustache?' giggled Helen. 'Does she bark out orders just like Daniel? Which one of them is in charge?'

Rebecca took a deep drink from her glass. 'None of that. She's actually quite attractive,' she said reluctantly.

'No!'

'Yes. She's made a real effort of course,' unlike me thought Rebecca running a hand through her hair which made it stick out even more. 'But she does look good.'

There was a pause.

'Really?' asked Helen unbelievingly. 'I mean, is she really pretty? And if she is, what on earth is she doing with Daniel? No offence Bec, but he's not exactly George Clooney is he?'

Rebecca sighed. She'd been asking herself the same question ever since she'd opened the door to see the pair standing on her front step. 'I don't know,' she admitted. 'I mean she's not stunning or anything.' She bit her lip, that sounded a little mean. 'What I mean is she isn't beautiful but she is okay. Well, more than okay I suppose and she dresses well and her hair is immaculate and her make up is just right and … well you know what I mean.'

'So what's the horrendous part about her then?' asked Helen intrigued.

'She's a bitch,' offered Rebecca taking another sip of wine. 'She keeps making all these unpleasant comments but with a smile on her face! Like how I'm still single and how we should be friends so I don't feel left out and that I probably eat macaroni cheese in the kitchen by myself!'

There was a brief silence.

'Okay,' said Helen slowly, 'I thought you liked macaroni cheese?'

'I do! It's not about the macaroni, it's the way she said it. That I sit here all by myself and eat it because I've got no-one to share it with.'

'I see.'

'And she said that she would love a kitchen like mine because she loves to entertain.'

'We'd all love a kitchen like yours Bec.'

'Well yes I know, it's a lovely kitchen but she said she would make the most of it, she would cook and entertain and that she would invite friends round whereas I'm single so I'm wasting it!'

29

'Right.'

'And she's brought loads of luggage and said she likes to be prepared – and when she said it she looked at me!'

'Looked at you?'

'Yes! Like I couldn't be bothered. It wasn't that I couldn't be bothered, I didn't have time because they came early!'

'And she said she wanted to be friends?'

'Yes! She suggested that when they get married no-one will have time for me so I'd better be her friend so that I can be included in things.'

'She said that!'

Rebecca nibbled at her lip. 'Well, maybe not those exact words. But that's what she meant.'

'Bec darling, are you sure you're not just being a tad over sensitive? Because none of that actually sounds bad. She's probably feeling really nervous about meeting you and saying the wrong things but talking about macaroni cheese and suggesting that you two become friends doesn't make her horrendous.'

'You didn't hear the way she said it,' Rebecca complained.

'I know, I know,' soothed Helen. 'I just think that maybe you're both a bit nervous and got off to a bad start? I mean, I know I wanted her to look hideous and have a big wart on her chin and give Daniel hell, but if she is okay and wants you to two be friends, that's got to be a whole lot easier than fighting for the next 40 years. Perhaps you need to give her a break and be pleasant back?'

Rebecca thought for a moment. She was fairly certain she had been pleasant to Annabelle. She didn't need to be pleasant to Daniel. And Annabelle hadn't appeared in the slightest bit nervous, she looked very much in control as she walked around Rebecca's kitchen grilling her about her lack of social life and entertaining skills. And she had definitely implied that Rebecca's beautiful house was wasted on her and that it would be put to far better use if Annabelle and Daniel lived there.

'Bec?'

'I'm thinking,' muttered Rebecca.

Another small pause. 'I may have read more into her remarks than she meant,' admitted Rebecca grudgingly.

'It's just nerves,' Helen said reassuringly.

'But I think she was making a point about something. I'm just not entirely sure what,' mumbled Rebecca.

'Honey, if Daniel marries her you are bound to meet occasionally, you know birthdays, holidays etc, try and make the best of it for your sake.'

'She wants us to get together at Christmas!' said Rebecca indignantly.

'Well there's no need to take it that far,' said Helen firmly, 'just be pleasant to each other when the need arises and ignore her the rest of the time. Like every other ex-wife does.'

Rebecca sighed, knowing her friend was right. 'What about this man you promised me,' she demanded.

'Whoa, slow down! You've refused to meet anyone I've tried to introduce you to for months, what's the rush now?'

'Because I need someone,' Rebecca hoped she sounded firm and not desperate. 'I'm not having Annabelle think I'm a lonely cat woman. I want to meet someone and start again, and it would be really handy if I could meet him before they get married. Can you imagine the smirk on her face if I'm a still by myself when she's drifting down the aisle?

'Cat woman?'

'I need someone Helen, I'm finally ready. So please arrange something and let's get my new life on track.'

'Okay, okay. But don't rush …'

'Rush! You were the one to tell me I should stop being so fussy and get on with it.'

'I know but for the right reasons darling, not because Daniel is getting married and you've developed an obsession with macaroni cheese!'

'Now is the right time. Arrange something Helen!'

And then Rebecca heard footsteps coming down the staircase and the conversation ended as she hung up, downed her wine and re-boiled the kettle to make the long awaited cup of tea.

It was a long afternoon. They moved into the living room and Rebecca bit her tongue as Daniel settled in Rebecca's favourite corner of the cream sofa and Annabelle fussed around him, making sure he could reach his tea and dashing back to the kitchen to fetch his newspaper. When Daniel finally retreated behind the printed pages Annabelle snuggled next to him and Rebecca sank into one of the equally comfortable chairs. She watched as Annabelle pressed herself into Daniel's side and was rewarded with a smile. If Rebecca had sat so closely to Daniel he would have given her a sharp poke in the ribs and told her to give him some elbow room. There again, Rebecca wouldn't have cared whether he could reach his tea and she certainly wouldn't have gone running into the kitchen to fetch his paper.

'So,' she said brightly. 'How exactly did you two meet?'

She winced. It was such a banal question and she already knew the answer. Daniel had told her months ago that he'd met a woman called Annabelle at a friend's house. He'd asked her out to dinner and a few weeks later he'd phoned Rebecca up to advise her, quite formally, that they were now dating. Rebecca had been uninterested at the time and amused that Daniel felt the need to keep her in the loop of his new life. Now she was intrigued as to how he had found it so easy to meet someone new, invite her for dinner and start a new life with little of the angst that Rebecca was experiencing.

Annabelle smiled widely and Rebecca saw her hand slide into the crook of Daniel's arm. 'A friend of a friend,' she replied coyly. 'We met at a party he was giving and our eyes met across a crowded room!'

Rebecca smiled obligingly. What on earth had Annabelle been thinking to see Daniel's rather blood shot eyes from across the room and decide she needed to get to know him better. 'Right,' she said unconvincingly. 'That's nice.'

Annabelle giggled. 'The first night we went out I was so nervous I drank far too much wine and Daniel was so sweet. He took me home and helped me indoors and then said he wanted to see me again! I'd been worried that getting so squiffy on our first date would put him off me for ever!'

Rebecca nodded. Daniel always accused Rebecca of being an embarrassment if she had more than two glasses of wine. Not that Rebecca had much of a chance, Daniel had invariably made her drive because he said he could take his drink whereas good wine was wasted on her.

She watched Daniel look indulgently down at Annabelle as she spoke. What on earth had she done to make Daniel dote on her as he clearly did? Or more to the question, what had Rebecca failed to do?

'And then, after only a few months he took me out to the most amazing restaurant,' continued Annabelle with a dreamy look, 'and he produced an engagement ring.'

She held out a hand so Rebecca could admire the large diamond nestled there. 'And he asked me to marry him!'

Rebecca's engagement ring had cost very little, they hadn't had a bean to rub together at the time and Daniel had always been careful with money. Some years later, when money wasn't quite so tight, Rebecca had suggested an eternity ring but Daniel had recoiled at the thought of spending money on an unnecessary token, as he had described it. It would seem his attitude had changed with the new woman in his life.

'How lovely!' declared Rebecca, trying to sound sincere.

'And you?'

'Me?'

'You haven't found anyone new, are you finding it difficult?'

Good grief, was her ex-husband's new partner going to give her relationship counselling?

'Of course not,' she answered sharply.

She tried to ignore the look that passed between her ex and Annabelle.

'I mean there have been men.' That didn't sound quite as she had intended, plus it was something of an exaggeration. There had been Richard. The handful of others who she had dated barely counted. 'I mean a man,' she corrected. That sounded just as bad. 'I have had relationships.'

'Of course,' nodded Annabelle sympathetically. 'We're just very lucky I suppose,' she said throwing an adoring smile at Daniel. 'So lucky to find each other. I suppose it shows that money can't buy everything.'

'What?'

'Oh Rebecca darling, even if you have all the money in the world it can't necessarily buy you love.'

Was it Rebecca's imagination or did Annabelle look ever so slightly smug.

Her shoulders tensed. 'Well I wouldn't put it quite like that. I just haven't found anybody I want to start a new relationship with yet,' she said stiffly.

'Of course,' said Annabelle soothingly.

Rebecca tried to smile but it was difficult with clenched teeth.

'How's business going?' she asked the newspaper that was covering Daniel's face.

'Oh he's doing so well!'

There was a grunt from Daniel as he turned the page.

'He's already expanded and had to find a second showroom,' Annabelle said with pride. 'And he's getting a real reputation amongst car dealers. He got a call from someone in Scotland a few days ago- they'd heard about him and they want Daniel to find them a very special car.'

She was smiling widely and Rebecca had to admit, albeit grudgingly, that she certainly seemed invested in Daniel and his career. More interested than Rebecca had ever been. Was there some kind of life lesson unfolding here, she wondered?

'That's good.'

There was a pause and Rebecca cast around wildly for something else to say.

'Do you have any plans while you're in Leeds?'

Annabel looked surprised. 'We've come to see you Rebecca,' she said pointedly.

'Right. Good.'

Another pause.

'Rebecca,' Annabelle relinquished Daniel's arm and leant forward slightly. 'I realise this is difficult for you.'

'Difficult?'

'Yes. I mean you're the ex Mrs Miles and I'm the new Mrs Miles …'

Rebecca couldn't help herself. 'Mrs Miles to be.'

'Mrs Miles very soon to be,' came back Annabelle.

'Regardless,' Rebecca continued smoothly. 'It's not at all hard Annabelle. Daniel and I split up two years ago and I'm happy for him – happy that he's met you and wants to get married.'

Annabelle raised her eyebrows in disbelief. 'That's very kind of you to say so Rebecca. But it must be hard,' she insisted firmly, 'knowing that Daniel has found true love and seeing him move on must be difficult when you're still – alone.'

Rebecca opened her mouth to tell Annabelle that life alone was infinitely preferable to life with Daniel.

'But that's part of the reason we've come to visit. We want there to be no tension in our family,' continued

Annabelle. 'We want everyone to be included and know they all have a place.'

Rebecca wanted to point out that the family Annabelle was referring to belonged to Rebecca and the only source of tension right now was Annabelle herself, but she swallowed her words and smiled stiffly instead.

'That's why I feel it's important that we get to know each other, become friends and share each other's lives,' continued Annabelle dreamily as Rebecca winced at the thought. 'Won't it be wonderful – us popping up for a long weekend, the children joining us for barbeques and Sunday lunch. All part of the family.'

Rebecca thought it sounded horrific. She had managed quite well without Daniel in her life for the last two years and if the children ever felt the need to visit their father they could travel down to Devon and do exactly that. She had felt no inclination to invite Daniel to join them for Sunday lunch, in fact if Rebecca had told either of her children their father was arriving they would probably have cancelled their visit

'Of course it would be lovely to be able to reciprocate,' Annabelle was continuing with a sad look on her face. 'But I'm afraid Daniel's circumstances are quite different.' There it was, that note of censure again. Rebecca didn't care what Helen said, this wasn't a nervous Annabelle saying the wrong thing, she definitely had a bee in her bonnet about something.

'I'm afraid our little house just isn't up to that kind of entertaining. Goodness me, we wouldn't be able to find bedrooms for you all,' she laughed, the little tinkly laugh that was starting to grate on Rebecca's nerves. 'No, this is the house.' She waved her arm around the spacious living room with its huge wood burner and elegant cream furniture. 'This is where we'll need to have our little get togethers. We need to get to know each other Rebecca my dear, we'll be spending a lot of time together from now on,' and smiling happily Annabelle sat back again, leaning against Daniel's arm and squeezing him fondly as she looked around the room with a contented expression.

Chapter 5

Rebecca's plan had been to make a chicken casserole but when she told her guests, Annabelle had cast her a rather startled glance.

'Oh, I see. You were going to treat us to home cooking tonight! How quaint.'

'You don't want a casserole?'

'I'd just presumed we would be going out tonight. To celebrate.'

'Oh I see. Well if you want …'

'Oh no Rebecca darling. Please don't change your plans for us! I'm sure chicken casserole will be lovely. I bet you make wonderful casserole!'

'Well, it's okay.'

'So that's settled! We'll forget about going out tonight and we'll stay in and eat casserole.'

Rebecca wondered why the offer of homemade chicken casserole suddenly sounded quite mean and thoughtless.

'No! No, I think we should go out. You're quite right.'

Annabelle's hands fluttered. 'You think so?'

'Absolutely,' said Rebecca firmly. 'We're going out.'

Daniel was reading another paper and ignoring the conversation but when Annabelle announced the change in plans, he looked up and smiled approvingly muttering 'for the best I think', before casting a reproachful look at Rebecca.

Smiling rather manically, Rebecca had suggested several restaurants but the final choice was made by Daniel, choosing somewhere they had visited once or twice in the past. Overpriced and somewhat pretentious, Rebecca wasn't surprised it was one of Daniel's favourites. But she put a brave face on and agreed with enthusiasm, leaving Daniel to phone and make a reservation in that overbearing voice he used for such occasions with Annabelle nodding enthusiastically next to him.

'I think I'll have a quick bath before we go out,' Rebecca announced, relishing the thought of an hour on her own even if it was in the bathroom. She stopped in the doorway, hope in her eyes. 'Maybe you two would like to go on your own?' she suggested brightly. 'You can have a lovely meal and celebrate without me.'

Two pairs of eyes met her own.

'Bec old girl, we've come here so you and Belles can get to know each other. Not going to work if we go anywhere without you is it?'

Annabelle had clutched her throat and asked in a soft, tremulous voice, 'Is it because you don't want to spend the evening with us Rebecca? Have I said something …?'

In the ensuing rush for Rebecca to reassure Annabelle that her company was very much desired and Daniel to tell Annabelle that Rebecca was just a little thoughtless sometimes and Annabelle to allow herself to be soothed and placated, Rebecca's head had begun to pound even as she insisted vehemently that of course she wanted to join them.

'Of course I'll come with you,' she insisted. 'I was just trying to …'

She sighed, it wasn't going to work. 'Of course I'll come,' she said bravely, 'wouldn't miss it for the world,' and she went into the kitchen in search of some painkillers - or Annabelle killers as she now decided they should be called.

So a few hours later they had arrived at the restaurant, sitting on hard chairs around an undersized table containing more glasses and cutlery than Rebecca had ever seen in one place.

'Menu old girl?'

She had also decided that if Daniel called her old girl once more she was very likely to stab him with the nearest thing to hand, which at that moment was the butter knife. She was sure she could exert the necessary force to turn it into a deadly weapon.

She relaxed her grip on the knife to take a menu and watched Annabelle slide her hand into Daniel's and give him a loving smile. 'What an excellent choice darling,' she cooed looking around admiringly. 'This is lovely.'

No it wasn't thought Rebecca, it was old fashioned and dimly lit with waiters who looked down their noses, no atmosphere and very little on the menu that Rebecca wanted to eat

'Champagne!' squeaked Annabelle, 'that's what we need darling, champagne!'

If Rebecca had demanded champagne Daniel would have told her she was mad. She watched his face as it melted into a smile and he patted Annabelle's hand. 'Then champagne we shall have my darling,' and he waved a hand imperiously at the head waiter and told him to be a good chap and bring a bottle of their best. Rebecca had cringed with embarrassment at Daniel's tone and sent an apologetic smile towards the expressionless waiter.

'And make sure it's chilled,' Annabelle had added with a silvery tinkle of laughter.

The champagne was delivered, chilled to perfection but Rebecca held her hand over her own glass and offered to drive them all home so Daniel and Annabelle could enjoy themselves.

'Ah,' declared Annabelle closing her eyes in appreciation, 'now that is wonderful champagne. How delicious. At last we can celebrate, to us my darling,' she said gazing into Daniel's eyes. 'And to our wedding!'

Rebecca hastily picked up her water glass, 'To you both.'

'To us,' echoed Daniel looking immensely pleased with himself. 'I'll order, shall I?'

Rebecca picked up her abandoned menu. 'I'll choose my own thank you,' she said firmly.

'Please yourself. You know you always wish you'd ordered something different once it arrives.'

Rebecca clenched her teeth. 'Well I've had plenty of practice choosing my own meals over the last few years Daniel!'

Annabelle didn't even glance at her own unopened menu as she set her glass down carefully on the table and gazed earnestly into Rebecca's eyes. 'Isn't this lovely?' she demanded. 'Isn't it wonderful the three of us being able to go out like this?'

'Yes, it's wonderful,' said Rebecca thinking exactly the opposite.

'Just don't order the sea bass, you don't like sea bass.'

Rebecca's head swivelled back to Daniel. 'I love sea bass! It's you who doesn't like it.'

'I don't expect to take your place in the family Rebecca, I will never replace you as Sarah and Toby's mother.'

'The last time you had sea bass you said you hadn't enjoyed it. But it's just like you to choose it again.'

Rebecca's eyes flew back to Annabelle. Did she really think that her children might suddenly decide they preferred Annabelle as a mother and stop visiting Rebecca? Did she expect they would start calling Annabelle mother and Rebecca would be left truly alone in her huge kitchen with her macaroni cheese.

The waiter was standing patiently by her chair. 'I'll have the sea bass,' she said defiantly as Daniel tutted.

'You won't be taking my place Annabelle,' she said firmly, passing her menu back to the waiter.

'And we do appreciate how brave you're being about Daniel finding true love,' Annabelle continued her warm smile containing infinite sympathy. 'We both want to thank you for being so welcoming.'

Rebecca gritted her teeth. 'I really don't mind.'

'But your husband is moving on with someone new Rebecca, I know that must hurt.'

'No - I *really* don't mind,' insisted Rebecca. 'Daniel and I split up years ago ...'

'And you're still alone while he's found someone new. So hard for you.'

'I don't mind!' Rebecca was almost shouting.

'Sometimes money isn't the answer is it? Sometimes what you need is someone in your life, like Daniel has.'

It was so accurate that for a moment Rebecca couldn't speak. She didn't want Daniel back, she didn't care that he was getting married. But Annabelle was right, for all her money Rebecca was lonely, the millions in her bank were not particularly good company.

'Really Annabelle …'

'Funny how it's worked out isn't it,' Annabelle was contemplating, 'Daniel leaves empty handed but he's the one that finds love.'

'Empty handed! Daniel didn't…'

'But it will all work out Rebecca dear. Because now we'll help you. We'll be your new family and help you find love, just like Daniel has. What happened in the past,' was that a hint of reproach in her eyes Rebecca wondered? 'What happened to Daniel, that's all behind us. Time to forgive and forget!'

'Forgive?'

'We don't begrudge your good luck. That would be small minded,' she continued staring pointedly at Rebecca, 'let's move on and start again shall we?'

'What on earth…'

And then the food arrived and Rebecca had no choice but to sit and silently fume as the waiters placed huge white plates containing tiny morsels of food in front of each of them and Annabelle fussed about the temperature of the champagne and Daniel complained about the lack of vegetables

She spent the next hour listening to Annabelle's high-pitched laughter that was beginning to sound less like a silver bell and more like a dentist's drill and Daniel's pompous declarations as to the quality of the beef, the richness of the red wine and how he was an expert in both.

She had not missed her ex-husband, she realised. She may be missing company, but she was not missing Daniel. As Annabelle excused herself from the table, Rebecca leaned forward to glare at him. He had lost weight over the last few years and his face had slimmed down a little. But there was still a double chin and a familiar smug expression on a face that was flushed with drink. Rebecca found herself fighting an urge to slap him. Perhaps there was a reason most ex-spouses didn't continue to socialise.

'Daniel,' she hissed, his attention sliding from the desert still on his plate to Rebecca. 'What have you told Annabelle about our split!'

Daniel looked surprised. 'What do you mean?'

'I get the feeling Annabelle thinks I threw you out and kept all the money for myself?'

'Don't be ridiculous Bec. You don't know what you're talking about.'

'Why does she think I'm heartbroken about the two of you getting together?'

'She doesn't, she's a very caring person and she doesn't want you to feel …'

'I don't care that you're getting married Daniel. Do you understand what I'm saying? I really don't care.'

Daniel raised his eyebrow. 'No?'

'No! And I won't have Annabelle constantly suggesting that I've somehow treated you badly. Speak to her Daniel! Speak to her and make sure she understands the facts. *Me*, treat *you* badly!'

'Oh relax Bec, I never said anything to make her think anything of the sort!'

'Then why does she keep suggesting I've wronged you somehow?'

'She's said nothing of the sort. You're imagining it!'

'I am not!' said Rebecca crossly. 'Annabelle seems to think I behaved badly and I won't have it. Speak to her Daniel, speak to her or I will!'

'Becs old g …'

Rebecca's hand curled round her desert fork. 'Stop calling me that!' she snapped.

Daniel sighed. It was his 'you're such a pain' sigh and with a slight roll of his eyes he leaned forward.

'Annabelle is a wonderful woman,' he began sternly. 'She wanted to meet you, she's been really excited about the whole trip and it will make life so much easier if we can all be civil to each other. Stop looking for trouble Bec, let's just try and get on shall we.'

'Looking for trouble! I am doing nothing of the kind!'

'Aren't you Bec? Aren't you just hoping you can find a reason not to like Annabelle?'

'No!'

'Because that's how it's starting to look …'

'Well you're looking in the wrong direction Daniel because the only person who seems to be a little upset round here is Annabelle!'

'Don't talk rubbish Bec,' suggested Daniel dismissively. 'Annabelle has done nothing wrong and I expected more of you!'

'What!'

'Belles darling! Found it okay?'

Annabelle was sliding back onto her seat looking immaculate.

'I did. Oh I have enjoyed myself tonight Rebecca, it's been lovely getting to know you.'

Daniel threw a triumphant look at Rebecca who bit her lip. 'Yes, yes, it's been lovely,' she muttered,' gazing down at the desert still left on her plate.

'I knew we would get on,' whispered Annabelle, putting one of her tiny hands on Rebecca's own. 'I just knew that with Daniel in common we'd be the best of friends.'

Rebecca refused to look in Daniel's direction and she tried to smile warmly at Annabelle, her teeth bared in what she hoped was a happy expression.

'Have you had enough to eat Belles?'

'I think so darling.'

Rebecca gazed at Annabelle's plate, she hadn't eaten more than two mouthfuls of any course that had been placed in front of her.

'Then we'll get going shall we?' and ignoring the fact that Rebecca still had most of her desert on her plate, Daniel stood up to take Annabelle by the hand and casting a disapproving look over his shoulder, he guided his wife to be towards the door leaving Rebecca, her desert and the bill at the table.

Rebecca glanced at the total and nearly fell from her chair as she saw how much the champagne had cost, plus the Remy Martin brandies Daniel had quaffed and the bottle of white he had ordered with the starters and the bottle of red he had ordered for the main course. For a moment she was tempted to send the bill to Daniel, now standing by the door declaring noisily that his coat was creased and that the cloakroom attendant should be more careful. But the effort simply wasn't worth it. All she wanted to do was go home to take some more painkillers and waving over the waiter she handed him her credit card and started counting the minutes until she would be home and in the relative peace of her bedroom.

Chapter 6

The next morning Rebecca looked for a quiet moment with Daniel to discuss Sarah's news. Although neither of the children had a good relationship with their father, Rebecca had urged Sarah to phone Daniel and tell him she was getting married.

She wanted to speak to Daniel about their daughter alone but finding Daniel without Annabelle hanging on his arm was proving a hard task and after stalking him along the hallway and lurking outside his bedroom door, she had to finally give in and raise the subject as they all sat in the kitchen.

'Yes she told me. Bit young aren't they? Have you met this Dominic chap? What's he like? Not after her money is he!'

Daniel gave Rebecca a reproving look. He had thoroughly disagreed with her giving their children a share of her winning ticket being firmly of the opinion they should stand on their own two feet.

'I've only met him once or twice, I must admit I hadn't realised it was quite this serious.'

'Mm. Can't be too careful you know, not when people know you've got money!' Daniel puffed up his chest importantly.

Annabelle reached over to take his hand and gaze lovingly into his eyes.

'That's why I'm so lucky I found Belles,' added Daniel gruffly, looking almost emotional and Rebecca watched in disbelief as he bent down and pressed a loving kiss on Annabelle's soft pink lips. 'So very lucky.'

Tearing her eyes away from the display of affection, Rebecca couldn't help the shaft of resentment. Daniel had barely cast a pleasant glance her way during the latter years of their marriage, this loving man indulging in public displays of affection was a mystery to her.

'Yes well, I'm sure Sarah knows what she's doing. Anyway, I've invited them over for the weekend, I thought it would give us chance to get to know Dominic a little better.'

'Oh,' Annabelle clapped her hands loudly making Rebecca jump. 'What a lovely idea. And we can talk weddings and dresses and plans can't we!'

Rebecca didn't answer and Annabelle bit her lip, leaning over to pat Rebecca's hand. 'Oh Rebecca I didn't mean to …'

'Yes well,' interrupted Daniel, 'it will be good to meet Dominic.'

'And of course,' added Annabelle in a sympathetic whisper, 'we don't have to talk weddings *all* the time.'

Rebecca closed her eyes briefly. 'Annabelle, please believe me, I am not upset that you and Daniel are getting married. I am not upset that Sarah and Dominic are getting married.' Her voice was rising and she stopped and brought it down a pitch. 'I am very happy for you all and I am more than happy to talk weddings. We can talk about weddings as much as you want.'

'Really! Do you really mean that Rebecca?' Annabelle was sitting forward in her chair, her hands fluttering in delight and Rebecca tried her best to smile pleasantly.

'Of course.'

'Oh you have no idea how happy that makes me. Because there was something we wanted to tell you but we didn't want to upset you in any way, not in any way at all. Not if it is going to make you sad or make you …'

'Just tell me,' snapped Rebecca a little more firmly than she had intended. At Daniel's reproving glance she nodded encouragingly. 'Just tell me.'

'Well,' began Daniel grandly.

Rebecca tensed, she had a feeling there was bad news on the way.

'We've made a decision about the wedding itself.'

His cheeks were puffed up as they did when he felt important, certain that all eyes were on him as he continued.

'We've decided to get married in Leeds not in Devon.'

'No!' cried Rebecca.

They both stared at her.

'I mean, why would you do that. Surely all your friends are in Devon?'

'But my family is in Leeds Bec. And it means more to me having my wedding here than back in Devon.'

Rebecca searched for help.

'Well, Toby is in Bristol,' she said desperately. 'And Sarah might not be in Leeds much longer,' she lied.

'No, we've decided,' insisted Daniel, taking Annabelle's hand in his own. 'Leeds it is.'

'But ... but ...' Rebecca was scrambling round for inspiration something that would tempt them back to Devon, many miles away. 'The children wouldn't mind travelling to Devon for the wedding. It would be nice for them to visit you at your home,' she lied, knowing full well that if Toby could find an excuse not to attend his father's wedding he would snatch it with both hands.

'But what about you Rebecca?'

'Me?' asked Rebecca startled.

'We want you there as well, of course.' Rebecca flinched. It hadn't occurred to her that she would have to attend the ceremony. Did ex-wives attend the nuptials of the ex-husband when marrying the new wife? She would look it up on Google as soon as she had the chance, maybe there was some etiquette that she could quote to avoid such an unthinkable invite.

'You want me to come?' she asked to avoid any doubt.

Annabelle laughed. 'Of course we do Rebecca my darling. That's what the whole visit is about, remember.' She frowned as though Rebecca's inability to remember this fact was a cause for concern. 'We discussed this yesterday didn't we,' she continued in a loud, slow tone. 'About how we wanted to keep the family together, just a little larger with the addition of a new stepmother. Unfortunately because of our tiny house,' she sighed and Rebecca wished Helen was there to advise whether Rebecca was being overly sensitive or whether Annabelle was having yet another dig, 'we can't have a family celebration in Devon. But here will be perfect.'

The back of Rebecca's neck began to prickle. 'Here?' she asked warily. 'What do you mean here?'

'Here!' laughed Annabelle, waving her thin arms around. 'Here in this glorious big house of yours.'

'You mean,' Rebecca was choosing her words carefully. 'You mean you want to get married *here*. In my house?'

Daniel looked over the top of the newspaper he was reading, his eyes suddenly bright and interested.

'We actually hadn't thought of that Bec old girl. Would you let us use the house?'

'Of course I wouldn't!' exploded Rebecca. 'What a ridiculous idea!'

Daniel shrugged and ducked back down beneath his newspaper, no longer interested in the conversation while Annabelle stared at Rebecca with a hurt look.

'I don't see why it's so preposterous,' she said with a sniff. 'After all, you keep saying how happy you are for us.'

Rebecca gritted her teeth. 'I *am* happy for you but it's just not – suitable. Using your ex-wife's house to get married. It's simply not going to happen Annabelle,' she finished firmly.

'Well that wasn't what I meant anyway although I'm a little upset that you would be so against the idea. I meant that the whole family will be getting together for our wedding and it's much better if we get married in Leeds because then we can use your house. We can all stay here, as a family. Unless you think that's a dreadful idea as well,' added Annabelle stiffly.

Oh yes, thought Rebecca, a truly dreadful idea. She'd had no intention of getting involved in Daniel's wedding and even less intention of holding a house party to celebrate.

'I'm not saying that you aren't welcome to stay here occasionally,' she started, 'but I don't think ...'

'Oh wonderful!' Annabelle sprang up and dashed around the table to place her arms around Rebecca, squeezing tightly. Rebecca felt a slight moment of panic at the feel of the bony arms around her neck and she let out a gasp of relief when Annabelle relaxed her grip.

'Thank you so much. That's wonderful! I told Daniel you wouldn't mind but he wasn't sure.'

Rebecca rubbed at her neck. She hadn't said yes, had she?

She closed her eyes for a moment, why couldn't Daniel have just phoned her up and told her he had gotten married. She could have said congratulations on the phone without any meeting needed. She didn't want to become Annabelle's new best friend. She didn't want them as part of her new extended family. She certainly didn't want them to visit her every weekend so they could celebrate their special bond. Maybe she should just offer to buy them a bigger house and hope they would spend more of their time there.

Annabelle was looking pleased with herself and Rebecca stood up wearily. 'I'm going to the supermarket,' she announced. Adding pointedly, 'I didn't have time yesterday.'

Daniel's newspaper suddenly went down. 'Get some more bacon old girl. And some beer – there's none in the fridge,' he said slightly aggrieved. 'And get some plain bread, I really don't like that stuff you get with all the nuts and bits in it.'

'Ooh, you should get some champagne. Then when Sarah and Dominic get here we can toast our weddings with a glass of bubbly. And could you get some skimmed milk please? I watch ever little calorie you know,' pouted Annabelle giving Rebecca's slightly rounded stomach a quick glance. 'And maybe some nice salad, I know you've got some things in the fridge but it's all a bit plain. Have you ever tried escarole? It's quite divine. And maybe some sunflower seeds and definitely some avocado and sun-dried tomatoes. I'm surprised you're not a little bit more imaginative in the kitchen Rebecca.'

Rebecca glared at them both.

'Anything else,' she asked sarcastically.

But Annabelle gave her a sweet smile and shook her head. 'Oh I'm sure you've thought of everything else,' and went back to playing with Daniel's fingers which we're still wrapped round his newspaper.

Rebecca took her time strolling around the supermarket throwing things into her trolley. She was tempted not to buy any beer for Daniel but decided to get some for Dom. She deliberately put in anther loaf of wholegrain bread, if Daniel wanted plain white he could go back to Devon to eat some. She refused to look at the fancy salad leaves and almost walked past the champagne, but then remembered that they would be celebrating Sarah's news so she added several bottles.

Eventually, with her trolley overflowing, she had to accept she had done and she paid, taking her time loading the car before driving home. As she pulled up outside the front door it flew open and Sarah stood there, smiling widely.

'Mum!' she said stepping forward to give Rebecca a big hug as she climbed out of the car.

'Hello darling. Give me a hand getting this lot inside. How lovely to see you,' and she wrapped her arms around her daughter and held her close for a moment.

'Annabelle said you'd gone to the supermarket. You should have let me know if there was anything you needed, Dom and I would have picked it up on our way over.'

Sarah picked up a couple of bags and heaved them out of the boot and into the hallway.

'Well actually,' puffed Rebecca as she followed with a couple of bags full of champagne and beer, 'I was quite glad of the excuse to go out.'

They brought in the rest of the bags and Rebecca shut the door behinds them. 'You've obviously met Annabelle?'

'Yes! Isn't she lovely?' said Sarah with a delighted smile. 'Really NOT what I was expecting!'

Rebecca stopped fiddling with the bags and stood up to look her daughter in the eye.

'Are you serious?' she asked with a half laugh.

'Serious? Well, yes. I think she's wonderful. Don't you like her?'

Sarah looked genuinely confused that anyone would think otherwise and for a moment Rebecca didn't speak. She thought back to the conversation with Helen and her suggestion that Rebecca was actually a little jealous that Daniel had found someone new.

'Er, well no actually.'

Sarah's stared as Rebecca continued. 'She's quite unpleasant, always making snide comments about me having it easy and not working hard enough and eating macaroni cheese.'

'Macaroni cheese? But mum, she's really nice. The first thing she said was about not wanting to take Dad away from us and how we should just see her as another family member. She really wants us all to get on, in fact she's already talking about Christmas and how wonderful it would be if we all came to visit you here and had a kind of extended family house party. I thought that was a wonderful idea!'

What was it with this woman and Christmas, wondered Rebecca.

'And you think that would be nice? Having your dad and Annabelle stay over Christmas?'

'Well I'm not Dad's biggest fan but maybe it's time we gave him another chance. And he does seem a different person with Annabelle, much more relaxed and nearly cheerful!'

Rebecca tried to smile. Oh dear God, is this what the future held? Family holidays, long weekends, Christmas – all spent with her overbearing ex-husband and his equally obnoxious new wife while Rebecca sat in the kitchen and generally kept out of the way until they had all gone? Perhaps she could go away for Christmas. She would go on a singles holiday to somewhere exotic and lay under a palm tree on the beach while they all rejoiced in time spent with their new stepmother. Actually, that sounded equally sad, spending Christmas alone with only a few palm fronds for company.

She stretched her mouth into a rather grim smile, 'Sounds great,' she said. 'We'll have to see.'

'It's really odd that Dad's getting married as well,' giggled Sarah. 'At least it gives me someone to talk weddings with!'

'Bec is that you? What are you doing – did you bring some beer home?

'We're coming!' trilled Sarah. 'Hang on,' and with a happy smile she picked up some bags and headed towards the kitchen leaving Rebecca to follow slowly.

'You took your time,' grumbled Daniel as she walked through the door. 'Maybe you should have gone to the supermarket before your guests arrived?'

Rebecca opened her mouth to snap that perhaps he shouldn't have arrived a day early but she realised she was wasting her time. Daniel had already turned his back, as he so often had in the past, and was whispering something in Annabelle's ear as he slid a hand around her waist. Annabelle giggled happily and reached out a hand to Sarah who was squealing in delight as she pulled out several bottles of champagne. Dom was smiling at Sarah's excitement and leant over to kiss her on the cheek and for a brief moment they were all linked, a joyous group, happy and smiling and focusing on the future. All except for Rebecca, still standing in the doorway and watching.

'Oh you're forgiven,' said Annabelle looking with glee at the bottles of champagne. 'Sarah, let's get this lot in the fridge.'

Forgiven, thought Rebecca. Forgiven for going to the supermarket and filling the fridge for their visit?'

'Hi Rebecca!' she realised Dom was standing in front of her, holding out his hand almost shyly.

They had met before, Sarah had brought him over to the house a couple of times the previous summer, for a BBQ and a game of tennis with Helen and Emma and a Sunday lunch with Toby and his girlfriend.

'Hello Dominic.' And then suddenly remembering that he was about to become her son-in-law Rebecca reached forward and gave him a hug. 'Congratulations!'

She closed her eyes chastising herself. Daniel's arrival seemed to have thrown her sideways. Her daughter had announced she was getting married and all Rebecca could do was moan about Annabelle and her insults.

'Let's get that champagne chilled!' she declared. 'We've got lots to celebrate this weekend.'

She shrugged off her mood and stepped forward, encompassing Sarah, Dominic and Daniel in her gaze. 'Our family is going to change for ever,' she said softly. 'And we definitely need to raise a glass to the future.'

'Oh Rebecca!' Annabelle was suddenly by her side, one of her skinny arms wrapped around Rebecca's shoulders. 'That's such a wonderful thing to say. Thank you so much for being so welcoming. Your blessing means the world to Daniel and I,' she sniffed. 'We know how difficult it is for you.' Rebecca ground her teeth but stayed silent. 'But to say something so beautiful, well it's more than we could have hoped for,' and she kissed Rebecca on the cheek, holding her close for a moment.

'We're very happy to invite you into our family,' said Sarah, smiling happily at her future stepmother. 'It's going to be wonderful.'

Chapter 7

They stayed in the kitchen, gathered around the table drinking champagne and chatting about weddings, dresses and honeymoons. Rebecca watched as Sarah basked in the glow of her new status as a bride to be, noticing how often she gently touched Dominic's arm as though to reassure herself he was real. Annabelle had produced a couple of wedding magazines and they were browsing through, occasionally exclaiming at a dress or a bouquet.

She watched Dominic from under her eyelashes. She had met him on a handful of occasions but without feeling that she had gotten to know him. Sarah leaned forward to say something to him and he twisted in his seat to look at her, a smile playing round his lips as she spoke and then a laugh erupting as she finished, Rebecca saw his hand slide under the table to squeeze Sarah's fingers as he gave her a look of tender happiness and Rebecca relaxed slightly.

'Are you okay Mum?'

Broken out of her reverie Rebecca looked round the table and smiled. 'Sorry, I was in my own little world for a moment.'

'Oh poor you!' exclaimed Annabelle and Rebecca couldn't suppress the groan.

'I mean here we all are,' Annabelle flung her slender arm out in an all-encompassing gesture around the table which somehow, quite amazingly, managed to exclude Rebecca. 'All about to start a new life, all this talk of weddings - so hard for you?'

Rebecca wondered what she would have to say to stop Annabelle.

'Oh I don't think it's hard for Bec.'

Rebecca swung round to face Dom who was sitting back in his chair watching Sarah happily read about how to choose the perfect wedding venue. 'After all it is her daughter who's getting married. That's something that most parents are thrilled about.'

'Well yes but you and Sarah aren't the only ones getting married, are you?' Annabelle pointed out with a little giggle. 'Poor Bec has to listen to me planning my wedding to her ex-husband.'

Rebecca put her glass on the table rather more firmly than she'd intended and watched the champagne splash over the edge and make a small puddle. 'I divorced Daniel. If it was going to be hard letting him go and potentially marry someone else I would have kept him.' She winced a little, he sounded like a stray dog that she'd decided to rehome. 'But I didn't want him and I really do not mind in the slightest that he is marrying again so please stop saying how hard it is for me!'

She saw Daniel flinch and briefly regretted how harsh her words sounded. Sarah stopped reading, staring at her mother in surprise and for once there was no tinkly laugh coming from Annabelle.

'And how lucky for me that you decided to - let him go!' said Annabelle sharply. 'It's made me so happy!'

Rebecca smiled. It was a tight smile that didn't exactly throw warmth and light into the room but it was the best she could do under the circumstance.

'So we all win then don't we?' she said lightly and reached out to recover her champagne flute. 'Congratulations to us all!' and she raised her glass and drank the last of the fizzy bubbles as the rest of the table hastily followed all murmuring congratulations as they drank.

It took remarkably little for some people to recover their equilibrium thought Rebecca as thrilled at the toast Annabelle raised her glass looking dreamy. 'Oh thank you every body,' she giggled turning to gaze into Daniel's eyes, 'we are so very happy aren't we my darling?'

And suddenly everyone was smiling again, Anabelle was back to her bubbly self and Daniel relaxed his tense shoulders although he couldn't help the slightly hurt look he cast in Rebecca's direction.

Berating herself for bringing the mood down Rebecca made sure she smiled and joined in as Sarah pointed out various articles to Annabelle and had a light-hearted argument with Dom about the best place to honeymoon.

'Finding a venue at such short notice could be tricky,' mused Annabelle. 'We want to get married this summer, but everywhere gets booked up months in advance.

Sarah nodded. 'I suppose it depends what you want. I'm sure you can find a lovely hotel or restaurant that could fit you in.'

Annabelle looked as though she had been slapped. 'Oh no! I couldn't possibly make do with a pokey little restaurant somewhere, fitting in between everybody else who was out for a meal.' She swung round to face Daniel, one hand clutching at his arm in distress. ''We won't be having that will we darling?'

'Whatever you want Belles,' announced Daniel grandly. 'We'll have the wedding you want to have.'

Rebecca couldn't help her eyebrows from raising. Where had this generous man come from, the one who just wanted Annabelle to be happy? What had gone so wrong in their own marriage?

'Oh I've just had an amazing idea,' squealed Annabelle. She turned to Sarah and Dom in excitement. 'Why don't we look at some venues tomorrow? We can choose some today and make an appointment. Daniel and I,' she smiled happily in his direction, 'really need to find somewhere as soon as possible and it would be lovely for you and Dom to get an idea of what's out there.'

Sarah sat very still, her magazine drifting to the floor as she thought.

'Look at wedding venues?'

'Yes! We can go see them together and imagine having our wedding there.'

Sarah's eyes had begun to shine. She turned to Dom who grinned at her excited face. 'Dom?'

'If you want to.'

'Really?'

'Of course. We'll need to find somewhere for our wedding when we set a date.'

'Then yes! What a lovely idea.'

Sarah looked so happy that Rebecca couldn't help but smile, her daughter was getting married and if Daniel and Annabelle weren't present to cast such a huge shadow over the event, Rebecca would be dancing round the kitchen.

'And of course you can come too Rebecca,' added Annabelle graciously.

'Why thank you Annabelle,'

Sarah looked quizzically at Annabelle. 'Why wouldn't she?'

There was the tiniest of pauses and not waiting for the 'how hard it must be for you speech' Rebecca jumped to her feet and grabbed her iPad from the kitchen counter.

'Why don't we all choose a place to visit,' she suggested brightly, distracting Annabelle who started clapped her hands in excitement.

'I'm sure we can visit three venues and still be home for Sunday lunch. You might even find somewhere you want to book,' she said to Annabelle optimistically, crossing her fingers under the table. 'And then you and Daniel can go straight back to Devon and start planning your wedding!'

That was enough for Annabelle who in a state of high excitement went tripping off to the bedroom to fetch her own tablet and for the next hour there was barely a sound in the house as the three women scrolled through wedding venues in Leeds to find their favourite.

Daniel moved into the living room with another beer and was soon snoring loudly but Dom joined Sarah in the search and there was the occasional low hum of conversation from them as they discussed the merits of each place. Eventually it was done and they had three venues listed to visit. Rebecca grabbed the phone and made reservations and Annabelle and Sarah sat smiling happily at the table. The search for the perfect wedding venue had begun.

*

The following morning they were all up and dressed early, ready to start their search and even Rebecca couldn't help but feel excited. The first place on their list was Sarah and Dom's choice. It was a country house hotel with a pair of sturdy iron gates protecting it from the main road and a short tree lined drive to a large canopied entrance. It was an attractive building, old and covered in ivy and Rebecca could see why Sarah had chosen it.

They were welcomed by Cindy, a young woman with her hair high on her head and a brightly coloured scarf complete with the name of the hotel around her neck.

'Welcome to The Great Hall Hotel,' she offered, ushering them inside where a tray of champagne filled glasses was waiting on the reception desk.

Politely they all took a proffered glass and a little sip as they looked around. It was a good sized space with a thick red patterned carpet and a large number of glass topped tables holding brochures proclaiming the virtues of the hotel and its facilities.

'How lovely,' trilled Annabelle, her eyes resting on the ornate flower displays and the large golden statues set at the bottom of the staircase.

Cindy gave them a few moments and then stepped smartly forwards.

'This is where we welcome your guests,' she advised smoothly, 'before directing them to the function room.'

She waved her arm towards a door behind the staircase and they all followed obligingly and waited as she led them across the thick carpet and into the function room. It was a disappointing space. Rather unexpectedly they were in a large single storey extension pushing out from the rear of the hotel which was bland and devoid of any of the character hinted at from the entrance to the hotel.

'We can of course arrange the catering,' Cindy continued. 'We have a superb chef who will be happy to advise you on the perfect wedding menu. And because of our wealth of experience we can recommend florists, photographers, car rental and everything else you may need.'

Rebecca stopped listening, wandering over to peer through the serviceable UPVC double glazing and behind the thick nylon window drapes which filtered the uninspiring view of the car park and the bins at the rear of the kitchen. She saw Sarah's shoulders slump slightly and knew she was disappointed. Take away the wedding finery and it could serve just as well as a conference room. It was soulless and uninspiring.

'Could we see the bridal suite please,' asked Annabelle reading through the leaflet Cindy had provided.

'Of course, please follow me,' and she led them to the lifts.

'The bridal suite is on the 4th floor,' she advised, 'it has a wonderful view over the woodland to the rear of the building and is quite tranquil.'

Leaving the lift, they trooped down a corridor with more red carpet and cream walls, which looked exactly the same as every corridor of every hotel Rebecca had ever visited.

'We had a team of interior designers work on this room,' continued Cindy, 'to create the feeling of luxurious splendour every bride wants to enjoy on their wedding day.'

Annabelle looked decidedly interested, picking up the pace so she was right behind Cindy.

'The result is a room we are very proud of,' Cindy waved her pass key in front of an arched door at the end of the corridor with a very elaborate sign in gold proclaiming it to be The Great Hall Hotel Bridal Suite. 'It has all the elements that we feel make us a very special wedding venue. Its er,' Rebecca saw her take a quick peek at her note, 'its attention to detail has recreated a romantic room straight out of a fairy-tale - with of course the added comforts of the 20th century.'

She paused for laughter, gave it a few seconds and continued. 'I'm sure you'll appreciate its romance and comfort,' and then finally threw open the door to let in a straining Annabelle who was leaning forward so much she almost fell into the room.

It was huge, built on the corner and with windows on two sides. The large ornate window to one side did overlook woodland, and also the flat roof of the single storey extension below. The other offered a view of the busy main road at the end of the drive. The bed was a huge four poster with a white chalk painted finish and laden with gilded cherubs and ivy leaves, all hidden beneath swathes of sheer white fabric.

Everything in the room had a heavy layer of gilt, even the tumbler glasses at either side of the table were embossed with the hotel's name in gold script. The curtains were thick and heavy, capable of blocking out any light and the chairs scattered around the room were cream velvet liberally decorated with golden peacocks.

'It's amazing,' gasped Annabelle.

It's awful though Rebecca. She glanced over to Sarah who was looking round the room with wide eyes. 'What do you think darling?' she asked in a whisper as Annabelle wandered away to stroke the velvet chairs.

'It's a bit over the top,' answered Sarah wrinkling her nose. 'A bit of a pimped Jane Austen look.'

Rebecca couldn't help the snort of laughter. Sarah was right, the basic idea of an old fashioned bedroom had been given a very thorough updating with disastrous consequences.

'So you don't like it?'

'God no. I really wouldn't want something like this.'

'Good,' whispered Rebecca. 'I hate it!'

Quelling their laughter they thanked Cindy and made their way back to the car park.

'Oh wasn't that heavenly?' asked Annabelle as they walked across the crunchy gravel.

'I thought it was awful,' said Rebecca candidly. 'The function room was quite disappointing and the bridal suite was a real shock.'

'Mmm,' offered Sarah. 'I agree with mum.

Annabelle turned to glare at them. 'You didn't like it?'.

'No.'

'Daniel,' Annabelle grabbed his arm as he started to open the car door. 'What do you think, did you like it? Wouldn't you like to spend our wedding night in that beautiful romantic bridal suite. Can't you imagine us there, in that wonderful bed?'

Rebecca shuddered, she really didn't want to think about Daniel's wedding night. 'Well just because Sarah didn't like it doesn't mean that you can't choose it,' she said hastily before there was any more talk of what may happen in the four-poster bed.

Annabelle sniffed. 'Well I did like it,' she pouted. 'And let's face it, the bridal suite is a very important part of the wedding experience,' and ignoring Sarah and Rebecca's fit of giggles, she climbed in the car and slammed the door ready to set off to the next location which was Annabelle's own choice.

Chapter 8

They arrived at the next venue and the comparison was startling. No thick gravel ready to catch your heels and snag your tights but acres of block paving next to what looked like an old stable block now transformed into a dedicated car parking facility. As they pulled into a space, a liveried coachman approached to ask if they had an appointment and then pointed them towards the entrance door at the front of the property.

A flight of stone steps rose to a pair of huge double doors which swung open as they approached and led them in turn into an entrance hall which was almost as big as Rebecca's house. No mass-produced art on the walls here, just centuries of history and oak panelling and an atmosphere of grandeur that made them all instinctively lower their voices.

'Good Morning.'

They all turned in the direction of the voice which belonged to a stunning young woman dressed in a severe black dress which set off the shimmering golden hue of her immaculately pinned up hair.

She was holding a clipboard and several brochures plus a tick list and Rebecca automatically felt herself standing a little straighter, paying full attention.

'Welcome to Bransome Manor, my name is Belinda and I will be taking you on a tour of the property today.'

Everybody nodded obligingly and Belinda set off towards the foot of the magnificent oak staircase, aligning herself at a perfect 45 degrees with the bottom step and waiting with a raised eyebrow for the group to gather in front of her.

'This is the entrance hall and it is here you will welcome your guests. There will be two footmen at either side of the door providing a glass of champagne as your guests enter. They will remain here until the bride and groom arrive and a formal greeting line will commence.'

They all looked round, nodding approvingly. You could hold a football match in the reception hall and still have space for the average wedding party.

'After twenty minutes the bride and groom will be asked to lead the way into the chosen drawing room.'

She stepped forward and walked across to one side of the entrance hall, standing neatly next to a large ornately carved door. The group started to follow but Belinda held up a hand to stop them as she continued to speak.

'You can choose the drawing room of your choice depending on the size of your party and of course,' she paused disdainfully, 'your budget.'

'This is the Bramwell room and we also have,' she took a step forward to point at each of three identical doors, 'the Henrietta room, the Danube room and the Windsor room.'

She walked back to the group standing uncertainly in the centre of the entrance hall and whipped a brochure from the clipboard, which after the tiniest of pauses she handed to Daniel. 'The charge for each room is shown here. This allows two hours of usage. If you feel you would like more, additional increments of thirty minutes may be added for an additional charge.'

Rebecca was starting to feel stressed. What if the bride and groom hadn't managed to greet all their guests in the allotted twenty minutes. What if there were some slow eaters in the wedding party and the two hours expired. Did they have to leave their food if no thirty minute increment had been arranged?

'After the meal you can, if you choose, withdraw to the orangery for a further period of relaxed celebration and access to the terrace for a photographic opportunity. Follow me,' and she clicked her way to the end of the entrance hall and yet another door.

Following meekly, Rebecca looked round at the richly decorated walls and the tables containing enormous bouquets of flowers in crystal vases and silver framed photos of what she presumed were famous past guests. There were chairs scattered around, all straight backed and stiff and acres of highly polished surfaces which would show every finger print and smudge. Rebecca clasped her hands nervously in front of her, it was far from a relaxed atmosphere.

'Bloody hell!' echoed Daniel's voice up the hallway and Rebecca turned around to see him reading the brochure Belinda had passed him. 'Good God Annabelle, have you seen these prices?'

Ignoring the outburst Belinda led them into a magnificent orangery, beautifully proportioned and awash with orchids and small bay trees and huge floor length sheer curtains which were held back with thick corded silk and lay in puddles on the glittering white floor. It was beautiful and quite overwhelming.

'If you elect to use the facilities of the orangery you may in addition purchase access the terrace which many of our wedding parties use for the more informal wedding photographs,' and walking to one of the glass walls she flung open huge French windows which showed a terrace wrapping half the house with its honey coloured stone, weathered and worn and quite beautiful.

'If you do choose the orangery and the terrace, the prices for each hour are contained in this brochure,' and swooping past Daniel she dropped another glossy brochure in his hand which he took with far less enthusiasm than the first.

Half an hour later they were back in the entrance hall having swung by the kitchens where Daniel was handed yet another brochure and up to the bridal suite which looked like a scene from a Marie Antoinette film and where Daniel was passed a glossy price list.

'I do hope you decide to use Bransome for your wedding,' enthused Belinda who didn't look particularly interested one way or another. 'We book up several months in advance, in fact we have a wedding booked here in three years' time.'

It would probably take someone that long to afford it, thought Rebecca, watching Daniel looking in horror at the pile of brochures in his hand.

'And I also have to mention that if you do choose to make a booking, we will require a credit reference.'

At the stunned look of the entire group Belinda continued. 'I'm afraid some people's enthusiasm for a wedding venue isn't matched by their ability to pay and rather than have unpleasantness at the ceremony itself, we make quite sure that no-one is - over reaching themselves financially.' She paused and cast an eye over Rebecca and the cashmere wrap covering her Marc Jacobs dress, 'not that I imagine it will be an issue for you,' she continued smoothly, 'just a matter of process.'

And then they were outside, another liveried coachman appearing to escort them to their car and firmly off the premises, at least until their credit check had been completed.

Nobody said anything as they climbed back into their car but Rebecca watched as Daniel flung his armful of brochures into the glove compartment and held up a warning hand in Annabelle's direction. He may be blinded by love but Rebecca could tell there was no way Daniel would part with that kind of money simply for a wedding, not even for Annabelle.

Driving slowly back down the drive, past the perfectly spaced trees, Rebecca met Sarah and Dom's eyes and they all broke out into slightly hysterical giggles.

'Oh my God,' Dominic remarked, 'I would spend the entire day with a stopwatch. God forbid you should take longer than your allotted hour in the orangery.'

'Oh it was awful,' agreed Sarah. 'Well the place wasn't awful but the whole set up was quite ridiculous. It would be so stressful!'

Annabelle was sitting in the front in a sulky silence. No doubt she had loved the place and wanted the most expensive reception room complete with several thirty minute increments and access to the orangery and the terrace. If Sarah had fallen in love with Bransome Manor Rebecca would have been more than happy to pay whatever was needed but she was secretly relived that her daughter had felt the same way as Rebecca about the overly formal and regimented structure.

Willow Court was down a long rambling road with woodland on either side, slightly more shambolic than the immaculately planted parade of trees at Bransome Manor. Brightly coloured crocuses and the occasional early daffodil were peeping randomly from behind the trees and a carpet of snowdrops mingled with the grass. Despite the potholes in the road, Rebecca immediately felt more relaxed.

They arrived at a stone archway, a little lop sided and with part of the brickwork missing but still impressive. Driving through into a huge courtyard, they had their first glimpse of the house sprawling before them. It looked warm and mellow. It also looked in need of more than a little tender loving care and a lot of repointing.

A sweeping circular drive with a central fountain, not working and looking a little green around the gills led to the entrance and large double doors which stood ajar. Gardens sprawled in every direction and to one side was a path leading down to an enormous willow tree and what looked to be a rather untidy reed filled lake.

Pulling up on the gravel they all climbed out to take in the view, breathing in the cold air and taking in the sound of birdsong.

Annabelle wrinkled her nose slightly. 'It looks very …'

'Welcoming?' suggested Sarah, her eyes taking in the honey yellow stone and the rampant ivy that smothered one side of the house growing untidily over the windows.

'Welcoming? No, it looks very … untidy.'

Rebecca knew what she meant. Flowers were grouped in messy borders, reaching upwards to meet windows that looked in need of a good wash. Weeds poked out of the gravel on the driveway, the brass on the door looked almost black and everything looked a little worn and tired.

She walked into a bright entrance hall which had a curved staircase and huge stained glass windows on either side of the door which let in floods of colourful light. It also accentuated the peeling wooden panels, the plaster that had started to slide from the walls in places and the water stained floor that was inadequately hidden by a collection of cheap rugs

'Hello?' she shouted. 'Anybody here?'

There was no answer although she could hear the faint sound of voices from somewhere in the house.

'Hello?' she tried again walking over to the reception desk in search of a bell of some kind.

'Oh I'm so sorry,' gasped a voice running into the hall, 'you must be Mrs Miles.'

The woman smiled holding out her hand only to quickly withdraw it as she realised it was covered in dirt and soil.

She blushed. 'I've been trying to keep some of the weeds down,' she apologised, hiding her hand behind her back, 'I lost track of time.'

Rebecca smiled reassuringly. 'We've only just arrived, don't worry. This is my daughter Sarah and her fiancé Dominic. They're the ones who are getting married.'

She glanced towards Annabelle who was staring with horror at the mop and bucket that had been left at the foot of a staircase. 'And this is Annabelle and Daniel, they're getting married as well.'

'Er right okay.' Grabbing an old duster to get the worst of the dirt from her fingers before holding them back out to Rebecca, she smiled. 'I'm Debbie.'

'And are you in charge of weddings here?'

'Hmm, well sort of. It was Laura you see but she left. A bit abruptly actually and we didn't have anyone to take over but we had two weddings booked so I stepped in to help. For a while anyway.'

Nobody said anything and Debbie rushed on. 'My mother owns the place you see but I have a new job in Bradford that I'll be starting soon so we'll be getting someone to replace Laura. I just don't know who yet, but that person will do your wedding, if you have it here. What I mean is if you have your wedding here it won't be me but someone else...'

Rebecca put her out of her misery and taking her arm moved her away from the reception desk. 'Well in the meantime perhaps you could show us around Debbie and we'll worry about who will be doing the actual job for us later.'

Relieved to be able to stop talking Debbie beamed at them all and nodded her head enthusiastically. 'Right, okay, so this is the hall.' They all nodded enthusiastically as though relived to be told. 'It's big as you can see,' more nods' so we use this as a reception area, drinks etc.'

They looked around at the dingy space badly lit by a chandelier that hadn't been cleaned in centuries and in severe need of a coat of paint.

Debbie followed their eyes. 'Of course you don't have to use this area,' she said hastily and there was a collective sigh of relief, 'we have other reception rooms, er, please follow me.'

They started in a drawing room to one side of the house, a large rectangular room lined with French windows and with light flooding in from the garden, amazing cornices filled with cobwebs and a Victorian ceiling rose from which hung a beautiful chandelier, and several cobwebs. The walls needed painting, the fireplace set against one wall was at a definite angle and several of the window panes had cracks. They looked round in silence.

'This is the main room that you would use,' explained Debbie. 'There is a chapel that some people like to use for the actual ceremony but it is a bit cold so it doesn't get used much. But you can use it if you want.'

'Does it cost extra?' barked Daniel.

'Sorry?'

'Does it cost extra to use the chapel?'

'Oh no, if you want to use it you're more than welcome.'

She paused and then continued. 'So this is the room that you could - well use. You know, after you'd got married and you were … er .. you were …'

'Greeting your guests?' suggested Rebecca.

'That's it, this is the greeting room.'

They all waited.

'And eating?'

'Yes! Right, the eating room, I mean the dining room is down here,' and off she dashed to another room a little further down the hall flinging the door open with gusto. 'The dining room!'

It should have been a magnificent room. It was covered in mahogany panels with an ancient fireplace in the centre of one wall and large windows topped with stained glass panels along another wall. But the ceiling had turned a slightly nicotine colour from years of misuse and several of the panels had broken edges and scratches or were missing altogether. The fireplace had a corner missing and the floor was wonky with an alarming dip towards the centre.

'We've taken all the tables out so we can give it a good clean and a coat of paint. Obviously it looks a lot better when all the tables are in here,' Debbie offered as she followed their eyes. 'A lot better.'

It would have to, thought Rebecca. 'And the bedrooms?'

'Right yes, well the bedrooms are upstairs,' said Debbie flustered. 'Please follow me.'

Without a word they wandered behind Debbie up the sweeping staircase which was mercifully still intact although with a rather wobbly handrail and onto another long dimly lit corridor.

'This is the biggest bedroom,' said Debbie heading for a door at the end of the corridor.

'The bridal suite?' asked Annabelle looking a little more interested.

'Er - yes, I suppose,' shrugged Debbie throwing the door open.

It was like a scene from Wuthering heights, all splendid glory gone to ruin. It was much cleaner than downstairs, the dust had been held at bay but the four poster bed was wonky and leaning slightly to one side and the faded velvet drapes were more than a little moth eaten. The furniture covered several different centuries, some propped up to keep the surface level, other pieces covered with fussy silk table runners to hide the scratches and water marks. The window was beautiful, tall and arched but with ivy growing across the panes making the entire room dark and lackluster.

Rebecca turned round to see Annabelle backing out of the room in horror as Sarah advanced into the middle intrigued.

'It could be lovely couldn't it mum?'

Rebecca nodded. 'It certainly could.'

They looked at a few more bedrooms, all much the same and then one by one made their way back down the stairs. Rebecca paused to examine the deep set cornices on the corridor walls and realised that she could hear voices from inside one of the bedrooms.

'So, are they going to sell then, has anyone told you what's going on? I need to know, if I've got to get another job I need to start looking now!'

'Can't see how they can do anything else,' said the second voice. 'There's no weddings booked and the old lady can't run it on her own when Debbie goes.'

'Well I need to know,' the first voice was truculent, 'there's other cleaning jobs I can take!'

Rebecca walked on quickly, not wanting to appear as though she was eavesdropping. Regardless of whether anybody liked the place, it was all irrelevant if it was about to close. Walking quickly down the staircase she turned right at the bottom and took several steps down the hallway before she realised she'd gone the wrong way. Swinging round, she headed for the front door only to stop in her tracks. A door stood ajar, with enough on view to catch Rebecca's interest. She looked around to see if anyone was present to ask permission and then pushed the door open a little further, sliding into the room.

Rebecca looked round in awe. The plaster was crumbling from the walls, great swathes of it laying on the floor. One of the window panes was boarded up and several of the original wooden frames had almost disintegrated. There was another ornate fireplace with a marble hearth that had great chunks missing.

But it was still a room of sheer beauty. There was a domed ceiling that rose high above Rebecca, its ornate plasterwork following a curved line to the very centre where there was an explosion of cherubs supporting the central rose from which hung a waterfall of crystal droplets. A huge bay curved outwards, echoing the line of the dome and was lined with arched windows. The intricate cornice could still be seen under years of neglect although one corner had come away completely and joined the plaster on the floor. It had been a room of beauty, a perfect wedding venue.

'Bec where the bloody hell are you?'

'Mum?'

She could hear the voices from the hallway and taking another long look at the ceiling Rebecca left.

They were standing by the door with Debbie and Daniel could hardly contain his impatience as he grunted and turned towards the car park.

'Thank you,' said Sarah smiling.

'Have we got a brochure?' asked Rebecca.

Annabelle looked at her as though she had asked for someone's head on a platter and even Debbie looked a little surprised.

'Oh er.. you mean you might want to book?' she asked doubtfully.

'Well it would be good to have details if we did decide to go ahead,' Rebecca replied diplomatically.

Shuffling round behind the chaotic reception desk, Debbie finally managed to locate a somewhat dogeared brochure and handed it over.

'And what are your bookings like? Do you have many?'

Rebecca heard Daniel's tsk of annoyance from over her shoulder but she kept the pleasant smile on her face as she waited for Debbie's reply.

'Well we do have a few spaces. Quite a lot actually. As you can see we are in a programme of … er renovation and not everybody wants to have a wedding with that in the background.'

Rebecca glanced round. The entire building was suffering from a programme of neglect and disinterest with very little signs of renovation. But for some reason, it intrigued her.

Chapter 9

They arrived back at Rebecca's house in a whoosh of gravel and as they all unfolded themselves from the car, Rebecca's head was still full of Willow Court. The house, as unkempt and dishevelled as it was, had made a significant impact on her and she couldn't help but dream how wonderful it must have looked in years gone by and how much work would be needed to bring it back to such glory.

There was a lot of noise coming from the kitchen where Rebecca's guests had gathered and she could smell the rich aroma of coffee as Daniel fired up the space age coffee machine. The phone was ringing and rather than compete with the voices Rebecca slipped into her study.

'Oh hello Helen,' she said dreamily, her thoughts still with Willow Court.

'Hi darling, I won't keep you I know you've got a houseful, but I wanted to give you plenty of notice.'

'Notice? For what?'

''The dinner party. It's all arranged, I'm introducing you to Charles!'

'Who?'

'Charles. The man I've found for you.'

'Man?'

'You told me that I had to find you a man – and quickly! Well I've found you the perfect person, don't tell me you've changed your mind!'

Rebecca had given little thought to her potential date over the last few days. Her mind had been occupied with other less than pleasant thoughts.

'Er, no of course not,' she answered not entirely honestly. Now that it was a fait accompli she suddenly felt quite nervous.

'Good, because I've told Charles all about you and he's really looking forward to you two meeting.'

'And so am I,' insisted Rebecca cautiously.

'You don't sound excited.;

'Sorry, it's been a busy few days. I am excited Helen, really. Just a bit worried that's all.'

'Well don't be. It's going to work out this time, I have a good feeling,' and saying goodbye Helen left Rebecca sitting at her desk her stomach a knot of emotions as she thought about forthcoming weddings, ex-husbands and new beginnings.

With her head whirling she left the study and was about to turn in the direction of the kitchen only to stop at the sound of raised voices. Daniel and Annabelle were in the living room having an argument.

'Belles darling, it's not about loving you or not loving you. I had no idea that weddings could cost so much. It's simply not reasonable to spend that kind of money on one day. I'm sorry but we'll have to carry on looking until we find somewhere more reasonable.'

'It's not fair,' shouted Annabelle, clearly upset. 'I loved Bransome Manor, it was everything I want my wedding to be.'

'But it's too expensive Belles, far too expensive. Even that first place you looked at is expensive. Can't we just get married in a registry office and find a nice hotel ...'

'No!'

Standing by the study door Rebecca winced. Annabelle voice was almost a scream at the thought of downsizing her plans.

'Okay, okay,' Daniel nervously backtracked. 'Sorry I didn't mean to upset you, we'll find somewhere that you like but not Bransome Manor.'

Rebecca realised he was making his escape and she slipped discreetly back inside her study until she heard his footsteps walking hurriedly past the door. Rebecca felt a moment of sympathy for Annabelle. She had truly expected Daniel to provide the wedding of her dreams and it clearly hadn't occurred to her that he would say no.

Rebecca nibbled on her lower lip for a moment then walked towards the living room.

'Everything okay?' she asked gently when she found Annabelle slumped on the settee, her mascara smudged beneath the tears.

'No it is not,' sniffed Annabelle standing up and facing Rebecca somewhat angrily. 'Daniel thinks Bransome Manor is too expensive and I loved it.'

Rebecca tried to look sympathetic. 'Well it was a bit on the pricey side Annabelle. But I'm sure there will be somewhere else ...'

'I don't want anywhere else,' snapped Annabelle. 'I wanted Bransome or somewhere just like it.' She glared coldly at Rebecca. 'Of course you don't have that problem do you?'

Rebecca sighed. Which problem were they talking about now. Rebecca's inability to find a new man, her lack of entertaining, her reliance on macaroni cheese, her bravery at finding her ex-husband was getting married again.

'You have all the money you'll ever need. You could pay for Sarah to have Bransome Manor without even making a dent in your bank account.'

It was true and if Sarah wanted her wedding there Rebecca would do exactly that.

'Actually Sarah wasn't that keen on Bransome Manor. She ...'

'That's not the point.'

Rebecca stopped. Her sympathy for Annabelle had already waned and she wondered why she hadn't followed Daniel into the kitchen for a coffee.

'The point is that you have the money – and Daniel doesn't,'

Rebecca remained silent.

'It's a pity you couldn't have been a little kinder to him,' Annabelle continued, glaring as she walked past Rebecca and in the direction of the hallway. 'If you hadn't been so mean with the divorce settlement Daniel would be able to afford Bransome Manor. We could have had the wedding of our dreams but we can't afford it and it's all your fault.' And with a toss of her head she walked out leaving Rebecca open mouthed with shock.

Rebecca's heart was thumping so hard it hurt her chest. Is that what Daniel thought? Is that what her family thought? Had she been mean in her treatment of Daniel? When she had finally accepted that their marriage could not be saved she had offered to split the money with him. But Daniel had refused. He had been truly horrified that she had finally discovered his affair and the reason for the wasted years spent in Darlington and he had been determined to walk away empty handed, a self-imposed punishment. Eventually he had agreed to a million pounds, more than enough, he had said, to allow him to begin a new life for himself. Had he changed his mind, she wondered? With time to think and a new relationship did he now regret walking away with only a fraction of Rebecca's winnings.

'Mum.'

Rebecca spun round to stare at her daughter.

'Mum, what are you doing in here by yourself. Do you want me to get started with lunch?'

Did Sarah think her mother had been greedy the divorce settlement, she wondered. Did Toby think she had been mean. They had both supported her at the time, maybe they had changed their minds?

'Are you okay?'

Perhaps Daniel thought she had been unfair, perhaps they all thought she should have given Daniel more.

Sarah laughed, taking her mother's arm and setting off in the direction of the kitchen. 'You've been lost in your thoughts since we got back. Shall I start peeling potatoes, do you want me to do the veg as well?' and with her heart still thumping uncomfortably, Rebecca allowed herself to be led away.

Soon the smell of roast beef was wafting through the house, wine glasses were filled and everyone was gathering back in the kitchen. Sarah and Dom were sitting at the table looking both secretive and rather pleased with themselves, Rebecca had spent the last hour in her study, still smarting over Annabelle's suggestion that she had been unfair with the divorce settlement. Returning to the kitchen and finding Daniel sitting at the table, she gave him such a stern look that he had looked around nervously for a reason for her bad mood. But Annabelle seemed to be putting a brave front on her disappointment as she allowed Daniel to get her a glass of wine and sit by her side.

'Which was your favourite venue,' she asked Sarah, sending a longing look at the discarded Bransome Manor brochure that still littered the table.

'Mmm hard to say,' said Sarah looking at her mother who was busy making gravy. 'They were all so different.'

'I loved Bransome Manor,' sighed Annabelle, clinging to her dream. 'You've got plenty of time to find somewhere. I don't know what Daniel and I are going to do,' she added despondently.

'Actually,' Sarah started nervously, 'we don't have that much time.'

Rebecca hadn't been taking much notice of the conversation but there was something in her daughter's voice that made her look up and listen. 'The thing is that having looked at some venues, Dom and I have had a slight change of plan. We've decided there's not much point in waiting. We've made the big decision – to get married. So we just want to get on with it, we're going to set a date and get married this summer.'

There was a slight pause and Rebecca realised that both Sarah and Dom were waiting for her approval. Did she approve? She still thought they were a little young to get married but that wasn't Rebecca's decision to make and if they wanted to get married this summer instead of waiting for next summer, how could Rebecca object.

'You're both sure?'

They nodded, holding hands tightly under the table.

'I know it's a bit short notice mum but it's what we want to do.'

'Then I'm very pleased for you, and I'm sure we can get you a wonderful wedding organised for the summer,' said Rebecca smiling at them both.

'How exciting!' chimed in Annabelle. 'Are you sure you don't want Bransome Manor. Don't the bride's parents traditionally pay? You're lucky in that respect,' said Annabelle sending a frosty sideways glance in Rebecca's direction. 'You won't have to worry about the wedding bill!'

Rebecca watched the look of alarm flit across Daniel's face.

'Oh er … look here Annabelle. That's an old, old tradition and I don't think Sarah would be expecting me to pay for her wedding!'

Annabelle looked a little shocked. 'Well of course she wouldn't Daniel. I meant Becky. She'll probably be paying for Sarah's wedding.' Her head swivelled in Rebecca's direction. 'You wouldn't want Sarah worrying about how to afford the wedding of her dreams, would you?'

Daniel was still looking a little pale at being involved in the potential cost of an extra wedding but everybody else was looking at Rebecca.

'Oh no!' said Sarah shocked. 'We can afford our own wedding, we don't expect mum - or dad - to pay.'

'Of course I'll be paying. I can't think of anything better to spend money on.'

'But mum we …'

'I wouldn't have it any other way,' her mum interrupted firmly. 'I'll be paying Sarah darling, you can have the wedding of your dreams.'

She looked at Daniel from beneath her eyelashes, 'I'm sure your dad would love to contribute,' she said cheerily watching him almost choke on his wine as Annabelle opened her eyes wide in alarm,' but he does have a wedding of his own to organise so I am more than happy to do this on my own.'

She took a step back laughing as Sarah flung her arms around her mother's neck. 'Oh mum! Thank you - but you know you don't have to! I wasn't expecting you to pay, I have my own money and I ...'

'Hush. I'm paying. And if you want Bransome Manor, that's where we'll have the wedding.'

Dominic stood up and offered his hand. 'That's very generous of you and we really appreciate your offer,' he said smiling.

'Oh!' squealed Annabelle. The hands were flapping and Rebecca steeled herself for whatever was coming.

'We could have a joint wedding! Just imagine that, a father and daughter marrying on the same day, together! How wonderful!'

Rebecca couldn't imagine anything more disconcerting. Surely there was no way Sarah would want to share her day with Daniel and Annabelle.

'We could get married at Bransome Manor, ON THE SAME DAY! How amazing would that be. And we could book all the rooms so we had plenty of space for everyone to stay over and we'd have the place to ourselves.' Annabelle was clapping her tiny hands together frantically. 'Isn't that an amazing idea?'

Even Daniel looked less than enthusiastic and Sarah's face had fallen quite dramatically.

'Oh well I suppose it's a nice idea Annabelle, but I really wasn't that keen on Bransome Manor actually.'

'Well the Great Hall Hotel would be lovely as well,' conceded Annabelle, trying to mask her disappointment. 'Although perhaps we should go back to both and have a second look. Maybe Bransome will appeal to you more now you can actually imagine yourself getting married there.'

'Er … actually I wasn't that keen on the Great Hall either. It was a bit impersonal and I would like …'

'Or we can go somewhere else,' agreed Annabelle waving her hand in the air. 'Don't worry, we'll start looking in earnest now you've brought your date forward.'

Rebecca was watching her daughter's face, she was such a gentle soul it was really difficult for her to tell Annabelle that she didn't want to share her wedding.

'Where would you have your wedding Sarah?' asked Rebecca, holding her breath as she waited for the answer.

'Well, I actually loved willow Court,' admitted Sarah.

'What! That dirty old place. No! That wouldn't do at all.'

Rebecca ignored Annabelle's outraged rejection and kept her eyes on her daughter.

'I know it isn't suitable, it's practically falling down,' giggled Sarah. 'But that sort of place, you know? Not stuffy like Bransome Manor or somewhere impersonal like the first place. Somewhere old and gracious but warm and inviting.'

'Well I'm sure we could find somewhere like it,' mused Annabelle, 'maybe a little bit bigger and certainly not somewhere so scruffy. Oh I know … a castle!'

'And if it weren't falling down?' asked Rebecca. 'If it had gone through the programme of renovation Debbie mentioned. Would it be somewhere you would like to have your wedding?'

'Oh yes,' said Sarah without hesitation. 'Absolutely.'

'Really?' asked Annabelle doubtfully, 'because even if it had a lick of paint I didn't think it was entirely suitable. 'Maybe somewhere with a little more grandeur. Somewhere …'

Well that makes my decision easier then.'

Even Annabelle stopped as all eyes turned to Rebecca.

'What decision?' demanded Daniel.

She smiled around at the circle of faces. 'I've been making some enquiries this afternoon, Willow Court is for sale and I've decided to buy it. I'm going to give it the renovation that it needs and restore it to an amazing wedding venue. I'm afraid a double wedding is out of the question Annabelle,' she said firmly. There was no way she would allow Annabelle to take over Sarah's wedding day. 'I was hoping that Sarah and Dominic liked the place as much as I had because it would be my absolute privilege to hold the most wonderful wedding possible for them in a newly renovated and restored Willow Court.'

'You're going to buy Willow Court?' asked Sarah stunned.

'Yes.'

'To renovate it for my wedding?'

'Yes.'

'Do you think you can have it ready in time, now we've brought the wedding forward?'

'I'm sure I can. One thing I've learned,' she said with a grimace,' if you throw enough money at something it's amazing how quickly you can get things done. A summer wedding it is and don't worry, I'll have Willow Court ready and looking amazing for you.'

'Oh mum!' and suddenly Rebecca was engulfed in her daughter's arms and disappearing under a flurry of kisses. 'That would be amazing, absolutely amazing! Thank you.'

'What a ridiculous idea,' scoffed Daniel. 'What do you know about organising weddings?'

'I don't need to know anything about weddings. I know how to renovate a building and restore a business,' Rebecca reminded him defiantly.

'You've done it once, it doesn't make you an expert.'

'I didn't claim to be an expert, but I am buying Willow Court and I will turn it back into a successful business,'

'Don't be ridiculous, you know nothing about ....'

'Be quiet!'

Daniel's mouth flapped open unattractively. 'But ...'

'No! It's nothing to do with you Daniel. We've been here before. You do not tell me what I can and cannot do!'

Rebecca saw Sarah and Dom exchange a worried glance and Annabelle clutch at Daniel's hand and glare at her. She stopped and took a deep breath forcing herself to smile and lifting her glass.

'Let's not argue,' she said lightly. 'Congratulations to Sarah and Dom. Here's to your wedding, at Willow Court this summer.'

His chin wobbling with indignation Daniel snapped open his newspaper and retreated behind the pages, muttering darkly as the rest of them raised their glasses.

'Thanks mum. We were thinking of August.'

Annabelle's face suddenly cleared and she clapped her hands in joy. 'But that's perfect! This summer is when Daniel and I are getting married. We can go to Willow Court as well, can't we Daniel?'

'What? Get married at Willow court? I thought you said you hated the place. You said …'

'I didn't say I hated it,' Annabelle interrupted with a little laugh, 'I said it needed an awful lot of work. And that's exactly what Rebecca is going to give it. It will be ready this summer for Sarah and Dominic so we can use it as well can't we?' She turned back to Rebecca who was watching her with amusement. 'We can be your second guests after Sarah and Dominic!'

'Depends on the price Belles.'

'The price?' she asked genuinely confused.

'Yes. The price. If Willow Court is going to be as extortionately expensive as that other bloody place you like it's just out of the question, quite out of the question.'

'But Rebecca won't expect us to pay!' Annabelle swivelled her gaze back to Rebecca. 'Would you? I mean we're family. She wouldn't want us to pay!'

Rebecca said nothing and Daniel threw down his newspaper.

'Of course we'll pay! I don't need my ex-wife to pay for my wedding,' Daniel shouted, his cheeks puffing out alarmingly. 'How on earth would that look. I can pay for my own wedding Belles, and I won't have it any other way.'

'But Daniel darling, Bec would be positively insulted if we tried to pay her. She would be mortified at the thought of charging family for using her wedding venue.'

'And I would be mortified if I didn't pay so maybe we'd be better off looking elsewhere.'

'No! I mean Willow Court is so beautiful, I really want to get married there.'

Rebecca allowed her eyebrows to raise a little. Annabelle's regard for Willow Court was growing by the second.

'Then we'll pay like anybody else would.'

Rebecca took pity on Annabelle and the bottom lip she was tearing at with her teeth.

'I don't plan on Willow Court being the same kind of venue as Bransome,' she advised, 'the prices won't be the extortionate kind that upset Daniel so much,' adding cheekily, 'and I'm sure I can offer a discount.'

'How much?' It was blunt and straight to the point, but Rebecca was already learning that when Annabelle wanted something she rarely held back.

'I haven't even bought the place yet Annabelle. It's a bit early to be talking wedding costs.' She bent down to take the beef out of the oven and Daniel seemed to forget his anger, licking his lips eagerly.

'So can we get married at Willow Court Daniel?'

'What? Well it still depends on the price and …'

'Wonderful!' announced Annabelle. 'How wonderful, Sarah, we've both got our venue sorted!' and as the roast potatoes appeared next to the beef, Annabelle took a sip of wine and smiled happily, watching the light dance from her diamond ring.

Chapter 10

Monday morning Rebecca wrapped up warmly and drove into Leeds to visit Richard, her bank manager. It was with a great deal of relief that she had finally waved off Daniel and Annabelle half an hour earlier. Annabelle had been making all sorts of noises about staying and helping Rebecca organise the purchase of Willow Court. She had even presented Rebecca with a list of other similar properties for consideration, all far more expensive, not in need of any restoration but all exactly the sort of place Annabelle would love to have as a wedding venue.

Rebecca had politely ignored her until her patience exhausted she took the ever-growing list from Annabelle and dropped it into the kitchen bin. 'I'm buying Willow Court Annabelle. If you don't want to have your wedding there that's okay ...'

'I do!' squealed Annabelle and quickly closed down Rightmove.

Rebecca had also managed a quiet moment with Daniel, not an easy task with Annabelle an ever present limpet attached to his arm. This was not a conversation she wanted to have but she had buried too many conversations with Daniel in the past to let this go. She had wasted too many years not speaking her mind.

'What?' he had asked impatiently as she stood in front of him, suddenly nervous.

'I wondered,' Rebecca cleared her throat and ignored Daniel's rolling eyes and pointed glance at his watch. 'I wondered if you were unhappy at the settlement we agreed when we split up.'

There was a moment's silence as Daniel looked genuinely shocked by the question.

'What on earth do you mean?'

'Well, I wondered if you wished that you had asked for … I mean if I should have given you more money when we divorced.'

She took her eyes away from the floor and looked at Daniel whose cheeks had gone a dull red and whose chin was wobbling alarmingly.

'Why are we discussing this Rebecca? I am perfectly happy. I was at the time and I am now. You know I didn't want to take anything from you. If you're suggesting that I …'

I'm not suggesting anything Daniel,' Rebecca placed a calming hand on Daniel's rigid arm. 'I'm just wondering if you regret only taking what you did. If now that a few years have gone by you wish that you'd taken more.'

'Absolutely not.' Daniel's entire body quivered with righteous anger as he continued stiffly. 'You were more than fair under the circumstances and I have never wished for more.'

Rebecca nodded and tried to smile.

A sudden frown knotted Daniel's forehead. 'And why do you ask?'

Rebecca considered not saying anything. But she had spent too many years remaining silent under the dominant presence of Daniel and now she had escaped she had no desire to go back there.

'Annabelle,' she offered bluntly. 'She appears to think I have been mean and treated you quite badly.'

'Ah.' More colour filled Daniel's face and he shifted uncomfortably from one foot to another.

'You'll have to excuse her. She is very much in love with me you see,' he took a moment to look smug before continuing, 'and although I told her everything that happened between us, she can't help feeling that I was er, that I took too little in our divorce settlement.'

Rebecca opened her mouth but Daniel held up his hand. 'I said Annabelle feels aggrieved on my behalf, I didn't say that I was unhappy.'

'She thinks I should have given you more money?'

'Er, well yes.'

'And you're sure you don't agree with her?'

Daniel fidgeted uncomfortably. 'I've told you, I am happy. I was then and I am now. And there is really no need for us to continue discussing this. Annabelle shouldn't have said anything, she is a little sensitive on my behalf.'

'So you don't think that I was – mean?'

'No! Absolutely not!'

'Right. So we're okay? I mean, you're happy with the ….

Absolutely!'

'And you don't want …'

'Absolutely not!'

And they both scurried back to the kitchen where for once Rebecca was glad to see Annabelle in situ and the conversation was well and truly ended.

And now they were gone. Daniel had been quite eager to leave after his conversation with Rebecca and as the door slammed on their retreating figures, Rebecca gave a huge sigh of relief as her house returned almost instantly to its quiet, soothing space once more.

Armed with the little information Rebecca had managed to find on the internet about Willow Court, she had phoned to make an appointment with Richard and he had agreed to meet her that morning

'Rebecca, how lovely to see you.' Richard unwrapped his long frame from behind his desk and looking genuinely pleased he gave her a kiss on the cheek and wrapped his arms round her briefly.

He looked at the folder in her hand. 'Do I feel another business proposal in the air?'

Rebecca grinned. She had missed Richard over the last year. His dry sense of humour, his wit and his gentle manner had all been a delight. But for some reason she had never been able to completely relax in his company, she hadn't been able to stop the past from intruding.

'Yep! Another house actually.'

'You're moving?'

'Not exactly. Well not at all, I still love my house.' Richard nodded, he had made no secret of his admiration for Rebecca's beautiful home. 'This is another business centred round a house.'

'Well it's what you seem to specialise in and look at the success of Parklands. So,' he was back in his chair, fingers steepled under his chin in a familiar gesture, 'another care home?'

'Not this time.' Rebecca laid the folder on Richard's desk with a flourish. 'A wedding venue.'

'A wedding venue? You mean as in a house where people have their wedding reception?'

'The whole wedding if they choose. This house has a delightful chapel...' Rebecca remembered the cold, neglected chapel, maybe delightful was the wrong phrase. 'It has a chapel that could be used. It has rooms for the reception and enough bedrooms to allow bride, groom and family or friends to stay.'

'Mmm.' Richard was already absorbed in the folder. Rebecca had searched for Willow Court and found it hidden deep within Rightmove. There had been limited details, no mention of the wedding business and few photographs, almost a half-hearted attempt to sell. But it showed enough to capture Rebecca's interest and she had carried on digging, finding photographs from many years before when it had been a successful business and blissful brides posed at the foot of the wonderful oak staircase. There was even a photograph of the domed room, the windows thrown open and sheer curtains floating in the breeze as a young couple danced beneath the magnificent ceiling. She had also searched for the registered accounts of Willow Court Weddings and discovered that until 5 years ago the business had been successful but that profits had been plummeting ever since. Rightmove listed the house at 1.2 million, making mention of a certain degree of updating needed.

'The price?'

'Too much, I'll pay 1 million and no more. It needs a lot of work, more than the photographs indicate.'

'Timescale?'

'Before August.'

'Next year?'

'This year.'

'Six months to buy and renovate a house of this size?'

'Yes. It's a necessity. Sarah is getting married ...'

'Congratulations.'

'Thank you. She's getting married and I would like her to be able to use Willow Court. It means I need to move immediately. I need the sale to go through as quickly as possible and start the work straight away. Not everything needs to be done straight away, but there is one room in particular that needs a lot of work and I want it restoring in time for Sarah's wedding. A handful of the bedrooms need to be finished in time but not necessarily all. The roof seems sound, I need to look at the electrics and heating of course.'

'Refurbishment cost?'

'I don't know yet, I will have to get a builder in. I'll probably have to pay over the odds for the timescale I need.'

'The wedding business?'

'I'll put in a manager, I don't know enough about weddings to run it myself. But it's a beautiful house and it was successful before. The wedding side of things should be possible to start up again. If not, I've got a restored house I can sell on.'

Richard continued to read in silence and Rebecca fidgeted in her seat slightly as she waited.

'Well?'

'You have a good eye for these sorts of investments Rebecca. If you knock the price down and restore the business, it looks like a sound investment. Your losses are limited, your potential good. It looks like an excellent idea.'

Rebecca breathed a sigh of relief. 'Oh good! Thank you Richard, that's such good news!'

'Tell me, what would you have done if I had said it wasn't a good idea?' asked Richard curiously.

'I respect your opinion. I may well have abandoned the idea.'

'May have?'

Rebecca grinned. 'Yes, may have. I believe in myself a lot more these days Richard.'

There was a moment of silence broken by the arrival of coffee and biscuits.

'How are you Rebecca?' asked Richard quietly.

How was she? Excited at the prospect of Willow Court. Delighted to have something to occupy her time again. Disturbed by the fact Daniel was getting married again. Envious he was moving on. Lonely.

'I'm good Richard.' Why hadn't it worked out between them she wondered. He was such a kind and decent man. Impulsively she reached forward and put her hand over his as it lay on the desk. 'And you?'

'Very good. Actually I, er …' Was he blushing? 'I er … I'm seeing someone.'

Rebecca withdrew her hand. 'Seeing someone?'

'Yes. She's called Laura. I met her a few months ago and well …' He was definitely blushing. 'It's actually going really well and we … we're moving in together.'

'Already?' Rebecca didn't like the accusing tone of her voice and tried again. 'I mean that's wonderful Richard. I'm really pleased for you. And the boys?'

'Oh they've fallen head over heels in love with her as well! Can't wait for her to move in and become part of the family.'

Why did she want to cry Rebecca wondered? Why did she want to put her head on Richard's desk and cry like a baby?

'Well that's good, really good, quite excellent.'

'And you?'

Rebecca squeezed one hand into a tight fist so that the nails dug into her skin and made her wince. 'Oh no!' She attempted a laugh. 'Not me. I'm still enjoying life as a single woman.'

Richard was too polite to say anything but there was a flash of pity in his eyes even as he nodded and agreed. 'I can't blame you,' he offered generously. 'Make the most of it.'

Rebecca brought the meeting to a swift close, hugging Richard again, smiling and nodding and trying to look as cheerful as she had when she arrived. Walking back to her car she blamed her watering eyes on the biting cold air but she had no excuse for the ache in her heart. Even Richard had moved on. What on earth was wrong with her? And blinking rapidly she joined the line of motorists all crawling along the icy roads out of Leeds and in the direction of Willow Court.

*

'I'm sorry, you want to what?'

'I want to buy Willow Court.'

Rebecca was standing by the reception desk with a shocked Debbie.

'I thought you wanted to rent it for a wedding?'

'Well we are having a wedding and we would like it here at Willow Court but I would like to buy it first.'

'Buy Willow court?'

'Yes. It is for sale isn't it.'

'Well, yes, sort of.'

Rebecca frowned. 'Sort of? How is it sort of for sale?'

'Well you see it belongs to mum and she's run it as a wedding venue for years and she knows it's not working now but she's finding it hard to let go.' Debbie paused, looking over at the water stained flooring at the foot of the staircase. 'She hasn't really got the money - or the energy to do all the work needed. I told her she needed to sell and she put it on the market to see what happened but as far as actually selling it is concerned ... I'm really not sure.'

'I see. Then I need to have a conversation with your mother because I want to buy Willow Court and I want to buy it straight away so I can get on with the work needed and have it ready for my daughter's wedding in August.'

Debbie's mouth gaped open.

'So is she here?'

Debbie looked blank.

'Your mother, is she here?'

'You really want to buy this place?'

'I do.'

'Straight away?'

'Yes.'

'And keep the weddings going?'

'Yes.'

Suddenly Debbie looked interested, in fact positively enthusiastic.

'Then come with me!' and almost running she led Rebecca up the staircase and down another long corridor, as dilapidated as the rest of the house.

'These used to be the servant's quarters but Mum had them made into a private suite of rooms years ago she could use all the other rooms for the weddings.'

She threw open a door with such vigour that a small yelp came from inside.

'Sorry mum but this is important. This lady ...'

'My name is Rebecca...'

'Yes, this lady, Rebecca, wants to buy Willow Court.'

The elderly lady in the chair opened her eyes wide but said nothing and Rebecca stood in the doorway looking round the room. She was fairly certain servant's quarters were not normally this spacious and she suspected that a couple of rooms had been knocked together to create a reasonable size sitting room with a small fireplace and a couple of cosy settees. The windows looked out onto the side of the house with the garden and the woodland beyond and was a pleasant living space.

'Buy Willow Court?'

Rebecca sighed. There seemed to a be a great deal of disbelief in her simple request.

'Yes Mrs ...?'

'Mrs Hemmings. Please call me Audrey.'

'Thank you. Audrey, I came to visit a few days ago with a view to my daughter's wedding.' She saw Audrey's eyes light up. 'But of course that won't be happening because, well quite frankly this building needs an awful lot of work before anybody would want to hold a wedding here.' Rebecca refused to feel guilty about the sudden tremble of Audrey's lip. 'But I can see that it was once a beautiful place,' she continued hastily, 'a really lovely building. So I went onto Rightmove, saw that it was for sale and decided I would like to buy it. I want to buy Willow Court from you and I want to buy it as quickly as possible.'

'You want to buy the house.'

'Yes, that's what I said, I want to buy Willow Court.'

Audrey looked down at her hands, laying slackly in her lap. 'It was lovely,' she admitted reluctantly. 'I know it's not so good now but it's still ...'

'Mum she wants to carry on with the weddings!'

Suddenly Audrey's hands became rigid and her eyes came back to Rebecca.

'You want to do weddings here?'

Rebecca bit her lip to stop the scream of frustration. 'Yes. I want to buy willow Court, restore it and carry on doing weddings. Before August,' she added desperately, imaging summer arriving and Audrey Hemmings still sitting in her chair asking 'You want to buy Willow Court?'

She watched the emotions chase across the other woman's face, she could feel how tense Debbie was beside her and she looked from one to the other in confusion.

'Mum really didn't want to sell this place to anyone who didn't want to carry on with the weddings,' whispered Debbie quietly over her shoulder. 'Everybody who has expressed any interest at all wanted it as a private house but weddings are part of the tradition of Willow Court and mum wanted them to carry on.'

Rebecca nodded. 'So…?'

'So you wanting to keep the weddings could be the prod she needs,' Debbie said hopefully.

Rebecca stepped forwards, thankful that she'd brought her laptop in from the car.

'Mrs Hemmings,' she said eagerly, pulling her laptop from its case and flicking it open. 'Audrey, I came across this photograph when I was researching your beautiful home.'

Frantically Rebecca scrolled and tapped until she found what she was looking for.

She bent down next to Audrey's chair and put the laptop gently on her knee. It was the photograph of the young couple dancing in the domed room, the enchantment on their faces as they were caught in a moment of time, sunlight dancing through the window, a glimpse of the ceiling above their heads.

'I saw this photograph and I decided that this is what I wanted for my daughter. I want the weddings to continue and the very first one will be for Sarah, my own daughter. I want Willow court to look like it once did and for my Sarah to dance in that room.'

Audrey stared at the photograph, her eyes misting over slightly as she touched the screen gently. 'I remember that young couple,' she whispered. 'It is a beautiful room isn't it?'

'No,' answered Rebecca bluntly. 'But it could be. Let me buy Willow Court and I'll get that room looking like that again. For my daughter. And before August.'

Part Two
Wedding Plans

Chapter 11

'No, I can't wait until September for you to start. I told you, I need it finishing by August!'

Slamming down the phone, Rebecca let her head fall onto her desk top. She would never have believed it could be so difficult finding a building firm who could do the work she wanted in the timeframe she needed. She had tried dozens and had failed miserably, to the point where she had researched alternative wedding venues the previous night, concerned that she would not be able to deliver Willow Court to Sarah as promised. She needed someone with the skill to restore some of the old plasterwork which had proved to be her first hurdle. One firm had announced cheerfully that it wouldn't be a problem, they would box it in and plaster it over, a coat of paint and it would be smooth as a baby's bottom in no time at all. Less cleaning as well once all those little nooks and crannies had disappeared.

Rebecca looked down at her list. All the names she had gathered had been crossed off. They had either proved unsuitable, been unable to begin the work until after her deadline or hadn't even responded to her voicemail offering them vast amounts of money if they could restore a country house within the next few months.

There was one name left to try. It hadn't been on Rebecca's original list but when she met Helen and Emma for lunch the previous day and updated them with her building woes, Emma had pulled out her phone, scrolled through her contacts and announced that she was going to text Rebecca a number.

'Drew and Luke are fantastic,' she'd announced, 'reliable and really good. And I think they might have a space in their schedule because Drew was telling us last week that a new build they were due to start was delayed because of planning permission. He was really miffed because he'd taken on extra help to make sure it was done on time and now he needed to find something for them to do or he'd be paying their wages for nothing.'

So the last number Rebecca had on her list was for A & L Builders and if they couldn't help she really did need to start panicking.

The number answered on the third ring - already a tick in the box. Rebecca had decided that getting a builder to answer his phone was akin to trying to give Brad Pitt a quick bell.

'Hello. My name is Rebecca Miles and I'm hoping you can help.'

'Hi Rebecca. I've been waiting for you to ring.'

'You have?' Was this some new kind of builder Rebecca wondered? Building by divination.

'Yeah, Emma told me what you needed and that she was passing on my number.'

'Oh of course,' said Rebecca feeling slightly foolish. 'So, do you need me to provide the details or are you ...'

'Emma described the job and to be honest I drove over and had a quick peek at the place yesterday.'

An efficient and proactive builder.

'It looks a big job and a deadline of August could be tight. But it would actually help me out of a hole myself. I need some work over the next few months.'

An honest builder.

'Obviously I would have to go inside, have a good look round and talk to you about your designs. You may need to scale back some ideas to get it finished in time but we could certainly have a look and see what we can do.'

A practical builder.

'Did Emma mention there was some old plasterwork that needed restoring?'

'She did. That's a big job in itself and never quick.'

Ah - same old builder.

'But I do have someone I use for this sort of thing. He's a master craftsman at restoring old plasterwork designs. We would get him started in that room straight away and leave him to get on with it.'

Ooh - sensible builder.

'Hello, Rebecca, are you still there?'

'Oh yes. Sorry, just thinking.' An image of the domed room with its ceiling restored, windows open and curtains fluttering in the breeze was drifting through Rebecca's head.

'You think it can be done?' she asked cautiously.

'Well I can't say without going inside but I think it's a possible yes. Ow!' he complained as Rebecca's squeal of delight hit his eardrums.

'Oh sorry, sorry. I'm just so relieved to hear someone say they'll at least look at it for me.'

Drew chuckled. 'Well seeing as the job is so urgent, can you meet me today and we can start assessing what's needed?'

Rebecca gave him directions and hugged herself with delight. It may just happen after all.

Promising builder.

An hour later she was driving up to the front door of Willow Court. It wouldn't actually be hers for another week yet, but Audrey and Debbie were quite happy for Bec to wander around, making plans and taking measurements. In fact Audrey had been caught up in Rebecca's enthusiasm and was as eager as anyone to have the renovation started. She had also taken Rebecca into the huge attic and showed her all the lengths of muslin, tulle and lace that they used to decorate the tables and chairs. Stacks of cream chairs covered with a soft golden brocade were stacked in one corner. They needed a little work but Rebecca had fallen in love with them, so much better than the plain conference hall type chairs she had seen at other venues. 'Shabby chic!' Audrey had declared with a wave of her hand. 'Good clean is all they need.' There was also a mountain of beautiful old china. You could get plain white,

I suppose it would be more practical,' sniffed Audrey, 'but I always went with what looked the prettiest. And you don't need to match the pattern across the whole wedding party, mix and match across each table.'

There were vases - lots of vases of every size and shape and hundreds of candle holders. Huge free-standing ones for either side of a doorway or fireplace, candelabra style ones to create an impact on a centre table and a mountain of smaller ones to scatter around the room.

It was like an Aladdin's cave and Rebecca walked through the piles, trailing her hand through the dust.

'I'll include it all,' declared Audrey. 'it will save you time looking for replacements.'

'Oh Audrey I couldn't! I don't mind buying them …'

'Nonsense. Absolutely no good to me. And beside they belong here.'

She had also taken Rebecca into a room she had clearly used as a study and where she unearthed a mound of drawings.

'These are the original plans.'

Flicking on a light she spread one page out across the desk and Rebecca saw to her delight that in the corner of the page was a detailed drawing showing a section of the plaster cornice for the domed room together with the ceiling rose and the fireplace.

'Oh Audrey, this is exactly what I need,' Rebecca had enthused. 'We should be able to use this to match up the repairs.'

So with the co-operation of the current owners of Willow Court, Rebecca had already gathered together drawings of the renovations needed together with a list of the more practical building work such as repairs to walls and floors, new bathrooms, replacement windows, a new kitchen, repairing the staircase - the list went on and every time Rebecca thought about it her heart did a funny little skip as she acknowledged the amount of work needed.

She was sitting in her car biting her thumb nail when a van pulled alongside her and two men climbed out.

'Rebecca?'

Rebecca scrabbled from her seat and held out her hand. 'Yes. One of you must be Drew?'

The older of the two took her hand. 'I'm Drew, this is my son Luke. It's our business'

'Right. And who is the A?'

'The A?'

'Yes. A & L builders?'

'Ah!' He grinned and Rebecca decided it was a good sign for a builder to have evenly spaced white teeth.

'That's me. Andrew Chance.'

'Chance?'

'Yes. You can see why we called it A&L builders can't you. Who would want to employ a builder's firm called Chance!'

Rebecca smiled back. 'Maybe not. Well it's lovely to meet you anyway and I'm really hoping you can help me.'

'It's a lovely old building,' admired the younger man. He looked very much like his father, just a little smoother around the edges, a little softer in the face. He had the same dark blond hair cut in a short no nonsense style and the same firm jaw line and wide shoulders as his father. His eyes weren't quite the same piercing dark blue but more of a cornflower shade and for some reason Rebecca took an immediate liking to both father and son. Luke was probably the same age as her own son and taking a quick peep at Drew she decided he was probably around her own age.

'It may help that I've got the original drawings which shows what the plaster work should look like and gives all sorts of measurement and details.

Drew nodded. 'Things like that always help,' he said looking up at the house. 'Can we go in?'

'Of course, sorry, come this way.'

As Rebecca took them inside she explained about Audrey and Debbie and then arriving in the hallway she stopped to let them look around.

For the next half an hour Rebecca didn't speak. She trailed after Drew and Luke as they walked slowly from room to room, Drew talking softly and Luke making copious notes. They examined the panelling, the chipped fireplace and the broken picture rails. They visibly recoiled as they took in a kitchen which hadn't been updated for 50 years and they both stopped for a moment and stared in awe at the domed ceiling and the beautiful plasterwork. They went upstairs and measured bathrooms and broken windows and then went back downstairs and spent a few moments in the cold, damp chapel which had several windows boarded up and little light or heat to warm the old stone. Eventually they arrived back in the hallway and stood for a moment looking at each other as Rebecca waited for the verdict.

'Can it be done?' she asked impatiently.

'It can be done. But what you are asking me is if it can it be done in time.'

'Yes. Can it be done before the end of August?' She had spoken to Sarah and Dominic and they had settled on the last weekend in August which gave as much breathing room as possible for Rebecca and Willow Court.

'It'll be tight,' said Luke doubtfully.

'Very tight,' echoed Drew.

'And the plasterwork?'

'Even tighter," sighed Luke.

'Mmm,' agreed his father.

'But can it be done?' Rebecca asked in anguish.

'We'll have to start as soon as possible, I mean the minute you've signed for Willow Court we need to start work,' Drew said.

'Brian needs to get on with that plasterwork straight away, he really will need to work every day between now and your deadline to stand a chance of getting it finished,' added Luke with a sigh.

'And we need to talk budget because every bathroom in the place needs replacing,' Drew said with a grimace.

'Surprisingly the wiring looks okay.'

'And some of it is cosmetic damage so it's a quick fix.'

'it might be tricky getting the windows matched up.'

There was a long silence.

'Oh please put me out of my misery!' pleaded Bec.

The two men looked at each other and then at her.

'Of course it can,' they said in unison and with a squeal Rebecca literally threw herself at them trying to fit two sets of very wide shoulders into her embrace as she hugged them in delight.

Wonderful builders!

They took another tour of the building, this time full of ideas and suggestions, choosing which bedrooms could be left until later, the order of work, ideas how to make it all come together in the shortest space of time.

Eventually, as the light faded Rebecca looked at her watch and gave a little yelp.

'Oh I need to go!'

They wandered back towards the front door and feeling full of optimism Rebecca shook both their hands. 'Thank you so much for meeting me,' she smiled. 'I suppose the next step is you give me a price?'

She didn't say that as they were the only builders who had even considered taking on the work, it was more or less a done deal.

'It won't be a quick quote,' warned Drew scratching his head. 'We have so much to cost up it may take a couple of days to get back to you. I don't want to let you down by finding something is more expensive than we originally thought.'

Conscientious builder.

'Okay, well as soon as you have some figures let me know. I exchange next week so hopefully we'll be ready to start straight away?'

Drew and Luke both nodded and smiling they all walked back to the car park.

'I'm sorry I have to rush off,' apologised Rebecca, 'but if you need any more information you have my number.' She looked at her watch again and walked a little quicker towards her car.

'Doing anything nice?'

She stopped to open her car door and then looked back at the two builders with a grin. 'I hope so,' she said with a flutter of nerves in her stomach. 'I've got a date!' and waving goodbye she jumped in her car and headed for home.

Chapter 12

Knocking on Helen's door, Rebecca wanted the street to open and swallow her whole. Why on earth had she agreed to this, she wondered desperately? She hated these dinner parties where the sole object was to find a new love interest for Rebecca Miles. It was highly embarrassing having everybody else in the room winking at each other and whispering as Rebecca and her prospective mate chatted self-consciously. If either of them spoke the whole room would listen, laughing uproariously at every witty remark as if to confirm what excellent company they were, agreeing enthusiastically with every comment made and generally hanging on every word. Everybody would emphasise what a wonderful couple they made, how natural they seemed together, how much they had in common, how they should definitely meet up again and the sooner the better. She started to turn away, she had an emergency she decided. Getting Willow Court sorted was her first priority, she didn't have time for meeting new men. She would phone Helen and apologise but emphasise just how busy she was at the moment and…

'Not so quick!' Her arm was grasped firmly and before she could take a step towards the gate she was gently pulled into the hallway by Tim who pushed the door shut with his foot to block off her escape.

'Tim,' she whispered urgently, 'I just came to say I can't come, I mean I can't stay and …'

'Not a chance Bec my lovely. Helen would kill me if I let you go now.'

'But …'

'No way.' He had taken off her coat despite her trying to hang on tightly to the lapels, taking the bottle of wine form her hands and putting it on the hall table so he could slide her arms out of the sleeves.

'It's not that I don't want to come, I'm just so busy. I do have a genuine emergency Tim and I need to go ….'

Coat off and hung up, Tim slid one hand under Rebecca's elbow, picked up the bottle of wine with the other and grinned at the woman he'd known for almost 20 years. 'It's not going to work Bec. Just give in and make the most of it,' and with a wink he propelled her into the kitchen where her audience were waiting.

'Bec! I was beginning to worry that you weren't going to make it.' Helen swooped towards her friend, wrapping her arms around Rebecca's tense body and kissing her on the cheek, pausing to whisper in her ear. 'Stop looking so worried!'

Dropping her arms she spun Rebecca round so she could see everyone else in the room. Emma was sitting at the pine table, glass in hand looking very pleased with life. She grinned at Bec and gave a little nod of encouragement.

'Bec darling this is Judith and Chris who live down the road. They're new to the village and we decided it was time they met a few of the gang. This is Charles, he works with Dave and lives close by so we decided it was time we got to know him better,' Helen waved her hand casually around the room, 'and everyone else here you already know!' Rebecca squeezed her friend's hand, silently thanking her for the understated introduction.

'Hello everyone,' she said shyly, scooting across to join Emma at the table.

'Drink Bec?'

'Oh I'm driving so just a small glass please.'

'Driving?' Helen had appeared by her side, her eyebrows drawn together. She sat down almost on top of Emma so she could address Bec in a soft undertone. 'I thought we'd agreed you would get a taxi and then you could have a few glasses of wine?'

Rebecca squirmed a little. Helen had told her she needed to loosen up and insisted she didn't bring the car when she met Charles for the first time. 'You can't relax and enjoy meeting someone new if you're sipping Perrier while the rest of us are knocking back the vino!' she had told Rebecca.

'I decided to drive,' admitted Rebecca.

'Why? Are you planning on leaving halfway through the main course? Again.'

'No! Not at all.'

Rebecca had only done that once before, when she had been introduced to Ralph whose hand had sought out her kneecap during the starter and as the evening progressed become as insistent and as hard to escape as a hungry mosquito.

Helen looked at her suspiciously. 'Hmm. Well you can always leave the car here and get a taxi home,' she announced sternly. 'You are enjoying tonight Bec, whether you want to or not.'

Standing up she gave Rebecca a reproving glance and then grabbed the wine bottle to fill up a few glasses leaving Rebecca to look at Emma in horror.

'I want to go home,' she whispered softly to her friend. Emma giggled, patting Rebecca's hand sympathetically. 'That's not going to happen honey,' she advised. 'Helen would quite literally tie you to the chair before she would let you bail out of tonight. Anyway, I thought you were up for it? Helen said you had decided to start dating again?'

Rebecca screwed up her nose. She had said exactly that. She had even insisted that Helen found her someone as quickly as possible. But now, sitting at Helen's table with Charles only a few feet away and a world of expectation in the room, she had most definitely changed her mind.

'It seemed like a good idea at the time,' she admitted. 'Now I'm not so sure.'

'He's actually really nice Bec darling. I've met him a couple of times before and he's just an ordinary bloke, pleasant, charming, good looking. Absolutely nothing to be so worried about. Give it a go honey. You may actually like him!'

She gave her friend a sympathetic smile and then in an act of ultimate betrayal she raised her voice and said loudly, 'Charles, why don't you come over here and meet Rebecca.'

Ignoring the horrified look from Rebecca, Emma slid onto the next chair round the table leaving Charles no option but to sit next to Rebecca.

'Bec, Helen and I have been friends for longer than any of us care to remember,' laughed Emma easily. 'We all lived in the village at one point and we can't seem to stay away.'

Rebecca tried to smile but her face felt as though it was set in cement. She could feel Helen's eyes watching her every move and was aware that the conversation level in the room had just dropped considerably as everyone watched the point of the evening.

'Hello Rebecca.'

Charles held out his hand and Rebecca had no option but to take it. 'How nice to meet you,' he carried on easily, as all conversation stopped and they became the sole focus of the room. No-one spoke, no-one moved as they all froze, watching the couple intently.

'You too,' whispered Rebecca nervously.

He was tall and slender, not reedy but a straight up and down sort of figure. His hair was a light brown and his eyes were blue, not a piercing blue but a pleasant, relaxing shade.

Emma was watching intently, her glass halfway to her mouth as she looked for any signs of immediate and intense attraction. Rebecca remembered reading somewhere that it in Nature it was always the males who had the extravagant display of plumage and they would sway and wriggle and show off everything they had to the chosen female. The whole room seemed to be waiting for Charles to fluff up his feathers and perform the mating dance thought Rebecca wildly. She threw a pleading glance in her friend's direction and taking the hint Emma jumped to her feet.

'So what's on the menu tonight?' she demanded loudly stepping forwards so Rebecca and Charles were partially hidden from view. 'What delicious offering have you made for us Helen?' she asked brightly.

Taking her cue, Helen responded equally loudly, almost yelling in the ear of her new neighbours, who looked slightly startled at the two women now holding a high decibel conversation across the kitchen. 'I decided to make a chilli con carne tonight Emma,' she shouted. 'Nothing too complicated. Didn't want to spend the day in the kitchen.'

'Absolutely not,' her friend agreed, nodding enthusiastically. 'Totally agree, don't you Dave?'

Taken by surprise her husband stopped the bottle of beer on its way to his mouth. 'Er, I suppose,' he answered a little baffled.

'Good, good.'

His wife nudged him hard and he struggled on. 'Er, a chilli is always a good option isn't it?' he asked Tim.

'Absolutely.'

Suddenly conversation resumed and as guests turned to each other to discuss the relative benefits of dinner menu meals, Rebecca and Charles became just two voices in the room.

'It's awful isn't it,' he asked putting his beer next to Rebecca's glass of wine.

She raised her eyebrows wondering if they were still talking about chilli.

'All this being introduced by friends. It makes me feel like an exhibit at the zoo,' he carried on. 'Everyone staring and listening and wondering what we'll do next.'

Rebecca giggled. Her shoulders relaxed and for the first time that evening she didn't feel awkward and desperate. 'I know what you mean,' she agreed smiling. 'I imagine I can hear David Bellamy's voice describing what we might be thinking and how we're behaving.'

He laughed and it was a nice sound. Not too loud, not too over excited, just a nice pleasant laugh and Rebecca couldn't help but join in. She saw Helen give them a quick excited glance at the sound but ignored her and brought her gaze back to Charles.

'Have you been to many dinner set ups?' she asked curiously.

Charles shook his head. 'Enough. After the first couple I refused to go to any more. It's excruciatingly embarrassing and it rarely led to anything worth the trauma.'

Rebecca nodded. 'Helen was always arranging them when I first split up from my husband,' she said with a sigh. 'Emma wasn't quite as bad but it got to the stage where every time I met either of them they had a new prospect in tow. And they were all awful,' she added darkly, before blushing. 'Sorry, I didn't mean that you were …'

Charles laughed again and shook his head. 'It's okay Rebecca. I know exactly what you mean,' and in a moment of total understanding they both took a sip of their drinks and smiled.

The meal was declared ready and they all gathered around the table. If it was planned it was executed with subtlety and speed and as the plates arrived and a large bowl of steaming hot chilli was placed in the centre of the table, Rebecca and Charles found themselves not only sitting next to each other but squashed together where they had no option but to rub elbows and share stories.

The evening passed quickly. Taking Emma's lead Helen made sure that the conversation never stopped and that the eyes of the group were anywhere but on Rebecca and Charles. Rebecca put her hand over her glass and firmly declined Helen's offer to call her a taxi despite admitting to herself that she was enjoying Charles' company. She caught Emma and Helen passing each other delighted looks as the evening continued and as they all cleared away the plates and refilled glasses before the dessert arrived, Rebecca found herself briefly alone at the table with Charles by her side. Their offers of help had been waved away and they had nothing to do but enjoy each other's company.

On impulse she put her hand on his arm feeling the crispness of his shirt sleeve. 'I've had a really nice evening Charles. Thank you.'

He smiled back, his blue eyes shining. 'It's not over yet,' he joked. 'I could still turn into one of those dinner pests.'

Rebecca grinned. 'I doubt it.'

And she did. Charles was charming. He was considerate and well-mannered but had a good sense of humour and a lovely smile. He also knew exactly how Rebecca was feeling about embarking on the dating game and they had found a common bond over Helen's spicy chilli.

They had briefly compared their history. Charles had been happily married for 15 years but his wife had died and left him feeling quite lonely and confused. They had no children and Charles admitted that at the beginning that was a relief. He had no need to be strong for others, he could wallow in his own grief without having to put anyone else first. But as time went by he began to regret the lack of any family that tied him to his wife. She had gone and other than his memories there was nothing tangible left behind that contained any part of her. Rebecca had provided a brief summary of her marriage. She left out a lot of the bitterness and heartache, the anger and the distress. But she told Charles that she had won a lot of money and was honest when she said that it had helped her escape an unhappy marriage but so far had been unable to present the second chance she so desperately desired.

Charles had looked at her with naked curiosity and asked how it felt to suddenly become so rich and have her life changed so dramatically. And for once Rebecca hadn't tensed and worried about any hidden agendas and she had described how she felt elated, relieved, happy, scared, overwhelmed and confused all at the same time.

Then dessert arrived and they were scooped back into the conversation once more and as laughter filled the room and the chatter continued, Charles quietly asked Rebecca if she would like to join him for a quieter dinner one evening, just the two of them where they could get to know each other a little better without quite so many pairs of eyes on them.

Rebecca looked up to see Helen frozen in place. She had obviously overheard Charles despite his quiet tone and her eyes were now on Rebecca, no doubt willing her to accept. Rebecca looked away, she turned to Charles and met the pleasant blue eyes waiting for her reply. And nodding, she said that she thought that was an excellent idea and she would be more than happy to join him.

Chapter 13

May arrived, not with a burst of sunshine and warmer weather but in a flurry of rain and wind and sharp, cold mornings. Imagining a summer wedding with the sun high in the sky and guests drifting around the gardens which where currently a mudbank, was proving difficult for even Rebecca's fertile imagination.

She pulled up outside Willow Court and ran into the house to escape the rain that was hitting the floor so hard it bounced back up a good six inches. Inside wasn't much better. There was no heating, Rebecca could see her breath in the hallway which looked as though it had been sacked and looted by a passing army. The basis of the room was still visible, the oak staircase and the magnificent panelling had survived but much of the flooring had been ripped up due to water damage and rampant damp, great swathes of plaster hung from the walls and the reception desk Rebecca had first visited had disappeared as everything that could be removed had been ripped out for repairs to take place.

She had received yet another text from Annabelle that morning, demanding a progress report and she was tempted to take a photo of the beleaguered entrance hall and send it winging to Devon. Seeing the sheer volume of work that was needed might stop Annabelle sending copious photographs of wedding settings, all of which she declared would look 'just wonderful' for Willow Court. The fact that one was in a French chateau and another in a Norman castle didn't seem at all unreasonable to Annabelle. All represented her perfect day and exactly what she was hoping Rebecca would produce at Willow Court.

Down one side of the hallway she knew she would find Brian in the domed room. He looked a little like Moses with an incredibly long grey beard and hooded eyes. He rarely spoke, Rebecca had chatted away to him when he first arrived but never received more than a grunt in reply. In the end she had given up and left him to his work which she found fascinating, often lingering quietly in the doorway as she watched him lay on the scaffolding and recreate the intricate detail. She always poked her head in the room and shouted a cheery good morning when she arrived and if she made a tray of tea for the many workers, she would leave a cup at the foot of his scaffolding. The work was slow, there seemed to be very little progress at all and Rebecca was already fretting about timescales and how she could still use the domed room for Sarah's wedding if it still had Brian tucked away in the corner and only half a rose in the centre. But she remained cheerful and never told Brian of her worries, not wanting to disturb a craftsman at his work.

She could hear voices in the dining room and a female laugh that sounded familiar and walking past the mountain of building supplies piled against the wall, she walked into the one room that was making progress.

'Sarah! How lovely to see you. I didn't know you were planning to visit today.'

Sarah was sitting on an upturned box sipping at a cup of tea and chatting to Luke.

'Well my exams are finished, I don't have to go to Uni at all now, Dom's working really hard and won't be home until after 7:00 so I thought I'd come and see if I can help.'

Rebecca wandered over to give her daughter a hug and waved away Luke's offer of his cup of tea.

She screwed up her nose. 'I'm not sure what you can do, I always feel I'm in the way a little when I visit,' she admitted. 'Drew and Luke know what's going on and I just wander around asking lots of questions.'

She looked around the room. Drew had drawn up a schedule which even he admitted was tight but it meant that all the main reception rooms and a couple of bedrooms should be ready for Sarah's wedding date. The floor in the dining room had been the very first repair carried out, Drew had been worried that someone would disappear through the alarming dip that had appeared in the centre and lifting the floorboards they had found an amazing parquet floor beneath that for some reason had been covered over years before. The ceiling still looked as though it had spent the last 50 years in a pub but new windows had been ordered within an hour of Rebecca giving Drew and Luke the go ahead and they had brought in an expert at panelling who was performing wonders with some of the cracks and chips. The room was still a mess but Rebecca could already see the promise beneath.

She smiled at Sarah, 'This is where you'll have your wedding meal,' she said softly. 'Isn't that a wonderful thought?'

Sarah nodded happily. 'Luke and I were just talking about how many tables and chairs we could fit in here. As a wedding venue you'll want the maximum number of seats available for the best return on your investment.'

Rebecca looked around. 'I suppose so,' she said uncertainly. 'How do you know how many will fit?'

Sarah jumped up. 'Well, a lot depends on the shape of the table. Round tables are much cosier and better for everyone to be able to chat. Rectangular tables are easier to organise but you may get less people per table. You can stack tables end to end and have a couple of really long tables which doesn't do much for conversation but certainly gets the most out of a room. And you have to leave enough room between the chairs otherwise guests won't be able to get from A to B without tripping over each other'

Rebecca listened to her daughter in surprise.

'If Luke can help me measure the space,' continued Sarah with a quick shy smile in Luke's direction, then I'll draw up a couple of plans as to the optimum spread. I'll measure the tables Mrs Hemmings left behind and see if we can keep them, though they'll need a bit of a makeover,' she added doubtfully.

'You understand all this?' Rebecca asked, impressed.

Sarah nodded. 'It was part of my course. We had to look at event management, which of course is just what a wedding is, and how to maximise resources, space and profit.'

Luke looked impressed and Rebecca had a sudden spasm of pride for her daughter.

'In that case, I take back what I said. You would be a wonderful help round here.' Her mind started to wander, thinking of the room full of delights Andrea Hemming had left behind. 'There's an attic room,' she began, 'full of all the things they used to dress the place for a wedding. Perhaps you'd like to look through it all, maybe make an inventory and see what we can realistically re-use and what we will need to replace?'

'Oh mum!' squealed Sarah. She put down her tea and ran at a surprised Rebecca throwing her arms around her mother's neck and hugging her tightly. Rebecca saw Luke grin and she laughed, removing Sarah tight grip.

'I can be part of the project.' said Sarah with shining eyes. 'I'd love to get involved and I do actually understand a lot of this planning business. An inventory!' she said breathlessly. 'How wonderful!'

Luke laughed. 'I've never seen anyone get so excited over making an inventory,' he offered, his blue eyes twinkling. 'Me and Dad draw straws to see who has to do ours.'

Sarah twirled round. 'Yes but yours is bags of sand and cement and shovels,' she giggled. 'This is lists of ribbon and lace and tablecloths and all sorts of interesting things.'

Luke shook his head. 'Still a list if you ask me. But seeing as you're so excited about it, let's get measuring and then you can officially join the team – along with your lists.'

Rebecca watched as they made their way upstairs, laughing and joking and she hugged her arms around herself, partly to keep off the cold and partly because she suddenly felt very positive. Willow Court would be ready in time, she decided. Not only did she have a great team onboard in the shape of Drew and Luke but with Sarah joining in, how could it fail. All was going well, and not just at Willow Court

She had seen Charles three times since their first meeting. He had taken her to dinner the week after Helen's chilli and they'd had a lovely evening, chatting away, finding points in common and generally getting to know each other. Charles had insisted on paying the bill and then walked her back to her car and although Rebecca was gnawing at her lip in anxiety he was courtesy itself, kissing her gently on the cheek and thanking her for a wonderful evening. On impulse Rebecca had asked if he wanted to join her at the theatre the following week. He had been delighted and they'd had another very pleasant evening. Again he had kissed her on the cheek although Rebecca felt this kiss had lasted a little longer and the squeeze he had given her hand a little tighter.

The following week he had asked her to join him for a meal but announced that it was time to face reality and he would cook for her so she would be aware of his limited skills in the kitchen. Rebecca had somewhat hesitantly said yes, happy to brave Charles' cooking but wondering what direction the evening would take. It had ended pleasantly. This time Charles had looked into her eyes as though asking for permission and then sliding his hand behind her neck he leant down and pressed his lips on hers. For a moment Rebecca remained rigid and then she allowed herself to relax into his body, lifting her head so she could return the kiss.

His arm was around her waist and as he stopped, leaning his forehead against hers momentarily, she suddenly felt very safe. Happy, safe and secure. She met his eyes and impulsively reached up to kiss him again, remembering just how good it felt to be in someone's arms, feel the warmth of their body against her own and the feel of their lips on hers.

They were meeting again the following day and this time Rebecca had said she would cook. Charles had asked if this was another dose of reality but Rebecca had giggled and said not at all. The only risk was that he wouldn't want to go home after he had sampled her cooking and realised what good food could taste like. She had been joking and Charles had laughed but there had been a little hint of something Rebecca couldn't quite put her finger on lingering in the air and she wondered if Charles thought she was inviting him to stay.

Would that be so terrible, she wondered now, staring out of the window at the rain slamming into the glass and the trees blowing in the wind. They were both grown people who enjoyed each other's company.

'Everything okay?'

The voice made her jump and turning around she found Drew watching her curiously from the doorway.

'I'm fine, thanks. Just thinking.'

'About Willow Court?'

Drew knew of Rebecca's passion about her new house, and her fears it wouldn't be ready on time.

'For once, no,' she smiled. 'Just about … er things. You know, life.'

'Ah. Life. That's an awfully big subject to be thinking about on a Friday afternoon.'

He grinned and Rebecca couldn't help but smile back. Drew was easy to talk to, although most of their conversation was about plaster drying times and flush volumes for toilets.

'Another date?' he teased, watching Rebecca blush slightly.

She nodded.

'That's,' he held up his fingers counting, 'the fourth one?'

Another nod.

'It must be going well?'

'I think so. I mean yes, it is.' She nibbled on her lip and watched Drew watching her. She knew he was divorced, that Luke had been 14 and had wanted to stay with his dad which his mother had refused to allow. But the very second Luke had turned 16 and was free to make his own decisions he had returned to live with his dad and although Drew had insisted Luke finish school and do the best he could, it was always understood that as soon as he was allowed, Luke would join his dad in work.

'How long did you leave it before you started dating again Drew?'

He pulled a face, scratching at his head in what was becoming a familiar gesture to Rebecca. 'It's not a period in my life that I'm very proud of,' he answered quietly. 'I was very angry with Susan when we split, especially because she wouldn't let Luke stay with me. I behaved quite badly for a while,' he admitted with a frown. 'I went out on the very first night she left and picked up with someone or other. Not even sure I can remember her name. And there were a few others after that, for the first year I saw a different woman every few weeks.' He shook his head and gazed out of the window, much as Rebecca had been doing moments before. 'Suddenly I realised all I was doing was confusing my son and making my wife all the more determined to keep him away from me. There were no relationships being formed, I wasn't in love with any of them. Maybe I was trying to punish Susan, prove I was better off by myself, I don't know. I just know it didn't make me happy.'

Rebecca nodded sympathetically. He may have reacted in a different way to herself, but it was still the reaction of someone to the loss of a relationship that, whether good or bad, had been a constant in their life for a long time.

'Anyway, I stopped seeing anyone. I decided Luke was my priority and the only thing I cared about. He came to live with me a few months later and I can count on the fingers of one hand the women I've seen since,' he admitted frankly. 'I'm happy in my own company, I have Luke and the business to keep me occupied. I leave the dates to others,' he finished grinning at Rebecca.

Sensible builder.

She smiled. She had done exactly the opposite, but it hadn't made her any happier.

'What's his name?'

'Charles.'

'Well, I hope you and Charles have a wonderful time together.' He gave a little bow in Rebecca's direction. 'And I hope that he turns out to be the man for you Rebecca, you deserve a chance of happiness, of that I'm quite sure,' and with another friendly grin he left, shouting up the stairs for Luke and the plans for the bathrooms.

Chapter 14

For once Rebecca wasn't racing to catch up with herself. She had refused to get involved with anything that may delay her and as a result she had everything ready well before Charles was due.

The house looked beautiful. It always looked beautiful but today it seemed to glow as though it knew this was a special occasion. The outside lights were on and although the rain still came down and the trees swayed in the wind, the garden lights shone through the branches creating a movie screen in the sky and the spring flowers were highlighted as they nestled in their borders and leant against the tree trunks for protection. The house was immaculate and the smell of freshly baked bread drifted down from the kitchen and into the hallway where the soft lighting gave a welcome glow. Rebecca had visited the hairdresser for a new cut that gave her hair bounce and the soft silken feel that only an encounter with a professional could create. She had scoured her wardrobe for the appropriate outfit, throwing every choice onto the bed until she came across a soft cream dress. It had a deep v neck and crossed over her stomach to fall in soft drapes to one side. It made her waist look several inches smaller and hid the top of her legs which she felt were a little dumpy, showing instead her knees down to her ankles which Rebecca gratefully acknowledged were still slim and shapely. She had taken care with her makeup and added a touch of her favourite scent to her wrists. Eventually she was ready and she nodded as she looked at herself in the mirror. Not too much, not too little. She looked like an attractive woman about to have a relaxed meal with a potential suitor.

Going back into the kitchen she looked at her watch. Charles would be arriving any time soon and for some reason Rebecca's nerves were stretched to breaking. She had a feeling that this night was important. They had been for a meal, been to the theatre, they had chatted and gotten to know each other. And now they needed to make some kind of decision, some kind of unspoken agreement as to what would happen next. Would they remain friends who met up occasionally, kept each other company at the cinema, went for dinner to have a catch up? Would they become lovers, partners, moving on to the next stage and then maybe the one after that and the one after that? What exactly did she want, wondered Rebecca? She thought back briefly to the conversation she'd had with Drew. He'd decided his life was full enough with his son and his business. He had turned his back on the thought of romance and a new partner. Rebecca could take a leaf from his book and continue enjoying her own company. But she had been alone for too long, she felt more than ready for something new. Opening the fridge door Rebecca peered inside then closed it again. She desperately wanted to pour a glass of the chilled white Sauvignon sitting inside but she was worried that by the time Charles arrived she would have downed her inhibitions along with her wine. She needed to keep her head clear tonight.

The doorbell pealed out and Rebecca couldn't help the little squeak of alarm and reprimanding herself for being so silly she walked swiftly down the hall to let Charles in.

He had brought two bottles of wine, a bouquet of flowers and a box of chocolates. Laughing Rebecca relieved him of the flowers and the chocolates and led him into the kitchen.

'You didn't need to bring anything. Tonight is my treat.'

'Well, I know you say you're a good cook but I thought I'd bring chocolates just in case it was an exaggeration. At least we would have something to eat.'

His voice was warm, his smile mischievous and Rebecca could feel herself relaxing even as she punched him lightly on the arm.

'What a cheek!'

She opened a cupboard door and pointed to a vase on the top shelf. 'Make yourself useful and lift that down for me. Then you can pour us a glass of wine while I check that the food is still edible.'

Charles reached upwards, almost leaning against Rebecca and she stood still, refusing to take flight and allowing herself to enjoy the contact of his body. He passed her the vase, a flash of something in his eyes as their fingers met briefly before Rebecca took it to the sink along with the flowers.

'Something smells good,' he said softly and Rebecca felt her breath catch in her throat because she knew he wasn't talking about the boeuf bourguignon that was simmering in the oven.

'I told you I was a good cook,' Rebecca threw over her shoulder. 'You won't be needing the chocolates tonight.'

Charles poured the wine and Rebecca took the simmering beef out of the oven and then checked on the potatoes. She had cut them into small squares and cooked them with garlic and herbs which gave out a divine whiff as she gave them a final turn.

A glass of wine appeared by her side and hoping her face wasn't too flushed from the heat of the oven she turned to face Charles, taking the proffered drink and smiling in response.

'Cheers Rebecca,' he murmured, sending her a sweet smile. 'Here's to an excellent evening.'

The food was glorious and Charles made her laugh with his noises of delight every time he took another mouthful. The wine was delicious and was flowing very easily. The conversation was natural and spontaneous with no awkward silences and half way through the evening Rebecca had to admit that she was very much enjoying Charles' company. She had a brief flashback to Annabelle walking round the kitchen, trailing her fingers along every surface as she berated Rebecca for her lack of social life, her lack of friends, her lack of anything worth having. Rebecca lifted up her glass to take a sip of wine and watched Charles across the table. Well so much for Annabelle she thought with a smile. She had to sit opposite Daniel's pompous face every night while Rebecca had the much easier on the eye Charles sitting at her kitchen table. After they had finished the main course Charles packed the dishwasher while Rebecca served up an Amaretto and raspberry trifle. They cleaned out their bowls, both admitting they couldn't eat another thing and wandered through to the living room. Rebecca had lit the fire before Charles had arrived and although the flames had retreated to a gentle glow, the room was warm and cosy with the light from the embers and the side lamps. Rebecca sank into her favourite corner of the settee and Charles dropped down beside her, sitting close and taking her hand in his own.

'That was a glorious meal Bec. Thank you.'

'Do you want a chocolate?' she asked with a giggle and received a gentle poke in the ribs.

'I doubt I'll ever eat again,' he groaned rubbing his stomach in mock horror. 'If I ate here every Saturday night it would last me all week.'

Rebecca nodded in agreement.

They sat for a moment in companionable silence and Charles took one of her hands in his, playing lazily with her fingers. Rebecca felt a little shiver run down her spine and took a nervous sip from her glass.

'Helen phoned me today,' he told her.

'Really? What did she want?' Rebecca had an idea, Helen had phoned her several times, demanding to know how their fledgling relationship was progressing and insisting on some details. She flushed a little, hoping it would be hidden in the dim lighting of the room. Surely Helen hadn't asked Charles if they'd kissed, when they planned on going to bed, how they felt about each other, all questions she'd asked Rebecca.

'Just wanted to know if we had been on any more dates. If we planned on seeing each other again.'

'Right,' Rebecca nodded. Nothing too embarrassing.

'She did ask if I'd stayed over yet.'

Rebecca gasped. 'She didn't?'

Charles laughed. 'She's convinced we make a wonderful couple and is monitoring us carefully to make sure we don't squander our chance.'

Rebecca determined to phone Helen up as soon as possible and tell her to stop her questions immediately.

Reading her mind Charles squeezed her hand gently. 'She's a good friend you know, don't be too hard on her,' he said still laughing.

'Mmm,' said Rebecca doubtfully. 'Personally I would rather she didn't phone you asking for details every time we have a date!'

They sat watching the fire as it cast its shadows across the room.

'I am hoping that there will be a lot more dates,' offered Charles in a quiet voice. 'I really enjoy your company Bec and it would be nice to think I'll carry on seeing a lot more of you.'

Rebecca's heart started banging against her chest. 'I would like that very much Charles.'

He put down his glass and turned to face her, keeping hold of her hand as he looked into her eyes.

'Good,' he said softly.

Her heart was banging so loudly she thought she might have to ask him to speak up and swallowing hard she put down her glass.

'And of course we don't have to share it all with Helen,' he added mischievously.

'I hope not,' she said fervently, then immediately worried in case he thought she was being presumptuous.

'I hope,' he carried on, stroking the back of her hand with his fingers and leaving her feeling quite tingly and more than a little breathless, 'that some of it will be too inappropriate to pass on over the phone.'

'Oh,' squeaked Rebecca her eyes wide as she watched him grin.

'But I suppose we'll have to wait and see?'

She was finding it hard to concentrate and she certainly didn't want him to stop stroking her fingers but looking into his blue eyes she realised he was asking her a question. His eyes were lovely, kind and cheerful, they twinkled as he spoke. Rebecca had already decided that she very much enjoyed looking into them. He was charming and funny but courteous, maybe even slightly old fashioned and Rebecca already felt incredibly at ease in his company. She felt the pressure of his fingers on her and thought about him sitting on her settee on a regular basis, the two of them relaxing in front of the fire with a glass of wine after a good meal. She decided it was a very appealing idea. He was a second chance and Rebecca deserved a second chance.

She nibbled on her lip, searching deep for courage. 'I think it's an excellent idea,' she said in a slightly tremulous voice. 'And I think we should start right now, don't you?' and standing up, she took him by the hand and led him up the curving stairway towards her bedroom.

Chapter 15

Once a week Rebecca would go to Parklands to have a meeting with Barbara Wendover, the manager. They would discuss any problems, wander around to check for any repairs or maintenance issues, discuss ideas and generally compliment each other on the success they had made of the once failing retirement home. Rebecca would always speak to her mother, sometimes share a cup of tea and have a chat.

But she would often pay a visit to Parklands simply to visit her mother Gwen. She would wave to Mrs Wendover but she would stay away from the office and not spend time looking at accounts or discussing menus. She would sit in Gwen's favourite corner of the room where she could see out into the beautiful gardens and they would drink tea and chat. Rebecca would update her on Sarah and Toby and anything exciting that was happening or they would sit in peaceful silence and enjoy the feeling of security that Rebecca's good fortune had brought to them both.

Today was a visit day. Rebecca had brought in a selection of pastries from the local bakers and they sat, looking out onto a rain-soaked garden and chatted happily for an hour.

'You look happy,' announced Gwen looking pleased.

Rebecca smiled. 'I am.'

'In fact, you look happier than I've seen you look in a while.'

Rebecca didn't answer. She hugged herself slightly as she thought back to the previous evening when she and Charles had gone to the cinema and then back to his house with a pizza, which had remained un-eaten on the kitchen table. They'd spent the rest of the evening in bed and when their stomachs began to growl in the early hours of the morning, they'd snuck downstairs like teenagers and warmed it up in the microwave before taking it back to bed giggling.

She couldn't help the grin that spread across her face at the memory and Gwen watching her nodded sagely.

'Ah, things with Charles are going well.'

It was a statement not a question and Rebecca simply smiled.

Reaching out Gwen patted her daughter's hand. 'And not before time if you ask me. You've been far too cautious since you and Daniel divorced. It's about time you had a little action in the bedroom.'

'MUM!'

'What? Do you think I'm so old I don't remember what it was like to have a man in my life?'

Rebecca blushed bright red, she wasn't used to this kind of conversation with her mother, who was sitting with a shawl around her shoulder wearing fluffy slippers and looking like any typical gentle grandmother.

'I remember it all very well my darling and I'm telling you that this is exactly what you need. I'm just glad that you've finally opened your bedroom door.'

'MUM!' repeated Rebecca, looking round to see who might be near enough to overhear her mother giving out advice about her sex life.

Gwen smiled. She was extraordinarily proud of her daughter taking over Parklands and making it into such a successful business and a home that was so popular it now had a waiting list in double figures. She had watched Rebecca struggle with her decision to divorce Daniel followed by years of worry about starting the new life she kept promising herself. 'Don't be silly,' she said calmly. 'I bet it's the sort of conversation you would have with Helen and Emma. Why is it so wrong that I agree with them?'

'Because you're my mother and quite frankly I can't think of anything more embarrassing than discussing my love life with you.'

Gwen squashed a smile. As long as her daughter was happy she was happy. 'Okay,' she said soothingly, 'we won't talk about it again. But I'm pleased you and Charles are – enjoying yourselves.'

Laughing, Rebecca said her goodbyes and jumped back in the car. It was still raining and although May was rapidly coming to an end there was no sign of any improved weather coming along to speed up the renovations at Willow Court. Her phone beeped to indicate a message and quickly checking before she set off, Rebecca saw it was from Annabelle. With a groan she threw her phone on the passenger seat and started up the car.

Annabelle's messages were reaching a whole new level, pinging onto Rebecca's phone at all times of day and night. She sent messages about everything – how the dining room should be decorated, how the bridal suite should look. She had sent a photograph of a pink Swarovski chandelier that she thought would look 'divine' hanging over the bridal bed, she had sent photos of curtains covered in little golden hearts that would look 'absolutely fantastic' in the drawing room. One morning Rebecca had answered the door to find a sample of china which Annabelle thought would be 'super' for the Big Day as she had started referring to her forthcoming wedding to Daniel. There were photos of brides reclining on a silk chaise longue or leaning against walls decorated with butterflies. Photos of cakes bedecked with flowers and ribbons arrived regularly along with photos of other random items such as a crystal bedecked bird cage inhabited by two love birds to represent herself and Daniel which she thought would look 'truly amazing' on the top table and a huge glass slipper she thought would look 'just perfect' filled with flowers and set at the foot of the staircase.

Rebecca hadn't bothered answering, deciding that the hole developing at the bottom of the staircase where the water damaged floorboards were curling upwards was slightly more important than a giant glass slipper.

She put her foot down, already late for a meeting with Drew and the latest progress report. Pulling up outside the door of Willow Court, Rebecca dodged the puddles and the mountain of mud everywhere and ran into the hallway. Nothing had improved. It was a dumping ground for all the materials and equipment Drew and his team were using and rather than the elegant and welcoming space Rebecca had hoped for, at the moment it looked more like a builder's yard. She sighed and tried to quell the agitation she felt at the general lack of progress.

'Mum, just in time.'

Sarah was coming down the staircase. She was casual in jeans and jumper but had an air of efficiency that made Rebecca smile. Just when had her daughter become so grown up and responsible?

'Luke and I are discussing the ensuite to the bedrooms.'

It had been decided that they would definitely renovate the bridal suite and three of the bedrooms before the wedding, more if time allowed and if not, it was a job for after Sarah and Dom's wedding.

'I think the bathroom in the bridal suite needs to be fairly spectacular. After all,' she grinned, 'I'll be staying in it and I would like a wow factor!'

Rebecca nodded. Sarah had the added advantage of being able to place herself in the shoes of a potential bride and a lot of her ideas came after she sat down and thought carefully about her own expectations of a wedding venue.

'But the other bedrooms – they just need a bathroom. They don't need copper baths or rainforest showers. Just a well-appointed bathroom.'

Rebecca was thinking back to her own wedding day with Daniel. They hadn't been able to afford a honeymoon so they'd gone to Blackpool for a couple of days and stayed in a little guest house near the front. It had been quite awful. They shared a bathroom with all the other guests on their floor and the early morning rush was akin to the pool side towel dash at a Benidorm hotel. It had become quite vicious one morning when there were accusations of queue tampering and the landlady had been obliged to allocate time slots and tape them to the door.

'Mum?'

'Sorry darling. Miles away. Yes, I quite agree.'

'Good.' Sarah's eyes went back to her black notebook and she started muttering something about low flush and corner suites as she turned around and made her way back up the stairs, calling Luke's name.

Shaking out her umbrella and leaving it near the doorway, Rebecca walked towards the dome room as she did every time she visited. Brian was there, as always, perched on a scaffold in one corner and other than the softest sound of his radio playing opera, the faintest of noise swirling round his head as he worked, the room was peaceful. He didn't seem to have made very much progress at all and Rebecca bit her lip. He had been huddled in the same corner for weeks and Rebecca was desperate to see some movement.

'It will be okay Mrs Miles.' Rebecca jumped. It was the longest sentence Brian had ever spoken and it floated down from the ceiling to join the faint hum of Madame Butterfly.

'What?'

'It takes time to get started. You have to find the start point and ease your way in,' Brian continued. 'You can't force it, the new and the old need to become one, join together. Once that's happened it will start moving along. Don't worry, it will be okay.'

Rebecca watched as his fingers slid along the beautiful plaster coving, sweeping and soothing as they went.

'Thank you Brian,' she said quietly. 'Thank you.'

Feeling a little calmer, she went in search of Drew. The house was so big they could wander for hours looking for each other and the kitchen had become the unofficial starting point for any search. Halfway along the corridor she heard voices. Frowning she started walking faster only to freeze at the sound of a silver tinkle of laughter. Oh dear God no, please tell her it wasn't so.

Practically sprinting down the hallway, she threw open the kitchen door to find Annabelle giggling girlishly and a confused Drew wedged against the fridge, his face alarmed.

'Rebecca!' the relief in his voice was loud and clear and as he spoke Annabelle whirled round, giving a little screech of delight.

'Becky darling!'

Before Rebecca could move Annabelle's, bony arms were wrapped round her and the overwhelming smell of Channel no 5 was clogging her nostrils.

Pushing her away as gently as she could, Rebecca sneezed and then smartly sidestepped a chair so Annabelle couldn't grab her again.

'Annabelle, what on earth are you doing here?

'Well I have been messaging you with ideas and questions,' Annabelle said wagging her finger at Rebecca. 'And there's been no reply.'

Ah yes, the messages, countless little pictures of Annabelle's perfect day. The ones she had been ignoring. Rebecca bit her lip trying not to let her guilt show. Was it too late to apologise and promise to start sending a polite response she wondered?

'I'm sorry,' she said. 'I'm so sorry Annabelle. I've been so busy. I meant to reply and tell you how wonderful they all were,' she lied, 'but I've just been so busy.'

'Mmm – not very busy if the state of the hall is anything to go by.'

'Well we are in the middle of a renovation, there is a lot to do you know. I can't really think about all the little details when I've still got floors that need repairing and walls that need building,' Rebecca said defensively.

'Exactly!' said Annabelle with a cheery smile.

'But I promise I'll answer all your messages from now on.'

'Oh I understand Becky darling,' giggled Annabelle. 'You have so much to do, it's just not fair.'

An alarm bell started to sound in Rebecca's head. 'Er, well, I don't mind …'

'No! I won't have it! I won't have you burdened with all this responsibility.'

The hairs were standing up on Rebecca's arm. 'Really,' she insisted weakly, 'I don't mind at all. I'm loving it!'

'Well you don't need to worry any more,' Annabelle continued with a dazzling smile in Drew's direction, looking immensely pleased with herself. 'Because I'm here. And I'm going to help you. Surprise!'

Chapter 16

Drew's lips were definitely twitching as he took his opportunity to climb away from the fridge and sit at the table to watch the unfolding scene.

'I'm sorry,' Rebecca said faintly, hoping she had misheard. 'You're here because ....?'

'To help you of course.' Annabelle tutted, shaking her head at Drew as though they were talking about a naughty child. 'Becky you need to get used to the fact that from now on I'll always be here for you.'

'It's Rebecca, or Bec,' murmured Rebecca automatically.

'And of course let's not forget, 'another giggle, 'I do have a vested interest. After all, Willow Court is where I'm getting married.'

'Yes but ...'

'And because you seem so reluctant to let me know what's happening, I decided that I would just have to come up here and find out for myself.'

'You drove all the way here to check up on the renovations?'

'Oh no.'

Rebecca's shoulders relaxed a little.

'I came on the train. I couldn't possibly drive all that way by myself and poor Daniel has lots of important meetings this week.

The shoulders tightened again.

'But Annabelle ...' Rebecca paused, trying to find the right tone. 'How do you think you can help. We're still knee deep in building work.'

'Oh it's never too soon to start planning. We need to think about colours and fabrics and decorations.'

'Colours?' asked Rebecca faintly. Very few rooms had the full compliment of four walls a floor and a ceiling as yet. Colour hadn't made it onto the list.

'Yes, and china and bed linen and flowers.'

'It's a bit early for …'

'Nonsense. You see that's why I've come, because it's never too soon to think about details.' Annabelle tutted. 'This is exactly what I was afraid off, that you wouldn't be able to organise all these things without my help.'

'But ….'

'So here I am! To guide and advise.'

Annabelle was smiling happily, even as Rebecca's head began to throb.'

'Are you surprised? Are you thrilled?' Annabelle demanded. 'Aren't you relived to have someone to share all this planning?'

'Annabelle!'

Sarah was standing in the doorway looking surprised but pleased. 'I didn't know you were visiting. Mum didn't mention anything.'

She turned to Rebecca who was still hanging onto the chair and looking quite pale. 'Mum, are you okay?'

'Oh she's fine,' tinkled Annabelle. 'Just surprised.'

'But what are you doing here?'

Annabelle pulled out a chair and was about to place her cream suede bottom on it before she noticed the dust and general dirt. Pushing it back under the table she waved her arms in the air instead, fluttering her fingers so her diamond ring caught the light and almost blinded Luke who was standing behind Sarah.

'I've come to help.'

'Help with the …?'

'The wedding preparations of course.'

'But we're not ready.' Sarah laughed, then stopped when no one else in the room joined in. 'Er, we've still got lots of building work to do before we can begin to think of the wedding side of things.'

'As I've just been telling your mother, it's never too early to start planning.' Annabelle said reprovingly. 'I would have thought that you would appreciate that Sarah, after all I bet you have your wedding mapped out, every last detail sorted. Well I'm having my wedding here too and I need to get my own plans underway.'

'Well, I haven't actually made a lot of plans ...'

Rebecca lifted her hand to stop any more conversation. 'Sarah why don't you show Annabelle round,' she suggested wearily. 'Why don't you start with the drawing room,' which was a bomb site because the entire ceiling had collapsed following a leak from one of the upstairs bathrooms. 'And then I'm sure she'd love to see the chapel,' which had had precisely no work done at all and was as cold, drafty and unwelcome as the first time Rebecca had visited. 'And make sure you show her the bridal suite,' which was another disaster area because the wall had been knocked down to the bedroom next door to allow for an ensuite bathroom and tiny dressing room and one of the windows was missing following an accident with a flying hammer. 'I'm sure she'll find it all fascinating,' finished Rebecca with a grimace.

Nodding in excitement Annabelle wiggled after Sarah, accompanied as ever by Luke, and Rebecca who had no qualms about dust and dirt, sank down onto one of the chairs.

Drew filled the kettle and made them both a brew. Pushing a mug in front of her, he sat opposite and waited.

'She is a total nightmare!' declared Rebecca eventually.

'Seems so, and er – who exactly is she?'

'Daniel's wife. Well fiancée. They're getting married in the summer.'

'Daniel as in your ....?'

'My ex-husband Daniel.'

'Of course. I see.'

There was a moment of silence.

Actually, I don't think I see at all. I thought you had bought Willow Court for Sarah and Dom to get married? But you bought it so your ex can get married to his new partner?'

'Absolutely not! I bought Willow Court because I could see it had been a lovely wedding venue and could be again. And Sarah and Dom said they would like to get married here so it all worked out perfectly.'

'Okay – and Daniel and Annabelle?'

'Like spectres at the feast,' sighed Rebecca. 'Daniel brought her to Leeds so we could meet and become best friends and become one great big happy family,' she pulled a face. 'But I don't think it's going to work! Anyway, Daniel won't shell out for the sort of place Annabelle really wants for her wedding and she knows I'll make Willow Court as wonderful as I can for Sarah, so she latched onto the idea of getting married here as well.'

'Aah... all making much more sense,' said Drew with a grin. 'And are you charging them for the use of Willow Court?'

Rebecca wrinkled her nose, 'Daniel wants to pay because he doesn't want to take anything free from me,' Drew's eyebrow raised and Rebecca shrugged. 'Long story. Anyway, he wants to pay his way but is shocked at how much it costs to have a top-class wedding venue so he's on board with Willow Court because I offered a discount and Anabelle thinks I shouldn't charge anything at all because we're now family.'

Drew grinned. 'Complicated.'

'Extremely. I've actually considered offering to pay for their entire wedding but only if they have it somewhere a long way from here!'

She stopped, hearing the high pitch of Annabelle's laughter somewhere above their heads and meeting Drew's eyes, they broke out into giggles.

'Good luck!' offered Drew ruefully. 'I think you'll need it.'

With Annabelle out of sight and out of mind, Drew pulled out the plans he'd had drawn up of the new kitchen they had planned which would extend the current space and take it into the twenty first century.

But eventually the sound of Annabelle's voice came back in range and Sarah and Luke soon appeared in the doorway with Annabelle following.

The laughter had disappeared and Annabelle looked more than a little shocked.

'Becky darling, this is dreadful!'

'I did try and tell you.'

'There is so much to do, so much. It's nowhere near ready!' Annabelle was pacing the room in agitation, twisting her diamond ring. 'We need a clear plan, we need schedules, we need time frames. We need reassurances that this work will be finished on time.'

'We?' queried Rebecca.

'Yes. This is my wedding we're talking about. These builders,' she stopped to throw a disgruntled look at Drew, her eyelashes no longer fluttering, 'they need to start actually building something. There are holes everywhere!'

Drew opened his mouth to speak but Rebecca put a hand on his arm.

'These builders as you call them, are working night and day to get Willow Court finished and it may surprise you to learn we do have plans and timetables and they're all being met!'

'It doesn't look very organised to me.'

'Well it is. They are following a careful plan ...'

'That's what they've told you.' Annabelle edged a little closer to Rebecca, giving Drew a wide berth and a frosty glare. 'But maybe they're taking advantage,' she said in a loud whisper. 'After all, like Daniel said, you're out of your depth and you don't know what you're doing.'

Rebecca saw Sarah flinch and Drew take a step forward to defend his reputation.

'I have absolute faith in my builders! They know what they're doing.'

'Then why isn't it finished?'

'Because it take time!' snapped Rebecca. 'It can't be done overnight.'

'But there are ceilings missing! How can I plan how I want the balloons arranging when there isn't even a ceiling where I can hang them?

'I know there are ceilings missing …. balloons?'

'Yes. I want golden balloons from the ceiling spelling out Daniel and Annabelle. Don't you think that will look wonderful?'

Rebecca ignored Drew's snort of laughter. 'Er, well maybe. But all those details will just have to wait for a little while.'

'But how much time? I don't want my wedding to be a disaster because you won't listen to advice. Perhaps you need some different builders?'

'I don't need new builders…'

'Well you need some help, maybe Daniel could organise something.'

'I don't need help and certainly not from you or Daniel,' thundered Rebecca. 'I've told you, it takes time. But if you are so worried about Willow Court not being ready, maybe you should think about booking your wedding somewhere else.'

'Oh Becky!' Annabelle's hand flew to her throat in distress. 'There's no need for that attitude.'

'I'm just being practical. You obviously have no faith in either me or my builders.'

'I just need to know Willow Court will be finished for my wedding.'

'Willow Court will be ready for Sarah's wedding,' Rebecca said firmly.

'Oh er, yes of course,' Annabelle turned to give Sarah a brilliant smile, 'of course I want dear Sarah's wedding to be perfect.'

'Of course you do,' said Rebecca.

'If you let me help you then darling Sarah can have an amazing day, I'll make sure of that. It will be like a fairy tale.' The sparrow hands fluttered in the air. 'Rose petals everywhere, doves cooing, butterflies fluttering,' she added dreamily.

'Doves?' asked Sarah in alarm.

'I want Sarah to have a very special day, and of course it's only fair if I have the same, don't you think? And I don't want to go get married anywhere else, Daniel will be quite upset when I tell him that you won't let us use Willow Court.'

Rebecca rolled her eyes. It was like threatening a naughty child with the return of their father. 'I didn't say you couldn't use Willow Court. I just said that ….'

'Are you sure this isn't you being a teeny little bit jealous Becky darling? I can only imagine what it must be like watching Daniel get married again when you're still alone.'

Rebecca wanted to take hold of Annabelle and shake her thoroughly. 'I am not in the least upset Annabelle,' she ground from between clenched teeth. 'And I am not alone. I have …'

'Oh you're being so brave! And we don't want to go anywhere but Willow Court. But you should let me take over all the little details so Sarah can have the day of her dreams!'

'That's kind of you Annabelle,' offered Rebecca trying to sound sincere, 'but we're on top of it all. Really.'

'Well I'm very disappointed you won't let me help Becky. For Sarah of course. I'm very worried that Sarah won't get the wedding she wants,' pouted Annabelle. 'But I forgive you.'

Rebecca's mouth hung open. 'You'll forgive me?'

'Yes for being so bad tempered. I can see you're very busy. All the more reason to let me get involved really,' she added with a sniff. 'I do hope this isn't going to be a bad time.'

Rebecca stiffened. 'A bad time for?'

'For what should be a happy occasion, I really wanted you to be as happy as I am.'

'What about?'

'But having rejected my offer of help so unpleasantly has made me quite worried,' Annabelle's bottom lip trembled. 'I can't help feeling that you've spoilt this moment for me.'

Rebecca rolled her eyes. 'For goodness sake Annabelle, what do you want?'

Annabelle picked up her handbag from the kitchen table and delved inside.

'This is a very special moment for me Rebecca. I was hoping you would appreciate it and be just as happy.'

She held out her hand and Rebecca looked down to see a thick cream envelope offered. Reluctantly she took it as Annabelle squealed in excitement.

'Open it, open it!'

It was a wedding invitation, heavily embossed with a great deal of very curly writing and decoration, it declared the forthcoming nuptials between Daniel Miles and Annabelle Crompton at Willow Court. No wonder Annabelle didn't want her wedding to take place anywhere else.

'Er, thank you.'

Annabelle was beaming. 'We wanted the very first invite to go to you. Of course I have one for Sarah as well but,' she smiled coyly and fluttered her eyelashes, 'we want her to be our bridesmaid so it's a different sort of invitation,' and she flourished an equally decorative invitation to Sarah, offering her the honour of a being a bridesmaid at the forthcoming wedding of Daniel and Annabelle.

'Oh! What a surprise.'

'But of course we would want you to take part in our wedding Sarah. This is after all a family event. Now Rebecca darling, we have included a plus one but you mustn't feel bad if you attend by yourself. We'll make sure you are looked after, we won't leave you alone in the corner. We want you to be there, even if you have no-one to bring.'

'Actually I do have …'

'It won't matter to us in the slightest. We'll arrange the seating so no-one even notices.'

'But I do have…'

'And are you happy for us?' demanded Annabelle. 'Have you recovered from your bad mood?'

Rebecca closed her eyes and admitted defeat. 'Thank you Annabelle. I'm very happy for you,' she said dutifully. 'Very happy for both of you.'

Annabelle nodded happily. Order had been restored

'What time are we going home?'

'I beg your pardon?'

'What time are we going home? I've been on a train all morning and I'm longing for a bath. What time are we leaving?'

'You want to come home with me?' For the first time Rebecca noticed the small overnight bag standing in the corner of the kitchen.

Annabelle looked at Rebecca as thought she had gone mad. 'Of course. Where else would I stay?'

Lots of places, thought Rebecca. 'You can't stay with me Annabelle'

'What do you mean?'

Rebecca glared at her. 'It's not convenient. And you should have asked.'

'Well maybe you should answer my messages,' snapped Annabelle, 'because that's exactly what I did!'

Rebecca remembered the ping of a message as she left Parklands. 'It doesn't count if you're already here!'

Annabelle shrugged. 'It never occurred to me you wouldn't want me stay over. After all, your house is big enough.'

Rebecca clenched her fists. Would it do Sarah irreparable damage if she were to see her mother punch her future step mother she wondered.

'It just so happens I have a date tonight, it's not a convenient time for you to visit. Which I would have told you if you'd asked. And I do have someone to bring to your wedding.'

'A date? You've started seeing someone?'

'Yes. Yes I have.'

'Who?'

'It doesn't matter who it is. The fact is I have plans for tonight.'

'That's okay, I'll come with you.'

'No! Absolutely not.'

'But maybe I should meet him and see if he's suitable.'

'Suitable?' Rebecca's mouth fell open in horror.

'You can't be too careful Rebecca. I'll come with you and check …'

'No you will not! I am going out tonight Annabelle, you are not coming. You can go home or stay in a hotel but you cannot stay with me.'

'Well really, wait until I tell Daniel!'

'Will you stop threatening me with Daniel. He is my ex-husband, I really don't worry what Daniel might say, he has nothing to do with my life anymore.'

Ignoring Annabelle's shocked gasp Rebecca carried on. 'Do you need a lift to the station to catch your train. I can always ask one of the boys to run you into Leeds on their way home?'

At the thought of a dusty builder's van taking her anywhere, Annabelle looked nothing short of horrified. 'I'll get a taxi,' she said hurriedly pulling out her phone. 'But I think you're being very difficult and Daniel will be most …'

'Okay, if you're sure. Now you must excuse me because we've all got so much work to do, we have a ceiling to repair you know,' and she stalked out leaving Annabelle in the kitchen furiously texting Daniel.

Chapter 17

Leaving the kitchen, Rebecca shot into the drawing room followed by Drew, her legs almost giving way.

'Hey,' a soft voice murmured in her ear. 'Come on, let's get you sat down,'

Pulling her into the room, Drew looked round and pulled a couple of buckets towards them, covering them with a length of wood. 'Sit,' he commanded pushing Rebecca gently downwards.

'Sorry, I'm okay really. She just ……' she took a deep breath. It would appear that Annabelle was having a rather severe effect on Rebecca's blood pressure.

Drew chuckled softly. 'Well, I certainly saw a whole new Rebecca Miles. Remind me not to get on the wrong side of you!'

Rebecca smiled ruefully. 'You know for years I never bothered arguing with my husband. My ex-husband,' she corrected. 'It just didn't seem worth the effort. It never changed how he behaved and I basically couldn't be bothered.'

'You don't strike me as the argumentative sort.'

'Oh believe me, there was a lot I could have argued about. But I just ignored him. And now, all I have to do is see Annabelle and I can't help myself!'

'Well I can't blame you there, she is hard to take.'

Rebecca snorted. 'You don't say! But it's partly my fault, it must be. Sarah thinks she's lovely.'

'Sarah thinks everybody is lovely,' smiled Drew.

Rebecca sighed. 'Annabelle is convinced that I'm heartbroken about Daniel getting married again.'

Drew's eyebrows flew up and Rebecca gave a wry smile. 'She can't believe that I can see the two of them together and not regret letting him go.'

'And is there any truth in that?' asked Drew cautiously.

'Oh God no!' Rebecca fidgeted on the makeshift plank. She had told Drew that she was divorced, he even knew about the lottery win but she had said little of her life with Daniel. 'Our marriage deteriorated over several years, when we divorced it was a huge relief, to both of us I think.'

Drew was listening to her, his blue eyes sympathetic as she spoke.

'Believe me, I really do not want Daniel back in my life!' Rebecca continued with feeling. 'But Annabelle wants us to be best friends and now Daniel seems to be more involved than when we were married He didn't seem the slightest bit interested in me then.'

'I must admit,' he scratched his head, 'I certainly wouldn't like my ex being back in my life.'

'Annabelle thinks I'm sad and lonely.'

'Are you?'

'No,' protested Rebecca. Except that she had been, before Charles. Maybe not sad but definitely alone, lonely.

'When they came to visit I wasn't in a relationship and Annabelle seemed to think that it was a sign of something.' Money not buying love was the phrase she used. It had hurt. It had been a suggestion that in her greed Rebecca had sacrificed any chance for love. 'Annabelle seemed to think that was an indication of my sad state of mind.'

Drew smiled gently. 'You seem to have a pretty sound state of mind to me Bec. In fact, you haven't seemed particularly sad or lonely since I met you.'

'Well of course not, I have Charles now.'

'Are you dating him because you want Annabelle to think you've found someone?'

'Of course not!' denied Rebecca. 'I like Charles, it's lovely having someone in my life again.'

She smiled, it was lovely. It was nice to have someone to talk to at the end of the day, tell them the highs and lows and listen to them in return. To have someone to sit next to and feel their hand in hers as they watched TV.

'I'm happy,' she told Drew earnestly. 'Charles has made a big difference.'

'I'm surprised you didn't take her up on her offer to vet him,' Drew said gravely. 'I would have thought you would have welcomed her input.'

Rebecca snorted. 'I don't think Annabelle's input is a good idea! Not with Charles, not with Willow Court.'

'Good. So I don't need to follow her suggestion of replacing those silly stained glass windows in the dining room with UPVC double glazing?'

'Is that what she said? How dare she …..oh'

Drew was laughing at her and grinning she slapped his hand as she realised he was teasing.

Funny builder.

'I don't know,' she said thoughtfully, 'maybe it is a good idea after all.'

Drew stood up, grabbing her hand and pulling her to her feet.

'As if!' he scoffed.

Except he didn't let go of her hand straight away and as he held onto her fingers Rebecca realised that the hairs on her arms had shot upwards at his touch. Staring down at their entwined hands she felt her cheeks flush with colour. She had just finished telling Drew how happy she was with Charles, this was hardly an appropriate reaction. She tried to think if she had the same reaction when Charles touched her. She was fairly certain she did, but for some reason she was having trouble recalling exactly how she felt when Charles was around. She stopped staring at their hands and looked up to meet Drew's eyes. Then as if by mutual consent their hands slipped away and they stood with their arms by their side self-consciously.

Disturbing builder.

'You're right, no PVC double glazing,' Rebecca said slightly breathlessly. 'Although it would certainly keep the costs down.'

'Well, I'll just stick to the plans shall I?'

Rebecca nodded. 'Er, yes. Best idea,' and with both of them looking anywhere but at each other, they disappeared in opposite directions with claims of jobs to do and people to find.

Rebecca didn't have to wait long for Daniel's phone call. Two days later, having missed several calls from him which she chose not to return, Rebecca was standing in the kitchen of Willow Court when his name appeared on her ringing phone. Resisting the temptation to ignore him again, she answered, straightening her shoulders and preparing for the disapproval.

'Hello Daniel.'

'Hello Rebecca,' was the rather stiff reply.

Well at least it was progress from old girl, she thought but it was clearly not about to be a jolly conversation.'

'I've phoned several times but you've not been answering.'

'Sorry,' she said insincerely. 'I've been very busy.'

'Yes, well as I tried to tell you Bec,' he began pompously, 'renovating a property and starting a new business isn't easy. I know you think you're an expert in both but it takes real knowledge to ....'

'Oh not with Willow Court,' Rebecca interrupted. 'With Charles. Did I tell you about Charles? He's my new lover.'

She heard him sputter down the phone and almost wished she could see his face.

'Really Bec! There's no need for that!'

She grinned at the phone. It had stopped him pontificating

'What do you want Daniel?'

'Well actually I wanted to offer an apology,' he began, the stiffness back in his voice.

'An apology?'

Rebecca was stunned, she had spent years with Daniel and she couldn't remember the last time he had felt the need to offer an apology for anything. Except for when she found out he'd had an affair and ruined her life trying to cover it up.

'I understand that you and Annabelle had – words during her recent visit.'

Words, now there was an interesting description thought Rebecca.

'And I wanted to apologise.'

Rebecca waited, intrigued.

'I know how passionate Annabelle can be when she's speaking about something she really cares about,' he continued, clearing his throat. 'She explained to me how she wanted to be a part of Willow Court. Purely because she wants it to be a success,' he added hastily.

'Well as you've just taken the time to explain, renovating an old business and restoring a business isn't easy work Daniel. I don't think Annabelle understands the challenges.'

'Hmm, yes, well,' blustered Daniel, 'like I said she is very invested in Willow Court and she wants it to be a success.'

No, thought Rebecca, she wants her wedding to be a success.

'Annabelle was quite upset that you didn't want her input.'

Ah, here was the admonishment part thought Rebecca.

'But I can understand that this is your project. She relayed your conversation and as such I have told Annabelle that we need to look elsewhere.'

'Elsewhere?'

'I think the best thing would be if we chose another venue to get married. I don't want you thinking that we are trying to influence your business or your profits,' he announced pompously. 'I won't have you thinking that we expect any favours, we can pay for our own wedding you know.'

'Annabelle gave me an invite to your wedding. It's for Willow Court.'

'Well that can't be helped.'

'You'll have to have your invitations reprinted.'

'I realise that.'

'You'll have to pay to have your invitations reprinted.'

'Then we'll have to pay.'

Rebecca's mouth hung open. How her husband had changed. Whether she liked Annabelle or not, she had to admit that she was certainly bringing out the best in him, whereas Rebecca had most definitely brought out the worst. This was wonderful, they could get married somewhere else. Rebecca could put all her efforts into Sarah's wedding and not have to give a second thought to Daniel and Annabelle. How wonderful, exactly what she wanted.

'Don't do that Daniel.'

She heard herself speaking even as her mind was screaming at her to stop.

'Please. I shouldn't have been so angry with Annabelle and it seems ridiculous that I own a wedding venue and you don't have your wedding here.'

Please stop, her brain was yelling, please, please stop.

'Obviously the renovation has nothing to do with Annabelle, absolutely nothing to do with her,' she emphasised. 'But you should have your wedding here. And I would like it to be your wedding present from me.' Oh my God, what was she doing? And was it really appropriate to give your ex-husband the present of a new wedding to a different woman. Freud would have something to say about this she felt sure. But she had suddenly felt a stirring of compassion for her ex-husband and maybe even a smidge of it was drifting towards Annabelle. Daniel had been quite firm that he was happy with his settlement but the very suggestion that she had been mean had given Rebecca a jolt that still reverberated in the region of her heart. Maybe she had an opportunity to make a gesture that could make the relationship between the Miles' a little easier over the coming years.

'Please Daniel, get married at Willow Court,' she found herself saying even as she pulled a face and begged herself to stop, 'I would really like nothing more.'

Chapter 18

'That was a lovely thing to do.'

Rebecca whirled around to find Sarah standing behind her.

'I have the feeling it was a very foolish thing to do,' admitted Rebecca. 'And it will come back to haunt me!'

Sarah gave her mum a hug. Her original view of her future stepmother as a wonderful person had been revised somewhat following Annabelle's visit to Willow Court. But Sarah was always quick to forgiveness. Strangely the one person she had found it hard to forgive had been her father. Both Rebecca's children had greatly resented the way the course of their life had been changed by Daniel's decision to move them all to Darlington with no consultation.

'She can be a bit demanding,' giggled Sarah. 'But if we can cope with Annabelle as a potential bride we can cope with anyone!'

'Agreed,' sighed Rebecca. She was already regretting her impulsive offer but it had been made and she couldn't imagine Annabelle refusing.

'I wanted to invite you and Dom over on Sunday. I'll make lunch and it will be a chance for you to meet Charles.'

Sarah had been encouraging and enthusiastic at the idea of her mum going out with Charles. Even Toby had phoned her and asked how things were going.

'We'd love to,' smiled Sarah.

'I was going to ask Drew and Luke,' added Rebecca. 'But I decided I'd invite Helen and Emma instead. Helen is desperate to see me and Charles together, she's claiming our relationship is entirely her doing.'

'Good idea. So you're not inviting Drew and Luke then?'

'No I'll save them for another day,' answered Rebecca. 'I think we'll have enough bodies there for poor Dom to meet, don't you?'

'Yes, I suppose you're right.'

'I'm surprised Dom hasn't been to visit actually, check on what's going on with his wedding reception and what's keeping you so busy.'

'Oh he's been busy as well. He's been given two new accounts,' said Sarah proudly,' but it means he's been working late an awful lot and he always has lots to do when he comes home. He said the other day that we were like a power couple,' she giggled. 'We eat and then he has one corner of the table to finish his work and I have the other half to carry on planning.'

'Does he resent you spending so much time here? Are you sorry you offered to help?'

'No!' insisted Sarah looking surprised. 'Of course not. And Dom is really proud of the work I'm doing. He said it was a fantastic opportunity to put into practice all the things I've been learning about over the last 3 years. It's nice that we've both got something to occupy us in the evening.'

'And you're still enjoying it?'

'I love it.' The words were simple but said with such emotion that Rebecca stopped and turned to look at her daughter. 'I really love it Mum. I love all the planning and watching the place turn into our dream. But I also can't wait until it's finished, and we can start running it as a business. Just thinking about all the wonderful weddings we can provide brings me out in goose bumps.'

'We?' asked Rebecca softly

Sarah bit her lip. 'Well actually, I wanted to talk to you about that. I know it's a bit cheeky, I know you let me help because it's for my wedding and I've got a job to start in September and I know that you'll want a manager whose got some experience and who can …'

'Sarah, would you like a full-time job at Willow Court?'

Sarah gasped, the black note book coming up to cover her heart. 'More than anything.'

'Well that's excellent because I really want you to take over when we've finished the renovations. I can't imagine anyone I would rather have in charge than you.'

'So she's accepted the job?' asked Helen later that evening when Rebecca phoned her with an invitation for Sunday.'

'Yes, I'm so pleased. I thought I might be imagining her enthusiasm for the place but she has fallen deeply in love with Willow Court and wants to carry on indefinitely.'

'How romantic, managing the place where you had the first wedding. And speaking of romance, how are things going with you and Charles.'

'Perfect,' sighed Rebecca, 'absolutely perfect.'

'How perfect?'

Rebecca laughed, 'How perfect do you want it to be?'

'Well I don't know. Is it the sort of perfect that brings about a change in living arrangement?'

'What! Steady on Helen, it's only been a few weeks, give us time.'

'Oh I know but when you get to our age, there's no point messing around and thinking too much about things is there? I mean, if you like being with him, go for it.'

'No,' said Rebecca firmly. 'Not yet. I'm having a lovely time with him Helen and you were right we get on so well together but it's far too soon for anything like that. And don't tell me I'm being over cautious,' she threw in the conversation hearing her friend take a breath, 'we'll move on in our own time thank you.'

She ignored Helen's disappointed tut and changed the conversation.

'I've told Daniel that he and Annabelle can have their wedding at Willow Court, as a wedding present.'

'You did what?' exploded Helen and Rebecca congratulated herself at steering her friend away from more talk of romance and moving in together.

'It seemed the right thing to do,' continued Rebecca. 'After all I can hardly open a wedding venue and ban them from using it.'

'Not only can you but you should!' advised Helen.

Rebecca sighed. 'But they were going to use it anyway and pay. I thought that it was a nice thing to do offering to let them have it.'

'You're paying for your ex-husband to marry someone else,' advised Helen. 'That's not a nice thing to do, it's a nutty thing to do!'

Rebecca wanted to argue. But she knew Helen was right.

'Oh I know,' she groaned. 'I really tried to stop myself but once you've said it you can't unsay it. She's going to be a nightmare, isn't she?'

'Yep.'

'All diva demands.'

'Yep.'

'Expecting me to wait on her hand and foot?'

'Yep.'

'I'm going to regret it aren't I?'

'So much Rebecca, so much.'

Half an hour later Rebecca was already regretting the foolish offer. No sooner had she put the telephone down on Helen than it rang again and Annabel was on the line.

'Rebecca, thank you!' she squealed.

Moving the phone a foot away from her ear so she wasn't deafened, Rebecca missed her chance to say it was okay and hang up.

'When Daniel told me I just couldn't believe it,' Annabelle was giggling. 'I was so happy.'

'That's okay.'

'I knew we would become best friends!'

'Well I don't think ….'

'But to say you'll pay for our wedding! That is so very special.'

'I didn't say I was paying for your wedding!' said Rebecca firmly. 'I offered to let you use Willow Court, my present to you both.'

'Same thing,' trilled Annabelle dismissively.

'No it's not …'

'So now it's sorted,' was there a slight tint of smug in her voice wondered Rebecca, 'we need to get on with the important things.'

Rebecca thought that getting a ceiling back in the drawing room, a floor in the reception area and a window in the bridal suite were probably the important things but she let Annabelle continue.

'Just because I'm having it at Willow Court doesn't mean that I'll be happy with second best,' she giggled. 'You need to start looking through my requirements now Becky darling. A wedding planner needs to be prepared.'

'I'm not your wedding planner. I simply said that you and Daniel could use Willow Court but we haven't even finished the building work yet Annabelle. I haven't got time to organise your wedding!'

'So I've made a list,' Annabelle carried on, 'of all the essential things we need to get sorted.'

'We've got to get the ceiling repaired,' reminded Rebecca.

'But don't worry, I've got lots and lots of photos to help you understand exactly what it is I'm looking for.'

'The bridal suite doesn't even have a bathroom yet.'

'And I've been thinking about the canapes,' mused Annabelle.

'Canapes? We don't have a kitchen Annabelle. Canapes will have to wait.'

'Wouldn't it be wonderful if they were all heart shaped?'

'Heart shaped?'

Yes! Isn't that a wonderful idea?'

No, thought Rebecca, it sounded time consuming and totally unnecessary.

'Annabelle,' she said firmly, 'These things will all have to wait.'

'But these are all very important details and they can't be left to the last minute.'

Rebecca realised she was grinding her teeth. She would need a visit to the dentist before Willow Court was restored. Annabelle was having a bad effect on her molars.

'Let's not forget, I'm giving you a chance to show how well Willow Court can organise a wedding.'

'That's very kind of you Annabelle,' Rebecca said dryly. 'But I have to concentrate on getting Willow Court finished or there won't be a wedding.'

'What about Sarah?'

'Sarah?'

'Well you must be organising her wedding. So why can't you do mine at the same time.'

'Because I'm busy! And she is my daughter.'

'And I'm going to be your …' Rebecca could hear Annabelle trying to work out their relationship.

'You will be my ex-husband's second wife,' she said firmly. 'Not really family at all.'

'Now you're being mean.' Rebecca could imagine the pout. 'Of course we're family.'

'No, we're not. And I'm too busy.'

'But this is exactly why you should let me help you. You can carry on with the building work and I'll be there, in the background,' Rebecca doubted if Annabelle knew what a background was, she'd certainly never been in one, 'sorting out all the details. Who knows,' more giggling, 'you might even decide that you can't manage without me. We could be partners! Imagine that, us running Willow Court together.'

The thought made Rebecca shudder. 'That's really not necessary,' she said hastily.

'But you keep saying you haven't got enough time. Maybe I should come and stay with you for a while and …'

'No!' yelped Rebecca.

'But my canapes!'

Closing her eyes, Rebecca's shoulder slumped. 'Okay, well I'll ask Sarah to speak to the caterers about heart shaped canapes.'

'And the name cards.'

'You want heart shaped name cards?'

'No, don't be silly.'

Rebecca rolled her eyes as Annabelle continued.

'Name cards are usually so boring but I want something a little different, something special so I was thinking roses.'

Rebecca screwed up her eyes trying to imagine writing names on a rose.

'I want each name card to be set in a rose, a perfect large pink rose with a name card tucked in the petals.'

'Right, well that would be a lot of roses.'

'That's the whole point Becky darling. This wedding is going to be amazing.

Rebecca thought longingly of the open bottle of wine in the fridge. She didn't need a glass, if she could just reach the bottle.

'I'll ask Sarah to look at rose set name cards,' she said with a sigh. 'But we don't have a lot of time and you may just have to scale back a few of your ideas.' Hopefully the ones involving matching thrones in the drawing room, the doves she wanted to sit on golden branches in the corner of the dining room and coo politely while the guests ate their heart shaped meal and the kaleidoscope of butterflies that had to be trained to erupt into the air as she cut into her wedding cake.

'I really can't see the problem. Oh! I understand.'

'You do? Asked Rebecca hopefully.

'Yes.' There was a tremble in Annabelle's voice and Rebecca could imagine the wobble on her lower lip.

'You don't want my wedding to be a success do you?' whispered Annabelle.

'What! Don't be ridiculous.'

'You don't want me to have a special day because I'm marrying Daniel.'

Oh God, groaned Rebecca. Please not this again.

'You don't want to help me because you don't want my wedding to be amazing.'

'Of course I do,' snapped Rebecca. 'For goodness sake Annabelle, of course I want you to have a lovely day.'

'Are you sure?'

'Positive.'

'Oh good. You had me worried for a moment Rebecca darling.' The wobble had gone. 'I'm glad we've got that sorted out. So I'll send you a list of all the things I want and if you could get started that would be a weight of my mind.'

Rebecca sank onto one of the kitchen chairs. She was beaten.

'And please no cutting corners Becky darling.' The little tinkly laugh came down the phone like a drill into Rebecca's head. 'I'm having my wedding at Willow Court but I expect it to be every bit as special as if I were having it at Bransome Manor. I want the perfect wedding Rebecca dear, and I know you can give me exactly that.'

Chapter 19

Suddenly, the weather broke. It was as though nature remembered summer was on its way and overnight the rain and wind stopped and the sun came bursting out. Within a week, everyone was complaining. It was too warm, it was too muggy, no-one could sleep. Rebecca felt relieved. She was sure that the renovations at Willow Court would pick up now the incessant rain had stopped. But it seemed that conditions were never perfect for a builder. Now the plaster was going off too quickly, the concrete was going to waste, the team that turned up every morning had to stop earlier because they were hot and tired. Bottles and bottles of water had replaced the trays of tea and Rebecca kept turning up with boxes of ice lollies in the hope of keeping them refreshed and capable of working a few extra hours. Even Brian on top of his scaffold was muttering about drying times and shaking his head and Rebecca wanted to scream with frustration.

'But it must be easier to get work done when it isn't wet and cold,' she demanded when she came across Drew sitting on one of the outside walls taking a break. Her tone was a little shaper than she had intended because she was trying not to look at the broad shoulders and perfect six pack as he threw his T-shirt onto the grass.

'It's hard work Bec.'

Typical builder.

He looked tired and Rebecca immediately felt bad. 'I'm sorry, Of course it is. Can I get you anything? A drink, a lolly. A hose pipe?'

'Well the hosepipe is tempting but a lolly would do.'

Telling him to stay where he was Rebecca went into the kitchen in the hope that were still some left in the ancient freezer that mercifully they hadn't yet thrown away. Pushing open the door, she could see Sarah and Luke's heads almost touching as they poured over the plans for the ensuite bathrooms. Luke was explaining something about lagging to Sarah and Rebecca noticed how comfortable they were with each other as Luke pointed out pipes and junctions and Sarah followed his finger nodding in agreement. They never seemed to be very far away from each other these days.

'Just looking for a lolly for your dad,' she told Luke cheerfully. She dug one out and then turned to face them again. 'How's it going?'

'Great,' said Sarah. 'I've actually learned a lot working with Luke.' She paused and cast a shy glance in his direction. 'All sorts of things I might not have taken into account if I hadn't been involved in the project so early.'

'Actually it's made me think more about the end result,' Luke added, 'I know exactly what Sarah needs so it's easier to plan.'

'Good.' Rebecca nodded her head and stood for a moment, watching as they smiled at each other in mutual admiration. 'Right, well I'll go give this to Drew,' and she left them to it.

Passing the lolly to Drew she sat on the wall next to him.

'So,' she said, 'tell me.'

He groaned, pushing the lolly in his mouth and looking up at the blue, blue sky.

'Really?'

'Really.'

Drew sighed. This was something that Rebecca liked to do every day. Even if there was practically no progress because the day had been spent demolishing rather than building, she liked Drew to go through each room and give her not just an update but a vision report.

'It's really hot Rebecca. Can't we skip today?'

Tired builder.

She tried not to look at his chest, the muscled frame that had already caught the sun.

'It might be hot for the rest of the summer. I'll still want updates,' she said reasonably.

Drew carried on licking his lolly, watching her from beneath his surprisingly long eyelashes but not saying anything.

'Okay,' relented Rebecca a smile playing round her lips. 'Two rooms, just tell me about two rooms.'

He pretended to be considering the suggestion and then stood up. 'How about I actually show you one room?' he counter offered.

'Show me?'

'Yes. Today we stick to one room but I won't give you a report, I'll show it to you.'

Rebecca gasped. 'Does that mean you've finished something? Is there a finished room?'

'Well you'll have to come with me to find out won't you?' teased Drew, holding out his hand, melting lolly dripping down the other one.

Quickly Rebecca jumped to her feet, pretending not to notice the hand. She tried not to touch Drew. It had a strange effect on her and she really didn't have time to sit down and think what that might mean, so she had decided the best thing to do was to avoid anything that might cause that funny fluttering in her stomach. Things, like touching Drew's hand.

Her eyes were shining with excitement as she followed him, expecting him to turn back towards the house. Instead they passed the doorway and the French windows to the dining room and carried on walking.

'The chapel?' she guessed. 'Have you finished the chapel?'

Drew didn't answer. Finishing his lolly he threw the stick expertly in the direction of a skip and simply smiled as he carried on walking.

'It is the chapel isn't it? It has to be!'

There was nowhere else they could be going and with a little skip Rebecca passed Drew on the path as they arrived at the chapel door. It was small and built entirely of stone. As a result it was freezing in winter and as most of the windows had been boarded up it was only marginally warmer in the summer. Annabelle had a point when she had declared it a waste of time. But both Rebecca and Sarah had fallen in love with the little chapel and they were convinced that if they had many others would. What could be more romantic, Rebecca had thought, than to be married in your own chapel and then walk across the beautiful garden and into Willow Court to greet your guests. Other than the fact that you would need thermal underwear to survive ten minutes inside and that the garden resembled trench warfare rather than romantic summer blooms.

She pushed open the heavy wooden door which had been given a makeover. The rotten edges had been replaced and the wood coaxed back to its original colour, even the climbing rose round the entrance looked happier.

'It's been so hot I've had lads fighting over who could work in here,' said Drew. 'They're all just sorry it's finished.'

Inside, the stone was old and mellow and it took Rebecca a moment to realise the reason she could see it so well was that all the boards had gone and the sun shone in through the windows, including an amazing stained glass window that stood at one end high above the altar. It was a wedding scene, with a blue sky and a yellow sun which cast shafts of light across the whole chapel and instantly made Rebecca feel warm.

'But where …' she began in confusion.

'It was there all along. When we took the boards down we found this, undamaged. We think it was boarded over to protect it, maybe before a storm. And because it doesn't get used no-one thought to take the board down.'

Rebecca carried on looking round. It had been cleaned, all the leaves and debris that had blown through the badly fitting door over the years had gone and the mould that had been climbing up the walls had disappeared. The pews were shining, sanded, polished and re-varnished. The ceiling beams curved upwards resembling the bow of a boat and every beam was clean and smooth, it's age and history shining through.

'It's so warm,' Rebecca wondered.

'Well it is very warm outside today,' laughed Drew, 'but it's now got heating so even a winter wedding won't be a problem.'

Rebecca walked along the short aisle, touching the pews gently as she passed. She reached the front then turned back to face Drew.

Wonderful builder.

'Thank you.'

'Well, it's what you're paying me for.'

'I needed this Drew, I needed something to let me know we could make this deadline. This means so much to me, so thank you.'

And for once Drew didn't laugh or scratch his head. He looked at Rebecca standing before the altar and his face was soft and gentle.

'It's my pleasure Rebecca, my absolute pleasure.'

When Rebecca got home that night she couldn't wait to see Charles. She had a shower to wash away the dust and grime from the building site that was Willow Court and then sat in the kitchen with a glass of wine until Charles turned up with the Chinese takeaway.

'You look happy,' was his greeting as he put the bag of food on the kitchen table and turned to kiss her.

'I am. We've got a room ready!' announced Rebecca in the manner of someone announcing an Oscar winner.

'Really? I thought you were a way off that yet.' He grabbed a glass from the cupboard and poured himself some wine.

'Yes, well, it's the chapel.' admitted Rebecca. 'It's not exactly a crucial room but Charles – it looks so pretty!'

He smiled at her excitement, getting out the plates and knives and cutlery as she curled up on the raspberry settee her eyes shining. 'It looks absolutely divine,' she sighed. 'It's exactly what I would choose for my wedding day.'

Her eyes met his over the rim of her glass. Did he think she was suggesting they got married?

'Er ... if I was thinking of getting married,' she added hurriedly, adding 'which I'm obviously not,' for good measure.

Charles grinned and carried on ladling Chinese onto plates.

'And I know it's only the chapel but it's the first room that's totally finished and it's something that a lot of other places won't be able to offer.'

Rebecca wandered to the table, grabbing a plate and fork.

'I think I'll get a pergola put up between the Chapel and the drawing room. If we get roses trained along the sides and the top it will give a little bit of shelter. Even if it was rainy you could still make it the few hundred yards into the house without getting soaked. How romantic would that be,' she said with another sigh, 'marrying in your very own chapel and then walking through an arch of roses to greet your guests in a beautiful reception room.'

Okay, it wasn't a beautiful reception room yet. It had no ceiling, very little floor and several broken windows but it would be beautiful, with a lot of hard work and patience.

'It sounds amazing,' said Charles softly. 'Absolutely amazing. Now eat,' and he pushed the plate nearer to Rebecca.

'I'll have to come and look at Willow Court soon,' he said as they both tucked in.

'Really?'

'Of course. I'd like to see it before it completes its makeover, so I can appreciate what you've achieved.'

Rebecca put down her fork and gazed into Charles eyes. 'That would be wonderful.'

Charles speared a piece of duck then slid his hand over Rebecca's own. 'I know it's going to look amazing, I can see how hard you're working on this, you and Sarah and Drew. But it would be wonderful to see it now, while it still has missing ceilings and no proper bathrooms.'

He was so understanding, thought Rebecca. He seemed to know more about what drove her than Daniel ever had. Maybe Helen had been right, maybe there was no need to take everything so slowly at their age.

'Why don't we go away for a weekend?' asked Rebecca impulsively.

Charles eyebrows shot upwards. 'What?'

'Let's have a weekend away, just the two of us. Somewhere romantic, somewhere we can forget about everything for a while and just relax.'

'Okay. It sounds wonderful but are you sure? You seem so occupied with Willow Court at the moment and I don't want you to regret leaving it.'

Rebecca grinned. 'Well, if truth be told I actually contribute very little. I wander around nagging about whether it will be ready and if they can work any faster. Drew will probably be delighted to hear I'll miss a few days, he won't have to go through the endless vision reports.'

'Vision report?'

Rebecca ducked her head shyly. 'Oh I got fed up of listening to him talking about plaster drying times and square footage of plaster board so I make him tell me the vision he has for each room the following day.'

At Charles puzzled look she carried on. 'You know, like, tomorrow the drawing room will have a ceiling. Once it has a ceiling we can paint it and then instead of a grimy old ceiling we'll have a sparkling white one that will show off the beautiful oak panelled walls.'

She stopped because it sounded crazy and a bit strange. What she didn't say was that Drew would tell her all this in a deep mellow voice that made the vision come to life.

That he didn't just say the ceiling would be painted, he would describe to her exactly how she wanted the room to look because it turned out that the first day they met and Rebecca showed him around Willow Court, he had listened to every word she had uttered.

'Sounds crazy, I know,' she laughed. 'Part of the reason he won't miss me for a few days. Sarah on the other hand, she actually helps. She is so involved in everything. She knows exactly what she needs to happen so she can turn the place into a top notch wedding event.'

Charles was listening intently. He had listened to Rebecca's dreams for Willow Court since the first day they had met, always eager to hear about her project, always encouraging. It was so different to the life she'd had with Daniel that it had become hugely important to Rebecca. Someone in her life that actually listened to her. Someone who thought she had something to say.

'So, shall we go away for a weekend?'

'I think that is a very definite yes,' smiled Charles pushing his plate away and leaning forward to kiss Rebecca, despite the noodle that was draped across her chin. 'Let's leave life and Willow Court behind for a few days and go somewhere where we don't have to worry about a thing.'

Chapter 20

Drew did indeed look vaguely relieved when Rebecca announced that she would not be visiting Willow Court for a few days. Even Sarah looked happy at being in charge for a brief period and a week later Rebecca was sitting on a hotel balcony, soaking up the summer sun and admiring the glistening waters of Monte Carlo bay. Charles had been more than happy to visit Monaco although when Rebecca showed him the hotel she had chosen he had turned slightly pale.

'It's very expensive,' he'd murmured. 'Shall we look at some others before we decide?'

Rebecca chewed her lip. 'But this is a beautiful hotel, right in the centre of Monte Carlo. And look at the pictures of the room. Isn't it wonderful.'

Charles had nodded but continued to scroll through the list of hotels.

'It is indeed, but there's probably more here that are much more reasonably priced and I think …'

Rebecca had gently closed the laptop, forcing his search to stop. She smiled at him, laying one hand on top of his. 'The hotel is my treat Charles.' She held up a hand to stop his protest. 'It's not going to work, we are not going to work, if we ignore the situation. I have money,' Rebecca shrugged her shoulders. 'There's no point ignoring the fact. And if you won't allow me to occasionally upgrade us and spend some of my money on you, how can we carry on?'

Charles had been scrupulously fair from the very first date, which was in part why Rebecca's attraction for him had grown. There had never been the slightest hint that he was expecting her to stand the bill for their evening out, visits to the theatre, takeaways etc. They took it in turns to pay for their meals, because Rebecca insisted. If Rebecca invited him to the theatre she would pay for the tickets. If

Charles invited Rebecca to the cinema he would pay for the ticket. Rebecca was very comfortable with their relationship and had never once had any doubt that Charles was with her because of the money in her bank account. When she had visited Charles's home for the first time she had been pleasantly surprised. It was a lovely Georgian house on the outskirts of Harrogate, large, airy and well decorated. He told Rebecca that both he and his wife had held down good jobs and money had not been an issue. There was also a reasonable amount of life cover in place and when Sylvia had died, Charles had been left in a very comfortable financial position. But Rebecca was determined that they were honest and open about the relationship and she did not want to have to go through life pretending she was not a wealthy woman.

She could see the struggle on his face.

'It makes sense Charles. I chose Monte Carlo, I chose this hotel. So please, let me pay.'

And so, here they were. Rebecca could hear Charles moving around in their room as she sat on the balcony vaguely wondering how work at Willow Court was progressing but mainly thinking back to the previous evening and the wonderful meal they had shared, before strolling through the streets back to the hotel and making love with the windows to the balcony open and a gentle breeze drifting across the bed.

If she looked to the left she could see the world famous Monte Carlo casino, high on the hill. To the right was the Grimaldi palace, exuding glamour and elegance. And in front was the sweeping bay littered with multi million pound boats and the homes of the rich and famous, it had been a wonderful few days

Charles' arms slid round her shoulders from behind and she could smell the fresh lemon of his shower gel.

'Happy?'

'Mmm.'

The remnants of the breakfast tray were still laid out on the table and although Rebecca needed to get dressed so they could visit the palace and pay a visit to the aquarium before checking out and returning home, she was perfectly content to simply sit and feel the sea breeze lift her hair as she admired the view.

'It was a good choice,' admitted Charles topping up their cups from the silver pot.

Rebecca grinned. 'I won't say I told you so - but I did!'

'Okay smarty pants. I was wrong, you were right.'

They sat in companionable silence for a few minutes.

'Seriously Bec, I have enjoyed this break so much.'

She sighed happily and nodded in agreement.

'I would like to think we could do this again,' he continued with the smallest hint of hesitancy in his voice.

'Absolutely! It's been wonderful.'

Charles nodded and Rebecca had a feeling there was more he would like to say.

'It's a risk, that first break away together.'

She stiffened slightly. 'What do you mean?'

'I mean that a weekend away like this often shows the flaws in a relationship. Sharing a bed is one thing, sharing a bathroom is quite another! But I've enjoyed every single moment of being with you Bec, my only regret about this holiday is that it's coming to an end.'

Rebecca watched him. She had felt incredibly comfortable with Charles throughout the visit and she knew what he meant. There had been no tension or uncertainty. They had walked around the town each evening, holding hands content to soak up the atmosphere. They seemed to know each other so well, Rebecca felt as though they had been together for far longer than a few months.

She leaned forward to drop a kiss on his nose. 'I know what you mean,' she said dreamily, 'it has been wonderful.'

'And something you would want to do again?'

She peeped at him from beneath her lashes. 'Well this one isn't over yet but, yes. I would very much like to go away with you again Charles,' and smiling companionably they sat and watched the glittering blue sea, holding hands across the table as they sipped their coffee and relaxed in each other's company.

*

Rebecca couldn't wait to visit Willow Court. She and Charles had arrived back to a still hot and sticky Leeds and they had gone out for a meal at a riverside restaurant to extend the holiday mood until the very last moment. If Rebecca had been entirely honest she would have preferred to stay at home and catch up with Sarah about the progress made at Willow Court.

But she had smiled and nodded at Charles' suggestion and they had spent a pleasant evening, even if Rebecca's attention wasn't always one hundred percent on Charles and their conversation.

She had politely suggested that they go to their own homes that evening and Charles had carried her suitcase up to her bedroom and then kissed her goodnight. And whilst Rebecca felt the tiniest bit insensitive it meant that the next morning when she woke up she could throw on some clothes and drive to meet Sarah and Drew with no time spent on anything else.

It looked much the same. In fact it looked exactly the same except that the mud had dried to leave a front garden that looked as though it were covered in dirt waves. Deep trenches had been left by the various heavy goods vehicles that had come calling, small dents and troughs from piles of bricks and cement were everywhere and walking across it was akin to trekking the Himalayas. Rebecca frowned, it would be a major job getting it flat, green and pleasant again and as the first thing any prospective bridal party would see, it was a fairly important area. Still, she didn't have to worry about that until Willow Court was in a fit state to hold a wedding and at the moment the garden was the least of her worries.

The reception hall looked even worse. The hole at the bottom of the staircase had been repaired but everywhere was knee deep in dust with trails of sand and cement and piles of plaster board and bricks and tools. The rain may have been a nuisance but at least the damp air had kept the dust in order. With nothing but unrelenting sunshine and without a breath of fresh air to be had, every particle of dust from the entire building seemed to be gathering in the hall leaving Rebecca wondering why she felt that Willow Court would make such a pleasant wedding venue. Sighing she walked down the hall to the dome room, always her first stop. There was Brian on his scaffold in exactly the same position he had been in when she had left, working on exactly the same corner.

'Morning Brian,' she called, hoping the distress didn't show in her voice. The last thing she wanted was for him to work any slower. She received the usual grunt in reply and sighing she turned away in search of a room where more progress had been made. Surely, she thought, there should be one.

Drew had left her a voicemail halfway through her holiday, telling her not to worry because all was going well and the dining room in particular was racing along. She had smiled at the time, partly because he knew her well enough to know she would worry and partly because she loved listening to his voice when he spoke about Willow Court. Sarah had sent her a couple of texts saying the same thing but Rebecca was beginning to think they had both simply not wanted her to worry her holiday away. Walking down the other side of the stairway in the direction of the kitchen, Rebecca wondered where they all were. She called for both Sarah and Drew but there was no answer, just the sounds of work coming from upstairs, the usual banging and shouting. She had expected a greeting of some kind, perhaps the two of them waiting for her, ready to show her some improvement. She poked her head round the kitchen door but it was empty, cups littering the surfaces and pizza boxes jammed in the bin but no sign of life.

Feeling somehow let down, Rebecca remembered what Drew had said and walked back down the hallway towards the dining room, tripping over a length of wire and climbing past two pallets covered in bags of something dusty. Surely something had happened in here.

She pushed open the door and took a step inside, only to stop and catch her breath. Drew, Luke and Sarah were all there, waiting for her. There was a tray with a bottle of bucks fizz, some rather grubby mugs and three smiling faces. But more importantly, as far as Rebecca was concerned, there was a room. A real room complete with ceiling, a floor that was perfectly level, windows that were without a single crack and a fireplace complete with all four corners.

It was dusty and it needed painting. A small patch had been cleaned in front of the fireplace to show off the parquet floor they had discovered but the rest was grey with plaster dust. The fireplace had been cleared of years of paint and sanded so that the intricate carving across its width was now visible but it still needed a good clean. The windows might be crack free but they were also dirty and smeared and the heavy curtain rails with the huge bronze finials were empty of the sheer curtains that Rebecca had planned to have drifting across the window. The wooden panels had been cleverly repaired so there was no peeling or cracking on display, just lots of dirt and fingerprints and there were still several spider's webs hanging from the corners.

'It's beautiful,' whispered Rebecca. 'It's the most beautiful room I've ever seen,' and she promptly burst into tears.

The next few minutes were all a flurry as Sarah wrapped her arms around her mum and started crying too and Luke looked alarmed and worried until Drew explained they were happy tears and managed to produce a pack of tissue from his pocket.

Efficient builder.

The buck's fizz was opened and they all raised their mugs to the first, almost completed room in Willow Court.

'When we actually finish we'll open a bottle of the real stuff,' said Drew, his eyes looking suspiciously damp, 'but as Luke and I have a full day's work ahead of us, this will have to do for now.'

'Thank you,' said Rebecca who was still sniffling. 'Thank you all so very much.'

More hugs and tears followed until Drew declared that the men must get back to work which earned him a slap on the arm from Sarah's black notebook and grin from Luke and then it was just Rebecca and Sarah in the room.

'I've got something else for you mum.' Carefully Sarah took a long piece of rolled up paper from the top of the fireplace and then spread it out on the floor. This is a drawing I did of how it will look when we clean it up and actually decorate.'

Rebecca knelt down next to her daughter and almost started crying again. 'Oh My God, it's amazing!'

And it was. The drawing banished the dust and grime and curtains were indeed drifting across the windows. The chandeliers were glowing, the fireplace was full of pine cones and flowers and the floor shone. Tables were set out surrounded by cream and gold chairs and covered with old fashioned china. It looked exactly as Rebecca had imagined it would the very first day she had walked into the damp depressing room.

'It's going to work isn't it,' she asked Sarah and the two hugged each other delightedly at the realisation that their dream was turning into reality and Willow Court was about to become a beautiful building once more.

Chapter 21

Other than the odd cloud passing high overhead, the warm weather continued. Warnings of reservoirs running dry had already begun and the evening news was now dedicated to the weather and its effect on public transport, the old, the young and those who had to sit in stifling offices from 9:00 until 5:00 every day. June had arrived and it seemed to Rebecca that it couldn't wait to leave again. She had never known the weeks go by so quickly and she wanted to grab each day and insist it slowed down. The drawing room was also now finished, the unfortunate ceiling had been repaired, the windows were intact and the walls resembled walls once more.

Brian was still in the corner of the domed room, although Rebecca noticed he had shifted his potion and was now working on the other side of the corner, which meant at the current rate of progress he would only need another 6 months. Sarah seemed confident and totally absorbed in the job in hand and Rebecca had insisted on an employment contract and an official wage which had reduced her daughter to tears of happiness. In view of her now official status of manager of Willow Court Weddings, Rebecca did not feel at all guilty in directing Annabelle's' many calls and demands in Sarah's direction and she had successfully managed to deflect several proposed visits.

Her main excuse was that she simply didn't have time, not only did she have the ongoing business of Willow Court to deal with, but she had a relationship. In Rebecca's head, the word was in capital letters and she couldn't help but enjoy the feeling of being part of a couple. She had refused a proposed visit for the coming weekend, by turning the tables neatly on Annabelle. 'I am busy Annabelle,' she had insisted. 'I'm in a relationship, I've moved on. Are you not happy for me?'

For once lost for an argument Annabelle had accepted the situation with bad grace and immediately phoned Sarah to grumble about the lack of progress and insisted on talking for over an hour about the exact shade of pink rose she wanted Sarah to plant now in the hope that in only a few weeks Willow Court would be surrounded by pink blooms.

The small lake at the back of Willow Court was getting lower and lower. And although it was something they had all agreed would remain on the secondary list, it was getting a lot of attention simply because it was one of the few relatively cool places to sit when taking a break. The huge willow tree cast its feathery fronds across much of the bank and the constant stream of workers who would lay there for half an hour whilst they ate their lunch meant the path down to the lake had become well used and much easier to navigate. A lot of the debris that had been building up on the banks had been cleared as everyone took back bits and pieces and threw them into the skip. A picnic bench had appeared under the tree, found in the overgrown garden, and it turned out that one of the plasterers Drew employed was something of an aficionado on wildlife ponds and he had been clearing some of the weeds and encouraging the lily pads to spread their cool shade to the fish below.

Sweating in the midday heat, Rebecca decided to take a walk down to sit under the willow and look at the latest accounts. Drew kept a very tight handle on the spending and other than a few unexpected costs, like the collapse of the drawing room ceiling, the spend was pretty much where Rebecca had expected.

Efficient builder.

Her main worry was the time they would have once the renovations were complete. The renovation was only the beginning of the transformation of Willow Court. Once the paint was dry and the scaffolding removed, the entire place had to return to the splendid wedding venue of its past, or it had all been a waste of time.

Walking along the path Rebecca could hear voices and knew she wasn't the only person to seek the shade of the willow that day. Lifting one of the heavy fronds she saw Sarah and Luke on the opposite bank, still in the shade but slightly detached from anyone else who may decide to sit by the lake. Sarah's black book was on the grass by her side and next to Luke was a handful of drawings and plans rolled and wrapped with elastic bands. Rebecca smiled, she really couldn't fault their dedication, they had both thrown themselves into the renovation with an amazing level of enthusiasm.

Half hidden by the trailing willow branches, Rebecca watched them for a moment. Sarah lay back on the grass and Luke sat by her side, his body tilted in her direction and they both looked relaxed and utterly at ease with each other. Luke said something that made Sarah laugh and push him away and he pretended to roll towards the lake.

The previous week Sarah and Dom had been to Rebecca's house to meet Charles. Helen and Emma had joined them and they had all spent a wonderful day in the garden, taking shade in the courtyard while Charles and Tim took over the BBQ. A game of tennis had been suggested but everyone had decided it was far too hot and they had spent the day lazing in the sun and chatting, mainly about Willow Court and the forthcoming weddings. Rebecca had heard the enthusiasm in Sarah's voice as she brought Helen and Emma up to date with the plans for the bridal suite and how wonderful the chapel looked and teasing Dom gently about how she was now in charge of a team of burly builders. Their relationship didn't seem to have changed in the slightest and Rebecca had felt relieved that Sarah's long working day was not taking a toll on their lives. They held hands, Dom kissed her cheek softly as he passed her a glass of wine and they had seemed as much in love as ever. Rebecca had invited him to visit Willow

Court one day and see what was keeping his fiancée so busy and he had said he would love to, if only he could find a free hour or so.

So why, Rebecca wondered, did she suddenly feel so unsettled at the sight of Sarah and Luke sitting on the grass engrossed in their conversation and each other.

'She stepped forward, making the willow branches rustle as she approached the lake and shouting a cheery 'Hi' in their direction.

'Mum. Come over and join us.

'Phew, it's so warm isn't it,' she said joining them on the grass. 'What are you two talking about?'

'Oh the usual,' groaned Sarah. 'Plumbing, seating, lighting, timetables and more plumbing and seating! It's all Luke and I ever talk about,' she grinned.

'She's doing a fantastic job Rebecca,' offered Luke shyly. 'Really keeping on top of all the plans. No-one would dream of changing anything without checking with Sarah first. We all know she has an exact image of how it will all look and woe betide anybody who messes with that.'

Sarah laughed, digging Luke in the arm. 'You make me sound like a tyrant!' she protested.

'Well if the cap fits.'

He ducked as Sarah picked up her book to hit him with and Rebecca's lips tried to continue smiling. They were so at ease with each other, so together and completely at one. Did Luke have any idea of the way he was looking at her daughter, she wondered, did he have any conception of the look in his eyes.

'Dom said whether he can come over for a visit?' she asked.

Sarah sighed. 'No, poor Dom. He is just so busy at the moment. But he makes me describe it all to him every night.'

And were her sentences littered with Luke said and Luke did wondered Rebecca.

'Annabelle phoned again,' Sarah said wrinkling her nose. 'She is really worried that we won't finish in time and she insist on me sending her a picture of the roses she asked me to plant on the path to the chapel so she can check they're the right shape.'

'Shape?'

'Yeah, apparently some roses can be far too fat and Annabelle does not want fat roses at her wedding.' Sarah tried to say it with a straight face but Luke's look of comical bemusement sent her into a fit of giggles. 'She also said that maybe this wasn't the time for you to start a new relationship. You really should be focusing all your energy on Willow Court and her wedding, not on galivanting round Europe with Charles.'

Rebecca snorted with derision. She visited Willow Court most days, in between keeping up with events at Parklands and visiting Gwen. Her focus was most definitely on getting the place ready for Sarah's wedding and other than their break to Monte Carlo there had been no galivanting.

'She won't stay away much longer mum, she is frothing at the mouth waiting to come and visit.'

Rebecca sighed. 'Well there's absolutely no point until the building work is finished,' she said firmly. 'The shade and shape of Annabelle's roses is something I refuse to worry about right now.'

'Perhaps we should have a finishing party,' mused Sarah.

'A bit like a wrap party?' queried Luke.

'Exactly.' They smiled at each other.

'We can even have it at Willow Court because there won't be anything to spoil. We'll finish the building work, have a party to celebrate before we start filling it with things we wouldn't want to get broken. What do you think Mum?'

Rebecca was only half listening. She was watching the admiring stare Luke was sending Sarah at her suggestion.

'Sounds like a good idea. Dom needs to see it as well.'

'Dom?'

'Yes. Let's not forget that it's his wedding as well darling.' Rebecca tried to laugh. 'The poor boy has only seen this place as a wreck. He's putting an awful lot of faith in us both, delivering the perfect wedding venue to him in only a few weeks.'

She ignored the slight downcast to Luke's mouth. Maybe he needed a little reminder that this wasn't just about renovating Willow Court, it was about Sarah's forthcoming wedding to Dom.

'I suppose you're right. I hadn't really thought about it that way.'

'Well anyway, I think it's an excellent idea. We'll have a 'finished the building' party and Annabelle and Dom can both see the place they'll be getting married.'

Rebecca wanted to rip her tongue out. She really could do without a visit from Annabelle. But perhaps it was time they all remembered why they were working so hard, they had two weddings to arrange in only a few weeks and one of them was Sarah's own and it did not involve Luke.

Chapter 22

'Are you ignoring me?'

Rebecca jumped and spun round to see Drew lazing in the doorway and grinning at her.'

'No!' she lied, 'just been busy.

'It suits you.'

Rebecca frowned. 'Being busy?'

'No, being happy.'

'Well you've done a great job Drew, at times I actually believe we might get this thing finished on time.'

'I didn't mean Willow Court,' interrupted Drew. 'I meant you. You seem much more relaxed and a great deal happier than when I first met you. I thought it was down to Charles but are you saying it's me that's brought that smile to your eyes?' he asked cheekily.

Rebecca blushed. The truth was she had been avoiding Drew. She had decided the tingle she felt along her spine whenever their hands touched and the funny little flip that her heart did when he smiled at her was something she should not encourage. She had wondered if it was a builder dependency type of condition. A little like Stockholm syndrome. She was so totally dependent on Drew to make this work for her that he had become an integral part of her life. Maybe lots of women developed a little crush on their builders and it was a perfectly normal condition. As soon as Drew and his tanned six pack, dirty blonde hair and infectious grin disappeared leaving her with nothing but a very large bill, the bond would be broken and she would no longer feel a definite shortness of breath whenever she saw him from a distance. She had meant to speak to Emma about it, her friend had employed her fair share of builders over the years as she had restored her beautiful Georgian home. Rebecca needed to check if Emma had developed any crushes on the men that held such control, albeit briefly, over her life. Although she seemed to remember the only emotion Emma had ever shown was sheer frustration and she had seen her friend actually banging her head on her immaculate stripped pine table when Mr Builder had phoned to say that because the weather was too hot/cold/dry/wet he was unable yet again to come and get on with the job in hand. And judging by the names Emma had called them, Rebecca was fairly certain that there had been no romantic thoughts involved. But there again, none of Emma's builders had been 6' tall and had piercing blue eyes that made you want to run your hands over their well-developed chest and abandon yourself to their will.

She realised that Drew was watching her, waiting for an answer and she struggled to push away all thoughts of the ruffled blond hair on a pillow next to her and recall what they were talking about.

'What?'

'Are you happy because I'm pulling out all the stops to get Willow Court ready on time – or is it Charles that's brought that twinkle to your eye? You can be honest,' he said solemnly, 'I won't take offence.'

Rebecca blushed. Had Drew noticed that she always became slightly breathless when he was near her. 'Erm, well,' she mumbled. 'Charles and I are very happy.'

Not exactly enthusiastic but the best she could do at such short notice.

Drew clutched his heart in mock pain. 'And I thought it was me that had your skin glowing.'

He laughed at her deepening blush and then stopped. 'Seriously, I'm glad for you Bec, really glad,' and he gave her such a warm smile that she nearly burst into tears although exactly why she was completely unsure.

'I have good news,' he announced grinning widely.'

'Oh, you mean …?'

'I mean the bridal suite is complete.'

Rebecca closed her eyes and gave a great gusty sigh of relief. 'That's wonderful Drew, absolutely wonderful.

Thank you.' She felt the tears rush into her eyes again and decided that they were caused by overwhelming gratitude that he was keeping on top of the job and nothing to do with the look he was sending her way.

'It's what you pay me for,' he said, kindly ignoring the tears.

Efficient builder.

'You want to have a look?'

He turned to walk out of the door and towards the staircase and Rebecca really wanted to shout out that it was okay, she would check it herself later. But they had a routine and she knew she had to go with him or have a good reason why she was standing in the doorway biting her lip.

He turned around to look at her with a raised eyebrow. 'Coming?'

'Of course.'

Following him up the stairs Rebecca took a few deep breaths and tried to calm her nerves. She knew what was going to happen and she knew the effect it would have on her. She needed to be strong and not blub like a baby or even worse swoon in Drew's arms.

The previous week, when the drawing room had been finished Drew had taken her by the arm and shown her the room, pointed out the work they had done and explained the changes that had taken place. His voice had been soft and mellow, wrapping itself round Rebecca like a warm summer's day. And then he had gone on to remind her of her vision for the room and she had almost melted at his feet.

'You wanted this room to be full of light and warmth,' he reminded. 'Well those windows, now they're repaired and clean will let the light flood in here all afternoon. Imagine a warm summer's day with the windows wide open and curtains billowing in the breeze. You can walk out onto the terrace and soak up the sun. Or if it's a winter's day, the fire will be full of applewood logs crackling away as your guests watch the frost on the stone outside. The chandelier will hang right here,' gently he had drawn her to the centre of the room, 'casting a glow across the whole room.'

Rebecca had stared upwards at the beautifully repaired ceiling ready to welcome home the chandelier which had been removed for cleaning. She had looked around at the smoothly plastered walls and the repaired fireplace with its huge black grate ready to swallow up as many logs as they could find. She imagined the room full of rich velvet armchairs and occasional tables, the brocade curtains that would hang floor to ceiling at each French window.

'It will be warm and cosy in winter and full of light in summer,' Drew continued, 'the bride and groom can stand by the fireplace and the guests can raise their glasses in a room that wouldn't look out of place in Downton Abby. It will look wonderful, Bec, absolutely as you wanted it to look.'

And that's when it had happened. That was the moment that Rebecca looked into those lovely blue eyes and felt so deeply moved that she wanted to throw herself in his arms and cry. He understood her vision perfectly. He understood everything that she wanted from Willow Court and he was doing his very best to make that happen for her. And she loved him for it.

Clever, clever builder.

Of course, she didn't really love him she had told herself firmly after he had left and she sat on the floor by one of the French windows. She loved the feeling he gave her, the optimism, the self-belief, the certainty that she was going to succeed. She loved him in the way people loved the doctor who had made them well or the driving instructor that had helped them pass their test, she decided. She ignored the little voice that reminded her that her driving instructor had been small and rotund and had worn a hairpiece that stayed perfectly still when he swivelled his head to look behind him. She had felt no love for him, only a slight resentment at the amount of money he was costing her and relief that she didn't have to sit next to him anymore. No, thought Rebecca, of course it wasn't actual love, it was just a form of extreme thankfulness for the work he was doing at Willow Court. All the same, she had been careful to avoid Drew as much as possible since that day and the last thing she needed was another moment when Drew's low voice would wind itself around her reducing her insides to liquid.

She walked into the bridal suite and stood, quite still, looking round.

'If you remember,' Drew started and Rebecca's heart began to do somersaults in her chest, 'the windows were being blocked by the overgrown ivy and several were cracked, the wall had water stains everywhere, and the floor was uneven,'

Rebecca did remember, she had stared around the dejected room, dark, dingy and far from appealing and thought how lovely it could be if it were painted cream and the view down to the lake wasn't obscured and the floor didn't tilt alarmingly when you walked from one side of the room to the other.

Drew was standing by her shoulder, his breath caressing the back of her neck.

'Well the windows have been cleared and repaired,' Rebecca could indeed see right down to the huge willow tree and the lake. 'The ceiling and the walls have been plastered, the floor is straight and that door over there leads into the new bathroom we've created from the room next door.'

Rebecca thought how even under the layers of dust she could detect the faint aroma of fresh sandalwood that he'd probably splashed on that morning.

'You wanted a relaxing and romantic room,' Drew said taking her arm gently to turn her around so she had a 360 degree view. 'You wanted a soft colour on the walls and crisp bedding with layers of velvet and silk to give the luxury of a bridal suite.'

Rebecca wondered what colour Drew's bedding was.

'You wanted a huge fourposter bed, on a nice firm floor!' he laughed and Rebecca's heart leaped and twisted in excitement. 'Over there will be the dressing table complete with an antique mirror where the bride can sit and prepare for her wedding day,' Drew instructed, 'and by the window will be a love seat so the bride and groom can sip champagne and look out towards the lake after the wedding is over. The carpet is on its way, thick and rich and cream as you wanted.'

Rebecca wondered if it would be inappropriate to kiss him.

'And of course the main difference is the addition of a bathroom and dressing area.'

Drew led her to the door now nestled on one wall as though it had always been there. Inside was a huge freestanding tub on Victorian claw feet standing in the centre of the room. 'A tub for two,' he grinned and Rebecca had to beat away the image of a naked Drew stretched out in its foamy depths. The window was large, arched and set high up the wall so anyone in the bath would have a view of the stars. 'A perfect place to relax away the evening,' he added dreamily making Rebecca almost gasp out loud as she pulled away, forcing a little space and common sense between them.

'And of course the dressing room,' he opened the door leading to the small room lined with storage and hanging rails and a large mannequin standing proudly against one wall, 'all ready to take care of the wedding dress.'

Quickly Rebecca walked out of the small space and back towards the much bigger bedroom. 'It's superb,' she squeaked before clearing her throat and taking a deep breath.

'Truly Drew, it's exactly as I imagined. You've done an amazing job.'

'And on time too,' laughed Drew scratching his head. It was a familiar action and Rebecca wanted to dash forwards and run her own hands through the dusty mop of hair.

'And the rest?' asked Rebecca trying to bring her heart rate back to normal. 'Do you think it will all be finished in the next three weeks?' That would give them 4 weeks to furnish the place and get it ready for Sarah's wedding. If it went ahead, thought Rebecca as she had a sudden flash of Sarah and Luke laid by the lake so utterly relaxed in each other's company. But perhaps it was exactly the same with Sarah, she was besotted with the man who was bringing her dreams to life. The best thing that could happen to both Rebecca and her daughter would be to get Willow Court finished and these two men out of their lives. Then they could revert to the business of being in love and getting on with no builder shaped distractions.

'Well I always said it would be tight Bec,' said Drew, serious for once, 'and it will. But bar any disasters, we should have it finished. Brian will need every last minute. He will probably be up in that corner until the day before the wedding! But we can carry on with the rest of the room and work around him and the main part of the house should be finished and ready to go.'

Rebecca thought back to the hallway they had just walked through which still resembled a builder's site. She couldn't help but feel doubtful.

'I know the downstairs looks a mess,' said Drew reading her mind. 'And it will until the very last minute. But once we move out all the supplies you'll be amazed at the difference it makes.'

Rebecca would be amazed but Drew hadn't let her down so far so she allowed herself to be reassured and nodded her head.

'I believe you'll do it,' she said sincerely. 'I know you'll get it done.'

'I wouldn't let you down Rebecca,' Drew said, his soft voice having an instant and chaotic effect on Rebecca's blood pressure. 'You know I would do anything to make you happy,' and he was gone, leaving Rebecca gasping for breath and clutching her pounding heart in alarm.

Sexy, sexy builder.

Part Three
Second Thoughts

Chapter 24

Rebecca did not have a good night's sleep. She had drifted off analysing Charles' words and wondering if she had imagined his intentions. How embarrassing if she felt he was on the verge of a proposal and in reality, he simply wanted to be able to go on a longer holiday without the demands of Willow Court calling her back. She went over everything that had happened during the evening. He had undoubtedly said he loved her. She had not responded, although she was quite determined that she would rectify that as soon as possible. She loved him and would make sure he knew.

He had seemed to imply that he wanted them to be together on a long-term basis, didn't that mean marriage? He wanted them to be there for each other, always. Surely that meant a proposal? She would feel extremely foolish if this came to nothing after telling Helen and Emma that she was going to marry him!

And to make matters worse, when she had finally drifted off to sleep it was Drew that she dreamt about. Willow Court was bedecked with white flowers and trailing greenery, the windows were open and muslin drapes were billowing in the breeze just as she had envisioned. They were dancing in the domed room although there was still scaffolding in the corner and Brian was hunched on top, listening to his radio and working on the cornice. As they twirled around the room she could see Helen and Emma looking at her in disapproval and there was Charles in the corner, dressed as a groom with a lovely pink rosebud in his lapel, watching as she danced with Drew. And although she was wearing a wedding dress that drifted around her legs as she danced, she realised that Drew was wearing his work clothes and his hair was full of dust. She caught sight of Sarah standing by the window, Dom's arm around her shoulders. But she wasn't looking at him. Instead she was watching Luke who was measuring the wall next to her and writing everything down in Sarah's big, black book.

Waking with a start, Rebecca sat up in bed feeling groggy and confused and looked at the pillow next to her. But it was empty, Charles had gone to visit his mother the previous day. They had spoken on the phone but he had returned home late and they had not seen each other. He hadn't made any more reference to their future life together and Rebecca hadn't been brave enough to bring up the subject. He had said he wanted them to think about their future once Willow Court was finished, so Rebecca decided that once Sarah's wedding was over and the weight of expectation had been lifted from her shoulders, he would return to his thoughts about them committing to each other. She shivered, even though the day was already warm. Charles was right, life would get much easier once a certain building company were out of her life and sliding out of bed she headed for the shower and another day.

She went over to Willow Court a little later than normal, taking her time in the shower, her head full of thoughts. She had presumed that if she married Charles he would be happy to move into her house but what if he didn't want to? He had a very nice house of his own, the one he had shared with his wife for many years before she died. Would he be happy to leave it behind when he married someone else? Or would he want to stay in the place that held so many happy memories? Would it be fairer to find a new house that meant nothing to either of them and create their own memories? Rebecca grimaced. There were so many things to take into account, not least of which was that Charles hadn't actually proposed as yet. Maybe it wasn't such a good idea after all, wondered Rebecca. And if Charles didn't propose, then what did it matter anyway and refusing to give any more time to such disturbing thoughts she climbed in the car and set off.

The site was busy as usual and as she walked into the hallway she had the distinct impression of more space. A lot of the piles of materials had disappeared. There were still tools everywhere and the whole area sat under six inches of dust. But there were definitely spaces appearing, identified by the almost clean outlines on the floor and if she stood very still and tilted her head to one side, she could feel a definite air of excitement drifting along the halls and down the staircase.

'Hi Mum,' grinned Sarah, book under her arm as always. 'The upstairs bedrooms have been signed off and the bathrooms just need a tiny bit more work so we've nearly finished!'

Rebecca hugged her daughter impulsively. 'You've worked so hard my darling, I'm very proud of you.'

But Sarah shook her head. 'No harder than you – or Luke or Drew. In fact, if it wasn't for all Luke's help I wouldn't have known where to start.'

Ah yes, Luke. Another case of builder lust, wondered Rebecca?

'But we're getting there and Luke said that by tomorrow the upstairs will be empty of builders and anything remotely resembling a bucket of plaster.'

Most of the rooms had been replastered but there had been too much dust and dirt in the air to really get to grips with any serious decorating and Rebecca knew that her daughter was desperate to start filling the rooms with the beautiful furniture that had been measured and chosen weeks ago and was just waiting to be rehomed.

'And you?' she asked.

'Me?'

'Are you able to remember that this is all about your wedding and be as excited as any bride should be?'

There was a blank look on Sarah's face that spoke volumes to Rebecca.

'To be honest, I do forget that I'll get married here,' Sarah began slowly and honestly. 'I want Willow Court to be amazing so that anyone who visits will want to have their wedding here. I want it to be any bride's dream location but I do forget that it's already mine.'

She looked around the dusty reception area and the carved wooden staircase rising upwards. 'It's an amazing place to get married,' she continued with a look of awe on her face. 'And I'll be the first.'

'Exactly! And you should be doing what all other brides do only a few weeks before their wedding. Choosing flowers and canapés and worrying about their hair and nails, not fretting about bathroom flush systems and having sleepless nights thinking about the ideal shape of tables for the dining room.'

'But I love it Mum! The whole thing, worrying about the planning and organisation, getting everything just right and making sure any wedding will go ahead flawlessly – it's the best thing that ever happened to me,' and grinning she walked towards the kitchen already lost in perusal of her book and the number of bottles that could be held in the cellar.

Rebecca watched her daughter walk away thinking that maybe the best thing that had ever happened to her should be Dom asking her to be his wife. But she was hardly one to talk and looking around to make sure she didn't bump into Drew, she slipped out of the hallway and set off upstairs to check on the bedrooms.

It was an hour or so later that she heard a car pull up the gravel driveway and automatically looked out to see what had arrived.

It wasn't a delivery but Dom, climbing out of a silver BMW and stretching himself out as he looked around. Rebecca peered out of the window to see where Sarah was and spotted her sitting on a wall by the chapel. And there was Luke, by her side as usual. They were looking at something Luke was holding, their heads almost touching and Rebecca watched as Dom's gaze found them in the still overgrown garden, staring as they laughed, oblivious to his presence.

Rebecca flew down the steps, catching sight of Drew in a doorway but for once ignoring him as she dashed outside.'

'Dom! How lovely to see you here!' she shouted loudly, making him jump. 'Sarah said you were trying to find the time to pay us a visit. She really wanted to show you how the place is getting on and how hard we've all been working.'

She was still shouting, and a couple of the builders working near the doorway stopped working and stared at each other nervously.

Sarah and Luke both looked up at the noise Rebecca was making and Rebecca's heart plummeted. Because it was very clear, to her at least, that Sarah didn't look particularly excited to see Dom, that Luke looked decidedly unhappy to see Dom and that the two of them looked equally put out at being disturbed.

Sarah recovered first, jumping off the low wall, leaving her book behind as she crossed the gravel. 'Dom! Why didn't you tell me you were coming today?'

She had reached his side and he bent down to kiss her on the lips, his eyes catching Luke's gaze as he did so. He took his time, sliding his arm around Sarah's waist before releasing her mouth.

'I just found a spare hour or so in the day and you keep saying come and visit so I did,' he announced, his voice level even though his eyes were still on Luke rather than Sarah.

'And it's perfect timing,' said Rebecca with forced gaiety in her voice. 'We've got so much finished in the last few days, it's starting to look like the sort of place you would want to have your wedding!' She laughed and winced at the high pitch.

'Sarah, you need to give Dom a tour, show him what all this hard work and time has produced.'

'Of course. Can you spare the time?'

Dom nodded, his eyes now back on Sarah. His suit looking sharp in the bright afternoon light, his tie straight and neat, his blonde hair immaculately combed. He looked every inch a successful young executive. So why was Sarah looking beyond him to Luke still sitting on the wall.

'Of course,' said Dom and Rebecca had a feeling that wild horses wouldn't tear him away right now. 'I want to see where we're going to get married, all the rooms you've described.' He laughed, turning to Rebecca, his voice loud and clear. 'She never stops talking about the place you know. I get the full run down on everything that's happened that day, whose done what, what's going where. Even when we've gone to bed it doesn't stop. Our pillow talk is now about plumbing and plastering!'

Rebecca was looking at Luke, at the sudden darkening of his face and she laughed loudly, deliberately stepping between Sarah and Dom and their view of the wall and its inhabitant.

'And now you can see it for yourself.' She was sweating and for once she didn't think it had anything to do with the heat of the day.

'I want to see the chapel where we'll make our vows,' said Dom looking into Sarah's eyes. 'I want to see the drawing room and the dining room. And of course, I want to see the bridal suite! I need to check out this double bathtub.'

Sarah was blushing and Rebecca saw Luke take a couple of steps forward out of the corner of her eye

'It's wonderful!' Rebecca trilled. 'I wouldn't mind trying it out myself!' and then she blushed even more than Sarah because she was reminded of the very vivid image she'd had of Drew and herself languishing in a sea of scented bubbles.

Dom set off towards the door. 'I can't wait,' he grinned holding Sarah's hand firmly. 'Let's go.'

There was a look exchanged between Sarah and Luke and Rebecca heard the crunch of gravel as Luke crossed the driveway to follow them.

'Luke, I need you to help me out.' Drew's voice was soft but firm, drifting from the doorway where he was listening to the exchange. 'Now is a perfect time, while Sarah shows Dom around.'

For a moment Rebecca wondered if Luke would refuse. His eyes were pinned on Sarah and Dom as they walked away and Rebecca's heart broke at the longing she could see there.

'Luke.' And the spell was broken, Luke's attention was caught by his father's voice and as Rebecca stood looking anxiously at the complicated scene unfolding before her, Drew touched his son on the arm and then guided him firmly away from the house.

Chapter 25

Rebecca sat anxiously on the wall, waiting for Sarah and Dom to finish their tour and for Drew and Luke to reappear, hoping the two events didn't happen at the same time. She heard voices behind her and saw Dom and Sarah walking towards her, still holding hands and looking cheerful.

'You've done an amazing job,' enthused Dom as he walked back to his car. 'It's almost unrecognisable.'

Sarah looked pleased with herself.

'It will be good when it's all over. I don't mean the wedding,' he threw a quick smile at Sarah. 'I just mean all the hard work. When you can come home and relax and not carry on worrying about how many walls need repairing and how many bedrooms you can finish.'

Rebecca had a feeling that Sarah didn't share that sentiment. She was loving every minute of the hustle and bustle and she would probably feel quite lost when all she had to do was manage a successful wedding venue.

'I think we're all looking forward to the hard work being over and getting back to normal,' Rebecca said with feeling. 'It will do us all good.'

Dom nodded, dropping a kiss on Sarah's cheek. 'I'll try not to be too late tonight darling,' he said close to her ear. 'Why don't I bring home a takeaway and we can open a bottle and forget about work for a few hours?' It was a remonstration, albeit gentle and Rebecca could see her daughter taking note.

'That will be lovely,' said Sarah with a determined look. 'Absolutely lovely. And neither of us will talk about work.'

They smiled at each other, in accord, and Rebecca took a step backwards, allowing them a moment before Dom climbed back into his car and wound down the window to wave goodbye.

Sarah watched him make his way down the drive and Rebecca moved forward to stand by her daughter.

'Everything okay?' she asked softly.

'It will be Mum, it will be,' and recovering her book from the wall she strode back into the house, already in work mode.

Moments later Drew and Luke appeared around the side of the house, coming from the direction of the chapel.

Luke looked sulky but Drew was striding ahead, quietly confident as always.

'We were just checking on the chapel,' he announced as he reached Rebecca's side. 'There are just one or two things still on the snagging list but Luke is going to clear those for us and then we can sign it off,' he finished with a cheery smile.

'Right.' Rebecca was watching Luke who was searching the reception area for a glimpse of Sarah. 'That's great, thank you.'

Luke nodded and disappeared and Drew let out a sigh.

'Everything okay?' she asked cautiously.

For a moment Drew watched his son's back before returning to look at Rebecca.

'Mmm. I'm sure it will be okay.'

'They've spent a lot of time in each other's company lately,' Rebecca advised, 'sometimes it becomes difficult to separate what's happening at work with reality. It's easy to get caught up in a fantasy but it doesn't last.'

Realising what she was saying, she blushed bright red as Drew stared at her. 'It will stop as soon as they're not spending every minute of the day together. I mean, they'll both get back to normal and forget what they felt,' she carried on hurriedly.

She was making it sound like a nasty case of measles she thought. And she wasn't sure at this point if she was describing her daughter or herself.

'You think so?'

'Oh yes,' Rebecca nodded fervently. She sincerely hoped so otherwise she was in a great deal of trouble. 'I'm certain.'

Drew looked unconvinced and they both stood for a moment, deep in their own thoughts. Rebecca decided that she needed to see Charles tonight. She needed to remind herself how much she loved him and she needed to make sure he knew how she felt. Perhaps it might make him bring the proposal forward. She hoped that a potential wedding date and a ring on her finger might just help her builder problem.

Drew was still staring at her. 'I'm not altogether convinced,' he was saying with a small smile playing on his lips. 'I think that some feelings are for life, not just for summer,' and he walked away, leaving Rebecca to take a long shuddering breath and wonder what on earth was going on at Willow Court.

Complicated builder.

When Charles appeared later that night, Rebecca was glad to see him. Being careful to avoid any mention of Drew, she told him about Dom's visit to the site and her worries about her daughter's forthcoming wedding.

Charles was sat at the kitchen table nursing a glass of wine as Rebecca put the finishing touches to a lasagne.

'You think Sarah's changed her mind about getting married?'

'No. Not exactly. Well, I really don't know.' Rebecca opened the oven and slid in the lasagne dish. 'I think she's a little confused. This has been her first job and she and Luke have spent so much time together.'

Rebecca and Drew had spent a great deal of time together this summer as well.

'And of course she is very young,' she added hastily. At least no-one could accuse her and Drew of being young.

'I think she may be struggling to forget about work when she gets home at the end of the day. That's why I'm so lucky having you,' she said pointedly. 'I can come home and get it all off my chest and then enjoy the rest of the evening.'

Putting down her oven glove she leaned over to give him a kiss. 'It makes all the difference you know.'

She thought that Charles looked a little relieved at her reassuring words and she carried on. 'That's why I'm looking forward to having Willow Court finished, so we can enjoy more time to ourselves.'

She met his eyes, willing him to say something. Surely a proposal was the last thing she needed right now with Willow Court almost there but not quite and Sarah seemingly unsure about her relationship with Dom and Annabelle straining at the bit to be allowed to make another visit. To throw another potential wedding into the mix was madness. But at least she would know. She could say yes and stop spending so much time during the day wondering if he did intend to ask her to be his wife. She would know for sure that Drew was nothing more than a crush because of course she wouldn't be able to say yes to Charles if she actually felt anything for Drew. And she could greet Daniel and Annabelle with a casual update about her own forthcoming wedding and tell Annabelle that there was absolutely no possibility of Rebecca being left alone and uncared for, because she now had her own relationship. No more macaroni cheese for one and lonely nights in the kitchen. It would be a new start for Rebecca, long promised and finally arrived. Her second chance.

She caught Charles' hand holding it tightly. 'Yes I'm really looking forward to having it all over and done with,' she said firmly. 'Then it will be time for me and you.'

*

The following day, Rebecca decided it was time to approach Sarah about her wedding. Or not. Timing it carefully when there was no-one else under the willow tree, she asked Sarah to join her and they sat on the floor, leaning against the huge trunk and watching damselflies swoop lazily through the air and land on the lily pads.

'When I first saw Willow Court,' began Rebecca, 'I decided that it needed rescuing. I could see how beautiful it had once been and I knew that it deserved to be returned to its former glory. I suppose I would never have even seen it if you and Dom hadn't been planning on getting married, but the minute I walked into the domed room I had a vision of what I wanted to do.'

They could hear the occasional gentle plop as a fish hovered under the surface or an insect hit the water, but there wasn't another sound to be heard.

'The fact that you loved it as much as I did and wanted your wedding here was an encouragement to get things moving as quickly as possible. But what you need to understand is that I would have bought this place anyway. I would have bought it and restored it in exactly the same way, well maybe a little slower,' grinned Rebecca. 'But I would still have bought it. And if you want to have your wedding here, nothing would make me happier.'

She felt Sarah shift uncomfortably by her side and reaching out she took her daughter's hand. 'But if you've changed your mind Sarah, if you've had second thoughts and decide you don't want to marry Dom, or you want to postpone the wedding, or you want to run off to Gretna Green and forget about drawing rooms and bridal toasts and dancing under the dome, I don't mind in the slightest. But it would break my heart if I thought for one moment that you were going ahead with this wedding because you felt you had to. If you get married it needs to be because you want to, want to more than anything else. And if you have doubts or second thoughts, then just say so my darling and whilst we will carry on with Willow Court, we'll simply rub your name out of the diary and forget all about it.'

She realised there were tears running silently down Sarah's cheeks and she pulled her daughter into a tight hug. 'Have you changed your mind darling? Do you want to call off your wedding?'

'No,' wailed Sarah. 'Maybe. I don't know. I'm just so confused'

You and me both thought Rebecca.

'I love Dom, I really love him and he's been absolutely fantastic about the whole renovation thing and me working all the hours I do and rabbiting on about it all the time.'

'But?'

'But I don't really think he understands what I'm doing, how much work we've had to do. He fell asleep the other night when I was explaining how we were having to redo all the plumbing because we were putting ensuite bathrooms in all the bedrooms. I could tell he thought it was really boring.'

Rebecca couldn't really blame him, her own eyes glazed over when Drew was explaining the finer details of the plumbing system and U bends.

'Dom has a job of his own, you've told me how hard he's working. Perhaps you should agree to leave work at work?'

'Oh I know. And I should. But I can talk to Luke about it all day long and he never looks bored or falls asleep!'

'Because it's his job. I bet if you tried to talk to him about florist bouquets and how many canapes you should organise per head and how many glasses of wine you should allocate per guest, his eyes would start to close.'

'Maybe,' Sarah said reluctantly.

'So are you telling me you don't want to get married to Dom because of your feelings about Luke?' asked Rebecca carefully.

'No! Of course not! I don't have any feelings for Luke. Not those kind of feelings. He's a friend, a really good friend and it's so easy to talk to him. He understands what's happening here and how I feel. We've become close, but that's all.'

Denial was not going to sort this out, thought Rebecca.

'I love Dom. I just spend a lot of time with Luke and I sometimes wish that Dom would talk to me like Luke does and … and that we could discuss the building work and …' she was running dry and Rebecca bit her lip as she heard the confusion in Sarah's voice.

'But Dom isn't a builder is he? He's an account executive for a marketing firm and if you wanted to talk about segments and returns and spread, he would probably stay wide awake, but you would be bored.'

'Maybe.'

'Do you listen to everything Dom tells you about his day at work?'

Sarah wriggled uncomfortably under her mother's gaze. 'Actually, he's really good about leaving work at work. He doesn't spend every night telling me about everything he did that day because ….'

'Because?'

'Because he said it's boring,' sighed Sarah.

There was a moments silence.

'I love Dom.'

Rebecca wondered who she was trying to convince.

'I don't have any feelings other than friendship for Luke. I want to marry Dom.'

'Are you sure?'

'Yes, very sure. I think I'm tired and a little confused. After all, you were the one who said I should be thinking about flowers and champagne and face packs and not worrying about all this building work. I just need to get it all finished and then I'll feel much better about the whole thing. I'm getting married,' she finished with determination. 'I want to get married to Dom.'

Kissing her mother, she jumped up and wandered back to the house leaving Rebecca to watch the lake and wonder what kind of magic Willow Court was casting over them this summer and if they really would be able to return to their orderly, planned lives once the building was restored. She sincerely hoped so because the alternative was chaos!

Chapter 26

Rebecca drove towards Willow Court her mind overflowing with thoughts. She had been to Parklands to visit Gwen and bring her up to date with the renovations but had deliberately not mentioned her misgivings regarding Sarah and her forthcoming wedding. Neither had she mentioned her own worrying reaction whenever Drew appeared in a doorway. She had enthused about her relationship with Charles, which was the one uncomplicated thing in her life but then had fallen silent as she wondered again whether she had misunderstood his intention to propose when Willow Court was finished. The effect had been a rather strained visit and Gwen had looked at her quizzically as they said goodbye.

'Anything wrong dear?' she had asked gently.

'No. Not at all. It's just busy, that's all.' And difficult, and confusing.

Gwen had smiled and patted her daughter's hand, not at all convinced but wise enough not to push and they had kissed and said goodbye.

Pulling into the driveway Rebecca raised her eyes at the activity by the front door as men and vans gathered and an awful lot of loading and general shouting was being done. She picked her way through mounds of tools and bags and men and had just reached the front door when Sarah came bursting out grinning widely.

'Mum! About time, how's granny? We've been waiting for you.'

Rebecca walked round a man carrying scaffolding planks to one of the vans. 'What's going on?'

Sarah stood in the doorway clutching her black book to her chest as Drew appeared at her shoulder.

'We've finished!' she declared dramatically.

Rebecca raised her eyebrows. She hadn't visited willow Court for a couple of days but the last time she had inspected the work, completion still looked to be a way off.

'Well,' Sarah modified, 'the building work is finished. Except for Brian. And the kitchen. But most of the work has been done and Drew is moving the team off site now.'

'Off site? They're leaving?' Rebecca turned to Drew in panic. 'You're leaving! But ....'

'Relax Bec, this is a good thing!'

Rebecca was struggling to see the good in Drew's team leaving her renovation before it was finished but she bit her lip and let him carry on.

'Sarah is right. The building work is finished. Even Brian only needs a few more days. And most of the work in the kitchen has been done, we're just waiting for the new units and Luke and I will fit those when they arrive.'

Rebecca frowned. 'But it didn't look finished last time I was here. It looked like it needed a lot of work and …'

Drew stepped forward and he took Rebecca's arm, guiding her towards the front door. 'It needs a major clear out and a really good clean, and that's hard to do when the place is full of bodies. When you get to this stage, the fewer people you have around the better it is. Believe me Bec, we've finished all the building work,' and reaching the door he pushed her gently forwards.

Now that the pallets of sand and cement and piles of wood and tins had disappeared, Rebecca could see the reception hall for the first time in many months. It had been repaired, replastered, repanelled and looked as good as new. It was a huge space with the central staircase sweeping upwards and a line of doors on either side of the hallway. The desk that Rebecca had stood in front of on her very first visit, had been returned and although it now looked far too small for the grandeur of the space, it gave the room a sense of purpose. The huge windows at either side of the door let in the morning light and despite everything being covered in several inches of dust and grime, Rebecca could see for the first time how beautiful it was going to look.

'Remember what you told me,' came a voice close to her ear and Rebecca fought the urge to lean back against Drew's substantial chest as he continued. 'That this would be a grand entrance hall, the sort you would expect to find in a country house. Warm polished wood gleaming everywhere, shiny brass on all the doors, full of light and grandeur, somewhere that took your breath away the minute you walked in the door.'

Rebecca looked up at the newly plastered ceiling and the electric wires hanging down waiting for the chandelier. She looked around at the wooden panels that reached half way up the walls, all in need of a great deal of Mr Sheen before they shone with warmth and colour, at the grimy walls that were covered with track marks of dust and plaster splashes. She looked down at the floor which was grey with the dirt. The doors were all closed, the brass plates tarnished and grimy and the desk was covered in tins of varnish and paint brushes.

'Oh yes,' she sighed. 'It looks perfect.'

Clever, clever builder.

They wandered through the rest of the house to admire all the finished rooms. The reception rooms, the bridal suite and three other bedrooms had been completed. The kitchen had been extended to incorporate two small larders and a washroom to make a wonderful large space, waiting for the new units and work surfaces Rebecca and Sarah had chosen a few weeks earlier, together with the industrial sized ovens, a bank of microwaves and a couple of immense 10 burner hobs which would be adequate for any wedding party.

There was dust everywhere. It hung in the air and covered every surface and as they wandered the now empty corridors Rebecca realised why Drew had sent his team onto the next job. A few days hard cleaning and

Willow Court would be finished – or at least stage one would be finished. There was the small matter of turning the freshly renovated building into a magical place that would make any bride smile with delight.

Rebecca realised that Sarah, Drew and Luke were all anxiously waiting for her to speak and she turned to face them with a face devoid of emotion. 'So this is it?'

Drew's face tightened and Sarah gave a little squeak of anxiety.

'This is Willow Court finished?'

'I gave you what you asked for Rebecca,' answered Drew. 'This is exactly as per your plans.'

Rebecca nodded, turning away to look around the reception area where they had returned.

'I see,' she murmured. 'That's probably why ....' she spun back round to face them all, keeping her face straight, '... I absolutely love it!'

Her face broke into a wide grin. 'It's perfect! I love it.'

She saw relief flood three anxious faces as they slumped against each other before relaxing, grins breaking out.

'Mum!'

'Good God Bec I was really worried for a minute.'

'Unfair!' shouted Luke.

Rebecca walked forwards, holding her hand out towards Drew. 'I can't thank you enough,' she whispered. 'I really couldn't have asked for anyone who understood what I wanted more than you did. Thank you Drew, from the bottom of my heart thank you.'

Excellent builder.

Drew took her hand and then pulled her into a hug, his arms sliding round her body as he pulled her into his grip, burrowing his face into her hair. 'It's been a pleasure,' he said gruffly, squeezing her gently, 'an absolute pleasure.'

Briefly Rebecca wondered at the hardness of his chest, at how very comfortable she felt in his arms. She imagined just staying there, using his strength to support her in everything she did. She pushed the image away and imagined instead going home and telling Charles that Willow Court was almost done, that they would have more time to spend together, nothing to distract them from moving on with their relationship. She imagined the pleasure in Charles's eyes and she fantasised about him drawing a small box from his pocket and flipping it open to reveal a ring as he asked her to marry him. Sighing she stepped backwards, feeling suddenly bereft as Drew's arms left her body.

'Oh no!'

Reluctantly she pulled her eyes away from Drew and towards Sarah who was clutching her phone. 'It's the cleaning company. They've got their dates wrong. I told them we would definitely want them this week but they've got us down for the first week in September. After my wedding date!' She looked around the dusty hall in horror. 'I can't get married with it looking like this! We'll never get another company in at such short notice. I'm so sorry Mum, I've let you down.'

She looked devastated, her mouth trembling as she read the message on her phone from the industrial cleaning company.

'Don't be silly,' Rebecca remonstrated firmly. 'I'm amazed that they were the only company to let us down. Normally something much more serious goes wrong with any renovation work.'

'But what are we going to do? I've even told Annabelle that we would be ready to start decorating and furnishing this weekend.' She looked guilty. 'Sorry, I hadn't gotten around to telling you that yet. She phoned and I was so excited at having the building work finished I sort of blurted it out. She and Dad want to visit as soon as possible to have a look.'

Rebecca grimaced. She knew it couldn't be avoided but another visit from Daniel and Annabelle was not something on her to do list.

'And I sort of said that it would be okay for them to stay with you. Sorry,' she added as Rebecca groaned.

'Annabelle said that you'd mentioned a hotel but she was sure you hadn't meant she should stay in one and all I said was okay and she took it to mean she could stay and …' Sarah tailed off, looking apologetically at her mother. 'Sorry.'

'It's okay,' lied Rebecca, 'I'm sure I'll cope.'

'But what are we going to do about this place? How am I going to get any cleaners in before the weekend and what will …'

'We'll do it ourselves.'

Sarah blinked. 'Really?'

'Of course. It would be nice to get a company in to do it for us but it's only cleaning. We can do it ourselves.' Rebecca looked around at the reception area, gulping slightly. It was a huge job but needs must.

'We'll help,' offered Drew.

'Oh no! I mean you don't have to and …'

'We'll help.' He held up a hand to stop Rebecca's protests. 'It's part of a builder's job to clean up after themselves. Me and Luke were going to stick around for a couple more days anyway to get the kitchen finished so we'll help. It's not an easy job,' he warned, 'and you'll end up as dirty as the house. But if we all muck in,' he grinned, 'no pun intended, we can get it done in a couple of days.'

'Oh thank you,' gushed Sarah, 'thank you, thank you.'

Rebecca was silent. She had just worked herself up to the idea that Drew would be leaving. That her heart would start behaving itself again and that she would be able to look into Charles' eyes each evening without that tiny feeling of guilt that sometimes joined them.

'Are you sure?'

'Absolutely!'

She nodded, it was a huge job and there was no doubt that it would be far easier with a few extra pairs of hands.

'Then thank you, again,' she accepted.

They got started, opening every window as they swept the dusty rooms, wiping walls and surfaces, sweeping again, wiping more walls and sweeping once more. They coughed as dust and dirt clogged their throat and got into their eyes. They wrapped cloths around their faces to keep the worst of it at bay and half way through the day they all walked down to the lake to plunge their feet into the cool water and try to inhale some fresh air before they carried on. They lay in the grass and relished the dust free air, but not for long as they all trooped back to the house to reunite with their sweeping brushes.

'It's never ending,' complained Sarah at the end of a long hard day when everything looked significantly better but was still far from clean and Luke grinned.

'Builder's dust is the worst kind. You think you've got it all and then it settles again and you're back where you started.'

'Trust you to have special dust,' mocked Sarah flicking him with the duster she was holding.

He retaliated by splashing her with some of the water from a nearby bucket and Rebecca couldn't help but smile as Sarah's shrieks filled the air.

'We probably need to leave it a while to settle,' Drew announced, looking upwards at the thousands of tiny dust motes in the air. 'Then we'll get back to it tomorrow.'

Rebecca wasn't sorry to hear that they could go home. She wanted a shower. She wanted to wash all the dirt from her hair and the grime from her skin. She nodded in relief.

'So we'll meet back here tomorrow to finish up?'

Drew nodded. Sarah and Luke were racing through the downstairs rooms, flicking water at each other and shouting with laughter.

'It could be our last day,' he said casually.

Rebecca didn't answer. She watched her daughter dive out of the drawing room with Luke in hot pursuit trying to wring a cloth down the back of her neck. It could be the best thing for all of them, she thought sadly.

'Luke and I will fit the kitchen as some point but if we get the cleaning finished tomorrow, that's it. The last day we'll work together.'

Rebecca had imagined feeling so relieved when this moment came. It meant that things were going ahead as planned and that Willow Court was on track. So why did she feel so sad?

She nodded, looking at Drew's feet rather than into his eyes.

'It will feel really strange not seeing you every day Bec.'

Rebecca bit her lip. She was hoping it would feel much better not seeing Drew every day.

'I'll miss you,' he offered.

And she would miss him, until she forgot about his tanned face smiling at her each day as she arrived on site, the strong arms he put around her when she needed support and the curious jumping of her heart when she caught a glimpse of him out of the corner of her eye. But she would forget and then her life would return to normal and her builder lust would be over. She hoped.

'But we've got tomorrow,' he grinned. 'And you do look very sexy in that outfit!'

She looked down at her shorts, dirty bare legs and the walking boots she often wore on the building site. Her shirt was unbuttoned as far as she dare and her hair was tied on top of her head with a length of green twine. Last time she'd caught sight of herself in a mirror, she'd had a smear of dirt down one cheek and her skin was several shades lighter than normal due to the covering of dust.

She grinned. 'You'll be okay if I wear the same tomorrow? It won't put you off the cleaning?'

Drew walked towards her, wiping the smudge from her cheek and standing so close Rebecca could feel his breath on her face. 'Unfortunately I find you distracting whatever you wear Bec,' he murmured. 'I can't see tomorrow will be any different.'

Naughty builder.

Chapter 27

The next day started in another blaze of sunshine with temperatures already high even as the morning commute got underway. Grumpy motorists lined the road with windows wound down, trying to get the odd wisp of fresh air into their cars. Birds were sitting listlessly in trees berating Nature for the heatwave and on the TV, the weather forecasters explained why Britain was still sweltering under an extended period of sunshine and why everyone should be grateful because it would soon be over.

Rebecca pulled on some clean shorts and a T-shirt. She resisted the urge to go through her wardrobe for something a little more flattering as Drew's words drummed in her head. She brushed her hair and tied it up, leaving a few stray curls to float around her face which she told herself was definitely not for Drew's benefit and she resisted the urge to get her lipstick from her dressing table, because she certainly hadn't bothered any other day she had wandered around Willow Court inspecting building work and poking into dingy corners and dusty alcoves.

She thought about the previous evening. Drew had been teasing, she told herself firmly. He had been teasing her because she had looked a fright and he was relived the end was nigh. The goose bumps on her arms had been because the sun had finally lost some of its heat and a slight breeze had appeared. She had imagined the look in his eye because she couldn't explain it and she didn't want to think about it. And she certainly wasn't going to spend any more time contemplating the shiver that had gone down her spine at the sound of his mellow voice saying how distracting he found her. Of course she was distracting, she always wanted to know what he was doing, when he would finish, if he was on budget. She was distracting because when she was there he couldn't get on with his work and he would be glad to see the back of her. That was all, nothing more.

So Rebecca got ready for another day of hard cleaning and picking up her car keys she left the house. Seconds later she dashed back in, taking the stairs two at a time as she flew into her bedroom to exchange the T-shirt for a gingham blouse before adding a quick swipe of lipstick and a spray of perfume and telling herself that it was a momentous occasion today and needed a little more effort.

It was another long, hot day and the four of them worked tirelessly cleaning Willow Court. They spoke little, their throats hoarse with the amount of dust in the air, they drank bottle after bottle of water and cleaned like demons. Mid-afternoon, Rebecca decided she could see the difference. Suddenly the dust they were moving wasn't landing back on the surfaces within minutes. It was disappearing and they were able to move onto the mile upon mile of wooden panelling. Later in the afternoon the Mr Sheen came out and in addition to cleaning, the dusting and polishing started. Not only was Willow Court looking dirt free, it was starting to shine. The upstairs bedrooms were spotless. The windows were still wide open to let in the summer air and the smell of lemon polish and fresh meadows overtook the smell of plaster and paint. The bathrooms gleamed and the brass fitting on every door was polished until it sang.

The downstairs floors were washed and scrubbed until they could see their faces reflected and everywhere started to sparkle.

Evening came but no-one made any suggestion to go home and Rebecca was in the domed room, giving the floor a final sweep. Brian still had his scaffolding in the corner and without his hunched figure in situ, Rebecca could see how close to finishing he was. The cracked windows had been replaced, the floor by the bay window had been repaired and even the walls were now smooth. The chandelier had been taken down, cleaned professionally and hung back in place and as the sky became darker it cast its flickering light over the entire room. The windows were open and the fresh evening air was starting to drift inside and Rebecca couldn't help but think back to the photo she had found with the young couple dancing, long white voile curtains fluttering in harmony at the windows, no thought for anyone but each other as they twirled across the wooden floor.

Her back ached, her eyes stung, her nails were ragged and her fingers raw with scrubbing and cleaning. But she couldn't remember the last time she had felt so content. They were all exhausted and about to grind to a halt but another half an hour and it would be done.

Drew had greeted her exactly as he always had, smiling widely and saying a cheerful hello. There had been nothing unusual in his manner as he had outlined the work they needed to do that day and allocated jobs and rooms to them all. Rebecca had been relieved. She was right, he had been teasing her. There was no edge, no lingering glances. Just Drew the builder trying to get the job finished so he could leave. She told herself that it was good to know that nothing had changed, that Drew was the same as always and the previous night had been a trick of the light, a teasing comment and nothing more. Although that didn't account for why her heart felt distinctly empty and why her eyes still swept every room she entered for a glimpse of him

She was staring out of the window, admiring the way the light from the room drifted across the stone terrace and wondering if she had the energy to drive home, when the sweeping brush she was holding was taken gently from her hands and an arm slid around her shoulders.

'Enough,' said that lovely deep voice. 'We've done all we can Bec. Time to stop.'

She looked around at the clean, softly lit room and agreed. There was still lots of work to do at Willow Court, but the hard graft was over. And Drew was right, it was time to stop.

Clever builder.

Blearily Rebecca peered into the hall. 'Where is Sarah? And Luke?'

'Getting something to eat and you need something too. Come on.'

He took her by the hand and far too tired to analyse the intense feeling of satisfaction she felt at the touch of his fingers, Rebecca allowed herself to be guided down towards the lake. Sniffing the air she realised that was not the smell of a summer's evening she could detect but the delicious aroma of pizza and her stomach growled loudly. Sarah and Luke were already there, laid out under the tree in the grass which was already starting to collect a little dew and was wonderfully soggy and cool. On the picnic bench were 2 large pizza boxes next to bottles of coke and the two of them were munching happily in silence.

'I ordered it when I realised we were nearly done,' Drew told her, pushing her towards the bench. 'We all need to eat, grab some and enjoy.'

The food was like nectar and Rebecca said nothing more until she had eaten two pieces and the hunger had started to fade from her stomach.

'What a good idea,' she sighed happily, grabbing a third slice and pouring some coke into a mug.

'Mmm,' agreed Sarah rubbing her stomach and laying back. 'I'm so tired. I could actually sleep here.'

Drew smiled and stretched contentedly as he contemplated another slice. 'We deserve it. We all did an incredible job getting that house cleaned and ready, congratulations to you all!' and raising his coke high in the air he tilted it in Rebecca's direction.

Sarah sighed. 'I must admit, there were a few moments when I thought we would never reach this point.'

'Like when the drawing room ceiling came down?' asked Luke

'Yeah, and when Tony's shovel flew through the bedroom window.'

'And the chapel door wouldn't go back on after we'd repointed the doorway!'

'And when the plumbers left and everything started leaking.'

'And Chris had given the wrong address to the delivery van and we spent two days waiting for the plasterboard to arrive.'

Sarah and Luke were rolling around laughing as the horrors of the build, now slipping into history, suddenly became funny.

For several minutes they sat and discussed the highs and lows of the last few months and what had kept them going. They cleared away the pizza boxes and wandered back to the house, Sarah and Luke arguing half-heartedly about who should empty the overflowing kitchen bins before deciding to do the job together. And suddenly Rebecca and Drew were alone, standing at the foot of the staircase where Rebecca intended to have a large plant winding its green leaves around the mellow oak of the handrail. The air smelled of polish and warmth and Rebecca knew that in a few weeks this space would look exactly how she had imagined. She was tired but happy, replete on pizza and coke and overwhelmingly relaxed after a pleasant hour.

'So, this is it.'

Drew was standing next to her, watching as she gazed around the building she had come to love.

Her eyes swivelled to his. 'I suppose it is.'

'You'll see us again of course,' Drew carried on, 'but for now, it's goodbye.'

Rebecca's heart was hammering so loudly she wondered if Drew could hear it.

'That seems very final,' she offered. And that was a good thing, she told herself firmly. No more fantasies about the hunky builder, no more work place attachments which wouldn't last.

'I suppose it does. We can keep in touch. Have the occasional coffee, even a meal out?'

Rebecca was finding it hard to speak. Her heart had leaped at the thought but her head was telling her it was a very bad idea.

'I mean, if you would like to?'

'That would be lovely.' What was she saying? She needed this to stop, to end so she could enjoy being in love with Charles, to marry Charles.

Drew nodded solemnly. 'I would like that too. I meant what I said the other day Bec, I will really miss not seeing you every day.'

And Rebecca would miss him, far more than he could ever realise.

'Oh I'm sure once you get started with your next job you'll soon forget me.'

Like she was hoping she would forget him.

'I don't think so.'

Was it her imagination or had he moved a little closer. There was no room between them. All she had to do was sway slightly forward and they would be touching. What a tempting thought.

'I think forgetting you might be very hard Rebecca Miles.'

'Really?'

Her voice sounded faint, far away.

'Indeed. I've grown quite attached to you, despite all the grief you've given me.'

He was joking, maybe she should laugh. Maybe she should stop looking at his lips as he was speaking and laugh at how funny he was.

Funny builder.

'You have?'

'I have.'

Rebecca wasn't quite certain which one of them swayed, all she knew was that suddenly they were in each other's arms and this was not a hug of support; a 'well done after a long day' hug, a 'glad you're my friend' hug.

She was pressed against Drew's chest, her arms around his neck as he ran one hand through the untidy tendrils of hair at the nape of her neck before tilting her face so he could kiss her upturned lips.

Rebecca remembered thinking briefly, very briefly, that this was not a good idea at all before she decided instead how wonderful it felt to be doing exactly this. Her head was swimming as he pulled her even closer and she couldn't help the tiny little gasp that escaped her as his lips explored every inch of her own and she felt as though she were about to melt in his arms. She felt his grip relax and realising it was about to stop, her heart cried out no even as her head said it was for the best. Reluctantly she let her arms slide away from Drew's neck as his lips left hers and he took a small step backwards.

'Sorry,' he said. He took another step back, hitting the newel post at the foot of the staircase. 'I'm sorry, I shouldn't have done that.'

Had he done it wondered Rebecca? She thought it might have been a joint thing, but she was happy to let him take any blame that was being apportioned.

'It was unfair of me, I know you and Charles are … Well I know about you and Charles.'

Ah yes, thought Rebecca. Charles. She seemed to have momentarily forgotten about Charles.

She peeped at Drew from under her lashes. Was he saying he was sorry he had kissed her, or that he was sorry because he knew about Charles and yet he had still kissed her?

They stood in awkward silence. Rebecca wondered if she should say she was sorry too. Or whether she should just kiss him again. She saw a movement outside and caught sight of Sarah and Luke. They were coming from the direction of the chapel, nowhere near the bins and as she watched she noticed that Luke had his arm around her daughter.

She turned away, she could only cope with one problem at a time and right now Drew's presence and her overwhelming need to step back into his arms was taking precedence. Willow Court was certainly weaving its magic tonight, she thought, watching Drew nibble on his lower lip. Would any of them find their way back to normality.

'It's not your fault Drew,' she said impulsively. 'I wanted you to kiss me.'

He didn't look surprised and Rebecca wondered if she hadn't hidden her feelings quite as well as she had hoped over the last few weeks.

'I mean, I was sort of hoping that you would. Well, at least I wasn't unhappy that you did. So, don't be sorry.'

Drew sighed, half smiling. 'I'm not sorry I kissed you Bec,' he said in a low voice that had Rebecca's blood scurrying through her veins. 'I enjoyed it every bit as much as I thought I would.'

'You've thought about kissing me before?'

'Many times.'

Oh dear, thought Rebecca. Her knees had gone very wobbly.

'Oh.'

'I'm sorry because I work for you and it's unprofessional to start kissing your employer.'

Was it, wondered Rebecca? Was it in the contract they had both signed – no kissing until the job was over? Well the job was over, almost. Did that mean they were free to start kissing? Something else she would check with Emma, once her builders had finished did she feel it was okay to end the job with a kiss?

'Well if I don't mind then …' Rebecca shrugged

'And of course there's Charles.'

Yes, she kept forgetting about Charles and she was fairly certain that he would definitely mind about the kissing. In fact, she was certain Charles would mind about the evening in general and she was being very unfair on him. She knew this was an infatuation with Drew, a temporary feeling of overwhelming lust that would disappear with him but that wasn't a conversation she really wanted to have with Charles.

'Yes of course,' she said, trying to organise her thoughts a little more. 'Of course it is unfair on Charles,' she said a little more firmly. 'And I do love him.'

Drew nodded. 'Do you?'

Rebecca stared in horror. 'Of course I do.'

'Right. It's just that when we were kissing you didn't seem to be thinking about Charles and I wondered …'

Rebecca blushed. 'I wasn't thinking about Charles,' she confessed, 'but I should have been. Because I love him.'

Then why were you kissing Drew, a voice in her head asked?

'Of course I'm very fond of you as well,' she added. 'I mean, we've spent a lot of time together recently and I have …'

Should she describe the feelings she had whenever she saw him? Maybe not.

'I think you are…'

Drew was not helping. He was standing very still waiting to hear exactly what she thought and Rebecca struggled on.

'I think that we….'

'Are you ready to go Mum?'

Whirling round in relief Rebecca found her daughter and Luke standing in the doorway.

'Absolutely!' Maybe that was a little too enthusiastic. 'Yes, let's go darling, I'm worn out and ready for bed.' Her cheeks were flushed and she was glad of the darkness that had now fallen. She realised that Luke and Sarah were standing with a great deal of space between them and that despite her words, Sarah's' eyes weren't meeting her own.

She sighed. Maybe hers wasn't the only illicit kiss stolen that evening.

'Thank you again Drew,' she said quite formally, reaching out her hand to shake his. 'And you too Luke. I know we'll see each other again but this feels like the appropriate time to say goodbye.'

Wonderful, reliable builders.

Did she detect a slight wince from Sarah?

'So, goodbye, thank you and good luck with … well everything,' and grabbing her daughter's arm she walked briskly towards the door. It was indeed time to say goodbye to A & L Builders and refusing to allow herself a last glance at Drew she hustled Sarah outside, neither of them speaking as they walked back to their cars and left Willow Court.

Chapter 28

Rebecca was having a dream. She was sweeping but the dust kept reappearing even heavier than before. She looked down at her feet and the dust and dirt was now covering her shoes. She swept a little faster but it made no difference and the swirling dirt was now up to her ankles and she was struggling to walk. She noticed that Drew was in the doorway. He was lounging against the frame smiling at her and holding out his hand. But she couldn't reach him, the dust was getting deeper and heavier and she couldn't move her feet anymore. Then she noticed that Charles was standing behind Drew and he was watching them both from the darkness of the corridor. Rebecca opened her mouth to call to him but she couldn't speak, her throat was clogged with dirt and as she tried to call out his name a cloud of dust erupted from her mouth, swirling in front of her face and clouding her view. There was a banging noise and she was trying to see if it was Drew or Charles but now she couldn't see anything but clouds of dust swirling round her face with a loud banging noise hammering from somewhere close by.

She jerked awake, sweating and anxious, instinctively wiggling her feet to see if she could move. She coughed but her throat was clear and although her mouth was dry, it was free of dust. She fell back on the pillow only to sit upright as the banging noise started again. Confused, Rebecca looked around the bedroom. Charles hadn't stayed over last night, she was in the house by herself so what on earth was that noise. Then the bell rang out and with a gasp Rebecca realised the banging was someone at the door, an insistent someone at the door.

Jumping out of bed and pulling on a dressing gown, Rebecca glanced in a mirror and winced at her hair sticking out at all angles and her pale face. Looking at her watch she saw it was 9:30, way past the point when she would normally wake up. But the last few days had been busy. She had suggested to Sarah that they work from home for a few days as the decorators swept into Willow Court wielding paintbrushes and furniture deliveries were organised. Sarah began to speak to catering firms, florists and wedding shops to begin promoting their business. She had attended a wedding fair a few weeks previously and had arrived home armed with contacts after doing an amazing job creating a lot of interest in their relatively small venture. And now was the time to start pulling all these strings into place and they had spent the last few days sorting out the fine detail of Willow Court. Neither of them said anything but time away from Willow Court and more importantly Drew and Luke, seemed important right now. Rebecca had caught her daughter staring out of the window lost in thought on more than one occasion and suspected that something had happened between Sarah and Luke that was causing some heart searching. But they had both smiled bravely and got on with the job, neither mentioning the reason for their frequent sighs and daydreams.

Walking down the stairs to the sound of more impatient banging on the door and the bell pealing out demanding attention, Rebecca rubbed her eyes and yawned. She could have done with another hour in bed this morning.

Opening the door, she stared in amazement at Daniel who had his hand raised to bang on the door once more and Annabelle who was clucking with impatience next to him.

'Bloody Hell Bec,' snapped Daniel, glaring at her as he started to haul bags into the hallway. 'What on earth kept you? Were you still in bed?'

He looked at her dressing gown with disapproval and pushed her out of the way so he could bring in more of Annabelle's matching luggage.

'What on earth?'

'Becky!' Annabelle slid in around Daniel and the cases sending an air kiss in her direction. 'We were starting to worry!'

'Worry? Why? What are you doing …'

Her phone rang and blearily Rebecca grabbed it from her dressing gown pocket.

'What?'

'Mum! Oh Mum I totally forgot to tell you yesterday, Dad phoned to say he and Annabelle would be arriving today. They want to see Willow Court.'

Rebecca sighed, counting the cases as Daniel kept heaving them through the door. 'So I gather,' she said wryly.

'They've already arrived haven't they?'

'They certainly have.'

'Sorry. It was when you'd gone to visit Gran and you left your phone at home. I meant to tell you but – I forgot.'

Rebecca wanted to tell her daughter it was okay and it wasn't a problem. But looking at the mounting luggage and listening to Daniel's mutterings about people who stayed in bed and showed a lack of care for visitors, she was finding it hard.

'Right, well we'll come over to Willow Court as soon as I've got dressed,' she mumbled. 'Er, is Drew there?'

'No. They've fitted the kitchen though, it looks great, loads of space. And the furniture has already started arriving. It's quite exciting!'

Rebecca wished she could drum up a little bit of excitement herself but was failing and saying goodbye to Sarah she closed the door as Daniel brought in the final case.

'Is that all?' she asked sarcastically as with a grunt he stacked the last one at the foot of the stairs.

'Yes. Weren't you expecting us?' asked Daniel grumpily, still annoyed at having to wait on the doorstep.'

'No.'

He stared. 'But I phoned yesterday and Sarah said she would tell you.'

'Well she forgot,' Rebecca was in no mood to be taken to task by her ex-husband.

'But Annabelle had already spoken to you and said she wanted to see Willow Court as soon as it was ready.'

'And I told her I thought a hotel would be a good idea.'

'A Hotel! A HOTEL! You want us to spend the next 4 weeks at a hotel? Well that's charming I must say. So much for family.'

'Well we're not family any more are we Daniel?' snapped Rebecca. 'And I don't see why you can't stay at a hotel like any other ex-husband would. Just a minute – four weeks?'

'Becky darling,' Annabelle's voice drifted down the staircase.

'It's Bec!' shouted both Daniel and Rebecca at the same time, causing Annabelle to stop mid stair with an expression of surprise.

'What are you doing Annabelle and what do you mean,' demanded Rebecca turning back to Daniel, 'four weeks. You can't stay with me for four weeks.'

'But Rebecca,' interrupted Annabelle, emphasising her name with a slight sniff, 'we can't possibly afford to stay in a hotel for four weeks. I spoke to Sarah and she assured me you would be happy for us to stay here.'

'Well it's not Sarah's house!'

'But I knew you wouldn't dream of putting us to all that expense and Sarah agreed.'

Rebecca glared at her through narrowed eyes. She was certain that Sarah would not have invited her father and Annabelle to stay for four weeks.

'She said,' continued Annabelle firmly,' that you were so kind and generous that she was sure you would welcome us with open arms. After all,' she sniffed again, 'we can't afford that kind of expense can we. Because ….'

'Oh alright!' growled Rebecca. She really didn't want to embark on another discussion about how mean she had been to Daniel with their divorce settlement.

'But I'm still very busy with Willow Court so you'll have to look after yourselves. I'm not here to cook and clean for you,' she said firmly.

'Oh of course. After all, we're not visiting are we. We're spending time with family.'

Rebecca closed her eyes. She was far too tired to start this again.

'Whatever,' she started wearily, turning towards the stairs in search of a shower. 'The spare room is …'

'Already made up! I know, I've just been up to check'

Rebecca stopped, Annabelle had arrived and gone straight upstairs to check out the spare room. Oh this was going to be hard, she thought, so very hard.

'You see,' tinkled Annabelle, 'I told you that would become our room! Our little room whenever we come to stay.'

There would be no more staying, decided Rebecca. Once the wedding was over there would be no more excuses for the two of them to arrive at 9:30 in the morning.

She ignored Anabelle and carried on walking up the stairs only to stop and turn back round.

'Why do you need to stay here for four weeks?' she asked puzzled.

'Why?' Annabelle's eyes were huge as though Rebecca had asked the most ridiculous question in the world. 'Why?'

'Yes Annabelle, why?'

'Because I am getting married. At Willow Court. I am marrying Daniel,' she continued slowly as though Rebecca were a little hard of hearing or slightly stupid, or perhaps both. 'I need to make plans, get everything sorted. I have very high standards and this wedding may be happening at a venue you own Rebecca, but I will still be expecting the very best of everything.' She laughed her tinkly little laugh and it was like a knife entering Rebecca's already aching head. 'I want the perfect wedding in the perfect location. And I will need the next few weeks to make absolutely sure that you can deliver exactly that Rebecca,' and smiling happily Annabelle set off in the direction of the kitchen demanding that Daniel make her one of those delicious little coffees and leaving Rebecca clutching the handrail of the stairs, her heart cold with dread. What had she done?

Chapter 29

When they pulled up at Willow Court, Rebecca couldn't help the glare she gave Sarah. 'You told her she could stay for four weeks?' she whispered angrily. 'Four weeks! How on earth can I cope with her for all that time?'

'I didn't!' answered Sarah defensively. 'She never mentioned four weeks. She just said she was coming to visit. Why does she need that long anyway?'

'Because,' said Rebecca grimly, 'she needs to make sure Willow Court is up to her exacting standards. Standards which cover perfection and little else.'

Sarah's face dropped in alarm. 'Perfection?' she asked nervously.

'That's right, perfection,' and then they had to stop and welcome Daniel and Annabelle as they finished inspecting the car park and approached Willow Court.

Annabelle had a large notebook in her hand, not dissimilar to Sarah's own book except that this was sparkly pink and had a little pencil attached via a length of silver elastic and sporting a bright pink pompom. Rebecca saw her daughter's eyes rest on it, twitching nervously.

'Sarah darling, how lovely to see you!' Annabelle stopped and presented her cheek for a kiss which Sarah obligingly provided.

'Isn't this wonderful? Can you believe it's almost time for our weddings? I was beginning to wonder if Willow Court would ever be ready,' she cast a reproving glance at Rebecca. 'But here we are at last. Have you had your final dress fitting? You must let me see it, maybe we should have checked each other's designs, we don't want to end up with identical dresses do we? Wouldn't that be awful! And what about flowers. I need to double check all the details now I'm here, I know exactly what I want and anything less simply won't do. As for the photographer,' she gave a little shudder, 'don't get me started on how hard it's been to find someone who understands the creative process I want to follow. But it's wonderful that we're doing this together, don't you think?' She linked arms with a rather startled Sarah and hugged her close. 'We can share the experience, isn't that amazing!'

Rebecca thought Sarah looked more overwhelmed than amazed but she had rather less sympathy than usual having had Daniel and his soon to be wife forced on her for the next four weeks.

'Right, shall we get started?'

'Started?'

'I want the full tour Sarah darling. I want to see every room and what miracles you've worked. I'm beyond excited you know but it's still important to remain focused isn't it? Neither of us want a lack of detail to spoil our big day.'

'Well no …'

'So let's have a good look round and see if there are any little tweaks needed. Oh and the party?'

'Party?' asked Rebecca puzzled.

'Sarah mentioned something about a party to celebrate finishing the work.'

Rebecca closed her eyes briefly then opened them to see an apologetic Sarah looking at her.

'Er, yes I did mention it a few weeks ago. It seemed like a good idea at the time,' she directed the apology at Rebecca, 'but I really don't think that …'

'Nonsense! It's an excellent idea. We can test out the facilities before the big day itself and besides, I've already bought a new dress.'

'I don't think we have the time to arrange a party with all the work still to do,' interrupted Rebecca firmly.

'Oh don't worry, I'll organise it all.'

'No!'

'No!'

Both Rebecca and Sarah spoke at the same time, Rebecca's far louder and a touch more aggressive than Sarah's alarmed squeak.

'That's very kind of you Annabelle,' Rebecca dredging up a smile, 'but if there is a party going to happen at Willow Court then I think we should organise it. We don't want anything to interfere with the wedding arrangements.'

'Oh definitely not. Okay, well I'll leave it to you both to set everything up for Saturday.'

'This Saturday?' asked Sarah looking very pale.

'Of course. The perfect time don't you think?' and with a tinkly laugh Annabelle grabbed Sarah's arm and carried on through the front door. 'Now let's get this tour started!'

The pink book and stretchy pencil were opened as Annabelle stood in the centre of the vastly improved reception hall.

'There's no chandelier.'

'I know, it's at the restorers and will be rehung next Tuesday,' Sarah advised.

Annabelle wrote something in her book and carried on looking round.

'Is that the final colour for the walls? What about the colour chart I sent you, didn't you like that luscious red colour that I circled? I thought that would be perfect for these walls, a little more colour than you've put on.'

Sarah nibbled on her lip. 'I think this colour looks lovely,' she offered nervously.

'Mmm, a little washed out don't you think?'

Sarah sent her mother a pleading glance and Rebecca sighed. She had seen Sarah deal with builders, plumbers, electricians and all manner of delivery men over the last few months. She had never doubted herself and had never given in to their demands. Annabelle seemed a step too far for Sarah.

She stepped forward. 'Red is not the right colour for these walls,' she said firmly but pleasantly. 'This is an old country house, it doesn't need red walls.' She looked round at the very soft and mellow buttercream colour that let the depth of the wood shine through and would complement the picture frames they had already chosen and the deep green of the many plants Rebecca wanted to have scattered around the hallway. It was calm and elegant and wouldn't clash with any bridal colour scheme.

Anabelle sniffed doubtfully. 'I would prefer more colour. I would prefer red.'

'But it's not your house Annabelle. It is my business and the walls will not be painted red.'

She could see Sarah's eyes following the conversation like a tennis match, her mouth a little O shape.

Annabelle sniffed and made quite a long entry in her book.

'The desk seems a little inadequate.'

Rebecca nodded. Much as she hated to agree with Annabelle about anything she was right. In the large open space with the pale walls, the desk which Rebecca had originally wanted to keep, looked rather small and plain in the corner.

'A new one is already on order.'

Annabelle nodded and scribbled in her book.

'You've done an amazing job old girl, quite a transformation I have to say.'

Annabelle looked around. 'I suppose it will look okay when it's furnished,' she said doubtfully. 'It needs a little touch of something though, don't you think? It's a bit plain. Oh – cherubs! Lots of cherubs would help! Lovely golden ones. And some gold chairs with red velvet seats,' she added in excitement, 'and a huge mirror somewhere that I …that the bride can stand in front of for an artistic photo shoot.'

Sarah gulped and started to move slowly, inching behind Rebecca.

'I did send you some amazing posts from Pinterest. There was a beautiful one of a castle decorated entirely in pink and silver. Did you see it? Wasn't it beautiful?' demanded Annabelle.

'No.'

'What? You didn't like it?'

It had been tacky, pretentious and quite out of keeping for a lovely old building like Willow Court, but Annabelle looked so crestfallen that Rebecca bit her lip.

'It didn't go with the feel we wanted for Willow Court,' she said diplomatically.

'But there will be pictures on the wall and lots of chairs and occasional tables scattered around,' offered Sarah in consolation. 'And we will have flowers everywhere.'

'What colour?'

'Whatever the bride chooses,' answered Rebecca smoothly. 'The flowers will be quite individual for each wedding.'

Annabelle looked almost mollified and writing furiously in her book she looked up and smiled at Sarah.

'Blush pink roses, Mokara orchid and white gypsum I think. Crystal vases on each table containing an arrangement, garlands above each door. A gold pedestal vase at each side of the doorway, minimum height 48 inches and a garland display along the staircase.'

'Right,' said Sarah faintly.

'I still think cherubs would be a good idea,' mused Annabelle. 'Please source some, I would like them at the bottom of the staircase.' She paused, her pencil in mid air, 'unless you managed to find the glass slipper I suggested?'

'Er, no I don't think ...' Sarah looked at Rebecca for guidance who shook her head slightly. 'No, no slipper.'

Annabelle sighed loudly. 'Okay, then cherubs please.'

Sarah's eyes were wide with alarm. 'You really want cherubs?'

'Yes, lots of them. All different sizes. Oh – I know, a cherub outside each door,' said Annabelle in excitement. 'Like a guardian!'

She wrote furiously in her book.

'Excellent. Now, can we look at the dining room please,' and closing her book with a snap, Annabelle sailed forth to leave a rather desperate looking Sarah to follow.

Opting to miss the rest of the tour, Rebecca announced that she had a lunch arranged and ignoring Daniel's suggestion that he should come with her, she jumped into her car and drove away as quickly as she could. She had a feeling that the only way she would make it through the next few weeks would be to put as much space between herself and Annabelle as possible.

*

After a lovely afternoon spent with Helen and Emma and with a bag containing her outfit for Sarah's wedding, Rebecca returned home to find a glum Sarah in the kitchen but mercifully no sign of Daniel or Annabelle.

'Oh my god Mum, she's an absolute nightmare!'

Rebecca flicked the kettle on and grinned at her daughter, 'I thought you liked her?'

Sarah pulled a face. 'I did. I do. Well maybe not so much now. She's so demanding!'

Rebecca chuckled. 'I know,' she said cheerfully.

'She has a list of requirements and she won't take no for an answer!'

'Yep!'

'And it's all about her, I really don't think she's given Dad a second thought at all!'

'Absolutely.'

'She's obsessed with having the perfect wedding.'

'I know.'

'But she doesn't seem to want to pay for anything! I mentioned the cost of the flowers and she looked at me like I'd gone mad and said that surely they were included with the venue!'

'Doesn't surprise me.'

'She even wanted me to get new bedding for the bridal suite because she particularly wanted a 'passionate red' theme in the bedroom.'

'I can imagine.'

'She wanted me to put up new curtains as well! Just for the night of her wedding because she finds the ones in the bridal suite 'a tad dreary'. They're beautiful but not dramatic enough for her.'

'That's what she's like.'

Sarah stopped and looked at her mother through narrowed eyes.

'And of course, you knew she was like this didn't you? When you told me she was awful, you'd already worked all this out hadn't you?'

'Yep.'

'I'm so sorry Mum,' she left the table to give Rebecca a big hug. 'I can remember telling you how nice she was and thinking it was lovely to have someone to talk weddings with. I should have listened to you.'

Rebecca smiled and hugged her back. 'I forgive you darling. Because now you're the manager of Willow Court and you're the one who has to deal with her and her demands,' and with a big smile Rebecca made a cup of tea and escaped to her bedroom for a peaceful hour before she met Charles.

When she returned to the kitchen to say goodbye, Daniel looked at her in surprise.

'Going somewhere?' he asked.

'Yes, I'm going for a meal with Charles.'

'Tonight?'

Rebecca glared at him. 'Yes Daniel, tonight.'

'Bit much isn't it? Going out when we've only just arrived.'

Rebecca clenched her fist, quelling the urge to throw something at him. 'I told you when you arrived that I would be getting on with my life. I'm not here to look after you and Annabelle, I have work to do and a life to lead. I thought I'd made that quite clear.'

'I know but it's our first night. We're quite exhausted from the drive and spending the day at Willow Court. It would be nice if you stayed in tonight and we had a meal together.'

'I've spent virtually every day of the last three months at Willow Court,' Rebecca snapped. 'I'm sorry that you've found one day so exhausting. And by meal together I presume you mean I should cook for you?'

'That would have been nice,' he sniffed.

'I'm sure it would be nice, having someone else to cook for you! Well Annabelle spent a great deal of time telling me how much she could do in a kitchen like this so now's her chance. She can make you a wonderful meal. I'm going out!' and she stalked out of the kitchen, slamming the door behind her.

Chapter 30

'She can't be that bad!' chuckled Charles as they worked their way through a rather delicious meal.

'Worse!'

'But what does Daniel see in her?'

Rebecca paused, the piece of steak on her fork hovering in front of her mouth. 'I've wondered about that,' she said thoughtfully. 'She's not at all like that with Daniel, she runs around after him and looks up to him and makes him feel special. Maybe that's what he always wanted.'

'And you didn't give that to him?'

Rebecca shook her head a little sadly. 'Not towards the end. Everything in our marriage was a battle. I clearly didn't treat him the way he wanted me to.'

'I think it's clear from what you've told me that he didn't treat you in the way he should have. Marriage is a two way process Bec darling.'

Rebecca put down her fork and smiled at him. He had made such a difference to her life over the last few months. It had been wonderful having someone she could talk to, who treated her with kindness and respect, who loved her and who made her want to love them. She hadn't seen Drew for several days now and she was waiting for the morning she would wake up and realise that it was a case of out of sight out of mind. Her builder had left and taken her fantasies with him. It was proving a little harder than she had imagined. She still half expected to see him lurking in a doorway at Willow Court, smiling up at her as she walked into one of the rooms. And when she thought about him, especially the feel of his lips on hers she felt clammy and shaky with a definite flutter in her heart. But it would go, she was sure, and in the meantime she had Charles.

'We're having a bit of a party on Saturday,' she remembered. 'At Willow Court, a sort of wrap party. You'll get chance to meet Daniel and Annabelle.'

She wondered if she should be nervous at the idea of her ex-husband meeting Charles. Far from being wary she was actually looking forward to the moment when she could finally eradicate some of Daniel's influence on her life, both past and present, by introducing him to his successor.

'You'll come?'

'Wouldn't miss it. And the weddings? Well Sarah's wedding, everything still okay?'

Rebecca sighed. 'I think so. I don't think she's spoken to Luke since they finished the building work. I have told her that she can change her mind anytime she likes but she still seems set on the idea.'

Sarah had been very quiet for the few days after they had all eaten pizza underneath the willow tree and Rebecca had been mentally preparing herself for the moment her daughter announced she wanted to call off her wedding. But suddenly the old Sarah had returned, bright, cheerful and focused. She had taken Rebecca with her as she attended her final dress fitting and her gown was hanging in her bedroom at Rebecca's house, away from Dom's eyes. She had the florist booked, the cake was organised and the wedding car arranged. She had made copious notes throughout the whole process and shown Rebecca the list she had been working on. If a bride chose Willow Court, Sarah wanted to be able to provide a list of potential wedding services that came with a personal recommendation. The caterers had been to see the kitchen and had been full of admiration for the way it had been organised and the facilities it now provided. Sarah had phoned them with a frantic request for a small scale party on Saturday and although they were catering for a wedding that afternoon, as it was a very small affair they had agreed to cover it and use the well fitted kitchen for the first time, calling it a test run.

'She still seems happy to go ahead but I don't know, she should be more excited about getting married. I would be.'

'Would you?'

Rebecca blushed. Nothing more had been said about their future plans or potential wedding since the night she sensed Charles was testing her response to a proposal and she had been avoiding any mention in case it looked as though she were pushing him into something he didn't really want.

'Yes I would. If I were her age and I was getting married for the first time, I would be incapable of thinking about anything else.'

'And you don't think Sarah is really looking forward to her wedding?'

'Maybe I was asking too much, getting her involved with Willow Court when she should have been concentrating on her own wedding. Maybe this is my fault,' said Rebecca anxiously.

'I think Sarah is quite capable of separating the two.' Charles had met Sarah and Dom several times and he had developed an easy, relaxed relationship with her daughter that made Rebecca very happy. 'Not everything is your fault or your responsibility you know.'

They'd had something approaching a small argument when Rebecca had phoned him to announce that her ex-husband and his future wife were staying with her for the next four weeks. He'd been of the opinion that they should have stayed in a hotel and that Rebecca had enough to do without playing host. Rebecca had been full of reasons why she had let them stay but in her heart she knew that she should have simply said 'No'.

'But Sarah is such a gentle soul, she really wouldn't want to make waves or upset anyone.'

'Give her some credit Rebecca. She may be a lovely person but she's not stupid and no-one gets married because they don't want to upset someone. They get married because they're in love, they love someone enough to decide to spend the rest of their lives together.'

He was looking at her intently and Rebecca wondered if they were still talking about Sarah and Dom.

'What if she's not sure?' she whispered.

'Then she should call the wedding off. She's not being kind to Dom marrying him under such circumstances, she needs to be absolutely certain that it's what she wants. That's only fair, to both of them.'

Rebecca nodded. 'I agree,' she said softly. There was a long pause as they both exchanged glances and then Charles took a sip of wine and changed the subject.

'So who's coming to the party?' he asked and the tension disappeared as they chatted about the evening ahead, the time constraint and what a pleasant evening it would be if the weather was still warm and they could wander out onto the terrace.

Rebecca decided to stay at Charles' house that night, partly so she wouldn't have an early morning kitchen encounter with her guests. Calling home mid-morning to get changed she crept into the house, her head tilted to the side listening for sounds of movement. She shouldn't have to behave like this in her own house, she thought running up the stairs. Charles was right, she really should have stuck to her guns and said no. There had been no sign of Daniel's car outside and she was hoping that they'd gone in search of pink roses or golden urns but just to be on the safe side she showered quickly, pulled on some clean clothes and shot off again before she could get roped into any of Annabelle's demands. She was on her way to Willow Court before it occurred to her that they may be there, measuring the windows for Annabelle approved curtains and she drove up the gravel drive quite prepared to turn around if she caught sight of Daniel's car outside the door.

Thankfully, there was no sign and she walked through to the kitchen to find Sarah at the table, her preferred spot for working.

'Good morning darling!'

'Is it?' answered Sarah darkly.

Rebecca peered over her shoulder at the list Sarah was working her way through, stopping as Sarah's phone started to chirrup.

With a groan Sarah picked it up and held it to her ear. 'Yes Annabelle?' she asked wearily.

Rebecca filled the kettle and sat opposite Sarah to smile encouragingly.

'But you said 'Double Date' was the perfect shade. You said that only 10 minutes ago!'

Sarah rolled her eyes and Rebecca watched as she drew a savage line through one of the items on her list.

'Too dark? But they're all pink!'

Sarah scowled at her mother and Rebecca could hear Annabelle's tinkly voice on the other end of the phone.

'Right, so 'Heaven' is the perfect shade. Are you sure Annabelle because once these roses have been ordered you can't change your mind anymore.'

'No, it doesn't work like that. We have no weddings booked after yours, not yet and even if we did we can't give the flowers you don't want to the next bride on the list!'

Sarah stabbed her pencil into her notebook and Rebecca tried to subdue her snort of laughter.

'What? You said you didn't want any buds in the arrangements, they all had to be in bloom but not,' Sarah consulted her list, 'not to have bloomed more than 24 hours previously.'

'Buds do what? Okay,' she heaved a sigh of impatience. 'Okay.'

Another line through one of her lists. 'So 20% buds and 80% blooms. Are you sure. I mean would you rather have 75% bloom and 25% buds? No, no, I was joking. Okay, Annabelle, leave it with me' and with a scowl she finished the call and put her phone and her head on the table.

'Apparently,' she ground out, 'roses signify perfect happiness which is the theme of Annabelle's wedding but buds mean new love and she's decided that she needs to include some buds so she can have new love with her perfect happiness.'

Rebecca tried and failed to look sympathetic.

'Is she giving you a hard time,' she laughed. 'You can always say no and tell her to organise her own wedding.'

'I could,' said Sarah slowly. 'And I may yet, but I'm putting it all down to experience. She won't be the last bridezilla to come through the door.'

'A bridezilla already.'

Rebecca spun round at the familiar voice. Drew was lounging in the doorway, his familiar face smiling as he listened to their conversation.

'Drew. What a lovely surprise!' Sarah stood up to throw her arms round his neck and Rebecca noticed the quick glance she gave over his shoulder checking if Luke were anywhere in sight.

'Just popped in to check a few things now the kitchen's been fitted. There was a small leak on the dishwasher, the plumber said it's fixed but I wanted to look.'

Efficient builder.

'And having spent so much time here over the last few months, it feels strange not to visit.'

Committed builder.

'And of course, I miss you both,' he added, his eyes most definitely on Rebecca.

Sexy builder.

'Oh I meant to phone you,' said Sarah with a big smile,' the wrap party – it's going ahead'

No! shouted Rebecca silently. No, it was meant to have ended, no more builder, no more builder fantasies.

'You will come won't you? You and Luke of course. It's on Saturday.'

Rebecca gave her daughter a quick glance but Sarah's face was impassive. Was this a ruse to get herself back in a room with Luke? But Dom would be there, surely she wouldn't want the two of them face to face.

'Sounds like fun.' Drew's eyes hadn't left Rebecca's. Did he want a reaction, she wondered? Did he want permission? She remembered his kiss and her cheeks flooded with colour. Her skin tingled as she returned his gaze and for a moment it was as though they were sharing the same memory and she held her breath, praying he would say no, that he had plans, couldn't make it.

'Of course we'll come.'

And with a long smile he continued to hold Rebecca's gaze. 'I wouldn't miss it for the world.'

Chapter 31

Willow Court looked stunning. Rebecca and Sarah had recovered several tables and chairs from the loft and scattered them along the stone terrace and in the drawing room. All the chandeliers had been rehung and now absent of years of grime, crystal droplets swayed in the breeze and shone and twinkled like a thousand candles. Elsewhere actual candles had been used in their hundreds, set along the stone wall of the terrace, huddled inside vases and lanterns of every description and casting a gentle shimmering glow.

There were no curtains anywhere, they would all be fitted on Monday, and very little furniture but it already looked magical. The walls had all been painted the same soft buttercream of the reception hall and the wooden panelling had been polished until it shone warmly in the soft light. The windows were open, allowing a summer scented breeze to drift in and the trees were rustling lazily as though playing a melody to the guests who wandered around the terrace in awe.

'I can't believe how good it looks,' said Helen dreamily, one hand holding her champagne glass and the other trailing through the myriad of shrubs and flowers planted in huge wooden boxes all around the terrace. 'I wish I was getting married, I would definitely come here.'

Rebecca had been touched by everyone's response to Willow Court. It had been hard work but as she looked around, she knew she would do it all again the very next day if needed.

She felt Charles' arm slide round her waist and she turned to kiss him. He had been her rock, encouraging her on the many occasions she thought she wouldn't get everything finished on time, listening to her when she had needed to talk through her ideas, never complaining when work came first.

'Thank you,' she whispered.

'For?'

'Oh you know, just being here, being you.'

They smiled at each other. Rebecca had insisted that they follow their usual routine and during the week she had invited Charles round as she would normally. Annabelle had greeted him with rather less enthusiasm than Rebecca had been expecting and he'd been grilled quite ferociously as they sat in the kitchen drinking wine.

'It's not easy to become part of someone else's family you know.'

'I realise that Annabelle, as indeed you must.'

'Oh I already feel at home, both in the family house and with Daniel's children.'

'But it's not really a family house is it? It's Rebecca's house.'

Annabelle's lips had thinned. 'I hope you wouldn't try to come between Rebecca and her family,' she'd gasped, one hand at the throat in mock horror.

'I wouldn't dream of coming between Rebecca and *her* family,' Charles had answered in a steady tone.

'But you wouldn't want them staying here, in the house?'

'I have absolutely no objection to Rebecca's children staying in Rebecca's house, none at all.'

'Good, because it has been suggested that we all have a lovely Christmas, here at home, where the family can all get together and enjoy the festive season.'

'Really?' Charles had raised an eyebrow and looked thoughtful. 'You may have to change your plans Annabelle. I think Rebecca is thinking more along the lines of a luxury cruise in the Caribbean this Christmas. Just the two of us. Isn't that right my darling?' and he had turned to face Rebecca giving her a naughty wink which had made her choke on her wine.

Daniel had shaken Charles' hand quite formally and given him a hard look before grilling him about his financial situation until Rebecca had decided enough was enough and told Daniel that how much Charles' house was worth was none of his business and that the two of them, yes just the two of them, were going out for a meal. She told Daniel and Annabelle that they were welcome to eat anything that was in the fridge, which seeing as neither of them had thought to make a visit to the supermarket since they'd arrived, was precisely nothing.

It had been quite a novelty having someone in her corner after years of Daniel's lack of interest and it had made Rebecca appreciate Charles even more.

'It does look wonderful darling,' he said now, looking into the drawing room and the guests as they relaxed in the comfy brocade covered armchairs Rebecca had found in the loft and had reupholstered.

Rebecca nodded and then cast another glance round her guests. Drew and Luke had still not arrived and although part of her was hoping they'd changed their minds, part of her was longing to see Drew's head appear round the doorway and see his lazy smile.

She caught Dom's eyes and smiled. He had his arm firmly around Sarah's waist and looked happier than Rebecca had ever seen him look. She wondered if that was in part because Luke had disappeared from their lives.

He was walking towards her, holding his glass up high in a silent toast.

'It looks incredible,' he said. 'Simply incredible.'

'I'm glad you like it.'

'How could anybody not?' Dom laughed.

Rebecca thought of all the notes in Annabel's book. Only this morning she had phoned Sarah and said that the flowers on the terrace would clash with her colour scheme and could Sarah arrange to have them re-potted. And she had been thinking about the dining chairs and she would like the large tulle bow on the back of each one dyed to match the shade of her roses. And would they mind painting the front door. A nice cream would be good rather than just plain wood.

'You'd be surprised,' she said to Dom with a smile.

'Well I think it's perfect and quite honestly I can't wait to get married here.' He smiled down at Sarah, still by his side and Rebecca's heart gave a little wobble at the slightly strained smile he received in return. 'Or should I say, we can't wait.'

Sarah nodded. 'That's right,' she said with an attempt at enthusiasm.

'And the chapel is a truly wonderful touch, I think you'll be booked solid as soon as you start advertising.'

'Well I sincerely hope so,' laughed Rebecca. 'It's a lot of work for one wedding.'

'Two Mum, don't forget Dad and Annabelle.'

Rebecca wrinkled her nose. She spent a lot of time and effort trying to forget Daniel and Annabelle.

'This does look quite lovely Becky darling.'

Speak of the devil thought Rebecca, waiting for the but.

'But I wish you would rethink the colour of the chairs. I saw some beautiful ones on Pinterest, I'm sure I sent you a picture. They were ever so slightly pink, almost the colour of my roses. Much better than those old things you have.'

The old chairs Annabelle referred to were wing backed armchairs, with a cream and gold brocade upholstery and they were supremely comfortable and fitted the style of Willow Court to perfection. She thought about replacing them with the rose pink, shiny monstrosities that Annabelle had suggested.

'They were just not the look we're aiming for,' chorused Rebecca and Sarah at the same time and then burst into giggles. Her daughter was learning, thought Rebecca proudly. She would do an excellent job managing Willow Court Weddings.

Watching Annabelle stalk off in a huff, Rebecca relaxed, determined to enjoy the evening. Drew had obviously changed his mind despite the very hot look he had sent her way when Sarah had given him his invite. She should concentrate on enjoying the evening. She had worked hard for this moment, as had Sarah. They had turned a decrepit old building around and it was something they should both be proud of. She was surrounded by her friends and the man she loved and for the first time in quite a while she was both happy and content with her lot in life. So she allowed Charles to fill her glass, ignored Annabelle sulking at the general lack of pink and wandered happily amongst her friends accepting their praise and soaking up the wonderful atmosphere of the gracious old building.

'Hello Rebecca.'

She didn't need to look round, she would recognise Drew's voice anywhere. Besides, she could see Luke hovering on the edge of a group of people including Sarah. She saw her daughter catch sight of Luke, the happiness on her face as she reached out an impulsive hand in his direction and then pulled it back quickly, remembering Dom was by her side.

She turned around.

It was the first time she had seen him without dust in his hair, dirt smeared across his cheeks and wearing smart clothes instead of his shorts and a range of worn T-shirts. He looked handsome, his blue eyes reflected in a light blue, short sleeved shirt and his lean body encased in a pair of smart jeans.

Sexy builder.

'Hello Drew.' Rebecca tried very hard to sound casual and welcoming. She wasn't convinced she had managed and she could feel the hand holding her champagne tremble slightly as he walked towards her.

'I didn't think you were coming.'

'We had a small problem on the new build. We had to stay a bit later but like I said, I wouldn't miss this for the world.'

She felt a blush touch her cheeks and she was glad of the fading light that hid the colour.

'What do you think?' she asked, trying to change the subject.

'Wonderful.'

He was still looking at her and she swallowed hard. 'Well it's down to you. Willow Court I mean,' she added hastily. 'Everything looks amazing because of you.'

'Willow Court looks wonderful as well.'

Rebecca's blush deepened. She was wearing a tea dress, cut low at the front and nipped in at her waist, it made her feel feminine and elegant, in keeping with the days when the inhabitants of Willow Court would change for dinner and congregate on the terrace for a champagne cocktail before dinner was served.

'Have you had a look around?' she asked breathlessly.

Drew shook his head, still refusing to move his gaze from hers.

'You should,' she said desperately. 'It's almost unrecognisable.'

'Show me.'

Her heart was galloping. That would be a very bad idea, she decided. Wandering from one candlelit room to another with Drew could only lead to trouble. She should avoid it at all costs.

'Okay.'

They didn't move, just carried on staring into each other's eyes, oblivious of the people and the conversation around them.

'Drew!' It was Emma, her voice making Rebecca jump although her gaze remained fixed on Drew.

'Hi Emma.'

'Well if I wasn't already giving your name to all and sundry I certainly would be after this job. It looks fantastic.

And Rebecca has shown me some of the before photos so I know how much work you've had to do.' Emma laughed, then her smile faltered as she looked from Rebecca to Drew and back again.

'Rebecca, you okay honey.'

Shaking herself out of her reverie, making herself leave Drew's eyes and the promise they held, Rebecca turned to her friend. 'Of course, I forgot it was you who gave me Drew's name,' she said trying to bring some normality to her shaking voice. 'Then you can take some credit for this as well!'

Emma was watching her through slightly narrowed eyes. 'Mmm. Shame I don't need a wedding venue. Shall I get you some water Bec, you look a little pale.'

'No, I'm fine really. Just been a long week that's all.'

Drew finally pulled his eyes away from Rebecca. 'I'll get myself a drink,' he said quietly. 'Maybe you can give me that tour later?'

Nodding, Rebecca watched him walk away.

'Bec, is there something going on between you and Drew?'

The directness of the question made Rebecca gasp. 'Of course not!'

'Really? Because I would swear that the two of you wanted to rip each other's clothes off right here and now and wouldn't care who was watching.'

'Emma! What a thing to say. I'm in love with Charles. There is absolutely nothing going on between me and Drew.'

Emma looked at her unbelievingly.

'Nothing,' reiterated Rebecca. 'Well, you know, just a little bit of builder's lust but that's all. I would never cheat on Charles.'

'Builder's lust! What on earth are you two talking about?'

Rebecca whirled round to see Helen, glass in hand, smile on her face as she perched on the stone wall next to her two friends. 'It sounds like someone's lusting after a builder,' she giggled. 'And if it's the one I've just seen walk indoors, I can't blame them. He is a hunk. So, come on, who is doing the lusting?'

She looked from one to the other, her smile fading as she realised that neither of them were laughing.

'Bec? What's happening? Is it you? Have you got builder's lust? What the hell is builder's lust anyway?'

'Just what I'd like to know,' said Emma grimly. 'But I suspect that Bec has fallen for Drew and from the look in his eye I think he's fallen right back at her.'

Helen's shocked face appeared in Rebecca's line of sight as she jumped up from the wall.

'What? No! Bec! I thought you were in love with Charles? I thought he was about to ask you to marry him? I thought you wanted him to ask you to marry him? What's going on?'

Rebecca bit her lip. She wasn't ready for this conversation.

'You know,' she said appealing to Emma.

'Me! Why would I know?'

'Well you've had lots of building work done.'

Emma stared at her. 'But I never fell in love with any of them!'

'I'm not in love with Drew! It's just a little crush. He's the handsome builder who made my dreams come true and it's entirely natural that I have a bit of a thing for him. Like you sometimes have for your boss or a teacher.'

Both her friends were looking at her blankly.

'But it doesn't mean anything, does it? I mean once they leave your life, once you move on and you don't see them every day, you just forget about them because it's not real, it's just a little fantasy, that's all.'

'You fantasise about Drew?' asked Helen cautiously.

'No! Not like that. I mean the whole thing is just a fantasy. He doesn't love me and I don't love him. It's purely because we've spent so much time together this summer, we've formed a bond but it's only temporary.'

Emma looked at Helen and back to Rebecca.

'Honey, I saw the way you looked at Drew and quite honestly I don't recall ever seeing you look at Charles like that. You're right I've had lots of building work done and the only fantasy I've ever had is that they might actually finish on time. That and the odd daydream about stabbing them. I think you may have to face reality Bec darling, you absolutely must not agree to marry Charles because you've fallen in love with Drew.'

Chapter 32

Rebecca stared at Emma.

'No! I love Charles. Drew is a …'

'Do not start on about builder's lust again Bec because there is no such thing. Builders are irritating, they never turn up when you need them to, they avoid your phone calls and charge you too much. No-one has builder's lust, they have builder's rage. If you feel anything for Drew it's because you love him, not because he's done a good job on your renovation project!'

But Rebecca was shaking her head furiously. 'Absolutely not. I love Charles. I've waited a long time to find someone who I wanted in my life and Charles is that person. Drew is a crush, nothing more. I am not in love with him!'

She held up her hand as Helen opened her mouth.

'No. Stop. You are ruining everything. Stop.' She glared at them both defiantly, 'I love Charles and if he asks me to marry him I shall say yes,' and not waiting for any more conversation she walked away, spying Charles in the doorway and grabbing hold of his arm, refusing to look behind her.

'Having a good time darling?' he asked

She nodded, not trusting her voice.

'Where's your glass, shall I get you some more champagne?'

More nodding and giving her a pat on the arm, Charles went into the drawing room.

'Everything okay Mum?'

'Wonderful!' That was a little over enthusiastic, she decided. She sounded more like Annabelle. 'It's a lovely evening isn't it?'

'Dom was just saying that his parents are coming to Leeds next week. They wanted to meet you before the wedding and Dad if he's still around.'

'Oh I imagine he will be,' said Rebecca dryly. Daniel had commandeered the study and had spent the last few days talking loudly on the phone explaining that he was at the family property in the North finalising the details for his wedding.

'Well, I had been going to ask if they could stay with you, but I don't think that's a good idea,' continued Sarah hurriedly, seeing the look of alarm on Rebecca's face, 'not while you've got Dad and Annabelle in the house as well.'

Rebecca looked relieved, she had enough to cope with right now without adding Dom's parent into the mix.

'Sorry,' she said apologetically to Dom. 'Under normal circumstances I would love to ...'

'Don't worry,' smiled Dom, 'I can see you've already got enough on your plate with Annabelle.'

Rebecca rolled her eyes. 'She is a handful but it's Sarah who is dealing with her.'

Dom laughed. 'She's been telling me all about Annabelle's demands. Fortunately my list is quite short. A lovely location – check. My family – check. And the girl I love – check.'

He bent down to kiss Sarah and Rebecca's eyes unaccountably filled with tears. It was a beautiful, romantic thing to say and she had no doubt of Dom's love for Sarah. Unfortunately, she had a rather large question mark over Sarah's love for Dom. Why, oh why was life so complicated?

The caterers had come up trumps and they walked out onto the terrace with trays of delicious canapes, sandwiches and more champagne. Rebecca watched Annabelle inspect each offering and then whip out her book to make furious notes. She watched Helen and Emma whispering furiously in one corner but ignored them. She listened to Emma's husband talking to Drew about the new building job he was on and Helen's husband tease Charles about working at Willow Court as a butler. She saw Sarah slip away from Dom's side and wander innocuously towards Luke and stand chatting to him with her back turned to the rest of the room. She tried to look happy, she tried to be happy. But her head was tumbling with thoughts and the memory of Helen and Emma's shocked faces as they told her she was in love with Drew. She caught Charles' eye and smiled at him, she caught Drew's eye and simply stared for a moment before turning her gaze away.

'Has anyone been down to the lake?' she asked loudly.

At the chorus of 'No' Rebecca put on her widest smile. 'Then follow me,' she shouted cheerfully and she set off down the stone stairs and across the grass. The terrace had suddenly seemed very small, she needed space, she needed to be able to look around without encountering Drew's eyes. Charles caught up with her and put a guiding hand under her elbow so she didn't fall in the long grass by the tree's roots. Dear Charles, she thought, wondering if she should stop drinking champagne now. Dear wonderful Charles.

Sarah had been down to the lake at the beginning of the evening and put hundreds of lanterns along the path and around the water's edge. The still water was bathed in light where insects, fooled into activity, plopped around the water and even the fish rose to the top to see what was happening. The strands of the willow tree trailed in the edges of the lake and for a moment no-one made a sound.

'It's beautiful,' breathed Helen, 'so, so beautiful.'

And the spell was broken as people wandered around, trailing hands in the water, sitting at the picnic table and chatting quietly.

Rebecca saw Drew walking towards her and turned to Charles. 'Isn't it romantic?' she asked.

'Absolutely.'

'A wonderful place to have some photos taken,' Dom added.

'You think so?' Annabelle looked unconvinced. 'Doesn't it look a little unkempt?'

'No, it looks natural and romantic and perfect for a wedding shot.'

Rebecca saw Annabelle perk up and whip out her book. She also caught a glimpse of Sarah walking away from the lake, almost hidden by the trees as she headed in the direction of the house. She looked round for Luke but couldn't see him anywhere and an uneasy feeling started to drift through her bones.

'It could do with being a little tidier though, Rebecca do you think you could do something about the path down here?'

'What kind of something,' asked Rebecca not really paying attention as she watched Dom look round for Sarah.

'Well cement it, pave it, whatever.'

Rebecca's head whipped round. 'You want me to cement a natural path that runs through woodland to a lake? Are you mad?'

Annabelle looked nonplussed. 'Mad? Why would that be mad? You can't have brides walking down here in their wedding dresses, wading through the long grass, tripping over roots and getting their trains and veils dirty from being too close to the lake.' She waved her hand towards the reeds that dipped towards the path and the willow fronds that trailed across passing shoulders.

'I think that's the whole point Annabelle,' Dom said in amusement. 'Not that anyone trips but that you come to a natural lake, surrounded by nature and have your photo taken.'

'Really?'

'Yes, it would make a stunning shot.'

Rebecca could see Annabelle was torn. A stunning wedding shot versus a potential smudge of dirt on her

257

wedding dress. She nibbled at the stretchy pencil and pulled a face, eventually scribbling something in her book.

Dom grinned at Rebecca. 'I'm just going to look for Sarah,' he said, 'I thought she came down with the rest of us but I can't see her.'

'I'll go! I'm going back up to the house anyway.' Charles stood up to join her. 'To the toilet,' she lied. 'I'll see where she is and send her down to join you.'

Dom shrugged and Charles sat back down. 'And I'll bring more champagne back with me so don't anyone go anywhere,' and waiting to make sure everyone had relaxed back into their positions Rebecca set off up the path. She reached the terrace but there was no sign of Sarah or Luke so she walked through the drawing room and into the reception hall. Poking her head round the dining room door and into the kitchen, she was about to go back outside when she turned around and went to the domed room. The scaffold was still in place in the corner and they had left this room in darkness, no candles, no lanterns to discourage visitors. Opening the door slowly, for a moment she thought she was alone. And then the moon erupted from behind a cloud and she saw Sarah and Luke, entwined in each other's arms their lips together and their bodies pressed so close they could have been one.

'Mum!' Sarah jumped backwards almost tripping over and relying on Luke's arm to steady her. She tried to pull her hand away but Luke hung on.

'Sarah!'

'It's not what it looks like,' said Sarah desperately, earning a hurt glance from Luke.

Rebecca shook her head sadly.

'I know it looks bad but it's nothing. I mean it's just a kiss. It just happened.'

Rebeca grimaced, she could hardly reprimand Sarah when she'd had her own unexpected kiss with Drew only a few nights before.

'I'm sorry Mum, I really am. We didn't mean anything to happen.' Her head fell and Rebecca could see tears rolling down her cheek.

Rebecca shook her head. 'Why are you apologising to me? I told you weeks ago that you shouldn't go ahead with this marriage unless you really wanted to. If you don't want to marry Dom that's entirely your business Sarah, but apologise to him, not to me. Speak to him about how you feel, sooner rather than later.'

'Rebecca …'

'No Luke. This is Sarah's decision, she has to decide, and she has to tell Dom, who by the way is looking for you.

Sarah nodded, wiping the tears with the back of her hand and straightening her shoulders.

'You're right Mum. I'm being very unfair to Dom. I just, well I suppose we just got carried away.'

'Sarah,' Luke began desperately trying to catch her hand again. 'Sarah please …'

Sarah shook her head. 'No Luke,' she pulled her hand from his grip. 'No. I need to think, I need to speak to Dom, I need ….' She shook her head in distress. 'I don't know what I need.'

Stepping away from Luke she avoided the hand he reached out in her direction. 'I'm sorry, I shouldn't have, we shouldn't have …' she took a shuddering breath. 'That shouldn't have happened,' she said quietly. She moved to stand by Rebecca's side. 'I love Dom.' Luke groaned but Sarah held up a hand to stop him speaking. 'I love Dom,' she repeated, her voice a little stronger, 'and I shouldn't have let this happen.' She and Luke exchanged a long look and then Sarah turned away and without looking back she followed Rebecca out of the door.

Rebecca felt her daughter shaking and she slipped her arm around her waist murmuring soothingly as they made their way back to the drawing room, just as the rest of the party appeared from the trees at the side of the house.

'What kept you?' shouted Charles. 'We ran out of champagne!'

Rebecca tried to smile through stiff lips. 'Sorry, I got distracted. You know what Sarah and I are like when we get talking about Willow Court.' She prayed Luke would stay where he was for a few more minutes. 'But there's lots of champagne, let's get some music on shall we?'

She watched Sarah pick up her chin and smile at Dom, walking over and taking hold of his arm as Helen squealed in agreement and a few moments later there was mellow music and laughter filling the terrace as Helen tried to instruct her husband the art of moving as though he could actually hear the tune.

Rebecca was exhausted. Her heart ached, for so many reasons. Her head ached from a surplus of champagne. She refused to meet Drew's eyes as she laughed and chatted and she took great pains to avoid Charles and Drew spending any time in close contact. They had met briefly one afternoon when Charles had called to collect her from Willow Court and Charles had shaken him by the hand earlier in the evening and congratulated him on the renovation.

Annabelle danced with Daniel on the terrace and looked overwhelmed by the occasion, but Rebecca suspected that was because Daniel had two left feet and was constantly standing on Annabelle's toes. She watched Emma watching her and Helen watching Drew. She saw Luke sit on the wall outside looking quite desolate and hoped everybody else thought he was merely taking in the evening sky. She smiled and tried not to think about what might happen with Sarah and Dom. Or think at all about Drew. Tonight truly would be the end. After this there would be no reason for her to ever see him again. She would concentrate on getting Willow Court ready for whatever weddings may come, although she was beginning to suspect that Sarah's would not be one of them. She would forget about Drew because Emma and Helen were both wrong and she did not love him. In a few weeks this evening would be forgotten by everyone and life would carry on at its own pace. She just had to get through the night without any more disasters, she really couldn't cope with any more drama.

The music changed and she saw Charles hold out his arms in her direction. Drifting towards him she put her hand in his and let him twirl her slowly around the room. He was looking into her eyes and she could feel his hands on her back, firm and reassuring. Everyone else stopped dancing and watched the two of them as they whirled and twirled and swept round the room. The music stopped and a little round of applause followed to which Charles gave a grave mock bow and Rebecca laughed in embarrassment. She started to move away, making space for others to start dancing again but Charles kept hold of her hand pulling her back towards him. He was smiling.

'I've been waiting for this moment,' he started to say to the room in general. 'The moment when Willow Court stopped being the most important thing in Bec's life.' There was a ripple of laughter at his rueful tone but Rebecca stayed silent, feeling her heart start to thump. 'I told Rebecca that once she had time to take a breath, when the hard work was over and she could think about things other than the plumbing,' another polite laugh, 'then it would be time for us to think about our future.'

He turned back to look into Rebecca's eyes, although all she could see was Helen's shocked face over his shoulder. 'And I can't think of any better time to do exactly that. Willow Court looks magnificent. Rebecca and Sarah have worked so hard and it's paid off. I think we can all get a sense tonight of how wonderful it would be to get married here.' Rebecca's heart was now beating so loudly she was having trouble hearing Charles as he drew her even closer and then put his hand in his pocket. 'So I'm hoping that on this magical, romantic night, Rebecca will agree to marry me. Here at Willow Court.' He pulled a small box out of his pocket and flipped it open to let the diamond ring that nestled in its depths wink under the light of the chandelier as both Emma and Helen gasped.

'So,' he slipped down onto one knee and offered the box up to Rebecca. She looked down at him, but not before she caught sight of Drew as he stood straight and silent, watching her intently. 'I love you Rebecca. Will you do me the honour of agreeing to marry me?'

Chapter 33

The sun was shining as usual. The heatwave showed no sign of breaking and there was talk of standpipes in the streets and a national crisis looming. It was on the verge of breaking, promised the experts. Any minute now there would be torrential rain and plummeting temperatures but in the meantime everyone walked around with perspiring faces and sun burnt arms. Rebecca got out of bed and stretched, watching the light catch on her engagement ring. She had seen Annabelle surreptitiously checking it out the minute it landed on Rebecca's finger. It was significantly bigger than Annabelle's solitaire and her mouth had pouted her disappointment. Rebecca watched it for a moment. It was certainly different to the tiny diamond ring Daniel had bought her many years ago. The central diamond was large and square flanked by two similar diamonds and it was exactly what she would have picked out for herself. Charles knew her so well, he knew her taste, he knew what she would like. That was why, she reminded herself firmly, she should marry him. It was why she was going to marry him.

Rebecca hadn't actually answered Charles when he proposed. It had been such a romantic moment that as he knelt down and held up the heart shaped box, flipping it open to let the brilliance of the diamonds burst into the room, everyone had immediately started cheering and laughing and congratulating them. And despite expecting the moment for weeks, Rebecca had been unprepared, too shocked to respond with anything other than a smile. She was watching Sarah, standing next to Dom and holding his hand, her eyes suspiciously bright which everyone would excuse as the emotion of the moment. She was watching Luke who stood slightly apart from the crowd looking at Sarah with such naked longing in his eyes that Rebecca wondered how the rest of the room could be unaware of how he felt. She was watching Drew, standing in the doorway, stiff and straight his eyes glued to hers as the scene unfolded and then his slight nod in her direction as he melted away. She watched Helen and Emma as they exchanged glances with each other before turning their eyes on Rebecca, waiting for her response.

Finally her eyes turned to Charles, still holding her hand after slipping on the beautiful ring, his eyes bright and shining, his love clear for the world to see. And she had continued to smile and nod and accept the kisses and congratulations from the room. Daniel had approached and quite formally held out his hand to Charles, nodding his head as though bestowing approval on the union. He had kissed Rebecca on the cheek and held her tight for a brief second before whispering a gruff 'congratulations' in her ear. Sarah had thrown her arms around her mum's neck and wept on her shoulder although they both knew it had little to do with Charles' proposal. Dom had hugged her and teased her about weddings and Willow Court. Even Annabelle tried to be excited although Rebecca detected a definite air of resentment about having some of the attention directed away from her own forthcoming nuptials. The only person she didn't speak to was Charles. Their eyes kept meeting, but they didn't speak.

Helen and Emma both appeared and looked her in the eye.

'Are you going to marry him?' asked Helen bluntly.

'Of course.'

'Even though you're in love with Drew?' It was Emma's turn.

'I've told you, I'm not in love with Drew, we've just grown close and I am attracted to him, but I love Charles.'

'You said he didn't make the earth move for you.'

Rebecca's eyebrow raised. 'I said I loved him, not in a fiery all guns blazing way that doesn't last, but in a quiet gentle way that will.'

'You're not marrying him because you're scared of how you feel about Drew?'

'No! I love Charles.'

Neither of them had looked convinced but they'd put their arms around their friend and offered their congratulations and said in that case they were very happy for her and they tried hard to spend the rest of the evening looking as joyful as everyone else did and making excited plans for yet another Willow Court wedding.

It wasn't until the party was ending, people were drifting away and goodbyes were echoing along the driveway that Rebecca finally found herself alone with Charles.

'You do know you haven't answered me,' he said with a small smile.

Rebecca knew. She had been aware all evening that although she'd let Charles slide the ring on her finger and had accepted everyone's best wishes, she hadn't as yet said the word.

'Shall I ask again, when we're not surrounded by people and you can tell me if you really want to marry me?'

Rebecca looked at him in shock. 'You think I would say no?'

'I think you would say yes, but I want you to want to say yes.'

Rebecca stared at him, 'I love you Charles, you do know that?'

He nodded his head. 'I think you do, but I'm not sure it's enough. I want you to marry me but only if you think you couldn't live without me. I want you to love me. I want us to spend the rest of our lives together Bec, but only if it's really what you want to do and not because you're worried about being lonely or because you're worried that you might not meet anyone else.'

'I wouldn't do that to you! I wouldn't marry you if I didn't love you.'

'And yet, you haven't said yes.'

Rebecca stood very still. They were framed in the doorway of Willow Court and the area around them was filled with the soft glow of candles that Sarah was still extinguishing. She looked at Charles and she wanted so much to say yes. She wanted to feel overwhelmed by his proposal, exhilarated at the thought of being his wife.

'Charles, I ...'

He pressed his finger to her lips. 'It's been a difficult few months Rebecca my love. Sometimes we think we know what we want and then when we finally get there, it turns out we were wrong. I think perhaps you should take your time before answering. Don't say anything tonight, make sure you know what you want, and then answer me.'

Rebecca could feel her eyes filling with tears. What did she want? She had no idea. She started to pull the ring from her finger but Charles stopped her. 'Leave it on. Get used to the feel,' he smiled. 'Decide whether you want to leave it there for the next 50 years or so.'

'I don't deserve you,' whispered Rebecca. 'I really don't.'

'Yes you do,' he kissed her gently on the forehead. 'I hope I deserve you but let's take our time and make sure that it's the right thing to do shall we?' and then he wandered off to help Sarah slowly extinguish the candle light from Willow Court.

Rebecca was wearing the ring, but as yet she still hadn't given Charles an answer. The last few days had been turbulent to say the least and her own wedding was still very much undecided. Getting showered and dressed she went downstairs and into the kitchen to find Annabelle pouring over menus and seating plans. She had changed her mind three times about the menu, much to the disgruntlement of the catering company who had demanded a final decision in the next 24 hours and no further changes after that point.

The sink was full of the detritus of breakfast but Rebecca simply ignored it and pushed her mug under the coffee machine. She had long since realised that Annabelle felt staying with Rebecca meant full board and lodgings including cleaning, washing and taxi duties. Rebecca's new tactic was to withdraw her services until they ran out of clean mugs, at which point Daniel would grumble loudly about the lack of organisation in the kitchen and Annabelle would look at Rebecca reproachfully and then fuss round making Daniel a coffee and a sandwich and restore order with much huffing and puffing.

'Have you decided on a wedding day?' she demanded of Rebecca as she saw her appear at the table.

Rebecca shook her head to Annabelle's loud tut. Rebecca could have put her out of her misery and told her that no date had been set, indeed no wedding as such had been set. But she knew that Annabelle was consumed with anxiety that Rebecca may just slide her wedding into Willow Court's empty bookings folder and pip Annabelle to the post. And she had decided that she was happy to let Annabelle live with the worry.

'Sorry Annabelle,' she said cheerfully. 'Nothing decided as yet although,' she paused looking thoughtful, 'I may just pop over to Willow Court and check out a few things.'

'What things? What needs checking? Are you looking at dates, do you think you'll …'

But Rebecca had already walked out of the kitchen, leaving Annabelle spluttering in alarm as Rebecca grabbed her car keys and set off on the all too familiar journey. As usual, the place was a hive of activity with several delivery vans parked outside and a jumble of workmen cluttering the hall. Except that now there was no dust clouding the air and no piles of building materials stacked at the foot of the staircase. The place shone and sparkled and one of today's deliveries was to return and hang some of the old paintings included in the sale together with several new pieces of art Rebecca had chosen, light and modern to mingle in with the portraits of previous owners that had decorated the walls for centuries. Plants were being arranged in all the reception rooms, fresh and vivid they added a splash of colour to the soft cream of the décor. A new reception desk was in place, larger and with a great deal more style, it looked perfect tucked to one side of the doorway. Tables were being unpacked and acres of muslin was being hung at every window, fluttering in the slightest of breezes that swept in through the open French windows. Even in the dome room, Brian had announced that the intricate repairs were finally complete and the scaffolding had already been dismantled and taken away. All that was needed was a careful coat of paint to match the chalky white of the rest of the cornice. Sarah's wedding date was eleven days away and there was no doubt that Willow Court was ready to be shown in all its wonderful glory.

Looking round for her daughter, Rebecca walked up the stairs and turned right to reach the suite of rooms that Audrey Hemmings had used as her apartment and where Rebecca had offered to buy Willow Court only a few months earlier. The door was slightly ajar and walking in she found Sarah sitting at the large dining table, surrounded by paper and lists and plans and invoices.

Her head was bent over her work and for a moment Rebecca watched. She had lost weight, her cheeks drawn and her shoulder blades prominent. Her hair was dull and her mouth permanently tinged with sadness. The day after the wrap party, Sarah had phoned her mother to say she was calling off her wedding. Rebecca had listened as her daughter sobbed telling her that she was making the right decision and although it was difficult now, difficult and sad, she would feel better in time.

'I love Dom,' Sarah had sobbed down the line. 'I haven't stopped loving him but how can I get married when I'm so unsure whether I really want to? And if I kissed Luke I must have feeling for him, how can I marry Dom when I'm happy to kiss someone else?'

Rebecca had been stunned into silence, not by her daughter's actions but her words. Didn't they echo what Helen and Emma had said the night of Charles' proposal?

'Perhaps we're too young or we've done it all too quickly, I don't know. All I know is that suddenly I want more than just a wedding. I want to make a success of this job, I want run Willow court and arrange other people's weddings. Dom has his career and I want mine. And I know getting married shouldn't change that but it feels as though it will.'

She had cried and cried and Rebecca had announced that she was driving over to comfort her daughter in person.

'I'm at Willow Court,' Sarah had told her between the tears. 'I couldn't stay in the flat with Dom after I'd just called off our wedding.'

So Rebecca had jumped in the car and driven in haste to find her daughter sitting by the willow tree watering the parched ground with her tears.

'He was so understanding about it Mum,' she had wailed. 'He said he'd had a feeling I was going off the idea and he'd been half expecting something like this to happen.'

'Luke? He was expecting Luke…'

'No! Not Luke.' Sarah blushed. 'We didn't really talk about Luke,' she said averting her eyes.

Rebecca stayed silent.

'I'm not in love with Luke. I think he may be in love with me, a little bit anyway.'

Rebecca remembered the look in Luke's eyes the night she had found the pair kissing and thought that Sarah might be underestimating the strength of Luke's feelings.

'I'm not calling off the wedding because of Luke. I don't really want to split up with Dom, I just don't feel ready to get married. I've loved doing all this work, being in charge, organising, making decisions. I think that was part of Luke's attraction, he was part of a new life I could suddenly see for myself.'

Rebecca let her talk, her own thoughts wandering to Drew, the feeling he aroused in her every time she caught sight of him. Maybe it was the same, Drew was part of a new life that Rebecca was creating, that's why she felt so drawn to him.

'You asked me if I was ready to get married, when I first told you about me and Dom and I said of course I was. But it turns out you were right. I was more taken with the idea of getting married than actually getting married.' She wiped her eyes and blew her nose. 'And I've hurt him, he said he understands but I've hurt him.'

Rebecca sighed and hugged her daughter close. 'You've been brave to call it off sweetheart. Better than blindly going ahead and regretting it all later. You have to do whatever is right for you.'

Was she talking to her daughter or herself, she wondered? Was Sarah showing her mother that a little hard thinking was necessary, that love wasn't always enough?

'I've said I'll move out of the flat, at least for now. Until we know what we want to do about - things.'

'Do you want to come home?

'Actually, I wondered if I could stay here?'

Rebecca looked startled. 'What, in one of the bedrooms?'

'No. In the apartment. I know we haven't done any work on it yet. But we always said it would be great as a live-in manager's flat. It doesn't need much work, maybe a lick of paint. I could stay here and start as I mean to go on, as the manager of Willow Court.'

'Are you sure you wouldn't rather come home? You'll be by yourself here, there'll be no-one to talk to in the evening, you'll be quite alone.'

'Sounds perfect' said Sarah firmly. 'Really Mum, a bit of time by myself, no-one to feel guilty about if I'm working until two in the morning. It's exactly what I need.'

So Sarah had moved into Willow court, the apartment was now full of her belongings and she was using the dining room as a temporary office and working harder than ever to have every possible nook and cranny of Willow Court ready for its first wedding, even though that was no longer going to be her own.

'Hello darling.'

Sarah jumped and looked up. 'Hi Mum, I didn't see you there.' There were dark circles under her eyes which looked sore from crying, but she smiled bravely.

'I was wondering if you needed any help with cancelling everything? It can't be easy phoning round florists and caterers and everyone else, all of them asking questions.'

There was the tiniest quiver of a bottom lip but it was soon brought under control.

'Actually Mum, I haven't cancelled anything yet.'

'Then let me …'

'No! What I mean is I'm not going to cancel anything, I won't get any money back at this late date anyway. So I thought I'd leave it all in place.'

'But what on earth …'

'You see,' grinned Sarah, looking almost like her old self, 'I have an idea!'

Chapter 34

'You want to do what?'

'Host a wedding. But not a real wedding, like a wedding open day.'

Rebecca stared. What on earth was a wedding open day? Was it for people who might pop in on the off chance and get married?

'We need to start advertising now, get our name out there. We've finished too late to get into any of the wedding fairs this summer and we can advertise but it takes a bit of time. I didn't dare do too much publicity before we knew for certain that it would be finished. So now is the perfect time.'

'Er right. The perfect time for what exactly?'

'To have an open day! We'll advertise like crazy and put it on the radio and hope that we get a good response. I think we will, from all the people who have decided this summer they want to get married next summer. After all, look at our family, three weddings decided on in the last few months! We may be a little over the national average,' Sarah laughed,' but people are setting wedding dates all the time and how lovely to get the equivalent of a dry run.'

Rebecca looked quizzical. 'I'm still not sure how it's going to work.'

'I've got everything booked. Flowers, catering, cake,' there was a definite wobble in her voice and Rebecca put her hand out in sympathy. 'So instead of letting it go to waste, let's use it. Let the florist come and decorate the chapel and the rooms, let the caterer turn up and fill the place with canapés and nibbles. And we'll invite people to come along and experience what a wedding at Willow Court would really feel like!'

Rebecca started to nod. 'I see,' she said slowly.

'I'll get in touch with as many wedding suppliers as I can and see if they want to join in, show their brochures, have a few wedding dresses on display that kind of thing.'

Rebecca was smiling. 'What a wonderful idea!'

'It's a wedding, just without a bride and groom.' Sarah's face fell and for a moment she had to work hard to keep the tears back. 'And it will be a grand opening for Willow Court!'

*

Sarah's wedding day dawned, bright and sunny. There was still no break in the weather although every weather reporter spoke of its imminence and the general public were turning to more and more unlikely sources of forecasting, from the behaviour of pigs to the tingling of Bert the farmer's little finger which he insisted had never let him down as a weather barometer.

Willow Court looked magnificent. Rebecca had invited the previous owner Audrey along to see the improvements and she had taken one look and burst into tears. At first worried, Rebecca had been relieved to discover that it looked as beautiful as Audrey remembered it 50 years previously when she had first moved in as a young bride.

The chapel looked like a scene from a film. The doorway was framed by a huge arch of cream flowers, spilling over with roses, lilies, daisies, sweet peas and more, all twining round ivy and trailing greenery. Inside the blissfully cool room with its mellow yellow stone, every pew had a matching waterfall of flowers with rose petals scattered along the short aisle. The sun shone in through the stained glass window and the whole space had an air of peace and beauty. The path from the chapel to the house had been widened and on each side were natural flowers, twining round the trees and hanging over the path with a sweet heavy scent. The staircase had a similar garland twisting all the way up to the landing with trailing fronds of greens that left a delicious smell hanging in the air. Comfortable chairs covered in brocade, velvet and damask were scattered around the reception area next to small tables, all covered in a selection of heavy cream and gilt invitation cards supplied by a local firm.

The dining room was a picture with a long head table, heavily decorated with flowers and several small round tables scattered informally round the room, every chair with a tulle bow decorated with a spray of ivy and a single cream rose. The tables were laid and crystal glasses twinkled in the light. Along one wall, the caterers had laid out a selection of food and plates of canapes and glasses of champagne were constantly being circulated. Every reception room was filled with flowers and gave the impression of a wedding in full flow, briefly suspended in time just waiting for its bridal party to return. The bridal suite had been filled with yet more flowers, a wine cooler holding a bottle of champagne sat on the dressing table, a veil lay on the bed and a pair of cream silk shoes discarded by the open window which let in the scent of the summer flowers and gave a view down to the willow tree and the lake. The cream and gold bed linen was turned back and a heavy gold throw lay across the bottom of the bed, pooling onto the floor. In the corner stood a vintage mannequin dressed in a silk and lace wedding dress. Sarah had been unable to put her own wedding dress on display, the tears had been unstoppable at that point, but a bridal shop in Leeds had been more than happy to put several dresses scattered around the bedrooms in the hope of gathering new customers.

It was the picture of perfection and Rebecca knew Sarah had worked every hour of the last eleven days to bring together an amazing display of 'what if' to Willow Court and Rebecca felt pride flood her heart.

Sarah didn't have time to mourn what should have been her wedding day. They were awash with visitors, and not a single bride walked through the large double doors without letting out a gasp of admiration closely followed by a demand for available dates. The diary was filling up rapidly and a flushed Sarah looked ever more pleased with herself as the day progressed. At one o clock, the time of her wedding, Rebecca looked around to make sure she was still okay and not finding her she went in search down by the lake to find Sarah crying silently underneath the tree. But she dried her eyes and pulled back her shoulders, getting back to the job of meeting and greeting the many potential customers that continued to pour through the door.

Taking two minutes to make a cup of tea in the kitchen, Rebecca slipped off her shoes and groaned with relief.

'Hard day?'

It was Drew. He was standing in the doorway, just as he had so many times before, when he would update her on the progress he was making.

Rebecca slipped her shoes back on and stood up, rubbing her hands down the side of her dress, unaccountably nervous.

'It's been busy.' She acknowledged ruefully, 'which is good so I shouldn't complain.'

Drew nodded then came into the room to stand a few feet away.

'I was so sorry to hear about Sarah and Dom,' he said gently. 'Is she okay?'

Rebecca sighed. 'She says so. She's keeping busy and carrying on with the business.'

'Was it … was it anything to do with Luke?'

Sensitive builder.

He looked concerned and Rebecca shook her head quickly.

'No. She decided she was too young, had rushed into it a little too quickly. She has enjoyed her time working here and there's no doubt Luke was a part of that. But as far as I know she hasn't seen him since she cancelled the wedding. He was a symptom, not the cause.'

Drew scratched his head in such a familiar gesture that Rebecca almost gasped. She hadn't realised how much she'd missed him until she saw him standing there, almost close enough to touch.

'I think Luke was hoping it was a little bit more than that,' he confessed. 'He's thoroughly broken up about the whole thing.'

'They're both young,' said Rebecca with feeling, 'they'll get over it.'

'And you?'

Rebecca could feel the colour starting to fill her cheeks. 'Me?'

'I'm sorry I didn't stay and congratulate you on your own forthcoming wedding.' The words were formal, a little stiff from a man who had always been so comfortable and easy around her. 'But I hope you'll be very happy with Charles.'

Rebecca stayed silent, looking at Drew's chest rather than into his eyes.

'Have you set a date yet? No doubt it will be here?'

'No date. No plans. No real ...'

Rebecca stopped herself short. She'd been about to say no real wedding. Not as yet. Only the night before she'd started to take the ring off again, telling Charles that it was unfair to continue wearing it without giving him an answer. But he'd stopped her once more and told her to wait, until after Sarah's alternative wedding day and Annabelle's wedding, when she had time to think about herself and herself only.

'No...?' asked Drew softly.

Rebecca shook her head. 'Nothing. We haven't had time to plan anything yet, that's all.'

They stood for a moment, neither speaking until Rebecca asked curiously, 'Why didn't you stay?'

Drew looked thoughtful. 'Because it would have hurt to say I was happy for you. Because I wasn't very happy at all and it seemed best to just stay out of the way.'

'You're not happy for me?'

'I wasn't,' corrected Drew. 'I've had time to get used to the idea now and of course I'm happy for you. If you're happy, I'm happy.'

'But why …'

Drew gave a rueful smile, ruffling his already untidy hair. 'I grew very fond of you Bec. I was rather hoping when the work was finished and you stopped being my boss and it was slightly more appropriate,' he gave her a grin although it lacked its usual joy, 'that we might find time to sit down and get to know each other a little more.'

'Oh.'

'I'm sorry, it was my mistake. I hadn't understood how close you and Charles had become, I certainly hadn't realised that you were on the verge of getting married otherwise I would never have, never …'

Never what, thought Rebecca. Never looked at her with that intense blue gaze, never smiled at her with that lazy smile, never kissed her, holding her in his arms and close to his chest so that she felt completely safe and never wanted him to let go. Suddenly she felt like crying. Not just for herself but for Sarah and Dom, Luke and Drew, Charles. What a strange summer it had been, so full of highs and lows. It had brought her the new start she had longed for and yet didn't seem to be filling her with the happiness she had imagined. So much had happened and yet nobody seemed particularly happy as a result.

'I shouldn't have kissed you,' finished Drew, watching Rebecca's eyes fill with tears. 'I am sorry Rebecca, truly.'

Should she tell him she wasn't crying because he had kissed her, rather that he had stopped kissing her.

'Please don't apologise,' she whispered.

'Mum, any sign of that tea,' said an exhausted Sarah appearing in the kitchen doorway. 'Oh hello Drew, I didn't know you were here.'

'Just popped in to see how you were doing, see if you needed a builder at all?'

Conscientious builder.

Sarah grinned. 'Well seeing as you're here, could you have a look at the tap in one of the bedrooms, it's definitely running a little and the door to the drawing room seems stiff. And …'

'Whoa,' laughed Drew, 'enough! Let me get my kit out of the car. Do I have to wear a wedding tux?'

Sarah giggled. 'Well there are a couple lying around, we could have you working incognito,' and leaving Rebecca in the kitchen listening to the thud of her heart, they wandered off, their voices drifting down the hallway as Rebecca wrapped her arms around herself and wondered what to do.

Chapter 35

Annabelle arrived in a sweep of gravel, almost falling out of the car in her excitement.

'Oh,' she squeaked excitedly as she walked into the reception hall. 'Oh yes! How perfect.'

Daniel nodded approvingly at the elegant and beautifully presented space before wandering off to inspect the windows and the pointing.

'Sarah! Sarah! Have you arranged that for me?'

Annabelle was waving her hand towards the staircase and its wonderful trail of twisted flowers.'

'Er no.'

'No! why not? I want it to look exactly like that on my wedding day. Well not exactly the same. All cream is a little dreary don't you think. The same design but with pink. And not a pale pink, I'm still a little worried that the flowers you've arranged for the centre pieces are a little washed out. I want a proper pink to brighten the place up. And more of them, let's make a real statement.'

'But Annabelle you've already reached your floristry budget.'

'And make sure there's plenty of green, have it trailing down the steps.'

'Annabelle, you've already overspent on your flower budget.

'And let's add some bows. Lots of pink bows along the top.'

'No. you can't afford it!'

At last Annabelle turned from her contemplation of the staircase to look blankly at Sarah.

'Can't afford it, what on earth do you mean?'

'Dad gave me the budget for the flowers weeks ago and it's all been spent. You added extra centre pieces on every table and you wanted those giant pots of lilies in the chapel. There's nothing left in the budget for a garland.'

Sarah looked up at the staircase thoughtfully, 'I suppose we could add the pink bows along the rail. That wouldn't cost too much.'

'I don't want bows, I want flowers. Like those, only more of them.'

'But ...'

'No! please don't talk about budgets again, increase the budget!'

'Er, right. Are you sure?'

'Of course I'm sure! I want it to look like this.'

Any minute now, thought Rebecca, she would stamp her foot.

'Okay, okay,' said Sarah soothingly, making copious notes in her book. 'I'll arrange a garland.'

With a beaming smile Annabelle sailed forth into the dining room and Rebecca and Sarah looked at each other and grinned as another excited squeal filled the room.

'This is exactly how I want the room to look Sarah. Well done. It's perfect. Now, we need to change the colours of course, and the tables seem a little haphazard.'

'It's a more informal approach ...'

'Can we get them lined up properly?'

Sarah flipped open her book and sighed. 'If you want.'

'And I really don't like the idea of all this vintage mismatched chinaware. I want matching plates, I've seen the perfect pattern in John Lewis. I'll send you a link.'

'You're going to buy a dinner service specifically for your wedding?' asked a shocked Sarah.

'No. I want you to buy one.'

'But Annabelle, we don't buy a different dinner service for each guest! You can have a matching set but it will be the one we have which is plain white.'

'Oh no, that won't do. You'll have to get a new one.'

'No,' interrupted Rebecca firmly. 'It doesn't work like that.'

Annabelle scowled. 'White won't do,' she snapped. 'I want a gold band at the very least.'

'Then paint one on,' snapped back Rebecca. 'You get to use what we've got.'

'This is most unsatisfactory,' hissed Annabelle. 'Not good enough at all.'

'Let me show you the bridal suite,' said Sarah, desperately stepping between the two. 'I'm sure you'll love it.'

Almost growling Annabelle turned on her heel and set off for the staircase. 'I've taken dozens of bookings today and not one of them has made half the demands she has,' muttered Sarah with feeling.

'Well,' sighed Rebecca, 'it will soon be over and hopefully she'll stay in Devon for a while,' and smothering giggles they followed Annabelle to the bridal room which she declared was absolutely perfect.

'Except for the throw. I really think you should have had a red one, red for romance and passion.'

Sarah's eyebrows shot up. She was unused to thinking of her father in the same sentence as passion and romance.

'And of course I want a bottle of champagne on the dressing table,' announced Annabelle, 'and a bottle of the good stuff, not the cheap stuff you're giving the guests.'

'Annabelle, you've chosen the most expensive wine we offer for your toasts!'

'And a few more flowers in here.'

'Okay.'

'And some chocolates. Oh, and some cigars!'

'It's a non-smoking hotel Annabelle.'

'Daniel is your father!'

Sarah looked at her in exasperation. 'And this is still a non-smoking hotel!'

'And could we upgrade the toiletries please. Jo Malone I think.'

Sarah sighed and carried on writing as Rebecca stared out of the window at Drew walking across the car park to get something out of his van.

'But it is quite perfect, well done.'

'Rebecca! Rebecca!'

She dragged her gaze away from Drew.

'I said it's all quite perfect!'

So perfect that Annabelle had asked for a change in every single room and added thousands to her bill in the space of a few minutes.

'Thank you,' inclining her head graciously, Rebecca decided she'd had enough of Annabelle's demands for a while and excusing herself with a smile she fled down the stairs and into the domed room which was blessedly empty.

She stood underneath the magnificent dome and looked upwards to the thousand sparkling crystals that fell like a waterfall from the chandelier towards the centre of the room. The plasterwork looked as though it had always been there, Brian's repairs merging seamlessly with the original and she closed her eyes and stood with her arms spread outwards turning in a small circle She recalled the photograph she had seen all those weeks ago, of a young couple dancing across the highly polished floor. The curtains had drifted upwards behind them, echoing their movements as they were caught mid spin, gazing into each other's eyes, full of love and the excitement of what lay ahead. They epitomised everything that Rebecca had wanted to bring back to Willow Court. And now she could join them, she could glide across that floor, held in Charles's arms as they danced and looked forward to their future. She concentrated hard, hearing the swell of music in the background, feeling the people gathered around watching. She could hear the swish of her dress as she spun and turned, she could see the twinkling crystals flash as she spun beneath them. The windows were open and the stone terrace, full of flowers, beckoned and she imagined the dusk falling and the guests spilling out into the warm evening air, still dancing, still happy.

Her hands dropped and she stood still, opening her eyes. There were tears trickling slowly down her cheeks and her heart felt heavy and suddenly tired. Because although she could imagine the feel of silk against her skin, the sound of music in her ears and the scent of the flowers in the air, the one thing she hadn't been able to imagine was Charles. She had tried to place herself in his arms and failed. She had tried to imagine his breath on her cheek and it wasn't there. No matter how hard she had tried, she had been unable to bring Charles into her dream. She was facing the windows, looking down the garden towards the lake and she thought she caught a glimpse of Drew's head in the trees. The tears became sobs. She had failed to make Charles materialise but there had been arms around her waist, there had been a head close to hers, lips grazing her own. And they had all belonged to Drew. She looked down at her fingers and slowly pulled off the ring nestled there. She couldn't marry Charles. Maybe she had always known she wouldn't be able to say yes because as her own daughter had told her only days ago, she couldn't marry one person if she was capable of having such feelings for another.

She stood in front of the open windows, clutching the ring Charles had given her and crying. It was over, she needed to tell him so. Perhaps she and Sarah would spend the rest of their days in Willow Court, forever planning the weddings of others whilst never managing to attend their own, like a modern day Miss Havisham. She realised that it had been Drew in the trees and he was now in the garden walking towards the house. Licking at the salty tears on her cheeks, her body shook with the effort of swallowing her cries. Rebecca saw his head tilt as he saw her. He paused and watched for a moment then vaulting the small wall he almost ran into the room and without saying a word he wrapped his arms around her and pulled her to his chest.

She sobbed until there was nothing left but the odd hiccup and then stood still as he gently wiped her face with his own sleeve. He unravelled her clenched fingers to look at the still sparkling ring in her palm and then curled them back over to hide it from sight.

'I can't do it,' she said her throat raw with tears. 'I can't marry Charles.'

'Why?'

'It's not fair.'

'Why? Why isn't it fair Bec, why?'

He put one finger under her chin and tilted up her head so he could see her face more clearly.

'Why can't you marry him?'

Rebecca's lip quivered. 'Because I think I might love you.'

A slow smile spread across his face. It got wider and wider until it was a definite grin. 'You do?'

Rebecca nodded, a stray tear rolling down her cheek.

'Y-yes,' she mumbled unhappily.

'And is that why you're crying?'

She nodded.

'You don't want to love me?'

'I don't know,' she whispered, 'I don't know what I want any more.'

Drew nodded gravely. 'It can be confusing can't it?'

Another nod.

'I know something that might help.'

'You do?'

'I think so,' and ever so gently he dropped his head and let his lips cover hers. Softly, so softly, then as Rebecca relaxed and leaned into his arms he kissed her with all the passion and love she had ever wanted.

Clever builder.

'Did that help?' he asked eventually as they stopped and hung onto each other for support.

'I'm not really sure,' gasped Rebecca. 'I forgot to think about anything.'

'That's not a problem at all,' replied Drew with another grin, 'we can keep trying.'

And they did until Daniel, looking to see where Rebecca had disappeared to, found them a long time later, standing by the window with their arms around each other and staring out at the darkening sky.

Chapter 36

Rebecca ignored Daniel's open mothered splutterings and waved him away, telling him she would be along in a few minutes.

Tearing herself out of Drew's arms, she wondered how it was possible to feel so happy and so sad at the same time. She felt so utterly complete in Drew's arms that she couldn't believe she hadn't spent her entire life there. But she knew she had to speak to Charles. She had never lied when she had claimed to love him. She still loved him, just not with the overwhelming passion that Drew had brought into her life. She had told Helen and Emma that the ground had never moved when she had been with Charles and it wasn't something that she needed. Their gentle and considerate love would last much longer than lust and passion. How wrong she had been, how could she have contemplated settling for so little.

'Stay!' commanded Drew, pulling her in for another kiss.

'I can't,' wriggling out of his arms Rebecca took a step back. If he didn't stop kissing her like that she wouldn't get anything else done.

'Then come back soon?'

Rebecca sighed, 'I have to speak to Charles. And Sarah. And Daniel will explode if I don't let him know what's happening.'

'So I'm well down the pecking order?'

'Yes, I'm afraid so. Just for today. And maybe tomorrow. But after that,' she carried on hurriedly at his groan, 'I'm all yours.'

His eyes lit up. 'I like the sound of that.' He stretched out a hand to try and pull her back into his arms but Rebecca sidestepped him swiftly.

'Later,' she promised breathlessly.

Shaking his head in disgust Drew let her think she had escaped him only to grab her and kiss her thoroughly once more.

'Stop,' she begged without conviction.

'I can't. I've spent most of the summer wanting to do exactly that and wondering if you wanted it too. And now I can, I don't want to stop.'

For once Drew was looking serious and Rebecca wanted nothing more than to drag him upstairs to the bridal suite and christen the new bed.

But she wouldn't do that to Charles and she knew that in his heart Drew wouldn't want it either.

So he let her go, reluctantly, and Rebecca went in search of Daniel and Annabelle who were standing by the front door. Daniel was pacing in agitation as Annabelle looked puzzled. Sarah was ignoring them both but as Rebecca appeared she looked towards her mother and then looked again. Maybe, thought Rebecca, it was because she just couldn't stop smiling. There was a ridiculously large grin on her face which she was finding it impossible to quell. Or maybe it was because her face was red and scratched from the thorough kissing Drew had given her with two day old stubble. Or maybe it was because she was quite simply radiating happiness. Rebecca didn't know which gave her away but Sarah was staring at her open mouthed. And when Drew suddenly appeared behind her Sarah couldn't have looked more amazed as she slowly put one and one together and came up with a wedding booking.

Rebecca looked over at Drew as he stayed by the reception desk, allowing her to go home and do what she must.

Oh my sexy builder, she thought grinning at him. She would be back soon.

'Come on then,' she said cheerfully to Daniel and Annabelle. 'Let's get off,' and with a little wink in Drew's direction she drove home.

The meeting with Charles was as fraught as she was expecting, although not the shock to him that she thought it may be.

'I've had to stop you taking the ring off twice Rebecca darling,' he had said sadly. 'That didn't bode well. I think I knew that you were going to say 'No', I just felt that the longer you kept on the ring and the longer you took to answer me, the more chance I had that you may decide to say yes.'

Rebecca had cried and hugged him as she apologised. She was honest and told him that she had been fighting feelings for Drew throughout the summer but had truly believed she loved Charles and her heart broke as he nodded and told her that he'd suspected as much. But as ever gracious and courteous, there were no accusations or raised voices, just a great deal of sadness as he wished her all the best for her future.

Eventually she had left him and returned home to find Annabelle making even more mess in her kitchen.

Two seconds after Rebecca appeared, Annabelle grabbed her hand. 'Where's your ring? Have you called off the wedding?' she asked hopefully.

Rebecca shook her head. 'No. Yes.' There had never been a wedding, she had finally given Charles his answer and it had been no.

Annabelle's mouth hung open. 'So you're not getting married. You're not even engaged?'

'No.'

Annabelle looked like a cat that had swallowed a rather large carton of cream. 'I see! So now it's just me and Daniel. No other weddings?'

Rebecca shook her head, no energy left for anger. 'No more weddings Annabelle. Just you.'

Smiling happily, Annabelle returned to stirring the rather grey Bolognese she was making. For someone who had declared that she loved to entertain, her skills in the kitchen had turned out to be surprisingly limited. She was much better at ordering takeaway and positively shone at ordering the most expensive meal in the restaurant.

'Oh poor you,' she cooed in delight. 'Well of course, you've still got me and Daniel. Actually, I didn't think Charles was suited to you. He really didn't seem to welcome the idea of our family being such a strong unit.'

Rebecca grabbed a glass and poured herself a generous measure from the bottle on the table.

'You mean he wasn't keen on the idea of you and Daniel using my house as a second home?'

'What? That's not a nice thing to say Becky. We're only thinking of you, we don't want you to feel …'

'Oh I think I know this one Annabelle. Let me guess, you don't want me to feel left out now that you've joined the family and my children are going to ignore me and call you mother and I'll be a lonely cat lady eating macaroni in my kitchen?'

Annabelle looked a little puzzled. 'I didn't know you liked cats?'

'It's a figure of speech Annabelle!'

Rebecca shook her head in frustration. Because the truth was that only a few months earlier when Annabelle had appeared on her doorstep, clutching Daniel's arm and spouting goodwill in Rebecca's direction, she had been worried about being lonely. And when Sarah had come sweeping in with her big smile and generous nature and taken Annabelle into their lives without a second thought, Rebecca had felt the stirrings of jealousy as the two of them had sat side by side pouring over bridal magazines and giggling as they planned their rosy futures. But that had been a life time ago and since then Rebecca had loved, lost and loved again and she knew that her life was going to be every bit as rosy as Annabelle's own and would include neither cats or macaroni, although she was open to the idea of a dog after Drew had told her his dream of the three of them sitting in front of a blazing open fire that winter.

'Right,' said Annabelle uninterested. 'Anyway, as I was saying, you don't need to worry because Daniel and I ...'

'I don't need to worry full stop Annabelle. The reason I'm not marrying Charles is because I'm in love with Drew. We're deliriously happy and looking forward to spending a great deal of time together, the rest of our lives in fact.'

She wondered if it would be too childish to add 'so there' but didn't need to because Annabelle forgot all about her now burning Bolognese as she stared at Rebecca in disbelief.

'You and Drew?'

'Yep'

'The builder?'

'Oh yes!' Her gorgeous, sexy, conscientious, dedicated, accomplished builder.

'But he's ......'

'I know,' grinned Rebecca.

Annabelle gaped like a fish out of water. 'But he might be after your ...'

'Don't even go there Annabelle. Drew loves me and quite frankly, as far as I'm concerned he can have all my money if he wants it.'

For a moment Rebecca thought Annabelle might actually pass out as she gasped for air. 'You're going to give him all your money?' she wailed loudly.

Drew had told Rebecca that one of the things holding him back over the summer had been that Rebecca was employing him. 'It just didn't feel right coming onto the boss,' he had said kissing her.

'Drew,' Rebecca had started seriously. 'If my money is a problem ...'

'Not in the slightest,' Drew had mumbled, more interested in going back to kissing her than talking.

'But sometimes men can be ...'

'Rebecca, I love you. I own a very successful business and I'm far from being a pauper. I don't have your kind of money but it doesn't bother me that you have it.'

'Really?'

Drew had shrugged. 'Do you mind?'

'No, I quite like it.'

'Then what's the problem? Look, you can hide it all away if you want, somewhere I'll never be able to find it. Or just carry on enjoying it. Let's face it, we can go on some pretty special holidays with what you've got in the bank.'

And Rebecca had thrown back her head and laughed because she could tell from the look in Drew's eyes that he really didn't care at all.

'As long as we're together Bec, that's the main thing. Money can't buy happiness, but when you're already happy it can certainly help! We will have a wonderful life together my love. But I want to be with you, not your bank account, just you.'

Rebecca smiled at the memory and watched as Annabelle covered her horrified mouth with her hand. 'You're going to give all your money to a penniless builder?'

'Don't be ridiculous Annabelle, although if I wanted to I would. What I do with my money has nothing to do with you.

'But Daniel …'

'And it has nothing to do with Daniel either.'

Glaring at her, Annabelle slammed the spoon she was still holding onto the surface.

'How could you be so selfish? How could you be so horrible? You would give your money to someone you met a few weeks ago but not to poor Daniel. You would leave him poverty stricken rather than give him a penny from your millions!'

Rebecca looked at her in astonishment. 'Daniel isn't poverty stricken. And I've asked him if he was happy with the settlement. He told me he doesn't want any more.'

'What?'

Rebecca took a step back at the sheer fury in Annabelle's eyes.

'He did what?'

'Er, he said he was happy with what he had,' said Rebecca warily.

Annabelle's lips twisted with rage. 'And what about me?'

'What about you?'

'What about whether I'm happy?'

Rebecca took another step back, putting the table between them.

'We didn't talk about you Annabelle, I was talking to Daniel about our divorce.'

'Well I'm part of this family now,' spat Annabelle, 'I think I need to be included in these conversations.'

'You're not actually part of my family Annabelle and I don't think my money has anything to do with you …'

She leapt back as Annabelle, incandescent with rage gave a small scream of anger.

'How dare you! I am marrying Daniel, I will be his wife and it has everything to do with me!'

'Er, maybe you should talk to Daniel,' suggested Rebecca warily, keeping as much space as possible between them.

'Maybe I should,' snapped Annabelle. 'Because this is not good enough. It's simply not good enough,' and leaving the Bolognese to burn, she stormed out of the kitchen

Oh dear, thought Rebecca, after all that hard work maybe there wouldn't be any wedding at Willow Court this summer.

Chapter 37

Rebecca dashed to the hob and turned off the heat, before following the sound of Annabelle's heels clicking down the hallway in search of Daniel. But as she drew level with the front door it flew open and to her surprise Sarah appeared.

'Sarah! Hello darling, I wasn't expecting you tonight.'

'No, but I wanted to see you,' said Sarah meaningfully. 'I thought we had some catching up to do.'

Rebecca blushed a little, the colour deepening as Sarah glanced down at her mother's hand to see an empty space where Charles' diamond ring had previously sat.

Raising her eyebrows, Sarah gave her mum a quizzical look. 'Do you have something to tell me?'

Rebecca couldn't help a small giggle from erupting, it was as though their roles had been reversed and Sarah was the mother grilling her daughter about a new boyfriend.

'Well,' she began happily, only to stop at the loud squeal that came from the living room, followed by an angry exchange of voices.

'What on earth ...'

'Oh Annabelle is a little bit cross.'

Another scream of anger.

'Well she's very cross actually.'

'Why?'

'Well I told her about Drew and ...' Rebecca screwed up her nose, she wasn't sure how a conversation imparting good news had deteriorated so badly. 'Well, she was worried that I was going to give him all my money.' Sarah's eyebrows shot up even further. 'She said I should give some to Daniel and when I mentioned that he'd said he was happy with his settlement and didn't want any more, she became quite angry.'

Sarah was staring at her open mouthed. 'We definitely need a catch up,' she gasped. 'So you and Drew are together?'

Rebecca nodded shyly.

'And you're going to give him all your money?'

'Of course not!'

'Okay, well your money, your choice,' shrugged Sarah.

'And you'd offered Dad some more?'

'Well not exactly, but I had asked him if he wished he'd taken more and he said he was happy with what he had.'

'Right. And how come I didn't know any of this was going on?'

Rebecca grinned. 'It's been a busy summer.'

'You can say that again!'

'You came by because you guessed about Drew?'

'Hard not to, when you left he couldn't stop grinning. He was wandering around singing and looking absurdly happy.'

Rebecca blushed again.

'Anyway, I needed to give Dad his invoice for the wedding so I thought I'd kill two birds.'

'Let's hand over the invoice then we can open a bottle of wine and have a chat,' Rebecca suggested. 'I've got so much to tell you!'

Impulsively she hugged her daughter. Sensitive to Sarah's own precarious emotional state she was trying not to be too obviously happy, but it was proving hard. She wanted to share her joy with everyone.

They walked warily into the living room to find Daniel standing by the fire looking harassed and Annabelle sniffing unhappily.

'Hi!' said Sarah nervously, looking from one to the other. 'Is this a bad time? I can come back.'

Daniel waved her in. 'Not at all. Do you have my invoice?'

'Er yes. I'm afraid it has gone up quite a bit since we last spoke.'

'Why?' barked Daniel.

'Well,' Sarah licked her lips. 'Annabelle has asked for a few extra things to be included and, well they were all expensive.'

'Invoice?' queried Annabelle in a sulky tone, cheeks still damp with tears.

'I asked Sarah to keep me up to date with the cost of the wedding.'

'Why?'

Daniel stared at her. 'Why? Because I need to know how much it's all costing?'

'But why? I mean Rebecca said she would pay.'

'She did no such thing and I thought I had made it clear at the time. She has very kindly given us the use of Willow Court for our wedding. That is all. I wouldn't dream of asking my ex-wife to pay for my wedding! I will pay Annabelle.'

Annabelle glared at Rebecca and Sarah standing close to each other by the doorway. 'Well she can afford it,' she said nastily. 'Why on earth shouldn't she pay? She has enough money.'

'Annabelle!' thundered Daniel. 'You are marrying me not Rebecca and how much money she has is of no concern to either of us.'

'But it is! She's so mean, she's keeping it all to herself and she should have shared it with you. We should have lots of money as well.'

'BE QUIET! We are not having this conversation again, do you understand me?'

Rebecca felt Sarah flinch at her side and saw Annabelle take a step back. She was willing to bet that this was the first time she had seen Daniel in this kind of rage. It had been part of Rebecca's everyday life during the later years of their marriage.

Daniel was quivering with anger, his skin mottled with colour, flecks of spittle exploding from his mouth as he spoke.

'Rebecca is my ex-wife. She is not my personal banker. She does not need to hand out pocket money to me. I have a very good lifestyle of my own and I will not be treated like a charity case. DO YOU UNDERSTAND?'

Annabelle's chin was wobbling alarmingly. 'But Daniel…'

'No!' he bellowed. 'I am paying for this wedding. I will pay my own way.'

Collapsing into the nearest chair, Annabelle let the tears roll down her cheeks unchecked. 'But I want a special wedding. You promised me a perfect wedding day.'

Daniel snatched the invoice from Sarah, glaring at Annabelle. 'Perfect doesn't always equal expensive!'

He started looking down the invoice and Rebecca winced as she saw his face darken even more, his cheeks turning beetroot.

'£10,000 on flowers! Dear God, you've spent £10,000 on flowers?'

Annabelle sniffed. 'The reception hall is so plain it needed lots of flowers to liven it up and the chapel definitely needs something, it's so dreary …'

'Champagne! You want every toast to be made with top quality champagne. £500 just for a toast!'

He clutched his heart with his free hand and Rebecca started to feel genuinely worried about his blood pressure.

'Are you mad?' he whispered. 'Have you lost your mind?'

'Everyone judges a wedding by the quality of the food and wine Daniel! I won't have our guests toasting us with some cheap plonk, what would they think …'

'You've changed the wine we chose, you've chosen a bottle that's twice the price!'

'Well, I tested it again and I really didn't think …'

'We decided on chicken, we chose chicken and you've changed it to fillet steak?'

'Oh Daniel, everyone has chicken. I wanted something special ….'

'£1500 for someone to play a harp while we wait for you to arrive?'

'It's quite the done thing …

'You're only upstairs! You will be in a room upstairs and you want to spend £1500 for someone playing a tune for the two minutes it will take you to come downstairs?'

'But guests need entertaining while they're waiting ….'

'Then walk quicker!' yelled Daniel.

Annabelle pouted. 'Brides are meant to walk slowly.'

'£148 pounds on bathroom extras? What the hell are bathroom extras?'

'Sarah said I could have Jo Malone in the bathroom. I didn't realise she would charge for it,' snapped Annabelle giving Sarah a reproachful look.

'Who the hell is Jo Malone and why would you want him in the bathroom?' demanded a shocked Daniel. 'No! don't answer. No, no, no!'

'Er, no?' asked Annabelle hesitantly. 'No to Jo Malone?'

Daniel looked up from the invoice with a glazed expression. 'No to Jo Malone, no to the harpist, no to champagne toasts and fillet steak and wine at,' he looked back done at the invoice and gasped, '£47 bloody pounds a bottle!'

Annabelle stood up in horror.

'Daniel what are you saying?'

'I'm saying no Annabelle. I'm saying a great big bloody NO! We are not spending this kind of money on a wedding. Absolutely not. NO!'

Annabelle was shaking, her hand was pressed against her mouth in genuine horror and her eyes were filling with fresh tears. Turing round she gave a venomous look at Rebecca. 'This is all your fault!' she screamed. 'If you weren't so mean …'

'SHUT UP!' yelled Daniel. 'Stop blaming her. You're marrying me Annabelle. Me, not Rebecca!'

Rebecca stepped forward, anxiety clouding her face. 'Daniel …'

'No!' He held up a hand. 'No, we've had this discussion before Rebecca.' He drew himself up to his full height and Rebecca was relieved to see a little of the dull red colour leave his cheeks as he took a deep breath. 'I do not want any money from you. I will not take any money from you,' he ignored Annabelle's little mew of distress. 'Thank you but no.'

Rebecca had been about to ask him to sit down while she got him a brandy but she smiled anyway. 'Okay.'

'But Daniel,' wailed Annabelle, 'just think how happy we could be if Rebecca gave you more money. Just think what a wonderful life we could have if …' her words trailed away at the look Daniel gave her and instead she sat in the chair sobbing quietly.

'Thank you,' Daniel said stiffly to Sarah, waving the invoice in the air. 'I think Annabelle and I need to continue our conversation in private.' He turned to Rebecca. 'And I think it would be better if we moved out. We'll move into a hotel,' he cast a severe look in Annabelle's direction. 'We'll move out tomorrow, I apologise for making such a scene in your house.'

'You don't have to do that, really you don't,' said Rebecca, deciding she really needed to work on saying what she was thinking. She would love them to leave, had been looking forward to the moment ever since they had arrived. She was beginning to forget what it was like to have her beautiful house all to herself.

'No, I think we've outstayed our welcome. We'll check into a hotel – what was the one you used to stay at, Quebecs?'

Rebecca nodded. The hotel had been her home from home when she had won her millions. In fact it had been in Quebecs that she had sat nervously opposite the lottery advisors who came to talk her through her win and how the money would arrive in her bank. For several weeks she had lied to Daniel about her need to visit Leeds, pretending she was visiting her mother when in fact she was relaxing in the delightful luxury of Quebecs hotel and planning her new life. She bit her lip. It had not been her finest hour, keeping her win from Daniel for so long, even if she had convinced herself she was doing it for all the right reasons.

'Annabelle was right,' she blurted out, 'I did let her think I was paying for the wedding. We had a conversation and I think I said something about er, the invoice and paying.'

She was aware that Sarah was staring at her, Daniel was looking at her doubtfully and even Annabelle couldn't hide her surprise.

'Because it had always been my intention to pay for the whole reception as a wedding present,' she continued. 'I mean everything, not just Willow Court. The flowers and the wine and the er, harpist.'

'That would be extraordinarily generous of you Rebecca,' Daniel said looking at her shrewdly. 'Of course I couldn't accept.'

'I think you should,' argued Rebecca gently, 'for old time's sake Daniel. Let me do this for you.'

For once Annabelle didn't speak, just looked hopefully from Rebecca and back to Daniel.

'We can discuss it later,' he eventually answered gruffly, 'but we are still moving out. I'll phone Quebecs tomorrow and see if they have a room.' He folded up the invoice neatly and pushed it into his pocket. 'Annabelle?' he pointed towards the door and with a final sniff, Annabelle stood up and followed him meekly out of the room.

Sarah released a great gust of air. 'Oh my God,' she whispered, waiting to hear Annabelle's heels make their way up the staircase. 'Do you think Dad knows?'

Rebecca sank into one of the chairs, quite exhausted from watching the scene played out before them.

'Knows what?'

'That Annabelle is marrying him for your money?'

Rebecca shook her head. 'I really don't know.'

'Is that why she wants to spend so much time here? So she can live your lifestyle?'

'I suspect so.'

There was a moment of silence. 'Poor Dad.'

Poor Daniel indeed, thought Rebecca. She thought back to a few months earlier when he had phoned her out of the blue to announce his forthcoming wedding. She had felt envious. He had moved on, found someone new and started a whole new life, exactly what Rebecca had wanted to do. He'd arrived with Annabelle clinging to his arm and Rebecca had actually resented the obvious love he had for his new wife to be.

'Do you think they'll go ahead with the wedding?'

Rebecca shrugged. 'Who knows,' she sighed.

'Let's hope this isn't an omen for the future,' said Sarah. 'Book your wedding at Willow Court and it's sure to be cancelled!'

Rebecca looked shocked then joined in with her daughter's gentle laughter.

'It's not been the best start, 'she agreed.

'But it could all change. You and Drew could break the curse?'

Rebecca snorted. 'We haven't even been on a date yet? It's a bit early for wedding bells!'

'Oh I don't know, you both look pretty smitten to me!'

They smiled at each other.

'Willow Court had quite an effect on us all over the summer didn't it?' asked Rebecca dreamily.

'It certainly did. But Luke and I didn't fall in love. Oh I know he has a bit of a crush on me but it won't take him long to get over it. I didn't call off the wedding because of Luke, Willow Court made me grow up and showed me how much there was out there. It was too soon to get married.'

'And Dom?' asked Rebecca gently.

'I don't know. I really don't know. I still love him, I'm just not ready to get married to him. Whether we can rescue anything is up for debate. I wouldn't blame him if he didn't want to talk to me ever again!'

Rebecca patted Sarah's hand. 'You both did the right thing, not going ahead with a marriage you weren't sure about.'

'And what about Charles?'

Rebecca sighed. 'I wanted Charles to ask me to marry him and I had every intention of saying yes. It's just that when he did I realised I was settling for something less than I really wanted.'

'Drew?'

'Maybe. He makes me feel so much more alive than Charles ever did. I thought it was a silly summer obsession and would soon disappear but after a while I came to understand that whether it was going to last or not, it's what I wanted out of life. I don't want steady and gentle and caring. I want passion and excitement, I want to feel breathless and impulsive and – well I want Drew.'

Chapter 38

The weather finally broke and in a flash the heat of the summer was replaced with torrential rain and plummeting temperatures. The farmers rejoiced, the water companies heaved a sigh of relief and Rebecca and Sarah stood in the doorway of Willow Court looking out as the grass became instantly greener and the fish in the lake swam round excitedly at the infusion of fresh water into their rapidly shrinking home.

Of course it didn't make hosting a wedding easy. The flowers that framed the chapel door were receiving a pummelling and the poor florist who had spent hours twisting and positioning every petal was now soaked and shivering in the kitchen cupping a hot chocolate. Inside Sarah and Rebecca had run around the rooms closing the windows which had been open pretty much the whole of the summer. The heating was turned on and they held their breath as the new boiler sprang into life. But Drew had done them proud and there wasn't a single leak to be found and within minutes the radiators were sending out a blissful wave of warm air.

Reliable builder.

The fire in the drawing room was lit and the room soon filled with the smell of applewood as the flames crackled and danced and sent out a comforting glow. The staircase was bedecked with flowers and in the kitchen the caterers were working their magic in the bank of new ovens. The dining room was set and every table glittered under a selection of gleaming crockery and sparkling glasses, the rain beating at the windows hardly noticeable behind the soft white curtains and the glow of the chandelier.

Rebecca was still in jeans and a T-shirt having been anxiously inspecting every corner and every room.

'Mum you really need to get changed. You're going to end up being late.'

'Do you think the bedrooms are warm enough, should we turn up the heating?'

'The bedrooms are toasty. The temperature is perfect.'

'What about the dining room, people might get chilly and …'

'The dining room is also toasty and don't forget it will soon be full of bodies and warm food. It doesn't need to be any warmer.'

'Is the chapel warm? All that stone …'

'Mum! The chapel is warm, the drawing room is warm, everywhere is warm! Stop fussing and go get ready!'

Rebecca stopped, looking round her. 'It does look beautiful doesn't it?' she sighed in relief. 'And I know I'm fussing but this is the first wedding at Willow Court and I want everything to be …'

'Perfect! Yes I know. You keep telling me!'

Laughing Rebecca heaved a sigh. 'Okay! It's done, ready, finished … perfect!'

She stood at the bottom of the huge staircase next to her daughter as they both took a moment to admire the sight. They had turned Willow Court around, restored its elegant glory, its beauty and timeless style. And today it would welcome the first wedding guests. It was a job well done and Rebecca felt a glow of pride at their achievements. Sarah hugged her mother as they silently rejoiced, then gently turned her around.

'Now will you please go upstairs and get ready! Drew will be here soon and you're still in jeans!'

With a last look, Rebecca ran lightly up the stairs, admiring the fronds of ivy that trailed down the staircase and the multitude of flowers that wound their way round every spindle. Her dress was ready, her shoes standing beneath and her makeup was spread across the dressing table. There was the slam of a car door, the first guest had probably arrived and she resisted the urge to peep out of the window to see who it was. They had hired several young men to escort each guest from their car to the chapel holding up huge umbrellas so their finery stayed dry and intact until they slipped into a pew in the warm chapel filled with the scent of flowers.

With a deep breath Rebecca started to get ready. Nerves fluttered in her stomach. This was the beginning of so much, a new business, a new life. How much had changed in just a few short months she thought, sliding her arms into her dress, how much had happened. And how much she was looking forward to the future. It was her second chance, her time to put the past behind her and start over again and she couldn't wait.

'Ready?' shouted Sarah and opening the door she found her daughter, in her silk bridesmaid dress, her hair brushed and a flower tucked neatly behind one ear.

'You look lovely my darling,' she said hugging her daughter.

'Hey, watch the flower and you don't look bad yourself now come on, let's get this show on the road,' and grinning they walked back down the stairs.

'I thought you two had decided to give it a miss.' Drew was standing in the doorway, watching the rain bounce off the floor and high into the air.

'There's been a lot to do,' said Rebecca with feeling. 'It's a huge test today, our first wedding!'

'Stop worrying,' and Drew pulled her into his arms, kissing her lipstick right off.

They both ignored Sarah's little tut as she whipped out a tissue for Drew's face and a lipstick to repair the damage to Rebecca's make-up. 'It's going to be fine Bec darling. There isn't a person here who won't think that this is anything less than perfection.'

'Becky! Becky!' the high-pitched voice swept down the stairs and the three of them rolled their eyes and suppressed their giggles.

'Well almost no-one,' whispered Drew as they all turned to watch Annabelle wiggle down the staircase in her dress, holding her veil over one arm as she waved a petulant arm towards the front doors.

'Can't you do something about this rain?'

Rebecca could feel Drew's body shake with laughter behind her and she poked him in the ribs as she returned Annabelle's gaze solemnly.

'What would you like me to do?' she asked gravely

'Well I don't know, you're the one who runs weddings.'

Rebecca gave a determined smile. She had promised herself that today she would not let Annabelle make her angry. Today she would be calm and pleasant. Today would be a day of celebration and happiness. Although she wasn't entirely sure she would be successful.

'I'm afraid the weather isn't in my remit Annabelle. But you look lovely,' she added dutifully.

'Well no thanks to Sarah!' snapped Annabelle. 'She's my bridesmaid, she should have been upstairs looking after me not running around down here.'

Rebecca tried to stretch her mouth into a smile. 'But Annabelle,' she reminded her patiently, 'you decided that you wanted all the dark pink roses taken out of the centre pieces and swapped for the pink daisies in the staircase garland. Sarah can't do that and brush your hair for you.'

'Well you could have taken over!'

At the hair brushing or the rose reorganisation, wondered Rebecca.

'Well it's done now and it looks lovely, as do you.'

'Is the harpist here?'

'Yes,' said Drew helpfully. 'I've just taken her over to the chapel and she's happily er, plucking away.'

'Good. Where's the photographer gone?'

Probably to put his head in the nearest gas oven thought Rebecca. Annabelle had been directing his every move all morning, demanding that he make her look happier, more excited, younger, prettier while she repeated the same pose with the same expression over and over again.

'Just getting a cup of tea I think,' said Sarah, knowing full well he was hiding in the kitchen with his hip flask which he'd already refilled once.

'And Daniel?'

'Just arrived and in the chapel with Toby,' reported Drew with a little salute that brought a snort of laughter from Sarah.

'Then it's time,' said Annabelle grandly.

'Er, time?'

Sarah whipped out a little schedule from the tiny purse she was carrying.

'Oh yes! Right, er let's move into position shall we.'

Drew raised his eyebrows at Rebecca who looked nonplussed.

'Right everyone, we are going to stand in the reception hall,' Sarah waved her arm vaguely around, 'and the photographer is going to take a series of shots with us all er – bonding before the wedding.'

'I'd like to do a little bit of bonding,' whispered Drew in Rebecca's ear.

Naughty builder.

She giggled, earning a reproachful look from Annabelle.

'This is going to show,' Sarah looked down at the notes, 'how we are all welcoming Annabelle into our family and into our er, hearts before she takes her vows,' she read.

Annabelle smiled serenely. 'Exactly.'

At that moment the exhausted photographer returned and the group gathered rather woodenly, with Drew earning a ferocious glare from Annabelle as he accidentally kicked over a large cherub who had been perched on the bottom step.

'Sarah!' snapped Annabelle.

At Sarah's blank look she sighed. 'Champagne! We should all be holding a glass of champagne!'

'Or, yes sorry,' and she dashed off to collect the bottle and glasses.

Rebecca watched as Annabelle arranged herself, spreading her long veil across the steps and the now fallen cherub. The day after Daniel and Annabelle had moved into Quebecs hotel, Rebecca had asked him to meet her. It had been a difficult conversation to have with your ex-husband, advising him not to get married to the woman he loved. But Rebecca had wasted far too many years ignoring the problems between herself and Daniel to shy away from this.

They had met in the bar of the hotel, Annabelle was at the beauty parlour being tweaked as Daniel described it.

He had ordered them both a glass of wine and he now sat stiffly, as though predicting the conversation.

'Daniel,' Rebecca had begun gently. 'Are you sure that Annabelle is marrying you for the right reasons. Is it a good idea to marry someone who is so clearly unhappy with – lots of things? Mainly money.'

For a moment Rebecca thought she had taken it too far and that Daniel was going to leave. But then his shoulders had slumped and he had run a hand wearily over his face. 'I'm sorry Bec, it was unforgivable of her to speak to you like that.'

'I'm not worried about how she spoke to me! I'm worried about you, and Annabelle, and your forthcoming marriage.'

There had been a tiny pause. 'You mean because she thinks marrying the ex-husband of someone who has as much money as you, means she will get to share in it all?'

Rebecca winced. It was brutal. True, but brutal. 'Well, yes.'

'When I first met Annabelle, I was under no illusion that she had fallen for my looks or my witty demeanour,' he began. 'I own a successful business, I have money of my own, a certain lifestyle. That was a big draw to Annabelle. She's had a hard life,' he said apologetically, 'her first husband buggered off and left her with nothing but debts and she's had to work hard to recover her life.'

Rebecca had stayed silent. She felt a great deal of sympathy for Annabelle's first husband and was certain he'd heaved a sigh of relief when he finally escaped. And she was equally certain the debts were more than likely due to Annabelle's own outrageous spending, but she had nodded encouragingly and let Daniel continue.

'So I'm sure money was an initial attraction. But then, I fell in love with her Bec. I suddenly realised that I was lonely and wanted a partner in life.' Rebecca had given him a small smile, she understood that feeling. 'I asked her to marry me but first I told her everything. About the affair, moving to Darlington. About you not telling me about the money, for all the right reasons,' he'd added hastily. 'I told her how I behaved over buying White's and – oh everything. I was honest, and I told her how badly I had behaved and how you had given me a million to start a new life.'

He'd taken a drink of wine, staring thoughtfully into his glass for a moment. 'It was then that she first suggested that I should ask for more. She thought I should phone you up and tell you we were getting married and ask if you would give me more money now I had a new wife and more expenses.'

He'd emptied his glass. 'I told her straight away it wasn't going to happen Bec, I never encouraged her to think it was a good idea I never…'

'I know, I know,' Rebecca had said soothingly.

'I didn't realise she was taking it quite so far,' Daniel had groaned. 'She became a little obsessed about the whole idea.'

Rebecca bit her lip. 'So you think she's marrying you for your- my money?'

'No! No, I don't. Well not entirely. I think it is an added advantage.'

'And what are you going to do now?'

Daniel had looked at her in surprise. 'I'm going to marry her.'

'What? Knowing that she's after ....'

'I do love her you know. Not in the same way I loved you.'

Rebecca's eyes had opened wide in surprise.

'I loved you Rebecca. I loved the life we had, I loved our children, I loved everything about our time together. I ruined it all and lost everything. And now I have a second chance with Annabelle and she may not be perfect but then neither am I. I want Annabelle to marry me and I'm hoping she still will.'

Sarah reappeared with the glasses and the champagne and started pouring out the fizzy bubbles as Drew slid an arm round Rebecca's waist.

'Penny for them?'

'Just feeling sorry for Daniel really. Marrying someone like Annabelle because he thinks it might be the only chance he gets.'

'Is that why you've settled for me. Last chance saloon?'

Rebecca twisted in his arms so she could look into his face. They had spent every night of the last week together, waking up each morning delighted to find themselves face to face. She knew without hesitation that she loved Drew. But after Charles she had no intention of rushing anything. They were both enjoying themselves far too much.

'That's right,' she said seriously. 'I know I'm not going to get anyone better.'

Drew smiled, that lazy smile that made her heart beat a little bit quicker.

Her beloved builder.

'I love you,' he whispered into her hair, drawing her close.

'Are we all ready? Drew you shouldn't be in the shot, you're not family. Rebecca I want you standing over here, on the step below me I think.'

'Do we have to stay here all day?'

'I have a wedding to organise Mr Chance!'

'Shame she's in the bridal suite, we need to try out that bath tub.'

'Rebecca, come here! The photographer is ready. Sarah, stop grinning!'

'They all leave tomorrow. Back to Devon thank God. Maybe we could spend a couple of days here?'

'Sounds good to me. We can have our own party.'

'Is anyone listening to me? You, what was your name again? Stop taking photographs of them and take one of me. I'm the bride!'

Rebecca imagined the moment when all the guests would depart, when peace and quiet would reign again at Willow Court. It had been a strange summer and it looked as though it had come to an end she thought as a rumble of thunder played overhead. But she and Drew would have the domed room to themselves, the music would play, the fire would crackle and the light would drift in the shadows from the crystal droplets overhead. They would wrap their arms around each other and dance the night away, looking into each other's eyes as a young couple had many years ago.

'Sarah, please stop them and bring your mother here. And you – stop wasting my wedding film on them. They're not getting married, I am!'

'I can't wait,' breathed Drew, sharing her vision.

'Me neither,' answered Rebecca and she lifted her head to meet his lips as the thunder crashed around them. The rain, Sarah's laughter and Annabelle's fractious voice all drifted far, far away. She had her second chance and she wasn't going to waste a single moment.

The End

Other books by Julie Butterfield

Did I Mention I Won the Lottery?

Rebecca Miles has won the lottery and is now living a millionaire lifestyle. The only problem is, she hasn't told her husband. So at weekends she's a dutiful wife in Darlington, working at the local deli and making shepherd's pie for dinner, but during the week she's living in her new mansion in Leeds spending her days shopping whilst her husband thinks she's looking after her sick mother. Will she get the courage to tell him before he finds out for himself? And can several million pounds in your bank account save a failing marriage?

Google Your Husband Back

Kate has the perfect marriage, a handsome husband and a beautiful new baby - so she is more than a little surprised when one Monday morning Alex announces that he's leaving. Shocked and distressed at both his absence and his silence, Kate turns to Google for some answers. Why has her husband left and more to the point what can she do to make him come home? Together with her faithful friend Fiona they come up with a strategy to persuade her errant husband to see the light and return to his loving wife. Unfortunately for Kate, even Google doesn't have all the answers.

Printed in Great Britain
by Amazon